INVENTING THE FUTURE

INVENTING THE FUTURE

ALBERT CORY

Edited by SAMANTHA MASON

Illustrated by JONATHAN SAINSBURY

Photography by SCOTT MCKENNON

CUBBYBEAR PRESS

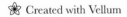

To all the people who made the Xerox Star, and especially those who are no longer with us; to Samantha Mason, my dedicated editor without whom this book would not have been written; and to Dave Liddle, who hired me for the best job I ever had.

The best way to predict the future is to invent it.

— ALAN KAY

CONTENTS

FOREWORD

DAVID CANFIELD SMITH

In the 1970s a "perfect storm" of creativity and empowerment occurred in Palo Alto, California. Out of it came the
first personal computer with a graphical user interface, laser
printing, the Ethernet, and networking with shared mailing,
printing, and filing servers. On the technical side, it introduced
bitmapped display screens and what-you-see-is-what-you-get
editing, and used object-oriented programming. I was fortu-
nate to be part of that storm for nearly a decade. It was the
most productive period of my career.

The Xerox Corporation under the visionary leadership of
Peter McColough recognized in the 1960s that while it had a
near monopoly in the highly profitable business of plain-paper
copying, the world of information creation and distribution
was going digital. This posed an existential threat to companies that relied on paper, just as digital photography threat-
ened the existence of companies that relied on film.
Accordingly in 1970, Xerox formed the Palo Alto Research
Center (PARC) with the goal of creating "the paperless office
of the future." What a glorious charter! In other words, they
were to embed themselves firmly in the state of the art of

computing and drive it forward to something better for human communication. This was tremendously inspiring.

Not only was the mandate inspiring, but the organization was executed brilliantly. Xerox chose Dr. George Pake, a respected physicist, along with its chief scientist Dr. Jack Goldman to found the center. The first thing Pake decided was that he wasn't going to micromanage it. He would hire the best computer scientists he could find and let them decide how to proceed. Pake's role would be to keep the goal in focus and to facilitate progress towards that goal. Not one organization in a thousand is so intelligently run. (Google comes to mind as another.)

Pake convinced Goldman to locate the center in Palo Alto to be near Stanford University and, it is apparent in retrospect, to be as far away as possible from Xerox's corporate offices in Rochester, New York. Thus was formed the "perfect storm" of productivity:

✓ Creativity – the broad goal of the paperless office of the future provided ample room for people's ideas.

✓ Empowerment – a generous budget provided the resources and people necessary to develop those ideas.

✓ Execution – once PARC implemented Alan Kay's idea for the Alto personal computer, there was—there's no other word for it—an explosion of creativity, a vast chaotic turbulence of new ideas. People saw with their own eyes what other people's ideas could become, which inspired them to implement their own ideas, which in turn inspired others, in a giant whirlpool of productivity.

It worked better than McColough could ever have hoped. During the 1970s PARC had the attention of the entire computing world. It was the center of progress in personal computing.

I had two personal experiences with the Alto. First, I wrote the first nontrivial user program in Alan Kay's new Smalltalk programming language on the Alto. I implemented my Ph.D.

thesis *Pygmalion* on the Alto, using its bitmapped screen as an "executable electronic blackboard." (Incidentally, that's where the concept of computer icons came from.) It would have been impossible to implement it on any other computer of the day.

My second experience was somewhat different and even more personal. Or rather, more personal for my wife. She was pregnant with our second son Jeff. (See the cover of this book.) She was two weeks overdue and getting increasingly impatient to get it over with. One night after work, as a distraction from the pregnancy, we went to PARC to play MazeWar, a popular video game implemented on the Alto by one of the researchers. In MazeWar, each player is represented by a giant bloodshot eyeball, a scary image in its own right.

The players wander the corridors of a maze. At any moment you might turn a corner in the maze to discover an eyeball staring at you. That is almost always fatal, since eyeballs can shoot out an instantaneous deadly ray. The tension of never knowing when an eyeball would appear together with their fearsome appearance was too much for my wife. It sent her into labor. Within 3½ hours Jeff was born— the fastest delivery of any of our three children by far.

Star

After a few Altos had been built and distributed to everyone in PARC, and to some Xerox executives, Xerox decided about mid-decade that it looked promising enough to turn into a product. Thus was formed the System Development Division (SDD). Half of SDD was located in Palo Alto just down the street from PARC; the other half was in Los Angeles 400 miles away (a stupid idea that caused the engineers endless headaches). That's when I joined the project. SDD completely reengineered the Alto, both its hardware and its software. The new computer that SDD built went through several names before eventually settling on "The Xerox 8010 'Star' Information System," which unsurprisingly came to be known simply as Star.

In addition to PARC's mandate to build the paperless office of the future, a second requirement was added for Star: it had to be acceptable to people in an office who not only had never used a computer but were generally afraid of them. Furthermore, the conventional wisdom was that "managers don't type." So that left them out. (Nowadays, computers have become so empowering for management that any manager who doesn't use one will quickly find himself becoming obsolete.) The target market for Star was "knowledge workers" in an office: staff, researchers, analysts, even secretaries. These people at least realized that they had a problem dealing with the increasing amount of information being generated every day. But they were still averse to computers. The most serious reason was that they regarded computers as a threat to their jobs. Most of them had mastered the requirements of their jobs, were competent in performing them, and were well regarded within the company. What if they couldn't handle this computer that was suddenly given to them? What if they didn't have the "aptitude" for it? What if they hated it? It would be bye bye worker!

So unlike the Alto's users, who were brilliant computer scientists and people whose business was innovation, Star's users were skeptical of change and hesitant to embrace it. I identified with them. I've always regarded myself more as a passenger on the train than the engineer who made it run. The first thing I decided when I joined the Star project as a user interface designer was that I wouldn't try to force our users into the computer's world; I would try to bring the computer into the office world.

Fortunately I had the perfect tool for doing that. I would use the idea of icons from my thesis. Whereas Pygmalion's icons were programmer centric—representing variables, conditionals, loops, functions, etc.,—Star's icons would represent familiar office objects—documents, folders, file cabinets, telephones, clocks, calendars, and yes wastebaskets. I literally looked around my office and created an icon for everything I saw. (Most were implemented; a few weren't.) Since icons had both a visual appearance and machine semantics, we were able to model fairly closely the behavior of the corresponding objects in an office. For example, if you drop a document icon on a folder icon, the document disappears. It went in the folder! If you open up the folder icon, you'll see it there. If you drop the document on a printer icon, paper will start coming out somewhere. This became known as the "desktop metaphor," and it's one of my most satisfying inventions. It instantly demystified the computer. People would say stuff like, "I recognize those things. They work just like the things in my office you say? OK, let me try." The stress level immediately plummeted. It was almost like playing a video game, except that you could create real information, and print it on real paper, and mail it to real people.

While icons and the desktop metaphor were my main

contributions to the Star design, I made a couple of others that worked out well. I was always looking for ways to reduce the burden on the user's memory. Since everything in Star was an object, they all had attributes. For example a text character had a font, a size, face characteristics such as bold, italic, underlined, strikeout, etc. Rather than make users remember all those attributes along with a bunch of commands for changing them, I introduced the concept of a dialog box that showed you all the attributes for whatever was selected. It had a simple point and click interface for changing them. Thus hundreds of special purpose commands went away in favor of a single command Show Properties that displayed a dialog box. This worked so well that I introduced several other commands that also applied to every type of object in the system: Move, Copy, Delete, Undo, Again, Copy Properties, Open, and a few others. We called these "universal commands" because they worked everywhere in the system. They replaced hundreds more special purpose commands. Yet they didn't reduce the capabilities of the system; they just eliminated redundant commands. No computer interface before or since has done more things with fewer commands than Star. To paraphrase Winston Churchill, "Never has so much been done by so many with so few commands."

The universal Undo command was the final way that we attempted to reduce the stress level of operating Star. According to Star's functional specification, "Any operation in Star can be undone by pushing the Undo key." While this significantly reduced the user's fear of making mistakes, by unanimous agreement it was the single hardest sentence to implement in the entire design.

Building the Star was a grand adventure. Everything we did was new. We knew that with the Alto we were starting ahead of everyone else in the world, and that if we did our job well, we could accelerate the progress of personal computers for decades to come. Which is in fact what happened—thanks in no small part to the brilliant contributions later of Steve Jobs at Apple.

But that was in the future. When we started, all we knew was that we were doing things that no one had done before. And while we were confident in our abilities, there was still a lingering fear that we would fall flat on our faces and become the laughingstock of the office world. I'll always remember the day that the Vice President of Marketing for Star came into my office, a sad expression on his face. "Dave," he said, "I've got some bad news. We can't use icons in the interface. It's too different from what other people are doing. They make the system seem toylike, like a video game, instead of a serious machine. They're too much fun to use." [emphasis mine] "But but but," I thought (though I didn't say it), "that's the whole point!" Needless to say, he and I did not have much interaction after that. I went into my boss's office, the redoubtable Charles Irby, the best manager I ever had. "I'll handle it," he said.

The combination of extremely high quality people, an inspiring challenge, and great uncertainty as to how it would all end up made for a highly charged environment. It was like being in the middle of an electrical storm with lightning everywhere. You never knew if you would get hit. This book Inventing the Future is the best description I've ever read of what it was like to be there in those days. Its clever use of historical fiction enables it to capture the spirit of those times better than a dry historical account would. I know that all of us who were privileged to be part of the effort regard it as one of the best times of our lives.

November 2020

PREFACE

This book is about real events that I was lucky enough to take part in, along with countless others. Many are named in the Acknowledgments, and some are no longer with us. While history books usually feature a few important people, like Steve Jobs, Larry Tesler, Alan Kay, Chuck Thacker, Butler Lampson, and so on, Star was a herculean effort by hundreds who don't appear in those books. The people I worked with at Xerox are a community of lifelong colleagues; we still keep in touch with each other, meet in person for reunions (or did before the pandemic), and mourn when one of us makes the final journey. This book is for them.

Someone in the Lisa group on Facebook referred to this book as a new genre, "Engineering Fiction." I like that term. There are lots of scientists and space explorers in fiction, but there are few, if any, books about what it's really like to do Engineering. The people who write fiction seem to think it's boring. It's not boring.

There are several excellent histories of these events, e.g., *Fumbling the Future* and *Dealers of Lightning*. One might ask, why this book? Albert Camus, the great French writer, said, "Fiction is the lie through which we tell the truth." This book is fiction, but I hope it tells the truth about what it was like to actually be there, when we didn't know how it was going to turn out. We didn't know how many buttons a mouse should have, if windows should overlap, how you should use object-oriented programming, or what icons were really good for. We fought about all of that, because we knew it mattered.

All characters are fictional and are composites of people I've known, except that Dan Markunas is modeled after me. The other two main characters, Janet Saunders and Grant Avery, are completely fictional, and are not in any way representative of the real people who had their jobs. In the Endnotes, I make clear which events are real and which are composites.

As the Acknowledgments show, I depended on the help and cooperation of a large number of the Xeroids (as we called ourselves) who are still alive. For some parts, e.g., the Lightning Strikes chapter, engineers who were actually there or who designed the Ethernet hardware checked them for accuracy. The only change I made to the events was to insert my heroes into them. All dates are accurate, as much as it was humanly possible to make them so.

In this book, I'm inviting the reader to imagine what they would have done had a giant corporation handed them some epochal, world-changing inventions, and said, "Here you go, here are some great ideas. Bring them to the whole world!" It was fun; in fact, it was a gas.

THE FIRST DAY

D an Markunas couldn't wait to enlist in the biggest computer revolution the world had ever seen. IBM's stranglehold on the computer business was finally going to be broken. Today was his first day as a programmer at Xerox. He envisioned a future where humans would control their data instead of begging the computer department for it. The machine would serve *you*, instead of you serving it. And, you wouldn't have to come in at night for extra time on it.

Xerox was making a computer you didn't have to share. You wouldn't submit a request for data and wait a week— you'd just get it yourself. He'd read the *Business Week* article on "The Office of the Future," and at his interview, Xerox seemed to be doing it. He was ready to sign up then and there!

He parked in the lot on Aviation Boulevard in El Segundo and reported to the Security office as his offer letter had instructed. Security had the vaguely menacing look of a police station, with metal furniture, linoleum floors, and cork bulletin boards. After an hour or so of processing, his manager Tom Burnside came and picked him up.

It was December 27, 1976. Dan had quit Burroughs, his first job out of college, after working on their proprietary database for three years. Right out of school, he made almost as much money as his father did after 45 years at Swift & Co., but then again, his dad didn't go to college. Nonetheless, Dan wanted to do something more interesting than merely being the best of the Seven Dwarfs, as IBM's competitors were often called. And, the people at Xerox seemed way smarter than the ones he used to work with. He should have been here all along!

His new manager, Tom, was a mild-mannered guy, balding on top, slightly built, and about 5'9", the same height as Dan. They walked across Alaska Avenue over to his new home, with Tom playing tour guide, "We're headed over to the A&E building. Administration and Engineering that is. M1 here is mostly manufacturing. You know we used to build computers here, right?"

Dan hadn't met Tom during his interviews, but his politeness and reserve reminded him of all his interviews in college. "Yeah, what do they do in that building now?"

Tom was carefully matching Dan's pace, "Still building printers, I think. They also house the credit union and cafeteria."

They were silent as they entered A&E. Dan finally asked, "How long have you been here?"

"About six years now. XDS was sold to Honeywell and a lot of the people went there, but Xerox got to decide which of us they wanted to invite to stay. I guess I was lucky." The A&E building was one of those soulless modern buildings that sprang up in big cities in the 1960s, with more linoleum floors, fluorescent lights, and everything painted in some weird combination of gray and beige that cynics called greige.

Tom led them past an atrium that held a showroom-like display of Xerox copiers and down a hallway, where they stopped at an empty office. "Well, here we are. Welcome to your new home."

Dan's new office was generously sized, with walls, a door,

and a nameplate on the outside. Inside was a desk and office chair, guest chair, and a black metal bookcase low enough to sit on. The desk had a phone, the Employee Handbook, and other HR publications on it. Alongside that stack were technical books, including the Alto User's Handbook and some others he was looking forward to reading. There was no terminal, but most engineers didn't have their own terminal at his previous job.

"I'll let you get settled in, find the bathroom, and all that, and then, I'll take you around and introduce you."

Dan opened his briefcase, put his coffee cup and wind-up toys on the desk, and walked out the south doors to his car to put the parking sticker on his car's back bumper. The parking lot was still only about half-full at 10:30, and Dan wondered why it was so big. And then, he remembered that they'd laid off people when they left the computer business, so there must have been more cars here at one time.

Back inside, Tom introduced Dan to his new coworkers. Gwen had the office next to his. Tom knocked on the open door and stepped inside, "Gwen, let me introduce Dan Markunas. He just joined us today to help with the Office of the Future project."

Gwen stood and held out her hand, "Welcome, Dan! Where are you joining us from? Are you just getting out of school?"

"No, I've been working at Burroughs in Irvine for three years."

"Burroughs! Are you working in ALGOL?"

Dan was used to that question. Everyone in the computer industry had read about the B6700, how it had virtual memory long before IBM's machines, and ALGOL. "No, that's the Large Systems. Our group mostly does Medium and Small Systems. But once in a while, I worked on the 6700."

"And what do you, sorry, did you work on there?"

"I worked for two years on a database system, but then, I moved to datacom support, teaching classes and whatnot."

Gwen responded excitedly, "Database! Is that DMS? Do I have that right?"

That was the other often-asked question Dan could count on whenever he met someone in the industry. Burroughs had good PR that way. "No, another system called FORTE/2."

He was about to elaborate when Tom interrupted, "Well, we have a lot of people to meet. You two will have plenty of chances to talk later since you're so close." They continued down the hall toward the south wall, the one with the windows. He noticed that most people he met had worked at XDS, and there weren't many new folks.

The other conversations resembled the one with Gwen. When they reached the end of the hall, there was a hallway parallel to the south wall, with large offices. These offices had windows, although there wasn't much to see, just a few small shrubs and a large lawn, and then Hawaii Street and the parking lot beyond. The west wall had the loading dock and no windows.

The corner office had a name tag for Paul Juranick, apparently a Very Important Person. Besides Betty Franco, the secretary, and her desk, it had a small table with four chairs, a giant potted plant, and an inner door into Paul's office so that you had to walk past Betty to see Paul. It also had an Alto, which Dan remembered from his interview. The instructions for printing a document were taped to the wall behind the machine.

They went back to Dan's office, and Tom said he'd come by later and take him to lunch. Dan started in on his stack of technical books. He immediately noticed that they were of higher quality than the Burroughs manuals. They looked like actual books, with good-looking fonts and footnotes, not like a computer manual. He opened the Alto User's Handbook. It started with the Alto Non-Programmer's Guide by Butler W.

Lampson, a name Dan had heard of, although he wasn't sure where. He was reading the section about how to initialize your disk pack when Gwen knocked.

"Hi, are you getting settled in?"

Dan swiveled his chair around, "Yeah, reading about the Alto. Looks like fun!"

"Have you tried using one yet?"

"Going to right after lunch. So, how long have you been at Xerox?"

"Almost six years now. It used to be Xerox Data Systems, as you probably heard. XDS is gone now, but some of us were kept around to work on this new thing that you were hired for."

"What did you work on?"

"Oh, different things. The last thing was the FORTRAN compiler. I won't miss that!" She rolled her eyes.

Dan was curious but decided to let that go, so he changed the subject, "What are you doing on the Office of the Future project?"

Gwen looked sheepish, "I don't really know yet. Right now, just reading docs and trying to learn Mesa."

Dan knew he'd be programming in Mesa, but he hadn't read anything about it yet. He had the Mesa manual in his stack. "Mesa! Another manual I have to go through." He paused, "What was XDS like?"

Gwen brightened, "It was okay. Kinda weird, though. I don't know if you've heard of Max Palevsky?" Dan shook his head. "He was the founder of Scientific Data Systems, which Xerox bought. He used to stand by the door every morning at 9:00 so that he could see who was coming in late!"

"Wow. Really?"

She laughed, "Seriously. Of course, eventually he had to go to work, so the rule was, if you were gonna be late, be really late!"

Tom walked in, "Shall we go to lunch? Gwen, do you want to join us? We're just going across the street."

"I can't. I'm meeting someone. Nice talking to you, Dan!"

Tom and Dan walked back across Alaska Street to M1, where he'd started the day. Tom asked, "Are you learning all about the Alto and Mesa?"

Dan nodded enthusiastically, "Lots to learn. I'm anxious to get on the Alto and start trying it out!"

"Should be fun, but let me know if you get stuck. Not that I'll be much help. I can barely use that thing myself."

They opened the doors and passed the security guard at his desk, who nodded at them. Walking on, they heard the clang of dishes and hum of conversation on the right and entered the cafeteria. Tom said, "I'll meet you just before the cash registers."

The cafeteria reminded Dan of the sort of budget restaurant his parents favored, with a hamburger station and another station with the special of the day, which was ham and limas.[1] That was like the food in his college dorm, so Dan settled for a hamburger, fries, and glass of soda and met Tom, who paid for them both at the register. The price seemed pretty cheap, at least. Tom had the special plus a piece of apple pie and glass of milk.

Tom went back to narrating, "Our wonderful Xerox cafeteria! I see you opted for the hamburger."

Dan didn't want to criticize the food on his first day, "Not too hungry, I guess." They found an empty table. Looking around, Dan noticed that the men seemed to be in shirts and ties and the women in dresses or suits.

Tom picked up his knife and fork, "You're still living down in Orange County, I think?" Dan nodded. "You can take time off to look for an apartment if you need to. Might as well do that sooner rather than later."

Dan looked surprised, "Really? Great, I think I'll do that. I've always wanted to live near the beach! Where I am in

Santa Ana is not particularly close to anything. Where do you live?"

"We live in Downey. It's home for us. My wife and I have been there for almost 10 years now. We have two girls, 6 and 10."

"Downey? Never been there. How do you commute, the 91?" Dan knew that discussing the freeways was as safe a topic in LA as the weather. In fact, it was safer since the weather was pretty much the same every day.

"Afraid so. It's been getting worse and worse. When we first moved here, I could make it in 25 minutes, but lately, it's more like 45."

The cafeteria was emptying, with people bussing their trays to the conveyor belt. Dan and Tom chatted for a few more minutes and finished eating. Walking back, Tom resumed the conversation, "Do you follow sports at all? I'm an Angels fan myself, but I know they're not very good."

Dan decided after moving to California that it was more fun to follow a local team than try to *follow* the Cubs from 2,000 miles away, especially since you never saw anything but the box scores in the paper. And, they were hardly ever on TV, so he'd become a Dodgers fan. They chatted about last October's World Series, how the Reds had been so dominating, and the Angels' poor prospects for the coming year. They entered their building and walked around the atrium to Dan's office.

"Well, I'll leave you to the Alto. I have meetings now, but I should have some time after 3:30. If you want to come by and talk then, you know where to find me."

Dan walked to the Alto outside of Paul Juranick's office, hoping it would be free, and it was. This would be exciting!

2

THE ALTO

The Alto in Paul's outer office reminded Dan of a dorm room refrigerator connected to an oddly shaped screen, taller than it was wide. He already knew that the shape was meant to show a document the size of an 8½ by 11-inch piece of paper. Besides the keyboard, the computer had a wire leading to a small oblong piece of plastic with three raised rectangles on top, which was the mouse and its buttons. He opened his Alto User's Handbook.

Under Getting Started, it read, "To do anything with an Alto, you must have a disk pack." This was a circular object, 15 inches in diameter and 2 inches high, holding a little over 2 megabytes. But Dan didn't have one. Paul's secretary, Betty, was still at lunch, and Paul's inner door was shut.

While he was looking around the room, Mark Banks, who had interviewed Dan, walked in and put out his hand, "Dan! You made it, welcome! I have to go to this meeting, but I'll talk to you when I get out."

Fortunately, Betty returned and was happy to check out a blank disk pack for Dan and showed him where the master Basic Non-Programmer's Disk was. Finally, he was in business.

He put the master disk into the drive labeled 0 and the

blank disk into drive 1 and pressed the Boot switch on the back of the keyboard. Some time elapsed, and then the > prompt appeared, just like the manual promised. He typed "NetExec," which apparently ran programs from somewhere else, and then "CopyDisk" and went through the steps in the manual to copy the master disk onto his blank disk. He typed "Quit" and pressed the LOAD switch on each disk drive. After about 25 seconds, the lights came on, and he pulled out both disks, gave the master to Betty, and wrote his name on the little card that slid out from behind the plastic on his new disk.

Betty asked, "Do you need any help? I'm not very good at it yet, but I did type a letter in Bravo for Paul!"

"Well, I might take you up on that if I get stuck, but let me see how far I get. Thanks!" He went back to reading about the Executive, files, Scavenger, and other necessities, occasionally trying out the commands. Paul's inner door opened, and the people came walking out, Tom among them. Tom introduced Dan to everyone and then said, "Do you have some time now? No hurry. Whenever you're at a stopping point."

"Good timing… I just copied my disk!" Dan followed Tom to his office.

"So, you're an Alto expert now. You can do about as much on it as I can."

"Well, I just made it past square zero."

"Do you have everything you need so far? Office supplies? Betty can order anything else you need."

"I think I'm okay for the moment. Tomorrow, I'll probably take you up on your offer to look for an apartment. Might as well take care of that if I can."

"Sure, it's a holiday week anyway, lots of people gone, might as well."

"So this Alto… it's not the machine we're selling, right?"

Tom smiled, "No, a lot of folks ask that. What the people in Palo Alto tell us is that it doesn't have virtual memory, it's not made for mass production, and Xerox can't support it out in the field, so they're building a new machine. You should have the PrincOps (he pronounced it "Prince Ops"), or Principles of Operation, in your copious stack of manuals, if you want to see what we're really doing."

"I guess I'll be reading that, but how is it different from the Alto?"

Tom hesitated, "Well… I'm probably not the best one to answer that, but you'll be going to Palo Alto soon and can talk to some of the folks up there if you want. I think the PrincOps machines will have virtual memory and some other goodies."

"Okay, great! Will we be going there soon?" Dan was used to travel being an infrequent thing at Burroughs. He'd gone on a few domestic trips, but usually, they were multi-day affairs.

"It could be as soon as next week. We have another new person starting next Monday, and the two of you can go up together."

"Great! Another thing I was wondering… what operating system will it run? Is it something I've heard of?"

Tom smiled again, patiently. These were the same questions he had asked his own bosses when the job was first proposed to him, and he'd been answering them almost every day since. "I doubt you've heard of it unless you have friends up in Palo Alto. It's called Pilot, and that should also be in your stack of manuals."

To Dan, it seemed that everything was still to be determined. He wanted *some* rock to stand on! He tried, "Do we have some kind of simulator for Pilot?"

Another on Tom's list of often-asked questions, "No, that's something we've been asking for, but so far, they haven't committed to anything. We'll keep trying, though."

Dan was intrigued by all this newness. In most programming jobs, all the technology was already set. Of course, some glorious new thing was coming along *real soon now*, as the engineers said sardonically, but usually, you were handed a stack of manuals and told to read them. And then, you started on your training project, and when that was complete, you received your first real assignment. But here, he had a chance to be in on the ground floor!

At Burroughs, two of his colleagues had quit to join a little systems house, as they were called, and were messing around with minicomputers, compilers, and languages. One of them told him they were "happy as pigs in shit." Systems software had a special mystique, and people who did it felt immensely superior to mere application programmers. He'd always been afraid that he was doomed to do applications his entire career. But now, maybe, he'd finally be a first-class citizen!

Still, he wasn't sure what exactly he could *do* beyond reading and thinking. He thought of all the Alto software that did cool stuff. That must be written in some language. "What language is Bravo written in?"

"Bravo is written in a language called BCPL, but we've been told we're not using that in our products." He glanced at his watch. "I have to run to a meeting in a few minutes, but I think Mark is free now. Unless he's in the meeting, too."

At least some things were the same here as at Burroughs— managers were always in a meeting or heading to one. Most offices were still empty, but Mark was at his desk. Dan knocked and walked in. Mark glanced up. "Dan, great to see you here! So, are you a master of the Alto already?"

Dan smiled, "Not quite yet. I did make my own system disk, though!"

"Well, you're almost there. Did you move up to LA County yet?"

"No, I'm going to look for an apartment tomorrow. Where do you recommend?"

"Jeez, it's been so long since I've looked for an apartment, I wouldn't know what to tell you. We've had our house in PV for six years now."

"PV?"

"Palos Verdes. You know, that big peninsula south of here that's a million miles from anything." Dan was about to ask Mark what his role was on the project, but Mark spoke first, "So anyway, what do you think about the project so far?"

Dan didn't know quite how to answer. Mark was controlling this conversation, though. "Oh... it seems pretty ambitious! I mean..."

Mark interrupted, "You mean the new hardware, new operating system, new programming language, no product spec? Other than that, what's ambitious about it? Just another programming project!" He laughed.

Dan also laughed, "Yeah, we should be able to knock this out in a year or so! I better go get on it."

"There you go. Well, I have to finish some stuff before we have yet another meeting, so if you'll excuse me..."

Back at his desk, Dan picked up the Mesa programming language manual and started reading. Programming languages hadn't evolved much since the 1960s, as far as he remembered, but then he didn't read most of the literature either. PL/1, which was his first language in college, came out in the 1960s, and ALGOL did, too. FORTRAN and COBOL were invented in the late 1950s. Burroughs, of course, was famous for ALGOL, but outsiders didn't know it was only on Large Systems, the B6700 series. His division supported that series, but only so they could say they did. Most Burroughs customers used Medium and Small Systems. Anyway, at least he had a new language to learn.

The first example of Mesa was the gcd, greatest common divisor, algorithm, and it went like this:

```
IF m = 0 AND n = 0 THEN gcd ← 0
ELSE
  BEGIN
  i: INTEGER
  UNTIL n = 0
  DO
```

```
r ← m MOD n;
m ← n; n ← r;
ENDLOOP;
gcd ← ABS[m];
END;
```

So, it used ← as the assignment operator! He'd seen that in some languages' documentation, but in reality, most keyboards didn't have that character. He didn't remember if the Alto keyboard did. This would at least eliminate using = for two things—testing if things were equal *and* assigning something to a variable.

It used lowercase letters as well as uppercase! The keywords were all capitalized. Already this was much more forward-looking and less a relic of the world of big clunky IBM machines.

He read on—the usual data types, constants, and operator precedence stuff that every language had. But then, whoa! You can invent *new* data types? Now, he was really getting interested. He had heard of this before but never really worked with it. You defined records and pointers to records. Records were the big deal with COBOL and a big reason why that stupid old language was still hanging on. Legions of business programmers wrote record definitions for files on tape and disk.

Onward. Mesa *did* have the GOTO statement. At Burroughs, there had been a continuing controversy about Edsger Dijkstra's 1968 letter, "Go To Statement Considered Harmful," and some managers tried to make Structured Programming their signature. Old-line programmers defended the GOTO and refused to do without it, but Dan was using it less and less anyway. To judge by the Mesa manual, he might be able to do without it entirely!

Dan was entranced, but he checked his watch and saw that it was after 5:00. He saw a stream of people heading for the door and decided it was time to call his first day over. He took a few manuals with him, just in case he became ambitious later. He felt guilty that he almost never read technical stuff at home, and his copies of *CACM* and *Computing Surveys* were piling up unread, but maybe now, life would be different. This stuff actually seemed interesting.

Under his windshield wiper was a printed form from Xerox Security, showing a list of infractions with "backing into parking space" checked. He didn't actually back in—he pulled through—but apparently, that was not allowed. The ticket instructed him to have his manager sign it and send it to Security.

"Oh, shit!" and ran back into the building. Tom's office door was locked. Dan searched his desk for some paper clips to attach a note to the infraction. No clips, and Betty's office door was locked, too. "*Damn it!*" Oh well, the ticket had his name on it, so hopefully, Tom would figure out what it was. He slipped it under Tom's door and left again.[1]

3

THE MISFIT

G rant Avery left the parking lot of Rickey's Hyatt House in Palo Alto and headed to his new Xerox office. He transferred from Xerox Dallas, and this was his first day at his new job. If this were any other Xerox location, he'd be in a suit and tie on his first day, but he figured, *"Hey, this is California!"* so he wore casual pants and a dress shirt without a tie.

9:00 am. He didn't want to arrive way before everyone else but figured the HR people probably came in earlier than the engineers. He drove down Arastradero past Gunn High, across Foothill, and then Hillview, the street he wanted. 3406 Hillview was the destination. Not many cars here yet. He entered and greeted the receptionist, who invited him to have a seat while she called the HR person.

Jacki came out shortly and led him to her office. "Welcome to Palo Alto! It says that you're transferring from Xerox Dallas? How's the weather there?"

"Colder than here. We do have snow once in a great while, which snarls everything. I guess I won't have to worry about that here, though."

"Well, we *have* had snow, but mostly it just rains in the

winter. Anyhow, you already have a Xerox badge, and I can do the paperwork myself. So, why don't I just walk you over to your manager." She led him down the hall to Michael Adams' office. "Michael's out now. Do you want to wait for him, or would you rather get settled in?"

"Might as well find my office and start bringing my stuff in." She walked him to an office at the end of the hall, which was much smaller than his Dallas office. But he was prepared for all that from his interviews, and anyway, corporate management promised him that he wouldn't have to spend more than two years or so out here. He wasn't supposed to tell anyone that, though.

Grant spent the morning bringing in his personal stuff, getting supplies, trying out all the features on his phone, although he knew that if he ever tried to do a conference call, he wouldn't remember how. Just as he was about to wander around the building, his new boss, Michael, poked his head in.

"Grant, glad you made it. Welcome! Sorry I missed you earlier… I was in a meeting when you arrived. Do you need anything?"

Grant shook hands with Michael, "I think I'm almost all set up, thanks. Where do people go to lunch around here? I didn't see a cafeteria anywhere."

"We usually walk over to the PARC cafeteria. Do you want to join us?"

"Sounds good. When are you going?"

Michael glanced at his watch, "Give me 10 minutes or so, and we'll swing by."

Ten minutes later, Michael came by and introduced two other guys, Richard Boddington and Patrick Wolfe. Richard was about 6' tall and stocky, blue-eyed with a large, unruly mass of light-brown hair, with an air of East Coast WASPi-ness. Patrick was taller and thinner, had a full beard, and his reserve somehow said gentleman. He recently joined after completing the Ph.D. program at Stanford.

They walked up Hillview to the PARC building. Grant regaled them with stories about the Rochester office and how Xerox, the progressive rebel, had turned into an Old Guard company.

Richard told them all about visiting Rochester and how everyone wore a tie, making him feel *very* out of place. At the cafeteria, Michael pointed out where everything was and said he'd meet Grant at the cash registers.

Grant took it all in. It seemed much more open and airy than other Xerox cafeterias. It featured a large salad bar, burger station, make-your-own sandwich station, and a station that had something called Omar's Feast, which was sort of a thin bread wrapped around some meat, cheese, lettuce, and tomatoes. He chose that. Michael paid for their lunches, and they joined Richard and Patrick at a table.

After some talk about the food, Richard inquired pleasantly, "So, I heard you're going to run the Pilot group?"

Grant glanced at Michael, "That's the plan, anyway. I met the team, including you Patrick, when I interviewed. Seems like a bright bunch."

Michael said, "We're looking forward to Grant starting because there's a lotta work to do."

Richard smiled, barely, and leaned over the table, "Have you had a chance to think much about what sort of operating system the Office of The Future should have?" He intoned the words as though they were capitalized. Michael looked ready to intervene to protect Grant, but Grant answered quickly.

"Not much so far. I worked on the OSs for the printers and word processors we're working on in Dallas, but that's about all. I'm looking forward to meeting with the team later today and really starting on the design process."

Patrick responded, "Yeah, I wrote up some preliminary thoughts about that. I'll drop them on your desk when we get back."

"Great… looking forward to reading them."

They finished eating, and Grant was curious about something, so he asked, to nobody in particular, "What's MAXC, or MAX, or however you say it? Some sort of big computer we all use, I guess?"

They glanced at each other, and Michael finally landed on Richard, "Richard, do you want to take this one?"

Richard seemed positively eager, "We wanted to buy a PDP-10 for research purposes, back when PARC was getting started. Since Xerox was in the computer business itself, as you may remember, the company refused to sign off on buying big hardware from a competitor. They wanted to give us an XDS machine. But the research guys here really wanted to run Tenex, because they needed the ARPANET, so we built our own PDP-10 lookalike instead."

"It had a huge benefit, too… we realized that *we* could build hardware. That's probably why we have the Alto."

Grant was shocked at this cheekiness about XDS and wanted to press him on that, but he hid it well. The name Max was an apparent reference to Max Palevsky, the founder of Scientific Data Systems, which Xerox had bought and renamed Xerox Data Systems. *Was it true what the Dallas office has warned him about?* They said the PARC people had their own agenda, and it wasn't Xerox's? He decided to reserve judgment for now. This was his new home, and he had to get along with these people.

Later that afternoon, Grant gathered the Pilot team, and they found an empty conference room. They waited for Grant to speak first.

"Well, I guess I met you guys when I came here before, but it's great to finally be here for real. I've been trying to read all the papers you gave me. Really interesting ideas! Why don't we go around the room, and each of you tell me a little about your background and what you've been working on here? I'll start. I'm Grant Avery, and I graduated from the University of

Missouri at Rolla in Mathematics in 1967. I've been at Xerox for nine years, mostly in printers and copiers, since that's what pays the bills. In Dallas, I headed up the software team for one of the word processor projects, and I'm really excited to be building The Office of the Future with you guys."

Since Patrick had just had lunch with Grant, he spoke next, "I'm Patrick Wolfe, and I received my doctorate from Stanford in 1974 in operating systems. I did a postdoc at Berkeley and then came to Xerox about nine months ago. And once again, welcome! We're very pleased to have you."

"I'm Arthur Hamilton, and I just transferred over from PARC a month ago, so I'm delighted to no longer be the new guy. Most of my work at PARC was in operating systems, and I studied that sort of thing at Cambridge, oh, hell, *too* long ago!"

"I'm Phillip Hansen, and I'm the newest Ph.D. here, as far as I can tell. I escaped last June from Berkeley. I did my dissertation on operating system security, which is a topic that I hope never to touch again as long as I live!"

Grant scratched out an imaginary item on his notepad and muttered, "Phillip… security. No," which made everyone laugh. He smiled, "According to the Xerox development standards, we're in the Exploration phase right now. How close do you think we are to exiting that?"

Silence. He continued, "Exploration is the phase before the Requirements writing starts. From reading all the papers, that definitely seems like where we are. What hurdles do we have to clear before we can proceed to Requirements?"

Grant wondered if he was speaking a different language than they were used to, judging from the blank looks. Nonetheless, he didn't have a better way to phrase the question, so he just waited.

Finally Patrick spoke, "Well, we don't have any formal requirements from the application software team, so we're kinda flying blind. We also don't have the actual hardware we'll be running on. I don't think we're anywhere close to getting those, but maybe Michael told you more than we've heard?"

Grant started to write on the whiteboard while Patrick was talking but thought better of it and sat down. Of course, he knew he was taking over an early-stage project when he accepted the job, but he'd thought at least *something* would have been settled by now. *"Okay, I get to be the fearless leader here. Stay organized."* He rose again and wrote:

```
1) Product Requirements
2) Hardware definition
```

"What else?"

Arthur said, "Well, there's the entire issue of address spaces, which we've been talking about a lot lately."

```
3) Address spaces
```

Arthur continued, "And support for multiple languages. I think the all-Mesa crowd is winning that one, but since we have a new manager, that should be reopened."

Grant looked puzzled, "Multiple languages? Isn't that a given? Well, let's just note that for now, and we'll come back to it.

```
4) Language support
```

Phillip spoke, "Contradicting what I just said about not wanting to work on OS security... there's the issue of how much protection against hardware and software errors we need, even if they're *not* malicious."

```
5) Process protection
```

Grant was becoming worried about this list. Was nothing settled?

Phillip continued, "And external programs. Do we assume that all the software comes from within Xerox, or do we allow for third-party software? A lot of things hinge on this."

```
6) Non-Xerox software
```

Grant put down the marker, "I think this is enough for now. Maybe if we can nail down most of these, we can make some progress. I need to talk to Michael and see where we are on the application software requirements and the hardware. Can I have volunteers for the rest of this list?" He waited. Everyone tried to seem eager, but no one raised a hand.

Phillip broke the silence, "I've already blown my cover on the security thing. I can take #5."

Grant wrote his name next to Process protection. "Excellent! Can we put you down for #6, too, since that sorta goes along with it?"

Grant continued, "Arthur, you brought up the multiple languages issue. Do you want to take that? I have some thoughts on it, so maybe you and I can work together on it." Arthur nodded.

"Finally, we have address spaces. Patrick, I don't fully understand the issues surrounding this, so maybe we can chat about it whenever you're free. Anyway, can I put you down for that?" Patrick agreed.

"Alright... that seems like a good day's work. Does anyone have any more thoughts before we break?"

They glanced at each other but remained silent. As they rose, Patrick spoke, "Sorry, there *is* something. In the background, we've been talking about this newish time-sharing system from Bell Labs for the PDP-11 called Unix. We're sorta wondering how much of that is really relevant for a personal computer. Our conclusion is not much. But I was wondering if you knew anything about that?"

Grant didn't. "I think I read something about that. My gut feeling is that you're right, and they're solving a different problem than we are. But we should talk about that a little more just to be sure we've covered all the bases. Thanks! See everyone... shall we say on Friday? I'm sure I'll be chatting with you all before then."

Arthur and Phillip walked side by side. At first, neither spoke. Finally, Arthur said, "Seems like a traditional corporate manager, doesn't he?"

"As compared to what?"

"Well, as compared to a professor. I mean, those guys at Cambridge didn't talk in terms of milestones and Requirements documents."

"I guess this is the *real world* they kept warning us about!"

"Okay, later."

Grant put the paper Patrick had given him in his briefcase, along with the other Pilot materials, and headed out to his car. He told himself that this was a management challenge, for sure, but no worse than problems he'd faced at Xerox already. Pretty soon, he'd have the group well along the path to IMO —Initial Machine Observation, the Xerox milestone that signified a finished product.

Driving down Hillview, he reviewed his relocation plans. He hadn't bought a house before coming, despite the company's transfer policy of offering a house-hunting trip because he wanted a better sense of the neighborhoods. He thought he'd just rent a house for the relatively short period he'd be here. House prices seemed insanely expensive, from what people had been telling him, especially for what little you got. He had driven around Palo Alto yesterday, and the houses were absolute garbage, especially compared to what $100,000 would buy in the Dallas suburbs. You could buy a palace on a halfacre, at a minimum.

At the hotel, he changed clothes and watched the local news. People at Xerox had told him that Chef Chu's was pretty good Chinese food, so he looked up their number in the phone book on the nightstand and called to make sure they were open on a Monday. They were, and he consulted the map to find it was at San Antonio Road and El Camino, a major street and very close by. Perfect. Almost within walking distance, but people didn't seem to walk here.

As he drove over, he noticed a Tower Records on the other side of the street and made a mental note to stop in and browse after dinner. The restaurant was large, with two stories, and busy, even on a Monday night, and the food was excellent. The Chinese Chicken Salad was the best he'd ever had. *"Maybe there are some redeeming things about this area!"*

Although they had Tower Records stores in Dallas, he always associated it with the Sunset Strip in LA, for some reason. They had snotty-looking clerks at the front desk and racks and racks of records. Grant wasn't the type to spend hours looking through the obscure records. He was more into keeping up with what he heard on the radio or records that someone might be talking about. He checked out the records near the front, *The Eagles: Their Greatest Hits, 1971-1975.* He had to have that. Every song on it was good. And, Paul McCartney had a new album, *Wings at the Speed of Sound.* He decided to wait until his stereo and the rest of his belongings arrived before buying those. A separate room, sonically isolated from the rest of the store, held classical music, and he spent some time thumbing through the Baroque section, then went to the hotel room and watched some TV before bed.

4

THE POWER COUPLE

On January 3, 1977, Janet Saunders called to her husband Ken as she grabbed the keys from the kitchen counter. Today was a special day—her first day at Xerox. It was the first job change for either of them since college.

"Bye! Wish me luck!"

Ken looked up from his cereal, "Good luck! Now, we can get free copies!"

She smiled thinly and closed the door. His jokes about working for Xerox, the copier company, were less and less amusing. Ken was outwardly enthusiastic about the job switch, but he seemed dubious. His comment when she interviewed was, "Xerox is getting back into computers? Didn't they just get out of that?" Her friends at TRW said more or less the same thing. When she turned in her resignation letter, her managers hurried her into meetings where they tried to convince her to stay, maybe with a transfer and a promotion, but she'd made up her mind.

Janet was a networking engineer at TRW, working on defense projects that she wasn't supposed to discuss, mostly about communicating with satellites. She'd joined TRW directly from MIT, where she earned a Bachelor's in Electrical Engineering and Computer Science two years ago. She was well-treated and one of a small number of women, enough that she wasn't a novelty. She always had the feeling her wedding rings kept the men at bay. The younger guys went out of their way to talk to her, invite her to lunch, and to play on the department softball team, but she never had the feeling that her technical abilities were being slighted. So far, her projects had gone well, and she'd received several raises already.

At the same time, she worried that the aerospace industry was dominated by bullet-headed older men, many of whom had served in the military or had worked at their companies for 20+ years, and she didn't see much chance of advancing very far without becoming a lifer. She knew a few women in senior management jobs, who were all in their 50s, lifers at their companies, and usually stunningly unattractive. Janet did not want to end up that way. She was so good-looking that she worried she intimidated some of the men, which was not a good thing if you wanted to become a manager.

Her husband, Ken, thought that becoming a VP at an aerospace firm was a perfectly fine goal for anyone, including himself. He worked at Hughes Aircraft as a system programmer on their DEC machines, a high-status job there. And, they had lots of friends from school who'd gone to work at MacDac (McDonnell-Douglas), GD (General Dynamics), Rockwell, or another aerospace giant.[1] They always joked about how everyone believed LA was all movies and entertainment, but they personally never met anyone in those fields and almost never saw a famous person. They met people who'd run into Dustin Hoffman in the Safeway, but they never had stories of their own.

Friends back East were always calling, wanting to come out and visit, especially during the winter. Ken and Janet didn't mind at first because LA had so many tourist attractions they wanted to see! They'd taken their out-of-town friends and relatives to Disneyland three times, Universal Studios, and the Queen Mary. Ken kept a freeway map on the wall at work to memorize the various freeways around the LA area. He especially enjoyed it when he could give complicated directions involving five changes of freeway.

They lived in an apartment in a large complex in Culver City, which they thought was close to Hughes and TRW when they chose it, although the traffic on the 405 still made it slow for Janet. The complex had several pools and lots of activities for the residents, which they had gone to when they moved in but were bored with now.

Ken and Janet had no kids yet, nor any immediate plans for any. When they were married, they told each other, "*When we have kids, someday,*" and that was as far as it went. Ken was climbing the systems programming hierarchy at Hughes, and once, he had even ridden in a fighter plane that used the electronics package he supported. He thought that Janet was in an ideal place to be promoted rapidly at TRW since the government was always pressing affirmative action. He used to annoy her by saying, "Hey, we can always change our name to Ramirez, and then you'll *really* be golden."

Later that morning at Xerox, after the obligatory visits to HR and Security, Tom took Janet around introducing her. She told the same stories about her background to everyone, explained that she wasn't allowed to talk about her work at TRW, received the introductory Alto lesson by a guy named Dan, and read some of the manuals on her desk. "*Typical first day in a new job.*" At the end of the day, she wasn't sure what to think, but it didn't have the air of a well-honed project. Nobody could say what it was, but they were sure it was earth-shaking.

At home, Ken was already fixing dinner on the cheap stove with electric burners that they both hated, but every apartment seemed to have. "Surprise! I thought I'd make dinner to celebrate your first day." It was his signature dish, spaghetti with meatballs. "So… how's the new job?"

Janet dropped her briefcase and purse by the counter and grabbed a Coke from the refrigerator. "Oh, the usual things… signed the paperwork, got my badge, met everyone, found the bathroom. You know."

"So… what kind of stuff will you be doing?"

"They didn't really tell me. It seems like they're just staffing up and figuring out what to do right now."

He smiled, "That's great! You can carve out a good job for yourself without a lot of competition."

She ignored that and sat down heavily at the end of the couch, "How was your day?"

Ken brightened, "Pretty good, actually. We had a presentation from our DEC representative on the KS10 they're planning."

He started explaining the way the KS systems booted compared to the KLs and the bus architecture when Janet suddenly walked over to the stove and interrupted, "My *God*, that smells good. Let me go wash my hands, and then we can eat!"

Over salad, Ken asked, "So… tell me about the job! Xerox is plotting to take over the office, is that it?"

"Something like that. They want to sell these little computers that'll fit on your desk, kinda like terminals, except they're *not* terminals. They're actual computers. I tried this prototype machine, the Alto, but they said that's not what they're going to sell."

"So what *are* they going to sell? Some kind of commercial microprocessor? Those things aren't very powerful."

"I'm not exactly sure, but I think they're building their own, not using something off-the-shelf. I have some docs that I haven't read yet."

"Interesting. What will it use for an operating system?"

She went to the counter and filled her plate with spaghetti

and meatballs. "Not too sure about that, either. That's another manual I have to read. You were about to tell me about that new DEC computer? When's it coming out?"

"The salesman wouldn't tell us, naturally. Sometime next year for the really important customers, which Hughes certainly is." He went into detail about the new bus architecture until they finished dinner and loaded the dishes into the dishwasher. He went into the living room and picked up the *LA Times*, opening the Sports section. Janet looked over his shoulder at Jim Murray's column, which was about the Dodgers' off-season moves. Ken had not moved his allegiances to LA yet, preferring to try to follow the Red Sox remotely. He wanted to turn the page, but she held it while finishing Murray's piece. Then, she took her work manuals into the other room, turned on the end table lamp, slouched down, and opened the Mesa manual.

It had the obligatory stuff on primitive data types and expressions. Okay, so Mesa made you declare the types of everything before you used them. Fine, that was pretty common. You used both uppercase *and* lowercase in names, and they were different. Great, *finally* we could ditch these lousy terminals that only did uppercase.

Then she came to Constructed data types. You could define new types and then use them!

`SignedNumber: TYPE = INTEGER;`

and then declare things to have that type:

`i, j: SignedNumber;`

Mesa had enumerations, records, pointers, arrays, subranges of arrays. This was pretty cool. At MIT, she had learned LISP, PL/1, Algol, APL, Focal, PLASMA, and assembler language for the PDP-10 and PDP-11. But this abstract data-type stuff reminded her a little of CLU, which she hadn't really used at school. Ken and she had attended a colloquium by Barbara Liskov about it soon after they met. When they reminisced about it, they argued about whether she'd suggested that as a date to impress him, or vice versa. Anyhow, neither of them learned much from the talk, but it was a great nerd date to kid each other with.

She hadn't seen abstract data types since leaving MIT. Software at TRW and other aerospace companies was mostly either FORTRAN, some other computation-heavy language, or assembler if it was time-critical. She thought Ken would be interested.

Ken was done with Sports and was now reading the front page. "Hey, remember that talk by Barbara Liskov we went to at school, about CLU?"

He closed his eyes, "Vaguely."

"Well, this Mesa language we're using has abstract data types sorta like CLU did!" She looked at him expectantly.

Ken was interested but not excited, "Really? What sort of language is it?"

"I haven't gotten too far in it yet, but it seems cool. It's a pretty high-level language, from what I can tell."

"Where did it come from? I haven't heard about Mesa before. Is anyone else using it?"

"It's something they invented themselves. They have a lot of Ph.D. types up in Palo Alto, I think."

Ken smirked. Hughes had a few of these Computer Science types, who usually wanted to invent their own version of *everything*. Generally, management guided them to some niche area safely off in the corner, like satellite photography, electronic warfare, or something, regardless of their research area. But at Xerox, they seemed to be running the show. "What kind of hardware does it run on? It sounds like a pretty demanding language."

Janet had asked Tom that very question, and he'd handed her another manual, The OIS Processor Principles of Operation. She'd only skimmed it, but it had all the basic instructions that the processors would have, the address structure, and so forth, just like any hardware manual. Xerox had clearly put some effort into this project.

"They're building that, too. I have another book with the hardware description, which I haven't read yet."

"Do those machines exist?" Janet laughed. She could see his skeptical, know-it-all self coming out. She usually humored him when he was in that mood. She shook her head. "Oh, great! And naturally, the operating system is brand new, too."

"You must have read my mind!" She bent over and kissed him and returned to the den. He turned on the TV.

5

DAN AND JANET LEARN MESA

D an and Janet's offices faced each other across the
hallway. They were at the far end of the second
corridor, counting from the west, radiating out from
the line of window offices. Paul had the corner office, naturally, and an office was reserved for Michael, the head of
Xerox's Systems Development Department (SDD), even
though he was usually in Palo Alto. Most of the offices were
occupied. Pretty soon, they'd be doubling up, Dan figured, but
for now, he enjoyed the luxury of privacy. Both of them had
their doors open, so he could have just yelled over, but this
would be a longer conversation. He knocked on her door, and
she looked up. "Hey! How are you coming with Mesa?"

"Plowing through it. What about you?"

"I'm ready to go find an Alto and start playing. I've never
really worked with user-defined types, except reading about
them once in school. You?"

"No, not really. I heard a talk by Barbara Liskov from
MIT once."

Dan looked puzzled, "Barbara Liskov? Don't know that
name. What does she do?"

"She's one of the creators of CLU. But I never used it, so

this is almost all new to me, too. Anyway, I'm gonna give it a try!"

Dan had been rejected by MIT, but he'd learned never to tell this to an MIT grad, else they'd feel superior, or maybe embarrassed. MIT was notorious for teaching LISP as their first programming language, to teach students to think the correct way. One of Dan's professors called it "man's most intelligent misuse of computers" and said that it stood for "Lots of Irritating Silly Parentheses."

But he decided to avoid that subject. Maybe he'd heard of CLU, once, but programming language theory was not his strong suit. "So, where are you from, originally?" Almost everybody in LA was from somewhere else, so this was always an interesting question.

"From the Detroit area. How about you?"

"I grew up in Chicago. Went to the University of Illinois. I got my Bachelor's and Master's there."

She brightened, "The U of I! Didn't HAL in 2001 say, 'I was born in Urbana, Illinois'?" voicing the last part in HAL's voice.

"He sure did. I had a class with one of the Illiac II designers!"

"The Illiac II! Isn't Illiac IV the latest? Whatever happened with that?"

"I think it's at Moffett Airfield. It's funny… there were all these campus demonstrations against it, but now, you never hear anything."

"What were they demonstrating about?"

"The military applications. You have to remember… this was during the Vietnam War."

"The other Illinois thing I've read about is PLATO. Did you have anything to do with that?"

"Not really. I used it once in a psych experiment, but PLATO was in a different building." He continued, "So, Detroit! Was your dad at a car company?"

"Yeah, 'fraid so! We lived in Bloomfield Hills with all the other car execs. I went to Cranbrook, or actually, Kingswood, the girls' school, with their kids."

Dan had never heard of Cranbrook, but she seemed to assume he would. He avoided asking what Cranbrook was, but later, he asked around and found out it was one of the top private high schools in the country. "What was that like? Did they have a computer class back then?"

"I think the boys' school did. We didn't." She glanced at her manual, "Well, guess I'll get back to Mesa! How far along are you?"

Dan took a step toward the door, "Just finished the part about data types, so I'll start with that."

A little later, Tom stopped by Janet's office to check in. "Hey, how's it going? I see you're learning Mesa. Maybe you can teach it to me!"

She laughed, "So, who is the Mesa expert in El Segundo?"

"Down here, that would be Gary. He wrote part of the manual, at least. Would you like to meet him?"

She stood, "Sure!"

"Why don't we grab Dan, too?"

They were about to go to Dan's office, but he'd overheard them and was walking over with his Mesa manual. They headed over to the next hallway to Gary's office. He was smoking his pipe and typing on his Alto. Almost nobody had their own Alto, so Dan figured this guy must be important.

Gary was a stocky 40ish man with large steel-frame glasses and short curly hair. He was dressed in a short-sleeved shirt with a collar and two front pockets, brown pants of some indeterminate fabric, and penny loafers. He tapped out his pipe in the ashtray and stood up.

Tom spoke first, "Gary Harris, let me introduce Dan Markunas and Janet Saunders." Turning to them, he said, "Gary and I worked together on the Sigma-7 operating system."

Gary shook both their hands, "So, what can I do you for?"

Tom answered, "Janet and Dan are both learning Mesa, and I was hoping you could answer some of their questions."

Gary was modest, "Well, I did help with some parts of the manual, but I wouldn't say I'm an authority! But I'll do my best." He motioned to the guest chairs just to the right of his desk. "Have a seat!" He swiveled to face them, and Tom left.

Dan looked at Janet to see if she wanted to go first, but she held out her hand to let him speak. Dan opened his Mesa manual to the table of contents, "I guess our biggest question is how much of this is implemented?" He pointed to the manual, "Like can we do the Modules, Programs, and Configurations stuff?"

Gary took the manual and examined those pages. He grabbed a pencil from his desk and checked Modules, Programs, and Configurations and muttered, "This stuff is pretty important. You should work with that."

"Let's see... variant records, yes. You can play with those, and you should. Signaling and Signal Data Types... I think there's a proposal for that." He rummaged through the papers on his desk and handed Dan the Signaling proposal. "You can make a photocopy of that. By the way, have you had the lecture on don't use Xerox as a verb?" He laughed.

"I heard that in my orientation! Anyway, what parts did you write?"

Gary grabbed his pipe, filled and lit it, and puffed a few times. "I wrote, let's see, hand me that manual again." He drew circles around the Introduction, Ordinary Statements, and Procedures sections in the table of contents. "I mostly reviewed what the other guys wrote. Are you flying up to Palo Alto soon?"

Janet answered for them both, "This Friday, we're going up for the day!"

"Good!" He puffed on his pipe. "If you get a chance, talk

to Jim Travis. He's real approachable, and he knows everything."

Janet had questions, "So, we write programs in Bravo on the Alto, and then run them in that same OS, right?"

"Yup!"

"How do we debug them? Print statements?"

"For now, it's good old-fashioned print statements. I've heard there's a debugger on the way."

Dan had been flipping through the manual while they were talking, "So, except for variant records, we can do the other basic stuff. Have you played with the process synchronization stuff? That looks pretty cool!"

Gary puffed on his pipe again, "I might have tried it once, but I wouldn't say I'm an expert. Bring that up on Friday when you're there."

Dan and Janet glanced at each other and decided that was enough for today and thanked Gary. They spent the rest of the day reading their manuals and scribbling Mesa on their scratch paper.

6

THE TRIP TO PALO ALTO

Dan caught the 7:00 am Pacific Southwest Airlines flight to San Jose from Orange County Airport. The airport was only a couple miles from his apartment in Santa Ana, but he'd never flown out of it before. It was just a day trip, and it felt weird to board a plane and not even bring a change of clothes. But apparently, this was going to be a regular thing at Xerox. On the flight, most of the men wore suits and ties, almost advertising "I'm a businessman!" He was casual, though. Programmers didn't wear ties in California.

Janet lived in Culver City, so she flew out of LAX, just a couple miles down the 405. She also noticed that most of the women were well-dressed, in power suits or dresses. She was in slacks and a long-sleeve blouse, the same as any other day. The flight to San Jose was almost full. This was a business flight, not a tourist flight.

Both their flights were about an hour, and they met at the San Jose airport, picked up their rental car, and drove down 17 and up 280 to Page Mill Road in Palo Alto. The 280 freeway was beautiful near Palo Alto. It had four lanes each way without a lot of traffic, even at rush hour, with green hills on the left and lots of trees on the right. You never saw scenery like that around a freeway in LA, where everything was all built up and ugly. They exited at Page Mill and still didn't see much development. There were no gas stations, no fast food places, and the speed limit was 50 mph. Coyote Hill Road, where they were supposed to turn, didn't have a light, and the sign wasn't very prominent. Dan might have missed it if he'd been on his own, but Janet was looking at the map and navigating. They turned right and saw no buildings at all.

Apparently, this was Stanford land, and now, they understood why Stanford students called the school The Farm. Janet read the directions out loud, "Turn right on Coyote Hill, go right on Hillview, 3406 will be on the right." On the left, they saw the sign for PARC, "Xerox Palo Alto Research Center," which they'd heard of already from talking to people down South. That wasn't their destination, though. The Systems Development Department (SDD), which they were part of, was supposed to bring PARC's technology to the world, and it had its own building.

The SDD building was one of a long line of almost-identical buildings set back from Hillview, surrounded by parking lots behind little hills. The spots near the road were mostly full, but they found a place to park and walked inside. The receptionist greeted them and called their contact. A trim, brown-haired man with a neatly clipped mustache and wearing an Oxford shirt with no tie came out. "Hi, welcome. I'm Grant Avery. How was your flight?"

Dan answered, "Short and uneventful, just the way I like them."

"Did you have any trouble finding the place?"

Janet said, "No, the directions were pretty simple. It's so nice around here! So different from LA."

"Yeah, I haven't gotten tired of it yet. All this land belongs to Stanford, which is why you see the horses grazing. Did you see PARC as you came in?"

"Yeah, we saw the sign. It looks like a big building."

"We'll have lunch at PARC. Shall we go to your first meeting? I'm afraid you have a full day ahead of you. There's a whole lot of technology, and we're going to throw a bunch of it at you. We'll stop by the restrooms and kitchen first."

After a short break, Dan and Janet settled uncomfortably into the beanbag chairs at the back of the conference room. Janet was glad she hadn't worn a skirt that day. Grant pulled up a chair and sat down nearby. The room had floor-to-ceiling whiteboards at the front and seemed full of light, such an improvement on the dreary fluorescent-lit conference rooms in El Segundo. They chatted about life in Palo Alto, which was new to Grant, too, since he'd recently transferred from Dallas. He was in the middle of explaining the various neighborhoods around Palo Alto when Jim Travis, a 30ish-looking guy in black jeans and a Levi's jacket, entered and started writing on the whiteboard.

Dan and Janet quickly realized that lying in a beanbag might *seem* cool and a throwback to the hippie era, but it wasn't a great way to actually participate in a meeting. They both struggled to stand. Grant extended a hand to Janet and pulled her to her feet, and they all sat down at the table near the front.[1]

Jim was the manager of the Mesa language development effort and was there to talk about Mesa. "How much do you know about Mesa so far? Grant, I know you've played with it."

Dan answered, "I've written a little play program that works."

Janet confirmed, "Me, too. It looks fun!"

"Excellent! So, I don't need to go over the overall syntax?" They both agreed that they knew how to write Mesa, more or less. Jim continued, "Let's talk about modules and defs files. Who's familiar with those?"

Dan looked sheepish, "I read it over." Janet nodded in agreement.

"Okay, then… let's talk about that. We're gonna write some *very* large programs in SDD, hundreds of people coding, so the Mesa team's spent a lot of time thinking about how to support that. Let's say you have a programming abstraction." He turned to the board and wrote Abstraction.

```
Abstraction: DEFINITIONS =
BEGIN
it: TYPE =...;
rt: TYPE = ...;
p: PROCEDURE;
p1: PROCEDURE [INTEGER];
pi: PROCEDURE [it] RETURNS [rt];
END
```

"You've probably seen this example in the manual. Abstraction is some sort of programming abstraction, and it exports two types, t and rt, and three procedures, p, p1, and pi. p1 takes an integer as an argument and returns nothing, while pi takes one arg of type it and returns an rt. Everyone with me so far?"

Janet asked, "So, another program that wants to use Abstraction can only use what's declared in the definitions file, right? Everything else is private?"

Jim had the look of the professor who got the answer he wanted. "Exactly! How often have you run into bugs where another programmer was reading your code and relying on something that you changed later?" They both raised their hands and looked rueful. "So, definitions files are a way of *hiding* implementation details from your users, or clients as we call them."

"Now, let's implement Abstraction." He turned to the board, "I'll just write PUB and PROC and so forth, and you'll know what I mean, but if not, ask. "

```
Implementer: PROG IMPL Abstraction =
BEGIN
OPEN Abstraction;
```

```
x: INT;
p: PUB PROC=(code)
p1: PUB PROC [i: INT]=(code)
pi: PUB PROC Ix: it] RET [y: rt]=(code)
END
```

"So, Implementer is what implements Abstraction. And, here's a pop quiz… can a client of Abstraction see the variable x?" He waited for an answer.

Both Dan and Janet said, "No!"

"You passed. You can stay. For now." He smiled as Dan pretended to wipe sweat off his forehead.

"x is PRIVATE by default, so clients can't see it. This is information-hiding, and it's key to keeping your code maintainable. You only expose things to clients who need to use your abstraction. Does all this make sense?"

They all nodded. Jim went on to explain binding, which seemed to Dan and Janet to resemble the linking they knew from other systems. You compile, separately, a bunch of programs that work together. At first, they have placeholders for the code outside themselves, and in binding, you put them together, and the Binder fills in those placeholders. Or not, if you were missing something!

They had lots of questions which Jim answered. He looked at his watch, "We have about 15 minutes left. Do you want to hear about where we're going with processes and coordination?"

Janet answered, "Definitely!"

Dan agreed, "For sure."

"Great! You probably noticed we don't have great support for parallelism right now." They didn't want to seem critical, so they didn't react.

"Anyway, our clients don't think much of what we have now!" he said with a smile. "What Mesa has is what we call hard processes, where the processes have to be statically declared, and the scheduling is non-preemptive. What are some problems with that?" Janet thought Jim must have been a professor at some point in his career because he seemed so confident in drawing them out.

Finally, Dan spoke up, "What if you decide you need more processes because the workload increased or something?"

"Yep, need dynamic forking and joining. What else?" He looked at Janet for the next answer.

She asked, "How can they share variables without stepping on each other?"

This was the answer he wanted, "Yep, synchronization. We have a yield primitive so that you *could* have well-behaved processes sharing information. But they have to be *cooperating*. This isn't a time-sharing system with arms-length programs. So... what's wrong with assuming that the software all cooperates?"

Grant had been sitting in the back and letting Dan and Janet answer, but now, he spoke up. "It means that we can't do our job in Pilot since any rogue process can freeze out everyone else."

Jim was expecting this from Grant, "Right, Grant. The operating system. What else?"

He looked at Dan and Janet. Dan answered, "Well, what if you had multiple processors so that they really *can* be running simultaneously?"

Jim was ecstatic, "Right! Exactly. We're not building anything like that yet, but this software could last for years. We don't want to constrain ourselves." He proceeded to explain the FORK and JOIN operators, and they were discussing those when Grant pointed to his watch, and Jim wrote his email address on the board. "Here's my email. I'm sure we'll be seeing you again. It was nice meeting you!" He shook their hands, went through the sliding glass doors, and lit a cigarette.

Grant walked up to the front, "Okay, we'll take a break, and then, I'll be talking about Pilot. Let's resume in 10 minutes."

In the kitchen, Dan couldn't help noticing the coffee was free. At the office down South, you were expected to put a quarter in a cup when you took some coffee, although it wasn't really enforced. Burroughs had been the same way.

Grant introduced Dan to a woman with curly brown hair and glasses, Rosalind. "Welcome to Xerox! So, you're gonna make a product out of all this stuff?"

"That's the plan. What do you do here?"

"I'm a user interface specialist. I'm supposed to figure out how people will actually use this thing. Whatever *this thing* turns out to be."

"Will we be seeing you down in El Segundo a lot?"

"Yes. I need to go down there soon! I've heard so much about it." Dan caught the teensiest bit of irony in her voice.

Grant interrupted, "We should get back for the next meeting."

Rosalind called over her shoulder, "Feel free to stop by later if you have any time! I'm right around the corner." Dan said he would.

In the conference room, they'd been joined by a new guy, who introduced himself as Charles Green, and said he was one of the Pilot designers. "Just hoping I might learn something." Janet figured he must be here to give Grant backup if he couldn't answer a question.

Grant began, "Operating systems! What are your experiences with them, just so we can calibrate things?"

Janet spoke first, "I worked at TRW on satellites, so it was mostly classified software I can't talk about. Hopelessly out of date! I'm eager to catch up with the rest of the world."

Grant smiled and looked at Dan. "I worked at Burroughs, but not on the B6700 you've all heard of. The business computers at Burroughs have some pretty conventional OSs, nothing much to talk about. I'll second what Janet said!"

Grant began, "Okay. I'll start by asking a question, 'What

important language feature do you *not* see much about in Mesa?' Who wants to start?"

Dan and Janet looked at each other. Janet said, "Files?"

"Right, the file system. That's a debate we're having right now in the Pilot group. PARC has been working on some pretty advanced features like transactions. We've been debating whether to include that in the Pilot file system. And virtual memory…"

Dan interrupted, "Transactions? We have that in the database system I was working on at Burroughs. But these would be in the file system?"

Charles, who had been silent up to now, jumped in, "Yeah, Butler Lampson and Howard Sturgis have this file system called Juniper that we're looking at. It has built-in transaction support."

This was the second time Dan had heard Dr. Lampson spoken of with such reverence. He wondered if El Segundo people ever got to meet this godlike person. Anyway, it felt great to be in a company that employed famous computer scientists.

Charles continued about transactions in Juniper, but Grant interrupted, "Juniper looks really interesting, but I'm not sure we can really support something that complicated on our dinky little office computers."

Janet thought Charles wanted to argue, but apparently, he decided not to, maybe because it was Grant's meeting, and Grant was his boss. Grant spoke at length about the difference between a personal computer operating system and the big multi-user systems they were used to. In a traditional OS, you had a limited set of resources, such as memory and processor time that multiple programs had to share, and thus, fairness was essential. But Pilot would be a single-user system. It could be oriented to serving its human user and not the machine!

Furthermore, Pilot only supported one programming language, Mesa. This was exciting and revolutionary for both

Dan and Janet. Dan recalled the final exam in his Systems Programming course at Illinois, which the professor had ended with, "Go forth and allocate all things to all programs." Traditional operating systems were all about being fair to all the programs. But this was the future, and there was only *one* user!

Charles had heard all this many times, so he read a paper he'd brought with him. After 15 minutes or so, Grant called on him to talk about processes in Mesa. Charles spoke about how Mesa was still immature and lacked the process infrastructure that a serious system like Pilot or the Office of the Future system needed. He spoke about monitors and condition variables, which Dan made a mental note of to research.

It all seemed very deep, and Dan and Janet didn't understand most of it, not to mention that their brains were almost full already. They were powerfully impressed that they would work with people as smart as Charles.

Grant stood up, "We're about out of time. Shall we head over to PARC for lunch? After lunch, we're going to throw even *more* stuff at you." They all agreed to meet in the lobby in five minutes.

Dan stopped by Rosalind's office on his way to the lobby. She had shelves of books and conference proceedings that almost all academic types had in their offices and a desk lamp instead of the overhead fluorescents. She looked up, "Hi, how's it going? It's Dan, right? Are you up to speed on Pilot and Mesa and all that?"

"God, so much to learn! We're going to lunch, and then it's more of the same this afternoon."

"I wish I could join you, but I already have lunch plans. Be sure and try Omar's Feast!" Dan had no idea what that was but figured he'd try it. It sounded more appetizing than ham and limas anyway.

Dan met up with Grant and Janet in the lobby, and the

three walked across Coyote Hill Road to the PARC building. Janet asked Grant about the process synchronization stuff that Charles had talked about, and he explained their origins in the computer science literature, citing Hoare, Dijkstra, Brinch Hansen, and others. He mentioned in passing that the PARC researchers had a metric of arrogance called the micro-dijkstra, where only Dijkstra himself was one million micro-dijkstras. It told you something that a group of people as arrogant as PARC researchers thought of someone *else* as arrogant! Dan felt again like he'd come to the right company if their coworkers knew the gods of computer science that well.

Now that Grant had them transfixed with the micro-dijkstra, he continued on to the milli-lampson, which was a unit of speaking speed. By now, they guessed, correctly, that only Butler Lampson could talk at 1,000 milli-lampsons.

Inside the front doors, PARC had a reception desk, but it lacked the big Security presence El Segundo had. They parted at the entrance of the cafeteria to get their food, and Dan grabbed the Omar's Feast Rosalind told him to try. It seemed to be a tortilla or some kind of thin bread wrapped around sandwich ingredients.

At their table, one of Grant's other engineers, Keith Lammartino, joined them. He had a bushy full beard, like Charles, and Dan and Janet were starting to wonder if that was the uniform up here for programmers. Keith had joined last year after finishing his doctorate from Berkeley, and he seemed to be the brains behind the process synchronization facilities that Charles had described. It was too noisy in the cafeteria to get seriously into technical stuff, though, so they didn't ask him about it.

Keith asked, "What are you guys going to be working on?" Dan wished someone would tell *him* that, "Not sure. The product plans are a little vague right now! "

Keith turned to Janet, "How about you, Janet?"

"Dan knows more than I do! Right now, I'm just trying to get up to speed."

Grant changed the subject, "Aren't we all? Anyhow, did anyone watch the Inauguration yesterday?" No one answered. It was a workday, so they weren't watching TV. "Carter got out of the limo and walked up Pennsylvania Avenue. Pretty cool!"

Dan made the whoop-de-do circle with his finger, "His first act was to pardon all the draft dodgers from Vietnam. Yay!"

Keith laughed, "But now, what's Chevy Chase going to do?"

It was Janet's turn, "I *love* his Gerald Ford impersonation! And, he doesn't even look like Ford."

Dan and Keith exchanged lines from NBC's *Saturday Night Live* skits for a while. "It's a dessert topping! No, it's a floor wax!"

"Did you see the show with Carly Simon? I *know* that song was about me!"

Everyone laughed. Grant proclaimed, "But the indisputably greatest show was the one with Neil Sedaka! I mean, come on!"

Dan thought for a second he might be serious, but something about the look on his face told him not. Janet responded, "I sang 'Breaking Up Is Hard to Do' at my going-away lunch at TRW!"

Keith and Dan both sang, "Comma, comma, down dooby doo down down."

Grant regained control of the conversation, "So, what do you all do for fun down in LA? Hang out on the beach, hobnob with movie stars, that sort of thing?" He looked at Dan and then at Janet.

Dan answered first, "I saw Mary Tyler Moore's car once. I *think* it was hers. It had a license plate MTM, at least."

Keith pretended to back away from the table, "Makes it all worthwhile, the smog and everything, huh?"

Janet said, "Nah, there's no smog where I live. That's inland!"

Dan remembered their drive from the airport and changed the subject, "I have to say, the drive on 280 is a lot nicer than down South. We had a guy at Burroughs who moved up to Sunnyvale and then came back, and he said it was just like Orange County!"

Keith's face looked slightly superior, "Well, he's right. I like to say Southern California begins at San Antonio Road!"

Dan and Janet didn't know where that was in relation to Sunnyvale. Grant had eaten at Chef Chu's at San Antonio and El Camino quite a few times since he moved here, so he knew. He objected, "But Chef Chu's is on the wrong side of that line! Do I have to stop eating there now?"

"Hmm. Hadn't thought of that." Keith turned back to Dan, "Anyhow, it's very important to me to work in a place where I can see horses grazing on my commute."

They didn't have a response to that, but Janet remembered her husband's warning that Bay Area people could be snooty, especially when the subject of water came up. Evidently, people here thought that Los Angeles was always stealing water from them to wash their cars and water their lawns. She steered the conversation to real estate, which seemed safer, "Where do you live, Grant?"

"I've been renting an apartment in Mountain View, on the wrong side of Keith's line. Haven't figured out where I'd want to buy around here."

"We haven't bought anything either. Are prices pretty high here?"

He looked pained, "I'd say. I could buy a palace on an acre of land in Dallas for what a three-bedroom costs here." None of them owned a house, so they all just looked sympathetic. They passed the rest of lunch comparing educational backgrounds, previous work experience, and people they knew in common, and then walked back to the SDD building. Keith said goodbye and returned to his office.

Grant led Dan and Janet to the conference room they'd been in before. "Okay, you know where the bathrooms and kitchen are. Be back here at 1:15." Grant went to Charles' office, where Keith and Charles were chatting. They went silent as he entered.

"So! What do you think so far?" he asked.

Charles didn't want to express an opinion about his new El Segundo colleagues, so he pretended not to understand. "About...?"

"Pretty sharp people? Do you think they can build the product?"

"Time will tell! What *is* the product, by the way?"

Grant had begun to realize this was all passive resistance. He noticed these folks asked questions instead of answering them and stopped whatever conversation they were having when he came in. In previous managing jobs, he'd encountered more overt opposition from his employees, but these people seemed a little more sneaky than his Xerox Management classes had prepared him for. He wanted above all to keep the upper hand and stay managerial.

He parried Charles' question, "I guess they'll tell us that. How's the Functional Spec coming?" That was the next milestone in the schedule Grant had given to his management. The team did not seem to be taking it as seriously as he wanted.

Charles turned to his desk and picked up a thick document, "We were just talking about the new OIS Processor PrincOps when you walked in. It has some new stuff about I/O and virtual memory that we really need to talk over."

Grant felt like they were always showing him some deep technical stuff that someone *else* was doing, and which his group just *had* to pay attention to, even if it meant putting off the milestone they were supposedly working toward. He just wanted to keep to the schedule, but he was starting to think that he was the only person who did.

"I have to get back to our guests. Do I have a copy of that?" pointing to the document. They assured him they'd left one on his chair.

In the conference room, Dan and Janet were sipping coffee and waiting for him. Grant left the door open, "Ready for some Ethernet?"

"Can't wait!" said Janet as Dan nodded.

In walked yet another late 20s guy with a bushy brown beard, "Hi, I'm Michael Campbell, and I'm working for Bob Metcalfe on the Ethernet. Bob couldn't be here today, but he sends his greetings."

"Another guy with a beard!" Beards had been a really radical thing up until the 1960s, and actually still were for the most part. His parents would comment on a beard with a strong note of disapproval, and it was utterly inconceivable that an IBM guy would ever have one. He'd never even considered growing a beard and didn't even know how it would look. Maybe someday he'd try it.

Grant introduced Dan and Janet and sat down in the back, as Michael turned to the whiteboard and drew three big circles with the numbers 1, 2, and 3, and the word AlohaNet in the middle. He faced them, "How many have ever heard of AlohaNet?" Only Grant raised his hand, but he'd heard this talk before.

"AlohaNet is a network in the Hawaiian islands. Bob saw it during a trip there and was inspired. As you probably know, the islands are separated by a lot of water, so laying cable is a bit more of a problem. So, what's the cheapest way to communicate?"

Janet raised her hand, "Radio?"

"Right! The AlohaNet is based on radio. Of course, it has more than three nodes, but we'll just make it simple here. Let's say Dan is on Node 1, and Janet is on Node 2, and you both want to transmit something to Node 3. What happens?"

Dan, who worked in Data Communications support at Burroughs, thought he knew the answer. "We both have to wait for permission to transmit? That's how terminals in a computer system work."

Michael asked, "You mean we need a traffic cop on the net?" Dan nodded. "But what if there *is* no traffic cop? What if the nodes are all equal? Or, the traffic cop goes down?"

Janet was getting interested, "You're out of luck?"

"Right. And… there's another problem. Can anyone see it?"

Janet asked, "The wait for permission. You spend most of your time doing nothing."

Michael was prepared for a long session of painfully pulling the answers out of them. He'd had a few of those, but these people were sharp. "Excellent! On a really fast wire with not too many nodes, the wait time might be okay. But the AlohaNet didn't want to do that, so they pioneered something else. Anyone?" No one knew. "We're going to do a live demo here. I hope this works!" He walked toward them.

"You two both start talking whenever you feel like it. Go ahead and say your names." Dan and Janet looked at each other and both laughed.

Michael said, "On three!" and held up one finger, then two fingers, and on three, they both spoke their names and laughed again.

"That got garbled. Both of you repeat what you just said!" This time Michael didn't give any cues on when to speak. They glanced at each other, then Janet said, "Janet Saunders," and Dan followed immediately, "Dan Markunas."

"Two things happened there. What was the first?" He had the feeling this tutorial was going to work. It didn't always work.

They both wanted to speak, but this time, Dan held out his

hand to let Janet talk. "You noticed we both spoke at the same time."

"Good, and I asked you both to retransmit. And by the way, you two noticed it, too, but we'll come back to that. Then what?"

Now it was Dan's turn, "We synced with each other?"

"Right. Now that part didn't quite fit real life because you two could just look at each other and sync. How else could we handle it?"

Janet looked tentative, "We could both wait for a second and then talk?"

"What if it happened again? And kept happening?"

Dan said, "Wait a random interval?"

Michael pointed at him, "Close enough! We just want to reduce the chances that it'll happen again." He went to the board and wrote Exponential backoff and turned to them again. "Anyone know what this means?" Neither did.

He went into a lengthy explanation of how each side waited longer each time a collision happened, and the times got *much* longer. He also explained how the way that they had noticed, themselves, that they were colliding was really important since a station on the Ethernet did the same thing. He used the cocktail party analogy, which was really popular in explaining Ethernet—two people both start talking and realize it and stop and just naturally work it out. Dan and Janet were riveted.

Michael was triumphant, "That was fun! I need to go make a quick phone call, and then, we'll get back into Ethernet."

They all stood up and stretched. Dan turned to Janet, "Was that great or what?" Grant looked proud of himself for organizing this. Dan tried to recall all the convoluted schemes for controlling terminals he'd learned about in his Burroughs days, generally with the computer playing traffic cop and telling each terminal when it could talk. It was something IBM or AT&T would come up with! They'd make it all big and expensive and dependent on a hierarchy emanating from some central intelligence, which *they* control, naturally. This scheme turned all that on its head! He loved it. This was what he'd come to Xerox for.

Janet was thinking of her experiences dealing with satellites and ground stations at TRW and also of her communications courses at MIT. None of them prepared her for this. She made a mental note to ask her husband, Ken, about it. He dealt with datacomm a lot at Hughes Aircraft.

Grant had heard all this before, and it made sense to him, too, as a business person. You shouldn't compete with IBM on their own turf because you'd lose. Ethernet was a more democratic solution, with no central intelligence in control, and that was the right strategy for an insurgent. He didn't have any particular attachment to *being* an insurgent, but as long as he was working for Xerox—hey, they gave the orders, he was just a soldier.

When they reassembled, Michael went into the physical construction of Ethernet. He held up a length of coaxial cable and a transceiver, which was about the size of a Coke can, and passed them around. Dan wasn't much of a hardware guy, but Janet had loved her circuit courses. She looked inside the transceiver, which wasn't sealed up like a commercial unit, and asked how, exactly, it detected a collision.

He did some math on the board on the capacity of the Ethernet—how long it was, how many stations were on the PARC version, how many on SDD. This was more up Dan's alley since he'd been a math major as an undergraduate. Janet continued looking at the circuitry as Dan walked up to the whiteboard.

Michael and Dan discussed the probability of two stations trying to transmit at the same time and colliding and how often it would have to happen before the Ethernet became useless. Dan could already imagine the future arguments. The stodgy, old-fashioned IBM guys would insist that this would *never* work, and you just had to have a traffic cop to keep order on the net. He loved it! No, you didn't, and they would never accept that without a fight. This wasn't a competing technology they could just appropriate and pretend they'd invented! They'd done that with virtual memory, a Burroughs invention, as everyone at Burroughs would tell you. What a great trip this was turning into!

When they finally wrapped up, Michael passed out copies of Bob and Dave's paper from last year, "Ethernet: Distributed Packet-Switching for Local Computer Networks," and said, "It was great meeting you folks. I'm sure I'll be seeing you around. Give me a call if I can help with anything." As he left, he turned to Grant, "Grant, nice to see you again."

Grant walked up to the front, "Are your brains full now?"

Janet said, "I'm wondering if I can go home and turn our TV antenna coax into an Ethernet!" They all laughed.

As they followed Grant out the door, he said, "That's all the formal presentations we have for you. You guys can go home early, or we can just walk and see who else is around. What time are your flights?"

Dan opened his binder and looked at the ticket envelope in the back folder. "Mine is at 5:00, so I have time."

Janet apologized. "Oh, I'm sorry! I made mine for 4:15. How long will it take to get to the airport now?"

"Dan, you can probably stand by for an earlier flight."

Dan had only ever stood by for a flight once before. Apparently, there were a lot of flights from the Bay Area to LA. This job was going to be so cool! They got in the rental car, with Janet driving this time, "Sorry I'm making you leave early!"

"No problem! It'll be good to be home early." They headed down Page Mill and turned onto 280. "What did you think?"

"It sure is a lot of new stuff, isn't it? What did you think?"

"I'm excited! My favorite was the Ethernet talk. How about you?"

Janet was thoughtful, "I'm wondering what happens if all the computers want to talk at once!"

"Michael and I talked about utilization and collisions quite a bit. I think the math works out."

"I've gotta talk to my husband about that. He works with datacomm a lot in his work."

They were silent for a while as they drove through Los Altos. There was amazingly little traffic, considering that 280 was a major freeway, and it was close to rush hour. In LA, it would be bumper-to-bumper. Dan put his finger on the radio's on-off switch, "Shall we check out Bay Area radio?"

"Sure."

He dialed around and found a station in the middle of "Where Did Our Love Go?" Oldies were always an uncontroversial music choice. Janet signaled her approval. The station was KYA, "Oldies Rock 'n' Roll." After some commercials, it went into "Born to Be Wild." Dan restrained himself from imitating the guitar lead and singing along, although it took some effort. She hummed along. They turned up 17 toward the airport, and suddenly, they found the rush-hour traffic that was missing on 280. They exited at Coleman, returned the rental car, and said goodbye at the terminal. Dan walked up to the gate for the next PSA flight to Orange County and put in his ticket for standby and sat down to read the Ethernet paper Michael had given him. The departure lounge was full of cigarette smoke, which he thought was one of the worst things about flying.

As flight time approached, they called the standby passengers, including Dan. This was so easy!

He'd brought a book to read on the plane, but he couldn't concentrate on it, as he thought about the day's events. This was really where it was all happening, and he wondered why they even needed the group in El Segundo when they had so many smart people up here. But everyone up here seemed to think that actually making a product out of all this technology was just not their thing. He wasn't sure El Segundo could do it, either, but at least he would learn a lot trying.

7

BACK IN REALITY

K en often wore a tie at Hughes. A lot of guys didn't, but then again, a lot still did, and it was one way of showing you were serious. The engineer stereotype was a short-sleeved white shirt, tie, and pocket protector with pens inside. But he figured you could never go wrong looking like all the older guys. But he *never* wore a complete suit—that was for the executives. Usually, he wore semi-casual pants, but never jeans, and something like a sports shirt instead of a formal-looking white shirt.

Today, he removed the tie when he arrived home, changed into his jeans, took a soda out of the fridge, and sat down on the couch with the *LA Times*. In Sports, they were rehashing the playoffs and talking about Sunday's Super Bowl, so the section was extra long. He had switched to the Comics when Janet walked in. He put the paper down, "So… how was it?"

"Exciting! We heard all about the hardware, the software, the network, everything!"

"Great, I want to hear all about it!"

Janet put her stuff on the counter, kissed him, and sat next to him on the couch, "But first, how was your day?

"Oh, the usual. Everything breaking on Friday afternoon. What's it like in Palo Alto?"

"Like a college building. The offices all look like faculty offices."

"Did you find out what kind of hardware your thing, whatever it is, runs on?"

Janet realized that the actual computer hadn't been covered in any talk. She knew what was coming next from her systems-programmer-guy husband. "No, next time. But we did hear about Mesa, Pilot, and Ethernet! Mesa's the language, Pilot's the operating system, and Ethernet is the network."

"But not the actual hardware? Do they even know what it is yet?"

"I'm sure they do. But there's only so much time in a day, Ken."

Ken noticed that Janet used his name, which was usually a warning from her, but he ignored it and pressed on, "I *think* I heard of Ethernet at MIT, vaguely. Remind me."

Janet already knew he was going to hate it. Since he started working at Hughes, he'd picked up that know-it-all attitude that all systems programmers seemed to have. But she felt, for the first time since they'd left school, that she was one up on him. The people at PARC seemed *way* smarter than their aerospace friends here in LA, as well as better looking. But then, he was the guy who actually worked with computers and terminals. With her job in satellites, she just used one channel for sending and one for receiving, so it was a little less complicated.

Janet recounted Michael's demonstration of collision detection and how nothing was in control on the Ethernet. Ken was suspicious. Communications was serious business, developed over decades by the phone company and the military, and it moved very slowly. People were always coming to his group with some whizbang new thing, and his team leader continuously shot it down. *You don't fuck with the datacomm*, that was his attitude. It cost a ton of money to rip out old wiring and put in new stuff, especially if the unions were involved, so you had to plan and budget for it years ahead.

He grilled her, "You want to use a single coax cable? How is it terminated? What happens if it breaks? How do you connect the people on one coax to the folks on another or across town?"

Janet had to admit they hadn't learned those details today. "They've been using it at PARC for a year or so, so I assume it works! We have Ethernet in El Segundo, too."

Ken moved on to the capacity of a coax cable, how much utilization you expected with Ethernet, and how you could possibly program a terminal when you didn't know when you'd be able to send your messages. He wondered how you wrote network software for something so unpredictable and how big and complicated it would be. How would it run on a dumb terminal, which was still what most people used? He had many, many questions.

Janet tried but didn't have answers for most of them, "I guess I'll find all that out!"

He thought this was enough hectoring for now. "Do they at least have a backup plan if this thing doesn't work?"

Janet was getting annoyed. Xerox was a giant company with more Ph.D.s in Computer Science than most universities. She was sick of listening to the old bald men at TRW, which was what this conversation reminded her of. Sometimes, she thought Ken was turning into one of *those* guys, sitting at their war-surplus steel desks in Hughes' World War II green buildings. Xerox, at least, started *after* the war!

"Don't know. I don't have anything for dinner. Do you want to go out?" She went into the bedroom to change clothes. Ken wondered if he'd gone too far with the questioning. It was her new job, so maybe he should just back off for now.

She returned, "Where do you want to go?"

"Jim and Steve and those guys are going to get a table at The Great American Food & Beverage Company. Do you want to go there?"

This was a semi-regular gathering. Ken and Janet were friends with a group of Ken's coworkers, who'd all moved out to LA after college. A few were married, most not. Their informal leader, Steve, lived in the Marina and had a boat, and he'd take them all out fishing during the summer. They met most Sunday mornings at Venice Beach to play volleyball, and now that it was skiing season, that would be a big topic of conversation.

"Sure! Do you think we can get in on a Friday night?" Then checking herself, "Oh, but wait, you said they were getting a table!"

At the Great American, a long line of people waited outside. It was still early, so the staff at the front desk were quoting only an hour wait. But Ken led Janet to the front of the line and told the server they were joining a party that was already seated. He was invited to look around and find them, and after spotting Jim, Steve, and the group in a back room, they found some chairs and sat down.

Steve called out, "Ken! Janet! Just in time. We ordered the plank feast, so there should be plenty for everyone!" He motioned to the waitress for two more glasses. Everyone raised their beer glass to them.

Besides Steve, who was a stocky guy with hair just longer than a crew cut and seemed to be the center of conversation, there was Jim, a Polish guy with thin, scraggly hair from the Chicago area who was Steve's understudy, more or less. Lisa was Jim's girlfriend and the only person other than Janet who didn't work at Hughes. Shelley, a secretary from another department, was recently divorced and had a very large Farrah Fawcett hairdo.

Steve was the social chairman of the group. All skiers at Hughes looking for a place to crash in Mammoth asked Steve first. Everyone liked him, which was why he was a great manager for Hughes. He knew the DEC system inside and out and was on friendly terms with all the various Engineering groups that used it.

Jim had worked for Steve as long as he'd been at Hughes. Steve had introduced him to all his friends when Jim had joined, invited him on group activities, and generally had been his sponsor at work and outside of it. Jim would do anything for Steve, and if you couldn't reach Steve for any reason, you told Jim. He received his Bachelor's from Illinois in Electrical Engineering and moved out to LA a couple of years ago.

His girlfriend, Lisa, was a former tennis player for UCLA and looked somewhat like Amelia Earhart. Jim was a chuck-the-football-around kind of guy himself but not particularly big or muscular, and he'd never been very serious about any sport. He loved that Lisa was better than he was at something and was proud to tell anyone who'd listen that when they played tennis, he was lucky to even win a point. They had a very non-touchy relationship, and it was rare to see them holding hands.

Shelley married just out of high school and had helped put her husband through college and law school, after which he'd promptly divorced her. She'd managed to finish her Bachelor's two years after that, and she was thankful they didn't have kids. After the divorce, she'd moved to the Oakwood apartments in the Marina, where nearly everyone was single, and there were constant parties and planned events. The group wondered if she and Steve were sleeping together, but they always had separate bedrooms when they went skiing.

When Ken and Janet sat down, Steve was in the middle of

coordinating the next ski trip, which was three weeks from now. They'd be going to Mammoth again, the second time this season, renting a condo together. They had to yell over the noise of the crowd and the occasional singing waiters, which was a signature attraction of the Great American. You actually had to audition to be a waiter, and if you didn't know some upbeat, crowd-pleasing song, you weren't hired. Periodically, one or two or more of them gathered and performed some song on various instruments, after which they went back to serving food. It was great for tips. Right now, they were doing an endless version of "Rubberband Man," complete with the Spinners' dance steps. Finally, they finished to thunderous applause, and you could talk again.

"Mammoth in three weeks! Be there or be square!" Steve yelled to them. Ken raised his beer glass, then looked at Janet. She hesitated a second, then raised hers. Just then, two waiters brought the plank feast and put it down on the table to cheers from everyone. This was a specialty of the house—a large pile of beef ribs, chicken, flank steak, corn on the cob, fruit, rice, veggies, and whatever else was ready in the kitchen, all heaped without dishes on the plank. Then, the waiters were joined by two others, and they all formed a semi-circle around Ken and Janet and broke into their "Happy Anniversary" song, to the tune of the *William Tell Overture*. "Happy Anniversary" was a staple, except that they sang "Welcome to Los Angeles" when Janet and Ken were new.

[1]Janet laughed and applauded along with the crowd. When they left, she said to the table, "But it's not our anniversary!"

Shelley yelled, "It is now!"

Ken said, "I guess Steve just wanted to hear the song again."

Steve held out his hands, palm up, "Dig in!" They all took turns grabbing food off the plank. After everyone had stuffed themselves, the conversation turned to the previous Mammoth trip and the upcoming one. The snow was late this winter, and Mammoth hadn't opened until just before Christmas. All of them had gone for the first trip of the year the weekend before last. Mammoth was the usual mob scene, with half-hour lines for the more popular lifts. They recounted which ski runs they'd done, how many runs they managed, memorable wipe-outs, how long the lift lines were, the number and depth of the moguls at the various runs, and all the usual topics. All were at least intermediate skiers, but Steve prided himself on being an expert, and Lisa was quite good, too.

Ken yelled over the noise, "So, Lisa! Are you going to do Scotty's Run this time? You were looking pretty good last time." She just smiled. Scotty's Run was a black diamond run named for a skier who died there. Only a professional, or someone suicidal, would attempt it.

Steve turned to Janet, "So, Janet, we hear you have a new job?"

"I do! Just flew up to the Bay Area today."

Jim put his elbows on the table and looked at her, "It's at Xerox? Are you going to put computers in the copiers or what?" He laughed.

She laughed, too. "I think somebody's doing that, but I'm not."

"Well, what *are* you doing?"

"I can't talk about it much, but it's a new computer that goes on your desk!"

Steve replied, "Wow! How big is it?"

"Can't say."

Ken was about to add, "That's because they don't know," but he restrained himself.

"Is it true they all hate us in the Bay Area?" Steve asked with a smirk.

Janet laughed, "I heard something about how we were stealing their water!" Jim picked up his water glass and looked at it.

Shelley jumped in, "We just replaced our Xerox machine with a Japanese thing. Ricoh or something."

Janet pushed her chair back and stood up, "You'll have to tell me about that at the condo! Right now, I'm exhausted, so I think we're going to call it a night. Right, Ken?"

Ken stood up, "Right! Long day today. See you all at Mammoth, if not before."

8

DAN MOVES TO THE BEACH

The day after the Palo Alto trip, Dan moved to Hermosa Beach, one of three towns just south of LAX that had "Beach" in their name, because he'd always wanted to live near the beach. It was the Southern California dream! Hermosa was the hippie of the trio, while Manhattan Beach was wealthy with upscale bars and restaurants. That was where flight attendants and newly divorced men lived. Redondo Beach was corporate and touristy, featuring a long pier with expensive shops and chain restaurants. But Hermosa, which was in between the other two, cultivated a scruffy, surfer image. It had a very wide beach and a long fishing pier that was always busy. It also had large monuments to famous surfers. The Strand was a sidewalk-like strip in between the sand and the houses that bicyclists, roller skaters, and runners used, and it went all the way to Santa Monica.

As long as he'd lived in Orange County, he yearned to move to LA proper. His friends from the University of Illinois, who all worked in aerospace, lived in LA, and it seemed that no matter what they all did together, whether skiing, concerts, backpacking, or whatever, it always required him to go to their neighborhood. Orange County had no culture, but finally, he was out of there!

His apartment was on Monterey, the third street up from the beach. There was a two-story building with eight apartments that faced the street, and in back, there was another, smaller building, with two second-floor apartments overlooking the alley, one of them his. His one-bedroom, which was surprisingly large for a beach apartment, was directly over the garage with his parking spot. It had hardwood floors, which hadn't been refinished in ages, so he made a mental note to buy an area rug for the living room. Wooden shutters covered the windows facing the alley, and the entrance had a decrepit screen door. Being near the beach meant the smog and mosquitos blew inland, and it never got excessively hot.

If you lived near the beach, you *had* to have your own parking spot since there was often no parking on the street. The door on his garage lacked an automatic opener—that was suburban nonsense! So, he had to get out of the car, unlock the padlock, and open the door. But at least it was a garage, and it kept the car's paint safe from the salt air.

The alley was a popular place to park illegally, and he was always running out yelling at people blocking his garage. Usually, they'd say they were only stopping for a couple of minutes, and if he called the towing company, they would, in fact, be gone before the tow truck arrived.

Walking down to the beach or the Pier was a great joy of living so close to the beach. Even in the middle of winter, it was never deserted like an East Coast beach in winter. The hassles of fighting the traffic and finding a parking spot that non-residents suffered was gone! He could grab food at any of the places with walk-up windows, have a drink at a bar, not that he went to bars much, see a classic movie at the Surf Theater, or hear jazz at The Lighthouse. The Lighthouse was a premier place for big-name jazz artists. He'd seen Mose Allison and Milt Jackson there before he even moved here, and he looked forward to being able to go whenever he wanted.[1]

A little way up from the beach on Pier Avenue was a very small bookshop, a local institution, the Either/Or. It occupied a multi-level building because the street sloped sharply up from the beach, and it stocked interesting arts, psychology, poetry, New Age, and history books. Charles Bukowsky used to autograph copies of his books. Dan spent a long time browsing the books. He was going to like it in Hermosa!

Back at the apartment, he looked through his technical articles from the Palo Alto trip. He read the original Ethernet paper by Metcalfe and Boggs, then thumbed through his old copies of *Communications of the ACM* and *Computing Surveys*, which were two of the scholarly publications of the Association for Computing Machinery. He felt virtuous to have the magazines, and usually when one came in the mail, he read the contents and resolved to read the articles later. He read a lot, but mostly fiction, history, politics, arts, and non-technical books, and he always felt guilty that he didn't read more technical stuff. These Palo Alto people struck him as the type who read it every waking hour! He'd need to up his game.

Computing Surveys had an article by Theodore Linden on "Operating System Structures to Support Security and Reliable Software" and one on "Fault Tolerant Operating Systems" by Peter Denning, which sounded like things he should read. And at the talk about Pilot on Friday, someone had mentioned *monitors and condition variables*, and that seemed vaguely familiar. He looked through his old *Communications of the ACM* and found "Monitors: An Operating System Structuring Concept" by Denning.

Dan read it quickly and thought he really needed to read it again more carefully, but what he absorbed was that a *monitor* let simultaneous processes avoid stepping on each other. If you had two or more processes that needed to access the same object, or *resource*, they had to enter the monitor first, and only one had it at a time. Your process had to wait if another process had it, and the *condition variable* woke you. Of course, there was much more to it than that. Sometimes, he loved that kind of stuff. It reminded him of studying calculus during his freshman year in college, which was the first time he ever thought that math was intrinsically interesting, instead of just useful.

He read that paper and gave himself a pat on the back. Then, he went to the supermarket and bought food for dinner. He hadn't made it to the bank to get cash, so he'd have to write a check. He wasn't sure they'd even accept a check from a non-local bank, but fortunately, they did.

After dinner, he watched *60 Minutes* and the other Sunday night TV, followed by the news, and then to bed.

Monday morning at the office, he dropped in on Tom. Janet was already sitting in a guest chair.

"So, how was it? Janet tells me you learned about Pilot and Ethernet and all that."

"It was great! I think we barely scratched the surface. Right, Janet?"

"Yeah, it was fun. It left me with a lot of questions about Ethernet, though." She didn't want to say that she'd told her husband about it since she wasn't sure what was supposed to be confidential. This stuff wasn't national-security-related like her job at TRW, but still, you never knew.

"Oh? Like what? I can try to answer them, but I'm not promising anything."

Janet thought for a second. Dan had questions of his own, but he waited. "Well, it has no central authority. How busy can it get? Won't you reach a point where everyone wants to talk, and they're just interfering with each other?"

Tom turned back to the pile of papers on his desk and dug out an article, "You're in luck. That, we have an answer for."

He stood up and handed it to her, "I have to head to a meeting now, but why don't we reconvene around 11:00?"

As they walked back to their office, Dan glanced at the article Janet was holding, "Can I read that when you're done?"

"Sure!"

In his office, Dan looked at the reading material he'd accumulated, including the stuff from Friday's visit. So much to know! Where to start? This wasn't school where you had a homework assignment or an exam, and it wasn't like a normal job where they gave you a training task, and you just had to learn the language and operating system. It was more like building an entire neighborhood, and you were supposed to help on the biggest building, but it didn't even have a rough sketch yet, let alone blueprints.

The Alto had fantastic programs, like Bravo, Draw, and Markup, but those were independent efforts, confined to a particular subject, and each had its own user interface. Whatever they were supposed to build for office workers needed a consistent user interface. What a massive responsibility to define that. Who would do it? He didn't know. Maybe *he* could do it! But how? And would people say, "What qualifications do *you* have to do this? You don't even have a doctorate. You didn't work at PARC." And anything that he did do, a hundred people with better credentials would argue about every last little bit of it. Everyone had an opinion here, about everything.

Still, Tom had encouraged him to play around and experiment, on the theory that anything he learned would be useful later on, even if it didn't lead to anything concrete right now. He'd never had a job like this!

Dan imagined explaining all this to his parents or his brothers, none of whom had gone to college. "You don't have any actual work to do? Sweet deal! You can go to the beach." was what his brothers might say.

His mom asked, "What time must you be at work? Do you get a coffee break? How long do you have for lunch?" She had worked at the Eastman Kodak factory on the South Side of Chicago as an assembly line worker before getting married, but then she never worked outside the house again. Her ideas of the world of work were a little limited.

His old neighborhood on the far South Side was heavily influenced by large-scale industry, such as Republic Steel, Chicago Bridge & Iron, International Harvester, and Pullman Car Company. In high school, the children of factory workers tended to be the greasers, and the children of white-collar workers were more likely honor students. His father was an office worker for Swift & Co., one of the giant meatpacking companies that built Chicago. The dream job description for the factory workers in his neighborhood was, "It's a nice inside job with no heavy lifting." The last thing they wanted was a job outside in the Chicago weather.

His thoughts returned to the pile of documentation in front of him. Actually, the heavy lifting for him was deciding what to do first. Read the articles? Definitely, but eventually, he wanted to *do* something. He might mock up some sort of user interface for all the features the product needed, but first, he'd have to figure out what they were. Various documents were floating around about that, but nothing final.

What could he create when the Mesa system was embryonic, at best, and the Pilot operating system wasn't even built yet? How did your program find out what the user was doing with the mouse, for example? Or the keyboard? And for that matter, what *kind* of mouse? The mice that came with the Alto had three buttons on them—was that what they were going with? The Alto also had a "keyset," a little five-key keyboard with keys about three inches long, and you could chord the keys, which meant pressing several at once. Some people in Palo Alto were very enamored with the keyset, and they'd even figured out how to type regular characters with it. Would the product have one? *That* would be pretty cool.

Dan picked up his Mesa manual and looked for something he hadn't read yet. Then, he started writing a program on scratch paper, which kept a simple database in a file, and headed off to look for an unused Alto. Soon, he'd have his own Alto!

9

GRANT BROODS

On Saturday, January 8, 1977, Grant checked out of the Rickey's Hyatt and drove to his new rental house in Mountain View. He didn't know if he wanted to buy a home here at all, let alone where, so renting was fine for now. The moving company would bring the furniture sometime next week. He took a break from carrying in stuff from his car, sat down on the floor, leaned against the wall, and pondered his new job. An hour went by. He thought about yesterday's visit from the El Segundo people, Dan and Janet. He'd known there were Pilot users at locations other than Palo Alto, but this was the first time he'd met any of them.

Grant tried to leave work at the office when he left. It was difficult with this job, though. It was so exciting sometimes. The technology was all new, and the people were so bright. Everyone was friendly, too. You didn't see the serious faces that everyone wore in Dallas or the dourness of the Rochester office.

Email was a big deal here and not only for work. All kinds of non-work-related mailing lists had sprung up, and he received maybe 50 emails a day, which occupied a significant

part of his time. Some topics were so common that there were
digests of them on MAXC, their PDP-10 lookalike, with
nothing but the collected suggestions for restaurants or bicycling routes. Another file collected Xerox folklore, some of
which he'd heard on his first day, like the milli-lampson.

It was easy to find people with similar interests. One girl
seemed to be continuously roller skating the hallways, and she
made a point of making him feel welcome. He wasn't sure
what, exactly, she did here, but she certainly brightened things
up. He hadn't gone to graduate school, but he imagined this
was similar but with better food and better pay.

On the business side, copiers were becoming a really
competitive business, after 20 years of being almost a Xerox
monopoly. The Japanese companies were flooding in, and
IBM had copiers, too. Xerox *had* to branch out into something
else, and the price of computer components was falling so fast
that maybe someday every office worker *could* have their own
computer! Who knew? Being on the ground floor of that
could be career-making. IBM's big advantage, supposedly, was
that their salesmen knew the important people in every
company, but then, so did Xerox's.

He kept replaying in his head his interactions with the
Pilot team, who were supposedly *his people*. Were they actually
keeping him apprised of what they were doing? Whenever he
talked to one of them, it came out that they'd had some deep
technical discussion with someone on the Mesa team, or the
hardware team, or the networking team, or someone at
PARC, and he hadn't heard about it. Or maybe, an email
discussion with PARC researchers happened, and he hadn't
been copied on it.

It didn't help that they loved stories about engineers
creating great products behind the boss' back and against
universal skepticism. "The world doesn't need photocopiers!"
was the industry's attitude that gave Xerox its opening. Gary
Starkweather developed the laser printer after his boss told

him it was a stupid idea. Almost everyone Xerox hired had a secret ambition to create the next big thing while no one was looking, and the countercultural fallout from the 1960s didn't help, either. That was why PARC had these stupid beanbag chairs that Grant couldn't stand.

His group, the Systems Development Department (SDD), was making good progress in taking over the PARC inventions that they needed to build products for, but good grief, was it ever a slow process. Taking over the Mesa language, for example. What did that mean? A language was more than just a compiler and a manual—it involved training new users, building systems to support very large programs, and lots of utilities like a debugger. Management, of course, wanted it all done in a few weeks of handover. His own people were doing that work and often not even telling him until he asked.

"*What this project needs is some old-fashioned management!*" He'd started to conclude that he was in the wrong job as manager of just the operating system. A better fit would be a job that used his organizational skills to deliver the product as a whole. He'd succeeded at that task before in Dallas, and the company had brought him out here to do it again.

Almost no one here devoted their attention to the overall product. They concentrated on their own little parts of it, like doctoral candidates on their dissertations. This was not surprising since most of them had been exactly that, Ph.D. students, in their recent past. But this was a giant corporation, not a research group. Not all the bright people at Xerox were in California, which they seemed to forget.

Grant wondered if he should talk to Michael, his boss, about changing his job. The Pilot operating system group should be run by some guy with an academic background in operating systems whom the team would all respect. And, Grant was not that guy. He should do what he did best and provide adult supervision and interface with the rest of Xerox. For example, he knew that the Dallas group had a new product coming out, a smart word processor. When he'd brought that up with Michael, he'd been encouraged to pursue it. Perhaps that was a hint?

Now that he had a plan to fix things, he felt better. It was almost 1:00 pm. He got in the car and went looking for a lunch place. After lunch, he took his bike out for a ride. He'd tried being a bike racer in Missouri after college, but he quickly discovered that the real racers had all started at around age 12 and were in way better shape than he was. As fit as he was, he was never going to be competitive with those guys, and fortunately, he had quit before he hated the very thought of bikes, the way some failed racers did. Now, it was just a fun hobby. He'd gone biking in Scotland a couple of years ago and had a great time, despite the rain and hurricane-force winds in places.

He'd been asking around and reading the file of bike rides on MAXC. Today, he thought he'd try the loop, which was apparently a very popular route over in Portola Valley. Part of riding The Loop was a stop at Zot's, which was what they called the beer garden whose real name was Rossotti's or The Alpine Inn, depending on whom you asked. He'd already been in several offsite meetings at Zot's. Biking was not popular in Texas, and you were always afraid someone would run you off the road accidentally. He might like California!

10

REAL WORK, SORT OF

D an was having one of his daily baseball talks with Tom. It was almost April, spring training was ending, and the season started soon. Baseball was their favorite conversation opener. They didn't follow basketball or football as much, and it had been a long winter with no baseball news except for some trades. Dan called that period *the void*. The void was almost over, and life was beginning anew.

The prospects for the Los Angeles Dodgers were bright. They had a new manager, Tommy Lasorda, replacing Walt Alston, who'd managed since they were in Brooklyn. Over the winter, they'd traded Bill Buckner and others to the Cubs for Rick Monday and another player. They had an imposing infield, finally, with Garvey, Lopes, Russell, and Cey.

Tom was a loyal California Angels fan, but he didn't have any false optimism about them. He would ruefully admit that they'd be lucky to play .500 ball this year, even though they'd signed some promising free agents over the winter, including Don Baylor, Bobby Grich, and Joe Rudi. The Angels just had *something* wrong with them, and most sports fans blamed The Cowboy, as owner Gene Autry was called after his most famous movie role. Dan and Tom were rehashing all that this morning.

Finally, they got around to work. Dan had been practicing his Mesa and reading every available bit of documentation since he'd been at Xerox, trying to follow the email traffic from Palo Alto, and flying up twice more since his initial January 7 visit. But now, he was itching for a real assignment. Surely with all this work to be done to create the Office of the Future, he could do *something* now!

Tom was not the sort of person to just grab a big idea and start doing it. He wanted formal permission from Paul, at least. If he'd had a personal vision of what their product should be and given it to Dan to prototype, Dan would have been ecstatic! But Tom was a corporate manager who didn't make waves, had no strong opinions of his own, and never, never offended anyone. That was why he had that job.

Today though, Tom had a small smile because he had good news for Dan. Tom had permission, amazingly enough! Not to go rogue and design the product itself, which was way too much to hope for. Rather, he had the authority to lend some of his people to an official effort to prototype it. He'd volunteered Dan and Brian Lerner, another engineer who'd been recruited from UCLA by Mark. Dan liked Brian, so he was pleased about this.

Dan had come to realize that Tom often knew a lot more than he told you initially, but he wasn't sure if this was ingrained management training or just modesty. Either way, you had to question him persistently if you really wanted to know what was happening. It took a good 15 minutes to drag it all out of him, but eventually, Tom confirmed that this project was intended to do what Dan had fantasized about, namely, create a proof-of-concept for this thing. It wasn't quite what he wished for, which was a live market test of the product to find out what businesses were willing to pay for it, but it was a start. They were supposed to produce the user interface the product would have, but with the Mesa language, the Pilot operating system, and all the other tools so that Xerox could see how it behaved.

Carroll Molnár was leading the project, codenamed Diamond. Dan hadn't met Carroll, but he knew that Carroll had written Bravo, the text editor that Xeroids used. He'd also noticed that the *á* in Carroll's last name was supposed to have an accent mark, but accented characters were a mystery to everyone except Carroll, so usually, it was just Molnar.

Dan and Brian were El Segundo's representatives on the project, and they would give El Segundo some early experience with the Mesa tools. What exactly they'd do wasn't specified yet, but Tom told Dan it might have something to do with printing. He encouraged Dan to go up North soon to start working with Carroll's team.

Dan was thrilled when he left Tom's office. Finally, a real task! He didn't know anything about printing, but then, nobody knew about *any* of these areas, so what the hell—he'd learn it. He sent an email to Carroll. He told him how excited he was to be working on Diamond, and they set up a day next week for Dan to come up. Friday, April 1 was a very auspicious day! Ever since Dan started working, he had an April Fool's Day tradition of pulling the same prank on his manager, usually a different person than the year before. He'd tape down the button on his manager's phone and then call him. His manager picked up the receiver, "Hello," and the phone kept ringing! Hilarious. He'd *hate* missing that this year.

In the meantime, Carroll gave him the names of the documents about print formats he should read. He found them on MAXC, transferred them via the FTP program to his Alto, and then printed them from Bravo. What a gigantic pain printing things was! But then, Xerox was obviously the best possible company to make it easy. That *was* their job, after all.

When he was picking up his documents at the printer, he ran into Brian, who was printing out the stuff for his project.

They walked to Brian's office. Brian was supposed to implement the Boyer-Moore string searching algorithm, which he didn't know anything about, but he'd just printed out the prepublication paper.

Brian was a cheerful, very good-looking guy who never spoke an unkind word about anyone, although he'd often laugh at your comments. He was way more likely to ask you how you were doing than to tell you anything personal about himself. He came from a large family in a small town where his father was a music teacher and went to a state college in that same town. He played the saxophone, but never jazz or rock, and no soloing. He played strictly orchestral or marching-band music. Brian read a lot of books on all sorts of nontechnical topics, so he and Dan had plenty to talk about. They were already looking forward to going to Dodger games with the other guys from UCLA.

Dan felt envious of Brian's easy-going nature and how everyone seemed to love him. Unlike Brian, Dan always disliked *someone* in any large organization, and even worse, they always knew! He had never been a joiner, and even as a kid, he'd dropped out of Cub Scouts. At Burroughs, he often felt it was high school, where being aggressively stupid was almost a requirement to be popular.

The best thing about Xerox, on the other hand, was that he actually *liked* a lot of these people, and they were smart, so it didn't take any superhuman efforts to be nice to them. Brian was one of those smart folks.

In Brian's office, they sat down and started reading their printouts. Dan looked up at Brian, "Press? You ever heard of that?"

"No, what is it?"

"It's apparently some sort of print file format. What's your project about?"

"Something called the Boyer-Moore string searching algorithm. From what I can tell so far, you first look for the *end* of the pattern, rather than the beginning."

"Oh, so then you don't have to look at every character in the string? Clever."

Brian was happy, "Okay, now I'm really looking forward to reading this!" Dan took that as a signal to go back to his office.

Later on, Mark, Steve Blewitt, and Randy Carter peeked in on Dan, "Lunch?"

Dan stood up, "Where to?" Although they might go to the Xerox cafeteria, especially if time was tight, that was so depressing that usually you'd say, "Across the street?" rather than "Lunch?"

Mark said, "We were thinking El Tabasco!" El Tabasco was their nickname for a Mexican dive in *downtown* El Segundo, whose real name was El Tarasco. Its "daily special" was the same every day—the Junior Super Deluxe Burrito. Since that part of town was directly under the flight paths from LAX and very close to the Chevron refinery and a large power plant, "downtown El Segundo" was a guaranteed laugh line in LA comedy clubs.

They stopped by Brian's office and invited him, walked out to the parking lot, and piled into Dan's car. He had a Volkswagen Dasher, not all that big but the only car that could hold all five of them. Brian had a Chevy Nova, which technically was large enough, but it was old with torn upholstery and chronically full of junk, and he made a big show of offering to drive while apologizing for the clutter. So, Dan usually ended up being the driver.

El Tarasco was about four miles away. On the way, they talked about the project and how clueless the Xerox management seemed to be. Mark, Steve, and Randy attended the interminable meetings with Tom and higher management, where plans were hammered out, or not, depending on what day it was. They never talked about it in any detail with Dan and Brian, though, unless a decision had been made official.

Power in the big company came from knowing something other people didn't.

Mark knew *everything*, it seemed, but he only told you stuff when he wanted to, so asking him questions was pointless. He knew all about Dan and Brian's projects, of course, "I hear you guys are gonna be working with Carroll. Sounds like fun." Brian answered, "Yeah, I'm excited."

Dan said, "Me, too! So, this is sorta a prototype of Janus?"

He'd noticed that Xerox had a codename for the thing they were working on. Every non-public project had a codename, and novice Xeroids always asked for a list of all them. If they asked a manager, they were told that any such document might be leaked, and then, a hostile actor would know what *everything* meant. So, no official announcement proclaimed that the Display Word Processor was now Janus.

Randy jumped in, "Yes, it's one more prototype of a mockup of a conceptual model of a think piece!"

Steve answered, "I think you left out taxonomy."

"Oh, right! And outline."

Steve said, "While they're recapitulating the taxonomy, maybe we should just build the stupid thing!"

Mark jumped in, "Now, now! Attitude there."

Steve turned to Dan, "So Dan, how do you think the Dodgers are gonna do this year?"

Dan laughed, "Well if they get some pitching, they could go all the way!"

Brian asked Mark, "When are we going to our first Dodgers game?"

Mark was the social chairman for the group, so he automatically answered these questions, "Well... who has the schedule?"

Dan reached into his wallet and pulled out the little schedule that convenience stores stocked near the cash register. "First homestand is with the Giants. We probably want to skip that. Braves are here April 11 to 13."

Mark checked the calendar in his wallet, "Maybe the 12th. I'll have to check with Jacki." Jaqueline, or Jacki, was Mark's wife.

The conversation turned to their colleagues who were still at UCLA and which ones they could recruit, the upcoming David Frost interviews with Nixon, the musical guests coming up on NBC's *Saturday Night Live* show, and the stupidity of the Security department in El Segundo. As they returned to the Xerox parking lot, Mark reminded him, "Now remember not to back into your parking spot, Dan!"

"I didn't *back in* that time! I pulled through."

Randy led them all in a chant of "Pull through! Pull through!"

11

ETHERNET AND SMALLTALK

J anet sat in her office, with manuals, papers, and research reports stacked on her desk. She finally had her own Alto, along with a rack for keeping the various disks she'd accumulated. After checking her email on MAXC and wishing they had a dedicated Alto program for mail, she looked at the Ethernet cable connected to the Alto. It was a regular coax cable, and it ran at three megabits per second. You'd pay the phone company thousands of dollars a month for a fraction of that! Granted, it was only that fast within a narrow radius, but still, most of your computing needs were local.

She'd heard that the product Xerox was going to ship was aiming for 20 megabits.[1] It was amazing. But, as people at Xerox explained, imagine an entire office full of knowledge workers with their own computers, sending documents and email to each other and to the printer. How much bandwidth would they need? A lot! Someone in Palo Alto had done a whiteboard exercise on the bandwidth required for teleportation, in other words, sending an entire human being through the wire. It wasn't that they took the prospect of teleportation seriously, but still, it was fun, and she enjoyed being around people who had fun at work.

Ken scoffed and insisted that Ethernet would never work. This was a recurring argument with them that was starting to annoy her, although usually she'd just smile and change the subject. He kept hurling the word *deterministic* as if it were a magic talisman. On the Ethernet, you weren't certain how long you'd have to wait to transmit your data. If the wire was busy when you wanted to talk, you had to wait.

If someone else tried to transmit *exactly* when you did, you both had to back off and try again. An engineer could give you the probabilities of various results, but no more. This was not real engineering, and Ken was offended by it. He was even offended by the word "ether" since any beginning physics student knows that ether was a bogus concept that was disproven ages ago.

The entire communications field that the two of them had studied at MIT was based on strict mathematical calculations and guarantees. For example, when you make a telephone connection, that circuit is yours until you're done. No other calls interfere with yours. The telephone companies had spent decades perfecting this system, and they had a monopoly. How could any company, even one as big as Xerox, hope to change that?

She tried telling him that packet-switching was a real discipline, and the Defense Department itself was backing it. It was originally designed to survive a nuclear attack that destroyed some of the military's communications lines. With packetswitching, the message was broken up into pieces, or packets, and the packets might arrive on separate paths. Ken didn't believe it would ever have commercial applications. People in aerospace had a low opinion of commercial stuff anyway.

Last night, Ken had told her that Hughes Aircraft was looking to hire more engineers, and of course, women were especially in demand. This was not his first attempt to entice her back to aerospace, and she was getting tired of it.

Janet had spent a lot of time with some of the Ethernet guys when she was last up in Palo Alto. They told her about the simulations that Bob had done several years ago that convinced him Ethernet worked, and furthermore, they had real statistics on PARC's usage for the past years. It was almost a settled issue for them.

Janet wanted to work on that *so* much! But how? The networking team was all in Palo Alto, and she was in El Segundo, and it was just too difficult to be a remote team member. You'd miss out on all the informal hallway chat. She'd talked to Tom about it, and he was sympathetic and promised to help. She believed him, but he had no idea what he could do, or when. In the meantime, she kept in email contact with the team and read all the articles they sent her about *local area networks*, which was a term she'd never heard before coming to Xerox.

But ever since Tom had offered her the chance to work on the Diamond project with Dan and Brian and she didn't take it, she still didn't know what she was going to do until the networking thing came through, if it ever did. She chatted with folks, and Mark told her there was this proto-type of a user interface in some language called Smalltalk, which a guy right here in El Segundo was helping with. Of course, Smalltalk was not what they were going to be using since Mesa was the official language. She was intrigued and asked Mark if he had any materials on it. He found a paper for her.

Smalltalk was a project at PARC. It was object-oriented, which was a term she remembered, vaguely, from her college classes. But the more she learned about it, the more fascinated she became. It was easy to produce overlapping windows, and most astonishing of all, you could look at the code for every-thing and even *change it on the fly*! You might to change the definition of the scrollbar to be blue, recompile it, and all the windows with scrollbars instantly changed.

She found the guy, Todd Clemens, who was working on that demo and knocked on his door. He was typing on his Alto with his feet on the desk and the keyboard on his lap and didn't notice her at first. "Oh, hi! What can I do for you?"

They introduced themselves and shook hands, "I hear you're working on Smalltalk."

"Yeah, I sure am. Would you like to hear about it? Pull up a chair!" He took his feet off the desk and rotated the display so that she could see it.

Todd was a blond guy who somehow just looked hippieish, although he was neatly dressed and didn't have particularly long hair. He had actually played guitar on the street in Santa Cruz. He'd gone back to school in Computer Science at Berkeley. Todd was very intense about computer languages and had done graduate work in them, had heard of Mesa before coming to Xerox, and was almost evangelical about Smalltalk. Janet had the feeling she was going to be listening to him for a while.

He explained that the new thing in user interfaces was *icons*. None of the PARC prototypes had them, but a Palo Alto guy, Henry Davis, had invented them as a way of representing common desktop objects, like folders and documents, and a few things that didn't exactly go on a physical desktop, like printers, trash cans, and file cabinets. The idea was that the computer was a representation of your desktop. Instead of you adjusting to the computer, the computer adjusted to you.

Xerox had *almost* completely bought into icons and the desktop metaphor anyway, but Todd and Henry were mocking it up so that people could actually try it. Their demo had icons that opened into windows, overlapping windows, scroll bars on the right side of the window instead of the left, and even a working document editor, which was just the Smalltalk text editor.

Janet had discovered already that when she told people outside Xerox what she was working on, she might as well be speaking Swahili. They usually just smiled politely and changed the subject.

To an ordinary person, a computer was either a spinning tape drive or a disembodied voice. HAL in the movie *2001* was a good example of the latter. They couldn't imagine a computer like that. They might have read somewhere that computers were getting smaller, but to them, that only meant they'd become refrigerator-sized instead of room-sized.

This stuff was the future. Todd continued, excitedly explaining what object-oriented meant. He quoted Alan Kay, the inventor of Smalltalk,

"Smalltalk's design—and existence—is due to the insight that every-thing we can describe can be represented by the recursive composition of a single kind of behavioral building block that hides its combination of state and process inside itself and can be dealt with only through the exchange of messages."

In a monolog that Janet didn't attempt to interrupt, Todd explained that everything was an object—a document, a window, an icon. Even a number could be an object, although you might not want to push it that far. If your object wanted to use another object for something, such as to open a window, it sent that object a message. You had no idea how it did what you asked, and moreover, you shouldn't! It might want to change its implementation, and that should not affect you. Objects were instances of *classes*.

He demonstrated classes and objects by bringing up the class browser and finding the ScrollBar and Image classes and Image class' Show method. A window showed the actual code for Show. Todd edited the code to add a black border, pressed a mouse button, which brought up a menu, and he selected compile. Moments later, all the scrollbars had black borders. Janet had the feeling that this was a standard demo that he did for everyone, but still, she was genuinely impressed. Todd handed her a stack of documents about Smalltalk. She started for the door but turned back, "I guess this is a dumb question, but I'll ask it anyway."

Todd interrupted her, "You're wondering why we aren't using Smalltalk instead of Mesa to build Janus?"

Janet laughed, "Well... yeah!"

Todd looked agitated, "No, it's not a dumb question *at all.* That's what I've been asking Henry."

"And what does he say?"

"Oh, something about how Mesa is a systems language that's tailor-made for our product, it scales to hundreds of programmers, the D-series hardware is tuned to it... that kind of thing."

"I don't know what D-series hardware means, but anyway, you're not buying it?"

Looking frustrated, Todd stood up, "I can give you the docs about the D-series, but you probably already have them. Anyway, no... I'm... not! Look at how easy it is to develop in Smalltalk. Granted, it's pretty slow with all that message-passing, but hell, we have a lot of bright people at Xerox. I'm sure they can figure it out."

"Makes sense to me. Have you raised this with anyone besides Henry?"

"No, not yet. Maybe I should!"

She smiled and turned back to the door, "Well, I have a lot of reading to do. This has really been great, Todd. Thanks!"

"Hey, no problem. Great meeting you!"

12

LET'S GET THIS SHOW ON THE ROAD

D an and Brian flew up to San Jose on the morning of April 1, 1977 for their first meeting with Carroll Molnár's group. Carroll was in charge of the prototype for Janus, and they were going to help! This wasn't some silly Smalltalk hack that bore no relation to the real thing, and it wasn't a tired old BCPL program inherited from PARC, either. It was in Mesa, and it was supposed to be a prototype as realistic as possible.

Carroll's group was busy working at their Altos when they arrived. He took Dan and Brian around and introduced them —Bill, a long-haired guy with glasses, around 6' tall; Joe, a curly-haired guy with a scraggly beard, about 5' 8"; and Jill, a petite woman with shortish hair. He gathered them all, found an empty conference room, and welcomed Dan and Brian. They went around the table and talked about what they were working on. Dan thought they were mostly recreating Bravo, the revolutionary text editor that introduced the term WYSI- WYG, what you see is what you get, meaning what you saw on the screen would be what came out on paper, but in Mesa. The graphics work was being done by a guy who wasn't at the meeting.

Dan had a memorable exchange with Carroll about WYSIWYG mode in Bravo at the meeting, before he learned to hold his tongue. He raised his hand, "WYSIWYG mode is kinda weird, isn't it? The characters look squashed." Nobody spoke for a few seconds.

Carroll replied, "We prefer to think of the other as non-WYSIWYG mode!" Everyone laughed.

While they were in a jovial mood, Carroll couldn't resist another story. "You all have heard this one," looking at Bill, Joe, and Jill. "But for Dan and Brian's benefit... a couple of years ago, I was giving a Bravo demo to a bunch of top-level Xerox executives. I forget who."

Carroll's group all had the "oh, not that story *again*" look on their faces. Carroll ignored them, "I was typing away furiously, showing how you used the mouse, how you could set fonts, all that stuff. It went on for a good 20 minutes. As we were walking to their cars, I asked one of them what he took away from this. Do you want to guess what he said?"

Brian and Dan tried to think of something witty to say but gave up. Carroll finally said, "I've never seen a *man* type that fast."[1]

After the laughter subsided, they turned to the Diamond project. Carroll's group seemed to be trying to make Mesa a suitable production environment. They'd created a cross-referencing tool, for example. All three struck Dan as *really* good engineers. Dan reserved judgment on the overall project, but it didn't seem as if they were actually trying to prototype Janus itself. Nobody talked about icons and opening, moving, or copying them, which was what he was expecting to see.

Carroll had written Bravo in BCPL, which was a very lowlevel programming language that Xerox was not using for Janus, and Dan suspected that he did not agree with the official choice of Mesa. Nonetheless, Carroll didn't care to refight that battle, so he was apparently trying to *prove* Mesa unsuitable by using it for an application already done in a different language. When Dan and Carroll were chatting, Carroll mentioned a new language out of Bell Labs, C, which he considered a better BCPL. Dan made a mental note to ask around about that.

The meeting never discussed their goals, though, at least not explicitly. Dan figured they must have talked about all that long ago because they appeared happy with their current work. When Dan and Brian spoke about their projects, they were interested and supportive. After the meeting, Dan took a walk with Bill and Joe outside. They all talked about their previous projects, which were many and varied. Joe mentioned a computer he'd worked on where they'd boot the operating system, then go up on the roof and smoke pot, and joke about how slow the OS was, "You can get loaded before it can."

Dan and Brian spent much of their day after the meeting talking to other Palo Alto folks who knew more about their areas. For Dan, it was the Press print file format, and for Brian, the Boyer-Moore string searching algorithm. Dan also dropped in on Grant, the guy who directed his first visit to Palo Alto in January, and Rosalind, the user interface expert.

Grant did not seem as upbeat as the first time they'd met. He apologized for not having a new version of the Functional Spec to give him, pleading difficulties with the Alto hardware and the Mesa transition. He answered Dan's questions about Pilot but didn't show much enthusiasm. Eventually, Grant glanced at his watch, "Whoops, gotta go. It was good meeting you again, Dan."

Dan walked down the hall and saw Keith, a guy he'd met briefly on his first visit up here. Keith was reading a journal article. Dan called, "Knock, knock!" rather than actually knocking.

Keith swiveled his chair around and stood up, "Hey! I'm sorry... I forgot your name. You're from El Segundo, right?"

"Right, Dan Markunas. We met back in January, I think."

"Oh right, sorry, I'm so bad with names. So, what brings you up here?"

"I'm working with Carroll's group!"

Keith didn't seem to be quite as familiar with this project as Dan had expected. "Right, Mr. Bravo! What are they doing, again? I know I've heard."

"It's supposed to be a prototype of Janus, in Mesa, as far as I know."

"Cool! So how's it going?"

"Well... hard to tell. This was just our first meeting. I'm supposed to do the Press output so that you can print stuff."

"Press, another thing I should know more about."

For Dan, every trip here was a chance to learn lots of new and interesting stuff. The Palo Alto people were almost always educational to talk to, so he asked questions as much as he could. "What are you working on?"

Keith looked pleased to be asked, and he wanted Dan to understand his answer. He paused and then said, "One of the big things we're wrestling with is address spaces. Should each process have its own, or should they all share a single space?"

Dan pondered, "If they're all in one address space, won't they interfere with each other? I mean... I'm sure you've thought of all that."

"Yeah, good point. We're thinking that once you throw out the idea of multiple, mutually-ignorant programs sharing the computer, a lot of things become possible."

"Like...?"

"Well, like task-switching. If you only have lightweight threads instead of heavyweight processes, then your program can spin off threads whenever it wants to, maybe thousands per second. It's not a big deal anymore."

"Okay, but you're not worried about having other programs that *don't* come from Xerox?"

Keith had heard this question many times, but it was a reasonable thing to ask. He didn't act condescending, "Well, so far, we've gotten very clear directions from above that we're not to worry about that. This will be a turnkey system, no installing other programs. All the software comes from Xerox."

Dan moved on, "A single address space, lightweight threads. What else have you been doing?"

"Mesa process primitives. You know that this is a singlelanguage OS, right? It only supports Mesa programs."

"Right. So...?"

"So, the Mesa language itself can handle some of the stuff that an OS usually does. Are you familiar with monitors and condition variables?"

"I read up on them after our January visit. Are you involved with that?"

"I've been on various committees dealing with it. It sounds like you already know the basics, right?" Dan nodded. "What we call the Mesa runtime is pretty hard to distinguish from Pilot itself." Dan nodded again. "And files! Fucking *files*. You wouldn't believe all the opinions about that." Keith looked pained.

"Well, they *are* pretty important, I guess."

"I'd really like them to be someone else's problem. As soon as we think it's all nailed down, someone brings up some new issue—file names and whether they're unique, what about file drawers, what about removable media, and on and on and on."

Dan remembered something Carroll had said about this C programming language out of Bell Labs. He had the impression that this was not a career-advancing thing to advocate since they were fully committed to Mesa, but he trusted Keith enough to mention it casually.

Keith laughed, "There's a sign on an office door over at PARC. It says,"

C: *All the control and flexibility of machine code plus all the type safety and abstraction of machine code*

Dan doubled over laughing, "Maybe it was the grade they got for it in their Language Design course." They both laughed. Anyhow, he figured he could safely forget about C.

Keith was not looking at his watch and hustling him off, the way Grant just had. They asked about each other's background, the way programmers always do, and he found that Keith had done a lot of work on operating systems at Berkeley, was married, and didn't have any single-consuming passion but was happy to talk about cooking, Dungeons and Dragons, cultural events in The City—as they called San Francisco up here—and was genuinely interested in what Dan had to say. Dan left his office thinking, "Wow, what a nice guy."

While wandering the halls, Dan ran into Brian, who also looked inordinately happy. Brian had been talking to an engineer who knew all about the Boyer-Moore algorithm as well as lots of other things besides, including the new *Star Wars* movie that was coming out next month. They agreed to leave early and stand by for an earlier flight.

13

BREAKING UP IS EASY TO DO

I t was Monday, April 4, and Grant had his weekly lunch with his boss Michael. Actually, it was *supposed* to be weekly, but for one reason or another, either Michael traveling, Grant traveling, or some bigwig from Rochester visiting, it had been months since they'd met for lunch.

They chatted for a while about recent goings-on with the Janus project, the codename for the Display Word Processor, but Grant's real agenda was his own job. He wanted a different one. But he'd been around the corporate world long enough to know that you have to present that as a positive, never expressing unhappiness with your current job. Everything must be presented as a logical move upward, not an escape from something else.

Grant started by asking a few questions about the future direction of Janus. Was the rest of Xerox on board with it? How did it relate to the work that Dallas was doing? He made sure to show his familiarity with the Dallas groups. Michael appeared to be familiar with all that, although Grant hinted that he knew more about it, while being careful not to show him up. Michael played along, asking him some easy questions about Dallas that he could answer.

For a while, they rehashed Xerox's history since the 914 copier came out to historic success—Chester Carlson, Joe Wilson, how an official forecast was that only 5,000 copiers could ever be sold, and on and on. This nostalgia was always a bonding experience for Xerox people. Xerox had made monopoly profits and turned "xerox" into a verb, and for a long time, they were the coolest company around. You could never go wrong by making everyone feel a part of that, even long after the monopoly had disappeared.

They were sitting in a remote corner of the PARC cafeteria away from everyone else, which discouraged people from visiting, but still, people were continually stopping by. It seemed like Michael knew absolutely *everyone* at Xerox. A pair walked by as he was saying something about the Dallas projects, and he glanced up, mid-sentence, and greeted them, "Hi, Barry! Hi, Melanie!" and continued.

When he finished, Grant asked, "Who were they?"

"Oh, sorry. Barry Lewandowski and Melanie Weber from El Segundo."

Grant didn't know how he recognized them. Almost everyone in El Segundo was brand new. He could barely remember someone he'd met yesterday. Michael had a gift that way.[1]

Having laid the groundwork and feeling more confident that this was going to work, Grant sprang. "It occurs to me that I might be able to help out more if I worked directly on that stuff."

Michael didn't seem surprised, "You mean… in addition to your work on Pilot? Or instead of it?"

"I can continue on Pilot if you need me to, of course. We have a guy joining who might be able to take over from me eventually, though."

"I think I know who you mean. He'd be an excellent choice to run the Pilot group. But yeah, I can definitely use some help with the corporate stuff."

"Great. When shall we announce this?"

"How about if you talk to your group, and let me know as soon as you have an acting manager?"

Done. Success! The rest of their lunch was spent talking about bicycling, the various people Grant and Michael both knew in Dallas and El Segundo, and Grant's other jobs at Xerox. He left lunch feeling great, as he always did after talking to Michael. You always felt like he thought you were terrific. Grant wished he could do that.

When Grant saw the guys from the Pilot team later that afternoon, they seemed more relaxed, somehow. It was as if they already knew everything. How did that work? It was too soon for any official announcement, and he certainly hadn't told anyone. At other parts of Xerox, it was a much bigger deal to make any job switch.

Anyhow, it was nice. Phillip, his operating systems security expert, who had never gone out of his way to be friendly, stopped by asking if Grant had gone bicycling this past weekend. Patrick joined them, and they talked about the beautiful spring weather they were having and what it was like in Dallas this time of year. No one said anything about work.

The next day, they had one of their regular group meetings, and since he didn't see any point in pretending, he said, "Well, I guess you all heard I'm transferring? Being kicked upstairs, as it were." No one appeared shocked.

Phillip said, "Congratulations! We knew you were destined for greater things!" Everyone laughed.

Grant went on, "Lawrence Adler is going to be the acting manager, assuming he agrees. I still have to talk to him."

Lawrence was starting on May 2, so this was a bit of a stretch, but he had struck everyone as the sort of bulldozer you needed in this job. If Pilot clients were overly insistent on having their needs met and Lawrence didn't think they were reasonable, he'd just tell them to piss off. If the PARC folks were arrogant about how operating systems *should* be designed, he'd listen but let them know how it was going to be. Diplomacy didn't need to be his strong suit.

Grant went around the room and had everyone give a progress report. For the most part, they hadn't been doing what Grant asked for, which was to write the Functional Spec. But for a change, he didn't care. Soon, it wouldn't be his problem anymore, and at the same time, they knew that if he, in his new role, actually wanted to make trouble for them, he could. He took an interest in their activities, asking a lot of questions about virtual memory and the Dolphin machine, which was supposed to become Janus. On their part, they went out of their way to show respect to him. The meeting adjourned, and they agreed to meet at Zot's after work to celebrate his new job.

14

CORPORATE POLITICS, HOT AND SOUR
SOUP, AND SOFTBALL

Grant was hitting his stride. His new job, as he'd sold it, was to bridge the gap between Palo Alto and the rest of Xerox. It wouldn't do any good if the California folks produced Janus, but the company didn't know how to sell it or, even worse, had other products competing with it. So, Grant had been working the phones to the big executives in El Segundo, Dallas, Rochester, and even Stamford, the corporate headquarters in Connecticut.

Calling them was like jumping from the warm sun into a freezing lake. Whereas the PARC technology seemed aimed at people with at least a Bachelor's degree, the Xerox execs were still citing papers from the early 1970s on the white-collar workforce, who mostly weren't college-educated. Xerox had to have a product for these unskilled office workers that could be sold by their copier sales force. PARC had it all wrong, in their opinion, and was ignoring the official guidance the company had given them. Grant made these execs feel like they had a friend in Palo Alto.

Michael was used to hearing all this, of course, since he'd dealt with these execs. Grant was extremely useful for absorbing all this criticism so that Michael didn't have to do it all. He had to at least pretend to take it seriously, but Grant was busy taking it *very* seriously.

One question the execs all asked Grant was, "How will your word processor stack up next to what's already on the market?" Xerox hadn't been a major force in the word processing market, so if it was going to enter it, they had to understand the competition. Grant had set up a comparative evaluation of the Wang 20, the IBM Office System 6, and the Alto-based prototypes they were using in Palo Alto. He'd convene a Management Review Committee meeting, which was a big corporate deal with high-level execs, where they could see what Janus was up against.

To do this, the local user interface group, headed by Martin Whitby, had to *get* a Wang and an IBM system and learn how to use them. They couldn't just order them from Wang and IBM since those companies were competitors, and Xerox didn't want to tip its hand. And besides, it would take too long for the hardware to be delivered. Martin and his group had to go somewhere that already had them. Fortunately, some divisions of Xerox had been using these things for a while. For example, the Legal Division in Rochester used the Wang for their contracts, and the Competitive Analysis group in Stamford seemed to buy one of everything.

Martin had to arrange for someone from his group to go to those offices and practice on them. "A dirty job, but someone has to do it," was what Martin said. He knew that in a big company like Xerox, you had to play these games, so he was a soldier about it.[1]

The word processor show-and-tell wasn't all Grant had been doing. Since he knew the folks in Dallas, he'd also set up a visit by Martin and some of the El Segundo people. They were going to learn about the Troy, a new version of the 860 word processing system that the Dallas people were marketing. It already had a specialized keyboard, a printer from Xerox's

Diablo subsidiary, and even training materials. They were way ahead of Palo Alto.

While he was talking word processors with the Dallas folks, he spoke to someone about the new copier they were building, the 9700, which used laser printing. That was a brand new technology that PARC was claiming credit for, and for once, they'd actually given Xerox something it could use. Grant thought that, if worse came to worst, he could always move back to Dallas and work on that. But for now, he needed to stick to the job he had.

This morning, Thursday, April 28, 1977, as Grant was writing up some notes on the Dallas visit for Martin, Dan from El Segundo knocked on his door, "Enter."

Dan walked in. After some pleasantries, he got to the point, "So, I heard you're organizing some competitive evaluations of the Janus UI against other word processing systems."

Grant paused a second, "That *is* an activity we're undertaking, yes. Did you have some questions about it?"

This wasn't a promising beginning, but Dan pressed on, "Well, I'm working with Carroll Molnár's group, and I was just wondering how our work relates to that?"

Grant crossed his legs and sat back in his chair, "We're having discussions with Carroll all the time. The competitive evaluations are a completely different thing. They're for Xerox executives to understand the market we're entering."

Dan realized Grant wasn't going to tell him much. This was how they treated you when you asked things above your pay grade. He thought Grant was a high-level tech guy you could talk to about stuff, but now, he realized he'd misread the situation. How to escape gracefully?

He tried to look unphased and nodded his head as if this made perfect sense, "Ah, okay. Well, thanks! I think I have a meeting in a few minutes."

"Okay, thanks for stopping by," Grant went back to writing his notes.

Dan walked down to Carroll's area on the lower floor, and they chatted about famous computer scientists that Carroll knew, a little bit of star worship that Dan permitted himself. Carroll referred to Niklaus Wirth as Klaus as if he just hung around, and maybe, Dan would get to meet him! Dan exchanged news with Carroll's folks, who were all sitting nearby, and then, they had their group meeting. Brian hadn't come up to Palo Alto with him today because he had a class on Thursdays. Thursday was softball day up here, and they'd invited Dan to play as a guest the next time he was up. He actually had his baseball glove in his briefcase.

Dan had been making good progress on his Press file module, which would let a Diamond user print complicated documents with graphics and text, so he had an easy time at the team meeting. Everyone else's project seemed to be coming along nicely, too, so it was pretty quick and over before lunch. Apparently, Carroll had expected this since he hadn't ordered lunch to be brought in. Dan was having lunch with Rosalind, so he excused himself and walked up to her office.

Rosalind's office reminded him of the teachers' offices he'd liked at college. The walls had shelves with lots of books and conference proceedings, and it definitely looked lived in but not slovenly. He grabbed a chair and sat down. She finished up a phone call and turned to him, "Hey! Do you want to go out to a restaurant for a change? I don't know if you have to be back here soon?"

"Sure! I don't have any plans for the afternoon until softball."

"Oh, you're playing in that? Cool. I don't play, myself, since I'm terrible at sports!"

"I am, too, but I don't let that stop me."

Rosalind picked up her purse, "That's the spirit. Shall we?" They walked out to her car. "I thought I'd take you to Hsi-Nan! You haven't been there yet, have you?"

"No! I'm guessing from the name it's an Italian place?"

Rosalind laughed, "Close! Szechuan. You're okay with spicy?" Dan was. She headed up Page Mill. "Hsi-Nan is a Palo Alto landmark. I've heard that all programmers *have* to eat there."

"Well, if I have to…"

"And, you *have* to have the hot and sour soup, too!" Dan pretended his arm was being twisted behind his back.[2]

"How are you liking Carroll's group?"

"It's been good so far. Everyone's been really nice."

"What does he have you doing?"

"I'm doing the printing, which is weird since I don't even need a printer to test it!"

"Oh, it's some kind of print file?"

"Yeah, a Press file. Do you know much about those?"

Rosalind looked a little abashed, "I think there was a talk about that over at PARC, but I didn't go to it. I'm sure you know a lot more than I do."

Dan always wanted to get Palo Alto people talking. But now, he wondered if maybe that was what they wanted, too. Perhaps they just liked to talk! Rosalind seemed actually interested in what *he* had to say, though. So, he decided to stay with his own experiences for a while and see what she thought.

"Yeah, I guess. Carroll's group is supposed to be doing a prototype of the user interface, isn't it?"

"That's certainly what I thought," she replied.

"But I don't see a lot of the UI people advising him! I keep expecting to see icons and stuff?"

"And you don't?"

"Not that I'm seeing. I take it you're not working with them?"

Rosalind replied, "No one's asked me to. I'm working with Gypsy to see whether we can use that sort of modelessness for Janus."

"What's Gypsy?"

Just then, they arrived at the shopping center parking lot where Hsi-Nan was and walked in. The place was almost full, with a crowd that was mostly men in jeans and T-shirts and longish hair. He knew they were programmers even before he heard snatches of conversation involving "booting the system" and "the compiler." It was programmer talk! The waiter pointed to an empty table, they sat down, and he gave them menus.

Dan said, "So... that study you're doing?"

"Oh, yeah, you wanted to hear about that. Sorry! Let's order, and then I'll tell you." She motioned to the waiter who walked over.

"Hot and sour soup," looking at Dan for confirmation. He nodded.

"And I'll have the Chinese chicken salad."

Dan said, "I'll have the Kung Pao Chicken."

The waiter asked, "How spicy do you want that?" Dan hesitated since he was never sure what that meant for a white person.

Rosalind jumped in, "They make everything spicy here. Medium is probably what you want."

He nodded to the waiter, who asked, "And steamed rice?" They confirmed, and he hurried off.

She leaned forward and put her elbows on the table, "What we're looking at is *modes*. You know Bravo has an edit mode and so forth?"

"Yup. That hazing ritual we pull on new employees, like type EDIT to start editing!"

She laughed, "Right. E for select everything, D for delete... I never get tired of that one! Anyway, I puts you in insert mode. Why can't you just start typing, instead of telling the computer, 'Hey, I'm going to type now!'"

Dan said, "I'm guessing Gypsy doesn't have any modes?"

"No, and Carroll is *really* interested in incorporating that in his next version of Bravo."

"Interesting. I'll have to ask him about that."

"Anyway, the other big thing going on is the Desktop demo." Dan didn't look as though he'd heard of that, so she continued, "You've heard about the Smalltalk demo, right?"

"Vaguely. I was talking to this guy Todd down South about it."

"Well, if you've seen it, you know how slow it is!" Dan just smiled. "So, Bill Beaumont's been translating it into Mesa so that we can use it for experimenting. I'm helping with that."

Dan had the feeling that any of this could be the subject of a multi-hour discussion, but he didn't feel like doing that during lunch, and he didn't think Rosalind did either. Their hot-and-sour soup arrived, and his first reaction to a spoonful was, "Oh my God!"

"Is that good?"

"This has to be the best hot-and-sour soup I've ever had."

They both consumed their soup in silence. Then the waiter took away their bowls and came back shortly with the main dishes.

As he picked up his chopsticks, Dan asked, "What did you study in school to be doing this stuff?"

Rosalind looked embarrassed, "Well, I kinda didn't know what to do with myself. I was in Psychology, and then I became interested in Computer Science, and then in grad school at Stanford, I got involved with human factors in computers."

"And here you are!"

"And here I am. What about you?"

Dan replied, "I was also in Psychology for a year!"

"Really? But you didn't stay in it?"

"No, I kept thinking, 'What will I do with a degree in this?'"

"So, you got out?"

"I did. I got into Math and Computer Science. But if I *had* stayed in Psych, I'd have been experimental like you."

"Well, you probably did the right thing."

"Why's that? You don't like what you're doing?"

Rosalind said, "I definitely do. But no one knows what a human factors researcher does. You're always having to justify yourself."

He didn't have an answer for that. It was true that everyone knew what a computer programmer did, so he didn't have that problem. Still, Dan had a lot of interests besides computers, and one thing he really enjoyed about Xerox was all the people like Rosalind.

They ate in silence for a while. Dan put down his chopsticks, "Where do you live?"

"My husband and I live in San Francisco. It's a long commute, but most of the traffic is going the other way, at least."

"Did you get your water ration from the City?" Dan had just read in the *LA Times* how outraged everyone in San Francisco was about their allotments.

Rosalind looked annoyed, "Yes, and we're seriously pissed off. We've always tried to conserve water, *unlike you folks in LA!*" She said it with an ironic smile, "So now, we have to cut the same percentage as someone who's just been wasting it."

"That's us! Washing our cars, filling our swimming pools, and whatnot," Dan was really going with it now.

"Anyway, shall we head back to ex-Rocks?"

Dan hung out in the guest office, reading his mail. At about 3:30, he noticed a higher pitch of activity in the hallways—a couple of guys throwing a softball back and forth, and people wearing their team T-shirts. It was time for softball! He went to the bathroom to put on his shorts and T-shirt and found it full of other guys doing the same.

Patrick greeted him, "So Dan, welcome to the Warthogs!"

"Is that my team? Thank you, sir, I'm honored!"

Ray Holmberg, another Palo Alto engineer Dan had met once or twice, hooted at that, "And remember, on the

Warthogs, it's no more than 10 errors or no champagne for you!"

Patrick replied, "Yeah, then he only drinks Anchor Steam."

Turning to Dan, "You probably have to catch a plane, right?" Dan nodded. "I'll drive you back here when we finish. Most people go to the Dutch Goose or the Oasis afterward, but I'm not going this week."

On the way over to Stanford, Patrick filled Dan in on the history of Palo Alto softball, "First of all, have you heard the Willie McCovey story?"

"Willie McCovey? No! What story is that?"

"You know who he is, right?" Of course, Dan did. "He threw out the first pitch of the season this year!"

"Oh, my God! How did that happen?"

Patrick explained that another team captain, Marcia, had found McCovey's home address and wrote to him, expecting never to hear another word about it. Then one day, she was called out of a meeting to take a call from the San Francisco Giants, who wondered how she'd gotten hold of Willie's home address.

"Long story short, he showed up on Opening Day! We were instructed 'No autographs!'"

Dan marveled, "What does Willie Mac look like these days?"

"He's *tall*, that's what everybody noticed. And *big!* He drives this tiny yellow Mercedes convertible, and somehow or other, he manages to get in and out of it."

"So, he threw out the first pitch…?"

"Oh, yeah. Some people couldn't help themselves and asked for an autograph, but he was gracious about it. And then, he threw out the first pitch and left!"

"Wow. You'll never top that one. Maybe you all thought he was going to give batting lessons or something?"[3]

Patrick laughed, "Wouldn't have helped most of us.

Anyhow, the other important softball fact to know is the timing of Opening Day!"

"It's not just springtime?"

"No, it's the first Thursday after the buzzards return to Hinckley, Ohio."

Dan laughed, "That's a big day, I guess. There really *is* such a day?"

"There is. It's March 15, usually, so yeah, basically springtime."

They were turning off Junipero Serra toward the campus. "Any special rules I should know about, or is it basically Jungle Ball?"

"Yeah, except you can't play in super-close when a weak hitter is up."

"Are there umpires?"

"No umps. We have a gentlemen's agreement when we have a dispute."

"Okey-dokey! This other team... what's the scouting report?" He smirked at the last words.

"They have one guy who played on the Stanford baseball team. So obviously, *he's* good. You'll know when he comes up."

"Then, the outfield backs up?"

"*Some* of them do. We have lots of outfielders."

"So, more than four?"

"Way more. You'll probably be one yourself!"

Dan thought, "*I'm not that good on fly balls*," but then he realized he probably wouldn't get many with that many players.

"Who decides which team you play for?" Dan was imagining, maybe, one lab in PARC against another or some kind of organizational rivalry.

"Good question! The captains meet every spring for a player draft."

"Wow. A chance for almost everyone to be humiliated!"

Patrick chuckled again, "It could be, but no one takes it

too seriously. Did you ever hear of the Hash House Harriers?"
"Nope."

"They call themselves 'A drinking club with a running problem.' That's us, except for softball."

They parked the car and joined the others playing catch and warming up. Dan played in the outfield as Patrick had predicted and only had one ball hit to him. The other team had a second baseman who brought two beers out to the field with him, and he noticed that indeed you did receive a glass of champagne if you made it to first. Since he had a bad habit of swinging too early, thereby either pulling a liner over third base or else a foul, he drank a lot of champagne. The rest of the game was a blur.

15

PALO ALTO EXPLAINS IT ALL FOR YOU

J anet wanted to work on Ethernet so bad! Eventually, Tom might work something out, but she wasn't sure what he could do. Ken was dead set against moving to the Bay Area, so that was out.

For the moment, she liked working on the Janus functional specification and was confident she'd be good at it. She'd spent weeks poring over the drafts and writing up ideas. But even that was a problem because the job was already spoken for—three guys down here and three in Palo Alto. They each went to the other's location once a week, making two days a week in meetings.

They didn't want to expand the group to an unwieldy size. She also suspected it was a boys' club, but it was hard to say for sure since they weren't adding men, either. Tom definitely felt that too many cooks spoil the broth.

In her regular talks with Tom, he was sympathetic, as usual, and suggested that she look into doing object-oriented programming (OOP) in Mesa. Smalltalk and its objects and methods were an *intellectual* success in Palo Alto. Everyone believed this to be the proper way to decompose large programs. With OOP, a small change in one place doesn't cause unpredictable effects in lots of other places, a problem they'd all seen in other jobs. It also gives you *reusability*, where some block of code that someone painfully wrote and debugged can be used by someone else more easily, and this is huge.

The Smalltalk demo of Janus was electrifying. You saw icons opening into windows and all that shiny new stuff. But it was pig-slow! For that reason, at least, Smalltalk wasn't considered the language for Janus. The question was whether Janus should be built in an object-oriented style. Could Mesa do that? The current hot topic was why it was so slow, and could Mesa keep most of the advantages of OOP and still run fast? She was intrigued. At TRW and Hughes, they wouldn't even bother asking those questions.

In a pure OOP system, which Smalltalk was, your code holds an object handle, and you have no idea what code lives on the other end of that handle. You just know your code can send messages to the object, and something will happen, but you have no idea how. This purity was part of the reason for the revolutionary excitement of Smalltalk and also why it was so slow! Whenever you do *anything* with an object handle, which is almost every line of code, the computer has to check to see what kind of object it is, where its data is, and how its methods are implemented. In a pure system, you have infinite flexibility. You can replace part of the system *while it's running*, for God's sake! This was science fiction to Janet. It made for a great demo, but you'd never find it in a real product.

A different philosophy, which she preferred, was to decide these things, or bind them, only *once*, when you compile your program, and then later, when the program is executed on a user's machine, they're already bound. That was the Mesa philosophy, which was a more practical, engineering-oriented approach.

Xerox, and any company designing software, had its starry-eyed optimists, who'd tell you that computers always get

faster. They thought it foolish to waste effort making the software fast *now* when in a year or three, all your speed problems
will be solved. They were deeply offended at *any* loss of that
infinite flexibility they prized so highly. But Janet realized that
they almost never win the argument in the end.

She read through the many, many emails discussing this
sort of thing, and soon realized these debates were so heated
because they were about philosophical questions that had no
answers. Janet found the starry-eyed optimists tiresome.
"We're building products *now*, not five years in the future" was
her attitude. She was careful not to take a position on either
side *too* overtly, though. She needed to avoid pissing anyone off
if she wanted to be a manager! She'd noticed that the big
managers in any company, not only Xerox, really marked you
down if you showed emotion about *anything.* "Cool and dispas-
sionate" was the way to be managerial.

So many big things were happening in Palo Alto! Since
travel between El Segundo and Palo Alto was actively encouraged, even without a good reason, she went up on Friday, May
20. Even though your reason for traveling didn't need to be
ironclad, you still needed a halfway-plausible excuse. So, the
justification to Tom was to talk to the various hardware
groups, including Ethernet, and also to see what the Mesa and
Pilot groups were up to. She was also interested in talking to
Grant, who had changed jobs since she last saw him. She
wondered what happened and what corporate political devel-
opments she should know about.

Ken asked as she left, "What time are you home tonight?"

She opened the envelope with the ticket and looked at the
summary sheet. "Around 7:00, probably, depending on the
traffic from the airport. Are you going to the Great American
tonight?"

"Umm... let's see. They usually meet at about 6:30." By
they, Ken meant his social group from Hughes, who usually
had dinner at the Great American Food and Beverage

Company on Friday nights. Janet and Ken had been playing volleyball, skiing, hanging out at the beach, playing softball, boating, and of course, drinking with this group for two years now, ever since they moved to LA. She wanted a change tonight.

"Do you want to go to Tito's Tacos tonight instead?" Janet and Ken had gone to this place, which wasn't far from their apartment, when they moved in, but they hadn't gone in years. At Xerox, whenever she told someone where she lived, they always mentioned Tito's. It seemed to be the first thing they associated with Culver City.

"You mean... skip The Great American?"

Janet almost said, "Well, obviously," but she knew that would irritate him. Instead, she said, "Maybe just this week? We'll see them all at volleyball on Sunday anyway."

For Ken, the plank feast at The Great American and plenty of beer was the perfect end to a week, but he didn't see a way to salvage it now since Janet was returning late. He wasn't exactly sure why she was going there today since no big meetings were scheduled, but he let it go for now. "Okay, Tito's it is! We haven't been there since... God, since we moved here!"

"See you tonight!" She kissed him and left. Ken finished his breakfast, put on his tie, and drove to work.

His manager, Steve, was leaving the machine room carrying a big bound stack of listings as Ken sat down at his desk. He dropped it on Ken's desk with a thud, "Happy Friday! We gonna see you and Janet at The Great American tonight?"

"Sorry, Janet's coming back late from Palo Alto, so we're going to go to Tito's tonight. I don't suppose we can talk you into that instead?" He didn't expect a yes.

"Tito's Tacos? Nice try. So, what's she doing in Palo Alto this time?"

Ken was embarrassed, "Not sure. Something about this

stupid language they use, or the operating system, or something."

Steve smiled, "They *still* don't have all that sorted out yet? What the hell are they doing?"

Ken wasn't in the mood for abuse from Steve right now, but he *was* saying what Ken was thinking. Month after month, he asked Janet when they'd see their production computer, how far along the design spec was—all those milestones he was used to in an engineering project. And month after month, they didn't happen.

The frustrating thing for him was that she didn't seem frustrated by that, no matter how much he tried to make her so. In fact, it was the opposite. She'd come home with some academic paper or internal Xerox report and settle happily into a chair reading it while he watched TV. Ken would ask what it was about, and it always seemed to be something *way* out of the mainstream of computing. *"But she seems to like that shit. Oh, well."*

Ken changed the subject and asked Steve what was wrong with the system today and why he was carrying around that stack of listings. They became so absorbed in the crash from last night and what caused it that they never returned to the evening plans.

Up in Palo Alto, Janet found Grant in his office, knocked, and sat down in his guest chair. After exchanging pleasantries, she came to the point. "I hear you have a new job! How's that going?"

"It's great! I'm introducing something they don't seem familiar with, the waterfall method." She looked puzzled, so he continued, "You know... first, you define what you'll do, and then, you do it. And that leads to the next thing. Basic stuff."

"Isn't that what we *were* doing?"

Grant momentarily took on a superior look, but he suppressed it, "Well, sort of. But Xerox has a product develop-

ment process," and handed her a thick binder labeled Phased
Program Planning.

She opened it, flipped past the pages marking it all as
Xerox trade secrets, and saw the table of contents. *"Is this
really the way Xerox does it?"* Janet figured she'd unearthed the
secret formula, the set of hoops that Xerox made you jump
through to bring a product out, and Grant knew them all.
This was a good person to know! She plied him with questions about the process. Where was Janus in the process
right now? What was the next milestone? What was the
danger point when the big execs might cancel the entire
thing? And most important of all, when was IMO, or Initial
Machine Observation, Xerox's term for when the product
ships?

Grant enjoyed it when anyone took this seriously. He was
used to the engineers smiling indulgently when he talked
about bureaucratic stuff. They imagined it was something that
happened to *other* people back East but didn't apply here.
Some were vaguely afraid of it, but confident that Michael
and his staff would handle it all—in fact, that it was *already*
handled. But Janet appreciated the seriousness of what he was
doing. He resolved to cultivate her as an ally.

"It looks like IMO is two years away, give or take. But so
much has to happen, and soon, if we're going to hit that
date."

"Like what? I mean… I can guess."

"Well, the hardware, to pick one. We don't have it yet, and
we don't even have a simulator for it."

Janet realized he was right. She'd heard that the Dolphin,
the first machine of the D-series, was coming along, but they
hadn't seen it yet. He gave her the names of some people in
SDD to talk to.

"And of course, the Ethernet, or Xerox Wire. You know
it's supposed to be 20 megabits, not the three that we have
now?"

She was keenly interested in that but already knew who to talk to about it.

"And then, we have Pilot, the operating system. I certainly know something about that!" He smirked.

Janet leaned forward, "Yeah, what's the story on that?"

Grant put on his "let me give you a line of corporate-speak" face. She knew this was a buffed-up version of the truth, and Grant knew she knew. But that was life in the corporation.

"I think they have a fantastic team, and they really need a leader with a research background. Michael and I both thought I could contribute more by getting us more aligned with the rest of Xerox."

She nodded enthusiastically and picked up the big binder again, "So, this development process is a part of that?"

Grant smiled. She was buying it. Excellent! "Indeed. And a few other things, like the competitive evaluations." She looked quizzical. "You know Janus could be considered a word processor, right?" Janet nodded, although almost no engineer ever called it that. She thought it was demeaning to put it in the same class as a Wang machine! "Senior management wants to see a competitive evaluation of the Alto, the IBM System 6, the Wang unit, and of course, Xerox's word processors. So... I'm setting that up."

"Great! When is that happening? And who's doing it on our side?"

"We're still getting the hardware together. Martin is the person to talk to about that. Have you met him?" She shook her head. "Martin Whitby. I can take you over and introduce you later."

"That'd be great! I think I have enough people to go see, but maybe I'll stop by later." She handed him the binder, thanked him, and stood up.

"Do you have plans for lunch?" he asked.

"None! Shall I come by here?" Grant nodded.

Grant noticed the wedding ring on her finger. *"That figures! Whenever one of them has her head on straight, she's already taken."* He'd had a total of one date since moving here almost six months ago.

Tony Webb was waiting outside the door. Janet didn't know how he'd figured out where she was, maybe heard her voice, but anyway, he was her contact in the Ethernet group. They shook hands and walked back to his office to drop her stuff off and then headed to the hardware lab.

The lab was as messy as any lab she'd ever seen at school, with soldering pens, oscilloscopes, and lots of other hardware she didn't recognize. She was thrilled! In school, she aced the circuit design courses and loved the stuff, but her life had been all software since then. It was exactly the same for Ken at Hughes. Software was where the jobs were. He'd be *so* insanely jealous if she worked on actual hardware! Could it be? She was about to find out.

Tony showed her the diagrams for the new 20Mbps transceiver he was working on. She didn't understand most of it since hardware design nowadays seemed to be finding a part in a catalog that did what you wanted, rather than soldering resistors, capacitors, and transistors. *"But obviously, they must do some soldering since they have the equipment lying around."*

He couldn't really demonstrate 20Mbps Ethernet very much. The transceiver wasn't developed yet, and there was no computer to connect it to, let alone software to use it. Janet asked a few questions about collision detection and maximum cable length, including something that many of the supposedly smart people around here never asked. "The 3MB Ethernet cable was at most one kilometer in length, right?"

"Yep."

"So, how do the computers here in SDD talk to the ones across the road at PARC? Do you have a leased line or something?"

Tony laughed. This was the dirty little secret, and she had found it. "We ran the cable under Coyote Hill Road!"

Janet laughed, "Really? Is that legal?"

He put his fingers up to his lips, in the shush gesture, "I think we talked to someone in the Palo Alto city government. Or maybe... it's because this is Stanford land."

She folded her hands in prayer, imitating Brother Dominic in the Xerox commercial, "It's a miracle!" They both laughed long and hard.

Janet had hoped that Tony wanted to recruit her to join the team, and this was a job interview, but it wasn't headed that way. For Tony, she was just another Xeroid to meet. He answered her questions about the Ethernet and its history, but it struck her as ordinary politeness. If Tom had ever approached his team about her joining, Tony obviously hadn't heard. Or more likely, he saw her as a software person, not a hardware person. If she'd ever designed digital hardware, that would be something else again, but taking a few courses in school didn't cut it.

She shifted gears. "*Never show disappointment*," she reminded herself. She asked a few more questions about the schedule for the new Ethernet transceiver and the integration with the Dolphin. Then, they dropped the shop talk and talked about the new *Star Wars* movie opening in five days. Tony asked her about the Janus software effort. He had almost no contact with the software world and imagined that it must be similar to hardware but not as well managed. "*Failing to plan is planning to fail!*" was his motto. Janet smiled politely. An MIT Computer Science Professor once said, "Hardware people always think they have the proper discipline, and software folks don't, and maybe if software was managed like hardware, it wouldn't always be so late!" She often remembered that and avoided arguing with them.

It was almost lunchtime. She was about to leave, and then remembered a cutting remark from her husband. She figured he was just being a jerk about the Ethernet, as usual, but she asked anyway, "Oh, before I go, every station sees all the packets, right?" Tony knew where this was going and just nodded. "So, could you look at everyone else's email and stuff, or is there some security that prevents that?" She was really hoping to put Ken in his place and tell him he was wrong.

"There's no security. If someone is snooping on someone else in the same company, that's an HR matter, not a network matter. Presumably, you'd be fired for that."[1]

She tried not to look crestfallen but apparently failed because he continued. "The HR department has their own private Ethernet for personnel matters. They unplug the corporate cable and plug in the HR cable when they want to be confidential."

Janet said, "Okay, thanks again, Tony!"

She went to Grant's office. He was on the phone but motioned for her to come in and sit down as he finished the conversation.

"Let's just go across the street, if you're okay with that. I have to be back here at 1:00." They walked over to PARC. After some chit chat about the flight to San Jose and the weather, which was utterly gorgeous this time of year, he asked, "How are things in El Segundo?"

"Oh, trying to stay busy, learning the tools, you know."

"Are you guys going to give us a product?"

Janet tried to see such questions as opportunities. *"You don't have to answer the literal question,"* she reminded herself. Anyway, what was she *supposed* to say to that? "We're planning it out, scoping the requirements, assessing the technology, all that management 101 stuff." There, she'd used the M-word! Even though she wasn't actually a manager and wasn't doing *any* planning, it was important to plant the thought in his mind.

"Very good! Same here," he answered as they entered the cafeteria and checked out what the chefs had for them today. Grant took a sandwich and a bag of potato chips and put them on his tray, while Janet chose one of the premade chicken salads.

After they'd paid for everything, they found a table in the mostly full cafeteria. Grant waved to three guys in suits at a table nearby. They both ate quickly, chatting about colleges, Grant's other jobs at Xerox, and Janet's previous job. Grant also asked what her husband did for a living.

Laying down her knife and fork, Janet put her elbows on the table, "You report to Michael Adams, right?" He nodded. "And who does *he* report to?"

Grant sat back, "Let's see," and looked at his watch. She laughed a little uncertainly. "I forget if it's Harold Hall, Bob Sparacino, or someone else today. They don't seem to last very long in that job."

She pondered that. Was he being cynical for a laugh, hiding some key information, or accurately representing the situation? Grant saw her confusion and sat more upright. "SDD has the charter to take PARC's technology to market. That much is stable. But the executives in charge of all that are, let's say, not in complete agreement on how to pull it off."

"What does Archie McCardell want?" She figured surely the preferences of the company's President ruled in the end.

Grant smiled, "I'm not sure anyone knows that, even Archie. It's mostly his senior VPs that we deal with. McCardell has much bigger things to worry about."

"Bigger things than the future of Xerox and the computing industry? Uh-oh!"

Grant knew what she was thinking, *"Welcome to the real world."*

He stood up, looking at his watch again, "I need to leave now. I'm really sorry." They returned to SDD, and he shook her hand. "It was great seeing you! Maybe I'll look you up when I'm down in El Segundo."

"That'd be great. Thanks, Grant!" She checked at the front desk for any of those "while you were out" slips and then went to the guest office and checked email. Martin had offered to move up her 2:00 appointment since he had some unexpected free time. He was on the phone when she arrived. He pointed to the beach chair, just inside the door, with a big umbrella over it, and she lowered herself into it. This was easier to rise out of than a beanbag, she thought, and anyway, she'd learned never to wear a skirt when coming up here.

He finished the call and turned to face her, "Welcome to Palo Alto! How's it going today?"

"Pretty good so far! I talked with Tony Webb this morning and had lunch with Grant Avery."

"Great! And now, you're here. What can I do for you?"

"Well... Tom Burnside, my manager, told me to walk around, talk to people, and report back. I always like coming up here, so that sounded good!"

"Do you want to hear about the Janus Functional Spec? I'm afraid I can't tell you much about the Ethernet." He reached for his copy of the current draft and handed it over. While she was leafing through it, he switched disks on his Alto and entered some commands. He moved his regular guest chair next to him, and she moved over to it.

"Have you seen the Desktop demo?" She shook her head and leaned forward to look at the Alto as Martin moved the mouse. It resembled Todd's Smalltalk demo, but this was *much* faster.

"This is the original Smalltalk demo that Bill Beaumont redid in Mesa for speed. You can see that we have overlapping windows like they did, text that reformats itself if you change the window boundaries, and now, we even have graphics! This isn't officially part of the Desktop yet, but I have a prototype of it. Do you want to try it?"

Janet took the mouse and tried to make sense of what she was seeing. She clicked down on a rectangle and tried dragging it. Nothing happened.

Martin grabbed the mouse to demonstrate, "Grab the control point. See?"

She figured out what to do and moved the rectangle, as the screen repainted. "Wow, what else can I do? Rotate it?" He explained the way to do that and smiled as she rotated the rectangle. Martin always tried to give a demo where the user succeeded at something. It didn't always work out, but today, it did.

"So, this is a vehicle for trying out user interfaces. You know that Mark, Steve, and Randy down in El Segundo are writing the actual functional spec with us, right?"

"Yep."

"Have you talked to them much?"

"I have." They'd been helpful in providing updates, but he never got the feeling they wanted any help. "*Everyone has an opinion!*" was their attitude.

"It's hard to know what to work on, though!" she said. "Everything's up in the air!"

Martin talked about other periods in history when the air was full of intellectual excitement, such as the Italian Renaissance and the Scottish Enlightenment. He spoke of Charles Darwin and the effect that his theories had on the Victorian mind. He stressed that this wasn't just another engineering job, but a revolution—this time in computing. *Of course* things seemed up in the air in such an era! But good God, how exciting it was to be a part of it.

But Martin paused because he knew what she must be feeling, despite all that revolution stuff! Everything *was* up in the air, including the product direction, the hardware, the software, the UI, everything! You couldn't expect her to automatically know what to do. He wanted to suggest how to be productive *now*.

Janet had the sense that he must deal with a lot of the big executives from back East. If she had to do that, she'd lie awake most of the night before. She knew that most of those execs only cared about copiers, and *maybe* word processing, and yet, they held the future of El Segundo *and* Palo Alto in their hands. She could learn a lot from Martin. He could gently persuade them and also deal on a technical level with brilliant but flighty Ph.D.s from fancy universities. Not many were able to do that. Some people could do the first part, like Grant, and they definitely had their place, but she felt that Grant wasn't quite up to the second part, the "brilliant but flighty Ph.D." part.

Martin tried a few ideas, "What are you interested in? Programming languages? User interfaces? Databases? Operating systems?"

Janet panicked, *"It's an interview! A male authority figure is asking what I want to do with my life! Oh God, now I have to say something!"*

"Well, Tom asked me to look into object-oriented programming with Mesa. So, I'm meeting with Ron Warrick after this."

Martin leaned back, "Good! Ron's a smart guy." She thought she detected a *"but he's a nut job!"* in his voice. But maybe she imagined it, and he probably wouldn't say that out loud anyway.

She was about to leave when a tall guy with tousled dark hair wandered in and put out his hand, "Hi, I'm Henry Davis. You must be from El Segundo."

"Uh-oh! Is it that obvious?" Janet figured that women were a small enough minority that the men had all studied the org chart and knew who she was, but she didn't want to come out and say that.

"No, no, I'm psychic! Anyhow, it's nice to meet you."

"Nice to meet you, too. Do you work for Martin?"

Martin interjected, "Working for me? That *could* be a great idea, Henry! We should talk about that."

Henry looked skyward, pretending to be thunderstruck with that idea, "I have some thoughts about graphics when you get a chance." Martin nodded, and Henry left, and a minute later, Janet did as well.

Sitting in the guest office, she thought about the two people she'd just seen. Grant was the consummate corporate warrior. He knew the procedures and believed in them. He was just the guy to sell Janus to the suits back East. But hearing about the exciting stuff the Pilot guys were doing, Janet doubted that any of it was his idea. In fact, he didn't even claim that it was. But he was doing important stuff now, like the competitive word processor evaluation.

Martin, on the other hand, was an intellectual who had polish. He could talk about politics or culture with as much enthusiasm as he gave to his research. That was what was so thrilling about Xerox. You met these folks who had so many talents and not just technical ones. It made her feel dissatisfied with her life since MIT! She and Ken and their friends did all kinds of Southern California fun stuff, but the intellectual part was definitely lacking. At MIT, they used to go to talks by famous people, one of the perks of a high-status university, and now, they never did. Ken didn't seem to miss it at all. After a few hours playing volleyball at the beach, she'd forget about it, too.

She went to Ron's office, and he bounded up and greeted her enthusiastically. She barely managed to say that she was looking into object-oriented programming with Mesa, and Ron launched into a half-hour explanation of OOP, Mesa, programming in general, file systems, atomicity of file transactions, and other topics she lost track of. Every five minutes or so, he'd pause for affirmation, she'd say, "Okay" or "Yeah," and off he'd go again. Eventually, she thanked him and was about to leave but then made the mistake of mentioning some differing opinions about objects she'd read on email. This set him off on another 15-minute rant until she resorted to looking at her watch and pretending to panic at her lateness.

16

LIGHTNING STRIKES!

Thursday, January 5, 1978. Janet was visiting Palo Alto again, something she never tired of. Today, she was just supposed to check in with people and learn whatever she could about the Pilot operating system, the product hardware, Ethernet, user interface, and all that.

In one of those magic changes of name that Xerox never officially announced because that would let an enemy keep track of code names, the product was now called "Star," She hoped she wouldn't slip up today and call it "Janus."

This time she took an earlier flight than she had been lately, the 7:00 am PSA flight out of LAX. She hated having to get up at an obscene hour, but really, if you took a more reasonable flight, you got to the office at 10:45 or later, and that made it a pretty short day. This morning, the roads were all wet and littered with tree branches and leaves. Apparently, it had stormed the night before.

She first went to Grant's office to talk about the latest marching orders from corporate management. Grant was pacing back and forth, frowning, holding the base of the phone in his right hand and the receiver in his left. He glanced at Janet, smiled briefly, and motioned to the guest chair.

"How much of the network is down?" The answer seemed to make him even more worried.

"Does Michael know? Okay, I'll tell him."

"Who's looking into this?" He wrote down some names on a yellow pad.

"Um, yeah. We have Peter McColough and Bill Glavin flying out tonight for a demo." He stared at Janet, knowing he just dropped the name of the Chairman of the Board.

Janet knew McColough was adamant that no exec would *ever* touch a keyboard—that was for their secretaries. The idea of an expensive computer like Star for knowledge workers, whatever that meant, was dubious to him. His rule of thumb was that you shouldn't buy a piece of equipment for a secretary that cost more than her annual salary. The execs were already a hostile audience. A bad demo was about the last thing Grant needed.

"I'll let you get back to it. Keep me posted." He hung up and turned to Janet, "The entire Ethernet is down. Excuse me, but I need to work this out." He started for the door, then paused. "On the other hand, do you want to help out?" Grant strode briskly toward Michael's office with Janet trying to keep up.

"What happened?" Janet asked. She had no idea whether this was a normal occurrence or not, but she knew bad things *always* happen at the worst possible time. *"It's life as an engineer. Naturally, if Peter McColough is coming out, everything will fall to pieces."*

"No idea yet. They're looking into it." He knocked on Michael's door and entered without waiting for acknowledgment.

"The Ethernet's down. All of it! Have you heard?"

Michael didn't look worried. "Yeah, they're on it. Unfortunately, swapping out transceivers isn't fixing the problem.

Usually, that does it." He was thumbing through his Rolodex. "Didn't we have lightning last night?"

Michael stopped flipping the cards, "Did we? What's that got to do with it?"

Grant had no answer, "Don't know. It's just... that's not very common around here, is it?"

"No, it's not. Anyway, the cable's not up on poles, Grant. Can you and Richard head over there?" Michael, of course, meant Richard Boddington, the guy in charge of the internal Ethernet. He surely needed to know about this if he didn't already.

He wasn't in his office, and Grant guessed he was already on the case. He led Janet down to the basement where Richard and three other engineers had gathered around a ladder, while another guy, Tim Field, stood on it with his head above the ceiling tiles.

After introducing Janet, Grant said, "What happened? Anyone know?"

Tim climbed down the ladder, "We're not sure. There's a short somewhere, but that's about all we know."

Grant was growing impatient but tried not to show it. *"I could tell them Peter McColough is coming tomorrow. That's what the executives in Dallas would do."* But Palo Alto didn't seem to work on fear. These were smart guys who were used to finding problems together and fixing them. And if Tim was here, you already had the best possible engineer on it. There was nothing more to do right now.

Richard clasped his hands, "Okay. Tim, what's the plan now?"

"We're replacing bad transceivers, but there's more than one. At this point, I'm not sure how many there are!"

"Got it, got it. Does anyone have a theory on what happened?"

No one did. Grant asked, "Could the lightning last night have done it?"

Janet had the impression they all considered this a dumb

idea but were too polite to say it. Tim finally said, "We're not ruling anything out at this point."

Richard said, "Okay, we'll leave you to it. Janet, can you help out here?"

Janet was thrilled. Grant and Richard left, and Tim climbed back up the ladder. He stopped and turned, "Janet, can you go over there and help Tony?" He pointed to the other end of the floor. "He might need another pair of hands." The two other guys walked off in a different direction, probably to do the same thing Janet was going to help with, on a different part of the Ethernet.

Tony was also up in the ceiling on a ladder next to a table with several transceivers on it, presumably bad ones. "Have you ever attached a transceiver to the coax?" Janet shook her head. "Here's a quick lesson," demonstrating how to attach the clamp to the cable and screw in the pin that penetrated to the center connector. "Here are some known good units," handing her a cardboard box full of Ethernet transceivers and other things she didn't recognize. "You can find a spare ladder and flashlight over there in the closet," pointing to a room that looked like a giant broom closet.

Janet retrieved the ladder and a flashlight. Tony climbed down and was going to help her carry it, but she was managing. He gave her a diagram of the Ethernet on that floor. "We know there are bad units between Tim and us because he's using the TDR."

"Time Domain Reflectometer? How does that work?"

"Basically, it shows you where there's a short in the cable. Here's another one," showing Janet a large piece of equipment with an oscilloscope-like screen. He continued, "Tim always says the Ethernet is like a string of Christmas tree lights. If one of them goes out, none of the others work, either. So, you can't really tell if any are good *after* the break."

"I split the Ethernet here so that we can find the bad transceivers from here on. What I want you to do is break it down there, and we'll just work on this segment. Tim and I could do this all ourselves, but we're under some time constraints."

Janet thought she detected a smirk. Tony must already know about the execs coming! "It looks like there's a junction over by the wall, right?"

Janet glanced at the diagram, "Yep!"

Janet took the ladder over to the wall, unfolded it, climbed up, pushed up the ceiling tile, grabbed it, and set it on the floor. She climbed back up and shined the light around, looking for a connector between two Ethernet segments. She found it, took a deep breath, and unscrewed the coax from each side. Then she yelled, "Ready!"

"Thanks, hold on!" A minute or so passed. Tony injected a pulse into the wire with his TDR and watched the results. "Okay, now what I need you to do is replace the transceiver closest to me."

So far, so good! She studied his diagram and found the transceiver closest to him, which corresponded to someone's Alto—no surprise. The owner wasn't around, so she moved the ladder there, repeated the drill with the ceiling tile, and replaced that transceiver as Tony had taught her.

Again, and again. Tony had her replace all the transceivers on that segment. When she was finished, he said, "You did great. Now, we'll clean up the mess. When we're done, we can reconnect the cable."

By *we*, he clearly meant *Janet*, so she reconnected the network. She noticed that the cable on the far side disappeared into some kind of conduit. "*This is the outside wall. Nothing on the other side.*" She shined the flashlight around the wall and saw a metal conduit with the cable inside it. Then, she saw a glint. It was something metallic that wasn't cable, conduit, or anything else legitimate. "*What's that?*" She had the person sitting nearby steady the ladder while she reached deep inside and retrieved it. It was a crescent wrench. "*Maybe this was supposed to be there? Nah! The last guy up here forgot to pack up his tools."*

She put back all the ceiling tiles and picked up the little bits of debris that had fallen down. When she finished, she returned to the table where Tim sat. It had pieces of electronics, metal casing and screws, and test equipment scattered around, and Tim was applying probes at various points in the circuit boards. All the bad transceivers had been replaced, and the network was back up.

He gave a running commentary as he worked. As she approached, Janet heard, "Another bad input transistor." Tim gave her a startled look. Janet expected another assignment, but he just asked, "Where did you find *that?*" pointing to the wrench in Janet's hand.

"Oh, some tech must have left his tools."

Tim paused and then resumed his debugging, "Thanks a lot, Janet." Everyone nodded. Janet walked back to Grant's office.

Grant was on the phone again. He was happier this time and gave her the thumbs-up, but then he turned his back and resumed his conversation. Janet went to the guest office to check her mail, which of course, she hadn't been able to do earlier with the net being down.

Ten minutes later, Kelly, one of the receptionists, knocked on the door, "Janet Saunders? Tim Field needs you."

Janet panicked, *"Uh-oh. I did do something wrong after all."*

As she approached the table downstairs with all the junk on it, Tim held the wrench, and they all looked at her. "Hi Janet, if you remember, can you show us where, exactly, you found this wrench?"

She worried for an instant that maybe the wrench was supposed to be there, and she should have left it in place. But no, that couldn't be true. "Sure, if I can remember," and led them back to the spot near the wall where she found it. Janet directed Tim on where he should set up the ladder. She climbed up, took out the ceiling tile, and handed it to him. Tony was carrying another ladder, and he opened it next to Janet's. Tim climbed up and gave her the wrench, "Can you put the wrench back where you found it?"

Janet tried to remember. She leaned it up against the metal conduit. Tim said, "Are you sure?"

"No, I'm not. I know it was around there, but I don't remember the exact position."

Tim moved one end of the wrench so that it touched the transceiver closest to the conduit. "Is there any chance it was like this?"

Janet closed her eyes and tried to remember, "Yeah, I think that was it. Not certain, though."

Tim took the wrench and climbed down the ladder, "I think we have our answer!"

Everyone stared. Tim said, "Remember when Grant said we had lightning last night?"

Smirking, Tony replied, "No. Who listens to Grant?"

Tim wore a thin smile, "We should listen to anyone with good information. Anyway, what would happen if the lightning hit on the SDD side of Coyote Hill?"

Tim was playing professor, which he enjoyed. Tony played along, "There'd be a massive change in the ground potential, relative to the PARC side?"

"And… this would affect the coax how?"

Tony thought hard and finally gave up, "I just don't see it."

Tim knew they'd *almost* had it, but he'd have to help them, "What was the wrench touching?"

"Well, one end was on the conduit, I assume, but we couldn't see what you were doing up there."

Tim realized they needed a hint, "The other end was touching the tap on the transceiver."

Janet still had no idea. Tony smiled, "So… the Ethernet was grounded through the wrench."

"Yeah?"

"Let's see. The lightning must have caused a big change in the ground reference voltage in one building, relative to the other building."

"And?"

Tony had to think hard, but this was life with Tim, "The voltage drop would be on the shield but not on the center conductor."

Tim looked pleased, "Why is this a problem?"

Tony stood up and almost yelled, "Because we have a transistor across that gap, and it can't handle that voltage."

Tim could have acted triumphant, but that wasn't his style. His voice was completely flat and emotionless. "Let me think about how to fix this problem permanently. Janet, you saved the Ethernet today! Thank you."

Janet laughed, "Hey, I just did what Tony told me to do!" Tim shook her hand, as did Tony.

Word spread fast among SDD and PARC. "Lightning took down the Ethernet!" Grant was annoyed that they didn't listen to him from the start. Janet didn't see how they'd have found it any faster if they did, and in any case, Tim *did* listen.

The rest of the day was a blur of Janet telling and retelling the wrench story. Michael sought her out and shook her hand. When Janet acted modest, he said, "Hey, sometimes noticing things nobody else sees is the mark of a great engineer!"

"*A great engineer*," Janet said to herself on the flight home. "*All I did was find a crescent wrench.*"[1]

17

BACK TO NORMAL

J anet felt like Tim, Tony, and she had just had a tickertape parade and received the key to the City. Michael's email to the division yesterday about the lightning incident had specifically called her out:

I'd like to thank everyone who helped with this crisis, but especially Tim Field, Tony Webb, and Janet Saunders. Janet never expected to be climbing up in the ceiling when she boarded the plane this morning!

Craziness. When she walked into work on Friday, she heard, "Congratulations, Janet!" as she went by, and people came out in the hall to shake hands. Paul, whom she'd virtually never interacted with during all her time at Xerox, stopped by and congratulated her, as did Tom. "We knew you had it in you, Janet!" he said with a wry smile. All morning long, they dropped by and said nice things. Janet was in a daze. She must have heard that she was having her "15 minutes of fame" every 15 minutes. After the third time, she started glancing at her watch comically, to check if the 15 minutes was over yet.

When the crush of well-wishers finally subsided, she thought, *"But this isn't even what I do here. I'm not a hardware person, and now, I'll be 'The Woman Who Found the Wrench' forever!"*

Dan came by later in the morning. After the obligatory, "Congratulations, Janet!" he sat down and asked some questions about what exactly had gone wrong with the Ethernet. She wondered for a while afterward if *maybe* he was a little jealous?

"So, why did a bolt of lightning bring down the Ethernet? I mean, I've heard the official story…"

"Well, as Tim figured out, there was a big voltage differential between the connector and the shield of the cable. It was going the wrong way across the collector junction of the input transistor and blew it out."

"And somehow, the lightning caused this voltage?"

Janet laughed. This was getting closer to the heroic part. "Well, the amazing thing is that the Ethernet goes *underneath* Coyote Hill Road!"

"It goes *under* the road? Does the city let them do that?"

She shrugged, "You probably heard about how I found the wrench?"

He stood up, "Of course! How did that happen? Were you looking for something?"

She looked embarrassed, "Wish I could say I was. Actually, I saw it lying near the conduit and gave it to Tim. The rest is history."

He sat back down, "So, it was an accident? The truth comes out!"

"The truth comes out, sadly."

"Well, you saw something out of place, and you didn't ignore it. That's the important thing!" Dan left.

Janet noticed that the crowd of well-wishers was gone. She had some peace and quiet for the first time this morning. It was ironic that she thought the Ethernet was so cool, and she wanted to be a part of it, and now she *had* been, but by accident.

It was still going to be hard to find a role on that team, not being a hardware engineer, but at least now, they knew who she was. She felt a rush of optimism, *"This might seem impossible today, but over time, I'll find a way. Some door will open."* She wasn't sure where, but it would!

In Palo Alto, Grant stood in the crowd of be-suited executives, as Martin conducted the demo that had been on the verge of disaster yesterday. McColough and Glavin had seen the Alto's famous programs, Bravo, Markup, and Draw, before, so Martin concentrated on the newer things like the Desktop prototype. The execs were mostly silent, and Grant tried to read their body language, but you don't become a VP by being transparent. He noticed they were not asking a lot of questions about the IMO or the commercial prospects, which he took as a bad sign. This whole computer thing was still a curiosity to them.

After the demo, Michael took them back to his office, and Grant was not encouraged to follow. He went back to his office and sat at his desk, lost in thought. His "bakeoff" of the leading word processors against the Alto had never come off, despite endless hours of trying to arrange it—calling executives' secretaries, enlisting Martin's group, and on and on. They did at least videotape the different systems, but it wasn't clear if anyone watched the video. Was he just wasting his time? He was starting to think so.

PARC had so much exciting new technology, stuff that the rest of the computing world had never even dreamed of. Was SDD really doing the right thing in trying to bring it all out at once? Okay, we had landed on the moon only six years ago with Apollo 17, so it was easy to believe that anything was possible. But NASA had a bit more money than Xerox did. Furthermore, Star wasn't even *all* of Xerox, just a couple hundred people in California. "*Maybe we should pick a more modest goal and concentrate on that for now,*" was an obvious idea.

What about the hardware for Star? The Dolphin did not seem to be going well. Whenever he talked to anyone about it, they became vague and suddenly remembered that they had a meeting. The new 20Mbps Ethernet was now 10Mbps, and it wasn't done, either.

Pilot, the operating system that he had been officially in charge of until last May, was chugging along, with a schedule calling for a first release in the second quarter of this year. Yet, they lacked even a complete design spec. For example, the Install Facility section said, "This section is a complete unknown; no one currently has responsibility for it."

What about the Star product itself, the grand unified machine that Xerox would actually sell? That had a Requirements doc, at least. However, the Functional Spec was, to be charitable, a "work in progress." Martin's group was working with Mark in El Segundo on that, and they had a good working relationship. But when was the spec coming? Who knew?

It was *not* a good sign to Grant that the FunSpec had a Direct Typing section, which detailed how the Star could function as a typewriter, meaning when you hit a key, a mark would appear on the printer. The rationale was that a secretary lacked space on her desk for both a Star and a typewriter, so the Star needed to replace the typewriter. Someone in the management team must not completely believe that knowledge-worker stuff.

Xerox upper management was in a constant state of flux, too. Archie McCardell, the President, had left. Which executive was actually in charge of Star? He had no clue. All this was old hat at SDD and career-limiting to harp on. "We're all in the boat, and it's time to row!"

But Grant wasn't in the mood for rowing at the moment. Since last May, he and Janet had talked on the phone now and then. She was a good audience, unlike most of the engineers up here. She appreciated what the Xerox Phased Program Planning manual was trying to accomplish, maybe because it reminded her of the big satellite programs she'd worked on at TRW. If he told her about the difficulties he was having, no apology was necessary. And, he still hadn't congratulated her for finding the wrench! He dialed.

"Hi, it's Grant. Let me be the *last* person to congratulate you for saving the Ethernet."

"Hi, Grant, thanks. It's been a whirlwind!"

"Yeah, when you came into my office, I had no idea *why* the network was back up."

"Me neither. Or rather, I thought it was just that we replaced some transceivers."

"Little did we know. Anyway, how are you? Other than being a hero, I mean."

"Oh, about the same. Ken and I are going skiing this weekend."

"Fantastic. Where, Mammoth?"

"Yeah, the usual. I forget... do you ski?"

"No, but I'm going to Tahoe for the first time in a couple of weeks."

"Oh, you'll love it! Tahoe's a little too far for us down here in LA."

Grant shifted the conversation, "What do you know about the various printer efforts in your building? I think they're on the second floor."

"*Now we come to the point of this call,*" thought Janet. "Nothing at all. Why?"

"Oh, I was just wondering. I know they're thinking of doing a printer that uses Mesa and a scaled-down version of Pilot."

"Really? Interesting. Why... you're not thinking of transferring down here, are you? Everyone here wants to move up *there.*"

Grant replied, "Yeah, I know. But it's the job that matters to me in the end. Anyhow, it's just research at this point."

Janet figured Grant must have some motivation for this sudden interest in El Segundo, but she doubted she'd find it out now, if ever. "Well, I'll ask around, *discreetly*."

"Thanks." They chatted some more about Star, the Functional Spec effort, the need for a Lead Design Team, which was being formed, and Grant's various attempts to lend some scheduling discipline to Star. He was vague about how much success he was having with the scheduling stuff, and Janet was tactful about asking. IMO still seemed to be two years away.

Janet had no idea what the rest of the A&E Building did. No all-Xerox social functions ever happened. SDDers might suspect that she wanted to transfer out if she asked them. She tried to think of anyone she knew who might know something, and finally thought of Gwen, whom she met when she first joined. Janet had chatted with Gwen a few times before she moved offices—didn't she join a printer project on the second floor? She looked her up in the corporate phone book. The office location looked right, so she dialed the number.

"Hi, Gwen, this is Janet Saunders. Hope you remember me!"

"Hi, Janet, sure I do. How are you?"

"Doing great. Hey, do you have a sec?" Gwen did. "I know a guy who was asking about the smart printer projects in El Segundo."

"Oh, really? Does he want to join? We might be hiring."

Janet laughed, "Good to hear. No, he just wanted some info. Are you free for lunch today?"

They made arrangements to meet in the cafeteria. Janet thought, *"This is a very good day so far!"*

Down the hall, Dan was *not* having a very good day. He was getting nowhere with his prototype of Star, and he was becoming very depressed about it. He knew that someday this would be totally obvious, but everything is obvious *after* you do it. Right now, it sure as hell wasn't. He didn't even know where to start, and it was a massive effort. But he still thought, "*Hey, I'm a smart guy, I should be able to do this,*" instead of admitting defeat or avoiding the task altogether.

He'd had a succession of officemates since there wasn't enough space anymore for everyone to have their own office. His first roommate, Benjamin—never Ben or Bennie—was extremely entertaining, although it probably would have pissed him off to be described that way. He had wild black hair and thick glasses and told anyone who asked that he was gay, although he wasn't terribly outspoken about it.

Benjamin had recently moved from Boston, where he'd worked for Digital Equipment Corporation (DEC) after graduating from MIT. Benjamin had worked on a publishing system for DEC, so he was familiar with some of what Xerox wanted the Star to do.

Dan quickly learned that mass transit and LA's lack of it was a hot button for Benjamin, so he avoided it. Most other people learned that, too. "Were you not aware that LA had no mass transit before you moved here?" was not a question you asked Benjamin.

Benjamin was also a serious backgammon player. He found a place in Westwood where backgammon players met to play for money. On their third day of sharing an office, Dan said, "Morning!" when Benjamin arrived.

"I am *so* pissed! I lost to this lousy player last night who kept rolling double-sixes exactly when he needed them."

Dan didn't play backgammon, "I guess that's bad, huh?"

Benjamin laughed, "Uh… yeah. I double him, he accepts when he should resign, and then he rolls the big Double Six."

More new terminology for Dan. Benjamin was probably not in the mood to explain. Dan sighed, "Ah, well." Benjamin sat down, fired up his Alto, and read his email.

This became a recurrent theme. Occasionally, he won at the tables the night before and was in a good mood when he came in, but more often, he'd been beaten by someone he considered inferior.

Music was another hot button for Benjamin, and on this topic, he and Dan were in complete agreement. Even though they differed in their preferred music, they were united in one opinion, which was that *disco sucks*. Dan learned that this was a great topic whenever Benjamin was angry about something. After a rant about how the DEC engineers were every bit the equal of the Xerox PARC ones, Dan changed the subject to the repetitiveness of disco. Benjamin's response was memorable, "I can see where this is going. I call it Tape-O! A loop of tape with a drumbeat and bass, playing forever." They laughed for a long time.[1]

Benjamin frequently argued with the other engineers about all sorts of topics, rapid transit being the most popular. Since he'd been at DEC and worked on publishing systems, he wasn't particularly impressed with Xerox's ambitions or credentials. He left in less than a year.

After Benjamin, Dan's next officemate was William, who was extremely reserved and formal. He had been in the Marines, and since the U.S. had officially lost the Vietnam War only three years before, many vets didn't advertise their service. William never did.

William was always unhappy about something on the Star project. There was no discipline—nothing worked, nobody was doing their jobs, the whole project was going nowhere. Eventually, this complaining won him the job of fixing the problem or at least the *bad Alto* part of it. He became the head of the Support group, and as a manager, he was entitled to his own office, so he moved out.

Dan was still an honorary member of the UCLA Mafia, and they didn't judge him as harshly as he judged himself for his failure to solve the Star User Interface problem. They understood that no one else had, either. They still went to lunch, attended Dodger games, watched big sports events on

TV, and always made fun of the more pretentious ideas that came out of Palo Alto. Their term for a really dumb idea was an RCI, for recto-cranial inversion, meaning head up the ass.

Whenever they went out to lunch, returning to the parking lot became the occasion for the *pull-through* chant so that they'd earn a ticket from Xerox Security. They especially enjoyed instructing visitors from Palo Alto to park their cars that way and then affecting surprise when they found tickets under their windshield wiper. Security was a regular topic of conversation since they all came in a side door, and usually after 9:00 am, the guards were gone, and they had to show their badges to the TV camera. One day when they came back from lunch, Randy said, "I bet you could show them a baseball card." Dan decided to try it.

He had no idea where you bought baseball cards anymore, but the next time he was in a 7-Eleven, he looked on the counter by the register, and sure enough, there they were. He bought a couple of packs. The Xerox badges had a red background, so he looked for a card with a lot of red on it. Tommy Herr, second base for the St. Louis Cardinals. Plenty of red on that card. The next morning, he held Tommy up to the TV camera. The door clicked. He was in![2]

Dan went to Janet's office and told her about it, "Okay, maybe *you* saved the Ethernet, but I got in here with a baseball card!" She laughed and agreed that they were now even.

Steve was in charge of the document management part of the Functional Spec, and records processing fell under that, so Dan spent a lot of time with him. Steve smoked cigarettes and affected a country-boy demeanor, although he was actually from the suburbs, as was everyone. Steve played guitar in their musical group, the Arcy Eyes, along with Dan on guitar, Randy on trumpet, and Brian on sax. He liked to stick his burning cigarette under the strings near the tuning heads on his guitar and always played "Pipeline."

In mid-January, Dan attended a meeting that included the

Functional Specification team, and a spirited argument about icons broke out. Should there be a trash can icon, and did people really keep their trash cans on their desktops? The conceit in Star was that the Desktop was, in fact, a visual representation of a real desktop, where the icons represented real objects like folders, documents, file cabinets, and printers. Of course, you didn't keep a file cabinet on your desktop, either.

Brooks Landon, the most intellectual member of Martin's group, said, "Let me recapitulate the taxonomy of this."

Steve turned to Dan, "Dan, how do you think the Dodgers are gonna do this year?"

Dan laughed, "If they get some pitching, they could go all the way." Brooks smiled slightly. Dan loved that making fun of each other was okay in this crowd, as long as it was goodhumored. These lines immediately became the standard response in El Segundo to any especially pretentious statement.

The discussion returned to icons and their taxonomy, and everyone realized that they didn't *literally* represent things on your desktop. The trash can icon was eventually eliminated in favor of a set of universal operations invoked by actual keys on the Star keyboard, which were MOVE, COPY, DELETE, and PROPERTIES (PROPS).

You did almost any action on the Star by selecting something and then hitting one of those four keys. For example, to change a word to italics, you selected it and hit the PROPS key. To print a document, you selected its icon and COPYed it to the printer icon—*or* should you MOVE it to the printer? Much time was spent debating this. Henry Davis, who reported to Martin, came up with the idea of the four keys for universal operations. The week before the "Let me recapitulate the taxonomy" meeting, Henry had sent out his latest thoughts on the user interface, and Dan dutifully printed it out. At the printer, he found Brian getting his copy.

"So, another RCI from Henry, I guess."

Brian was always positive about people and their efforts, although his *degree* of enthusiasm was what Dan looked for. "I don't know… this looks really interesting."

"Yeah, I haven't read it yet." Dan figured that with a real RCI, Brian would have been more measured in his praise. He admired that quality in Brian, but he thought if he tried it, it would just seem insincere. Dan was more the sarcastic type.

Dan read Henry's memo over and liked it a lot. This was one of Henry's better ideas, he thought. The function keys, as they were called, seemed intuitive, meaning that if you were a user trying to figure out how to do something, well, you didn't need to read a manual. At the same time, he'd learned that intuitive was a word to be careful about using inside the FunSpec group. It was likely to elicit a groan. They were past all the high-flown ideas, and now, they were trying to commit it to paper. Dan always thought that Mark, Steve, and Randy were the guys who kept the entire effort on track and actually got things done, but people in Palo Alto gave Martin all the credit.

Later that afternoon, Randy poked his head in Dan's office, "Arcy Eyes on Sunday night? My house, 7 o'clock." Dan gave the thumbs-up, and all weekend he looked forward to Sunday night. He had the sheet music to "The Work Song," which they had tried at their last session. He wrote out the chords on four sheets of music paper and worked out an arrangement where they changed keys upward several times. Dan didn't have a piano or any formal musical training, but he knew that on a guitar when using barre chords, moving up a key is a matter of sliding your finger up a fret. He assumed it must be the same for any instrument. He put the sheet music inside his guitar case and drove to Randy's house in Palos Verdes after he finished dinner on Sunday night, which was his usual chicken breast with Shake 'n Bake.

PV was a wealthy neighborhood and a long drive from the

405 freeway. On Los Angeles TV, Dan always saw commercials for car dealers or some other business where they advertised that they were freeway-close. He wondered if maybe the real estate sellers in PV made a point of saying freeway-*far*. On his way down Hawthorne Boulevard, Dan calculated how long it must take Randy to drive to the 405 every morning and figured it must be at least 20 minutes. "*My God, how could anyone live that way?*" Most driving in LA was either getting to the freeway or coming from it. Or, of course, driving on it.

Randy had a very large house with a giant living room. Mark, Steve, and he were all about seven years older than Dan and Brian, and they'd bought real estate back before the big boom in house prices. To Dan, it seemed insane. His dad had sold their house in 1969 for $22,000, after paying $13,500 back in 1950. To him, real estate was a dumb investment since if you worked out the annual rate of return on that, it wasn't all that great. This was definitely not the view in California. Dan was sticking to his apartment for now.

Randy and his wife, Jean, met him at the door and handed him a beer. Brian arrived shortly, followed by Steve and his wife, Jill. After a half-hour of socializing and deliberately not talking about work, they picked up their instruments. Dan had no amplifier, so he plugged his guitar into Steve's amp. Steve immediately jumped into "Pipeline" since he loved the opening dig-digga-digga-digga notes descending down the string. No one else had a part to play, certainly not the horns. But surf guitar was probably the reason Steve had learned to play guitar in the first place, so "Pipeline" was mandatory.

Dan brought out his sheet music for "The Work Song." Randy looked at the "music," which consisted of nothing but chords, and said, "What the hell is this?" Being a trumpet player, Randy had no idea of chords. Brian also played the piano, so he had that concept down at least.

Steve didn't play barre chords, which shocked Dan. He wasn't much of a guitar player, but he knew that much! Dan played through the arrangement with the key changes for them.

Randy cursed as he tried to work out how to move the notes up a half-step on his trumpet, "You know... this is not that easy on a horn, don't you, Dan?" Dan didn't know, actually. Brian figured out how to do it on his sax, and they played through "Work Song" with the key changes.

The conclusion was that it was good enough to keep in their repertoire, but it wasn't anyone's favorite. They talked about marching bands, which Randy and Brian had both been in, but Steve and Dan had not. Jill wanted to sing "White Rabbit," which she and Steve always performed together. Steve and Dan accompanied Jill as she did her Grace Slick imitation. This was real rock 'n' roll for Dan, and he loved it. Randy and Brian applauded. They chatted about real estate prices in the LA area, which was a big deal for Randy and Steve. Property taxes were skyrocketing along with them since if your house had doubled in value, so did your taxes, even though you weren't making any more money.

For some reason no one remembered, the Leonard Cohen song "Suzanne" came up. It was a lugubriously slow song made famous by Judy Collins, perfect for a late night in a coffeehouse:

Suzanne takes you down...

Randy recalled his trumpet teacher in high school, who was continually exasperated by Randy's obstinacy about rhythm and accused him of playing everything in march tempo. Brian laughed and said, "Hey, why don't we try Suzanne that way?"

Thus was born The Arcy Eyes' greatest hit—"The Suzanne March."[3]

18

A CELEBRITY IN OUR MIDST

On Monday, January 16, 1978, Xerox's internal PR group made a huge announcement. Judy Resnik, an engineer who was right in Janet's building, had been chosen to be an astronaut. She might even become the first American woman in space and definitely the first Jewish American.[1]

No one in SDD knew her or even had any idea what she did. After all, they had almost zero contact with the rest of Xerox, even groups in the same building. But her biography, which was distributed with the announcement, filled them all with envy. She'd turned down a chance to go to Julliard and become a concert pianist, instead earning her B.S. in Electrical Engineering from Carnegie Mellon and her Ph.D. from the University of Maryland. Now, she was blasting off into space.

Janet felt a rush of pride that this woman *in her building* had accomplished so much. After a period of admiration about Resnik's accomplishments, she started comparing herself. *"So, what am I doing with my life? Will I ever do anything that big?"* Judy was only a couple years older than her, 28.

Ken also heard about it. It was all over the news that day,

so you couldn't miss it. That night over spaghetti and garlic bread, he brought it up. The excitement about Janet finding the wrench and saving the Ethernet had worn off. Ken was not impressed with that feat, which she resented.

"Hey, do you know that Judith Resnik lady, the new astronaut?"

"No, wish I did! She's right in our building, though."

"What was she working on?"

"I have no idea. Something to do with optics, I think." Janet twirled her fork around some more spaghetti and lifted it to her mouth. She felt this topic was exhausted, but Ken persisted, "Optics? Like for xerography?"

She paused, "I assume. We really don't have much contact with that stuff." She resumed eating.

"Really? Isn't that what pays the bills?"

"*Where is this going? What does he want me to say?*"

"My paychecks don't bounce, Ken. What's your point?"

Ken missed that signal that she used his name. He pressed on, "I mean… you've been at Xerox a year now. When will they ship a computer?"

Janet was tired of smiling and changing the subject away from Xerox. On their recent ski trip with his Hughes buddies, the other folks were, occasionally, jerks about Xerox, and she felt he didn't support her. They quarreled about it, briefly, on the car ride home, but they were both too tired to fight in earnest. She laid her knife and fork down.

"Ken, I'm getting tired of this. I like it at Xerox. I'm not going back to aerospace. I wish you would stop nagging me about it."

Ken had too much frustration built up to let this drop. They used to have shared interests, a shared career, and a nice bunch of friends who kept them busy. Now, all that was disappearing. Janet was hanging around with a bunch of eggheads with Ph.D.s and jetting off to Palo Alto all the time. He felt, even though she never said anything, that she was starting to look down on him and his Hughes Aircraft friends. On their last ski trip when the entire group was at dinner, she drank an Anchor Steam instead of Coors, their usual. Hell, you still couldn't buy Coors east of the Mississippi! They always teased their friends back East about that.

"Nagging! How am I nagging? Don't engineers always talk about when their products are shipping?"

"Not like you do."

Ken paused for a second. He searched for some way to keep this from getting out of control. "Okay, you don't like being asked about Xerox. I get that. Sorry."

Janet didn't think this was resolved, whatever *resolved* meant, but she didn't relish having a big fight, either. "We're writing code pretty soon. Check back in a few months."

He was relieved, "Excellent! Are you done eating?" She nodded, and he cleared the dishes, rinsing and loading them into the dishwasher. "Ice cream?"

She jumped to her feet and reached into the cabinet below the counter, "I bought some Kahlua to put over the chocolate sauce. You have to try this!"

"Wow, okay." Another little bit of high culture she was bringing home, but he decided to let that one go. They didn't talk about work anymore that night.

The next day, Janet decided to go meet Judy. The crowds might have eased off, and she wouldn't have left for astronaut training quite yet. Around 9:30, she walked up the stairs and found Judy's office. She was just hurrying out the door when Janet arrived, but she shook Janet's hand and thanked her for her congratulations. *"A very nice person! I'm probably just one of a million people congratulating her, though."*

While she was on the second floor, she figured she might as well drop in on Gwen. Their lunch a couple weeks ago had been educational for Janet, beyond just getting the info Grant wanted. Gwen was at least 10 years older than Janet and had been at Xerox for a long time, and she'd been in a technical field a lot longer, too.

She wanted to learn so much from her. Gwen was probably curious about what younger women went through, too, after the feminist revolution made things theoretically easier for them. She knocked on Gwen's door. She was dressed more formally than Janet, in a skirt and blouse, which always made Janet wonder if she ought to dress up more, too.

"Hi, are you busy?"

"No, come on in, Janet. How are things down on the first floor?"

Janet sat down, "Oh, you know. About the same. I just came up to congratulate Judy Resnik."

"Judy! I'm *so* happy for her. Her life's about to change completely."

"Do you know her?"

Gwen admitted, "Only a little. Did you meet her?"

"Just for a second. She was on her way out."

"Oh, well." She closed the office door, "So… *really*! How are things down there?"

Janet sighed, "Well, you were in SDD. I'm not sure anyone knows what's happening."

"Still? I heard their new hardware isn't working out too well."

"*Gwen has better info than I do,*" Janet realized. "You must have good sources because I didn't know that."

"Yeah, I'm not surprised your friend is looking around. I don't think the big execs are all signed up for the Star."

Janet had heard all this before, especially from her husband. "*Old news. I might as well learn something new, if I can.*" So, she asked, "Your project. Is *that* an official Xerox project?"

Gwen shifted a little. This was a sensitive topic. "Well, nothing at Xerox is ever *official* until it's out the door."

Janet laughed, "So, Rochester bureaucracy…?"

"And Dallas. And sometimes, even Stamford." They both laughed.

Since the door was shut, Janet could say what was really bothering her. "So… you're divorced, right, Gwen?"

"Five years now. Why?" Gwen had her suspicions, but she didn't want to be the first to bring it up.

"Oh, I don't know. What was it like?"

Gwen paused and thought, "It was horrible. Hours and hours with lawyers, and that's if you have an *amicable* divorce, which ours was."

"Did you have kids?"

"One. He sees her every other weekend." Janet mulled that over. Gwen finally said, "Everything okay with your marriage?"

"Oh, yeah, we're fine. It's just that, sometimes…"

Gwen didn't want to play marriage counselor with someone she barely knew. Still, she could give Janet the benefit of her experience. "I'd never tell anyone to get a divorce. As I said, it's a horrible thing to go through. But it's *much* worse when you have kids."

"Which we don't. Well, I've taken enough of your time. Thanks, Gwen." Janet headed for the door.

"Anytime! Call me for lunch whenever you feel like it." Janet said she would.

She had a "while you were out" slip in her inbox saying that her dad, Len, called. She had a moment of dread. What was he calling about? She hoped to God that someone hadn't died. He left his work number, so that probably wasn't it. She called him back immediately, "Hi, Dad. You called?"

"Hi, sweetie! Don't worry… nothing's wrong," Janet expressed relief.

"I have a business trip out to LA this Friday. I just found out about it today."

"Oh, great! Can you spend the weekend with us?"

"Well, if it's not too big of a bother! I know this is short notice."

"Don't be silly. We'd love to have you!"

"Okay, well, don't go to any extra trouble for me. You can just go about your lives."

They worked out what time he'd come over on Friday and whether he had to be back in Detroit for work on Monday. Then, she called Ken, "Hey, guess who's coming to visit this weekend?"

"I don't know... who?"

"My dad! He has a business trip out here on Friday."

"Excellent. So, is he spending the weekend?"

She'd noticed that her dad and Ken weren't particularly close, but they seemed to get along okay. Len really wished Ken would call him Dad, but Ken said he'd feel funny about that as long as his own father was still alive. So, Len was the closest he'd come, and she always wondered if, secretly, he'd really prefer to call him Mr. Saunders.

Janet made up the extra bedroom for Len, and he arrived at about 6:30. Choosing a restaurant for him was always tough since he didn't like any ethnic food except Italian, and he always insisted on picking up the check, so she'd feel guilty if it was too expensive. She decided to make reservations at Victoria Station in West LA, where he could order prime rib.

"So, Ken, how are things at Hughes these days, now that Howard's gone?"

Ken was used to this question, "Oh, it's the same as before. It's the Medical Foundation that controls it, and he never even had much to do with that."

"So, no movie stars, huh?"

Ken just smiled. Janet rescued him, "Dad, how are things back in Detroit? I didn't see too many foreign cars on the roads last time I was there."

Len grimaced, "Goddamn rice-burners, excuse my French. They're eating our lunch. Every quarter, I have to work on the financial reports, and every quarter they get worse."

She laughed, "Ken keeps trying to get me to buy a Honda, but I'm still driving the old Plymouth Duster. I feel like I'm the last American car driver here."

"I couldn't help noticing all those rice-burners on the freeway today. They tried to give me a Toyota at the rental place, but I refused. Even a Ford Fairmont's better than that."

Janet thought they'd exhausted the subject of cars. Just then, their salads arrived, so she was spared from having to steer the conversation.

After the food was cleared, and they'd ordered dessert, Len leaned over, "Sweetie, tell me again about how you found the wrench and saved the day. Don't leave anything out!"

Ken stood up, "Excuse me, but I've heard this. I'll just go to the bathroom a sec."

Janet retold the story in exhaustive detail. Len listened raptly, occasionally interrupting with questions.

Ken returned to the table just as she was imitating Tim as he explained why the wrench had shorted out the transistors. He snorted, "Maybe if they designed their network properly in the first place, there wouldn't be an outage."

Janet put her hand over his, "I'm sure you're right, Ken, but Tim's a pretty smart guy." He smiled thinly.

Len asked, "This network you use... who designed it?"

She answered, "Mostly, it was a guy, Bob Metcalfe, who was at MIT just before us."

"He works at Xerox now?" She nodded.

"And, you all are using it now?"

"Yep. It seems to be working. Well, except for that lightning thing."

This was too much for Ken, "Tell him what happens if two computers start talking at the same time."

Len held up his hands, "Whoa, this is getting too technical for me! Here comes dessert." The waiter brought their desserts and asked if there was anything else. Len looked around to see if anyone wanted coffee and then asked for the check.

On Saturday, Janet and her dad went to Long Beach to see the Queen Mary. Ken begged off, claiming he had to go into work. That night, Len took them out to Chasen's because he'd heard that movie stars go there. They didn't see anyone they recognized.

19

WE HAVE LIFTOFF

I n the first half of 1978, the product effort was underway at last. A Functional Spec team was actually writing down how Star would work, with Martin's team in Palo Alto and Mark's team in El Segundo, and each team went to the other's location once a week. Some burning questions were still being debated on email, and it spilled out into the broader team. Mouse buttons, for instance. How many, and what would they do? The six of them wrestled with that question and many others.

For example, the PARC mouse had three buttons. Each system implementor did their own thing with them, and naturally, they thought of clever tasks for each button. If you gave a researcher a mouse with 10 buttons, they'd assign useful functions to every one of them and defend them to the death. That's what was going on now.

In Bravo, the main text editor everyone used, the left button was used for scrolling up and the right for scrolling down if the cursor was in the left edge, which was the scroll bar. The middle button was for thumbing, or scrolling the document to an approximate location based on the percentage of the document you wanted.

You used the left button to select a text *character*, the middle button to select a *word*, and the right button extended the selection. These habits became second nature to a Bravo user.

Another influential Alto program was Markup, for making diagrams. In Markup, the left button was used for *adding* information and the right button for *removing* it. The middle button popped up a command menu where you selected what you wanted to do. You also used the left and right buttons to rotate or scale the image.

The same was true for the other Alto programs that inspired Star. Each researcher did whatever made sense for them, but they didn't coordinate with each other. Star was supposed to combine all these great ideas into one consistent product, though. A user would have documents with text, fonts, graphics, and equations, and maybe images, too. No one had ever seen such a system outside of the publishing industry. No one was sure how text should flow around a graphics object or even if it should. And, how would you design software for all that unheard-of complexity? Dan had to admire the six FunSpec people for tackling the issues that everyone was so passionate about.

Obviously, Star couldn't have completely different rules for what the mouse meant depending on which part you were using. The rules had to be simple enough for an ordinary person to grasp without reading a manual. Intuitive was the word people hurled at each other, and it meant a user could internalize the rules just by seeing them in action. That was the holy grail of user interface. If a user grasped the concept behind your interface well enough to apply it to new situations, then you'd designed it correctly. Of course, how could you *prove* that your favorite idea was intuitive? That's what made the email debates endless. The FunSpec team had to get along with each other to make any progress at all, and fortunately, they did.

Email debates in SDD and PARC might have gone on

forever, but management didn't allow them to. The Human Factors research group added some scientific rigor by conducting experiments with real people, not Xerox employees. They tried one, two, and three-button mice, and tested users' ability to *point* for typing, *select* for text, icons, and graphic objects, and *extend* the selection, and measured both the time it took to perform the tasks and the error rates. Following this, the debate ended, and the Star mouse had two buttons. You might disagree, but that's how it was going to be.[1]

In parallel to the FunSpec effort was the Lead Design Team, which had to get the entire software effort started. This was a group of three who wrote sections of the Design Spec and handed them off to developers to code up. Dan's latest officemate, Jacob Rotmensch, was in the group, as was Gary, the XDS oldtimer Dan had met in his first week at work, and Randy, a member of the UCLA Mafia. Refreshingly, after all the grand philosophizing that had gone on, they decided to do what was possible now, rather than wait for the resolution of everything.

There was one burning issue they *had* to resolve, though— how to write the code. This was a grave question. The Star code was going to live for decades and be used by thousands of non-technical people. Furthermore, with a project this long-lived, every module eventually gets taken over by someone else, and that person has to maintain it. It would be irresponsible to be cowboy programmers and just write the code. You had to think hard about how to do it.

The Smalltalk language was influential on this, far beyond the few who actually wrote code in it. The object-oriented style was the way to go, and not only for its conceptual appeal. It gave the promise of reducing the amount of code because you could reuse it more easily. This was critically important because memory was still expensive. A hardware engineer could buy memory chips with 16 kilobits, but no more. The more chips, the bigger the circuit board, the more power it needed, and the greater the cost. Of course, bigger memory chips were coming, but Star wasn't living in the distant future —it was being designed now.

The Lead Design Team had to write the coding standards, and as the person with the most Mesa experience, Gary drew the assignment. He did not have the option of redesigning Mesa to be object-oriented, so being a practical engineer, he did the sensible thing, and now had to explain it to everyone.

In doing this, Gary knew that programmers are excruciatingly detail-oriented. Their job requires it. A simplified explanation wouldn't work for them, but for an audience of executives, it might be perfect. If the execs asked more detailed questions, he added the answers, but he didn't throw it at them all at once. Instead, he started with this:

Suppose you have a class of objects called "WheeledVehicle." All WheeledVehicles have certain characteristics. They have some number of wheels, and some mode of propulsion—motor, human power, or animal power. If your program has a WheeledVehicle available to it, your program can ask its wheel count, how it moves, and so forth.

We might create subclasses of WheeledVehicle: Car, Bicycle, where a Car or a Bicycle has additional properties. A Car has an engine, headlights, and taillights, and a Bicycle has two wheels, pedals, and handlebars. They both have the standard WheeledVehicle properties. In Mesa, it looks like this:

```
WheeledVehicle: TYPE = {
    type of vehicle
    number of wheels
    mode of propulsion
}
```

```
Car: TYPE = {
  WheeledVehicle: wv;
  engine data
  headlight data
  taillight data
}
Bicycle: TYPE = {
  WheeledVehicle: wv;
  pedal data
  handlebar data
}
```

Every Bicycle is also a WheeledVehicle, and so is every Car. Programmer Joe, writing the code for WheeledVehicles, needn't be aware of every type of vehicle that might come along later, and the programmers writing that code don't have to redo what Joe did.

The Star user interface was designed in terms of *objects*. A document is an object, and so is a graphics frame, and so are the graphics objects inside that frame. Every object on the screen can be selected and then have the MOVE, COPY, DELETE, or PROPERTIES actions invoked on it. Writing the code in an object-oriented style seemed the only way to do this.

When Gary presented his design for objects to the El Segundo engineers in the biggest conference room they had, he expected a lively discussion, and he wasn't disappointed. The high-level explanation for the execs wasn't nearly sufficient for this crowd. He stood at the whiteboard, and most people had brought their hardcopy of his proposal.

Gary had done design reviews before, so he was not nervous. He smiled broadly, "So... you've all read it. Are there any questions?" Everyone laughed.

Brian raised his hand, "Gary, can you walk through how methods are called?"

"Can you be more specific? Do you mean by a client of the object or an implementer of it?"

"Well, both, actually. Let's start with a client." Gary turned to the whiteboard and wrote:

```
bike: Bicycle ← (something);
   ctWheels                              ←
   WvDefs.GetCountWheels(LOOPHOLE[
       bike, WvDefs.Wv]);
```

"Since `bike` is a `Bicycle` and not a `WheeledVehicle`, we have to loophole it because `GetCountWheels` expects a `Wv`, not a `Bicycle`. But if we're calling a `Bicycle`-specific method, `bike` is already the right type."

He turned back and erased the "`WvDefs.Wv`" part, so it looked like:

```
ctWheels ← WvDefs.GetCountWheels (LOOPHOLE
[bike]);
```

"Since the compiler knows what type it wants, we don't have to tell it."

Everyone had an objection. Brian had the floor, so he spoke first. He laughed, "I guess you know what I'm going to say."

Gary did indeed, "What… you don't like the **LOOPHOLE**?" He chuckled.

Brian wasn't the type to argue endlessly, "Well, I guess we have to, given that Mesa doesn't have subclassing."

"Afraid so. If we want to do object-oriented programming, this is what we have to do."

David spoke up, "What's the chance of getting the compiler changed?"

Gary adopted a poker face, "We're talking to them, but I don't think there'll be anything soon."

Todd had been vocal about this before. "This really sucks. If the company is behind object-oriented programming, then the compiler should support it, or we shouldn't do it."

Gary was able to deflect that one, "You have a point, Todd, but this is the direction we've been told to go."

Todd was silent. This wasn't the right meeting to press that point.

Brian looked at Todd, "Can I ask the other part of the question now?" Todd nodded. "How about if you're the implementer of Bicycle? How do you call a superclass method?"

Gary turned back to the board and wrote:

```
ctDefs ←
WvDefs.GetCountWheels(LOOPHOLE[bike]);
```

"In other words, it's the same as if you're a client. You have to **LOOPHOLE** to the correct type."[2]

Other questions came up, mostly clever ways of avoiding the **LOOPHOLE** or inventing some new syntax where you declared that `Bicycle` was a subclass of `WheeledVehicle`, but Gary had thought of all that. He patiently explained why each scheme would not work. He was about to conclude the meeting, when Brian asked, "So, the people in Palo Alto. They don't use objects?"

"Not as far as I know."

"Why not? Are we ahead of them, or behind?"

Gary laughed again, but he was always diplomatic, "I guess it depends on what your application is. We're building something with objects… they're mostly not."

The meeting ended, and everyone filed out. Dan followed Brian back to his office, and they closed the door. "What do you think of all this?"

Dan answered, "You mean the **LOOPHOLE**s?"

"Yeah, the whole thing. It just seems… I don't know."

"Ugly? Is that the word you were looking for?" Dan laughed, and Brian did, too.

"Yeah, something like that."

"Well, I guess it's what we have right now. If Star's a success, we'll have whatever we want from Mesa."

Brian disliked the idea that business success had an impact on technical decisions. He was idealistic and just thought things were right or wrong. "I suppose. Thanks, Dan."

That same day, Dan was assigned his first task from the Lead Design Team. He was doing the Notification Queue, and he was thrilled to finally write real code.

The Notification Queue was a queue, or first-in-first-out list, of events to be sent to programs. An event was a mouse click, key press, or some other action generated by a human or another program, and it was kept in a central first-in-first-out (FIFO) queue so that the various Star applications could process them in order. Following the object-oriented style as Gary had just outlined it, the Notification Queue became two Mesa modules—NqDefs for the interface to the queue and NqPack for the package of code that implemented it. The interface was the definition of the functions that programs called but not the actual implementation, which was left to NqPack. This split between interface and implementation was universal at Xerox. It meant that if you were a programmer and wanted to use someone else's code, you only needed to read their Defs files, not the actual code.

This was a pretty simple task, but it had to work if two or more programs tried to handle an event at the same time. It wasn't literally the same time, of course, since the computer only had one processor. He could use the cool Mesa functions for multithreading: monitors and condition variables. Exciting![3]

Meantime, David, who was yet another engineer who'd followed Mark from UCLA, was busy implementing the desktop, which meant that icons were finally going to become a reality. David was one of the smartest programmers Dan had ever met and also one of the nicest. He seemed to have absorbed all possible information about Pilot, Mesa, and the Alto within his first week and was always happy to explain it to you.

He also typed faster than anyone Dan had ever seen. Dan noticed that this was true of almost all really good programmers he'd met—they all typed fast. Sometimes, he wondered if any people who typed fast were not great programmers, but he couldn't think of any. The converse was not true, or at least he hoped it wasn't, because he was only fast in short bursts, and then he needed to think. Maybe David dreamed in Mesa, or whatever language he was working in at the time, and his fingers just knew the right syntax.

Besides the Desktop, Brian was taking over text rendering from David. In the old world of terminals, which most of them had come from, and which Janet's husband Ken still lived in, your program just sent a text character to the terminal, and the terminal displayed it. It might be a little more complicated than that as terminals grew more intelligent over the years, but not much.

But in Star, it was not simple at all. The character came with looks, such as its font and whether it was bold, italic, underlined, a subscript, superscript, and on and on. Your program looked up the character in its font file, applied the other looks to it, any of which could change its width, and then transferred the bits to a buffer that was ultimately displayed on the screen. Maybe this character didn't fit on the current line of text given the margins, and you first had to output the current line and then start another. And of course, you didn't know that until you figured out the width of the character. David actually apologized to Brian for the complexity of his code when he turned it over to him.

Janet started out working on the file system, under Jacob's direction. Pilot, the operating system, did not give names to files, nor did it have directories or folders. A file id was only a 64-bit number, a uid, which was guaranteed unique, forever. The application, Star in this case, needed to supply names and directories itself, so creating a file system was a major task.

Janet had given up on transferring to the Ethernet team anytime soon since Tom told her she was needed on the Star effort. She still had a hard time explaining to Ken what exactly she was doing since, in his mind, an operating system *always* provides files and directories. What kind of OS doesn't? But at least she was writing code, so he couldn't nag her about that anymore.

20

MEANWHILE, BACK IN PALO ALTO

I n Palo Alto, Grant tried to keep the hardware effort on track. After all, the computer and its peripherals were most of what the accountants called COGS (cost of goods sold). Xerox made a Star for the COGS, and a common rule of thumb made the final price three times that. Once you had actual dollar figures, the big executives took a lively interest. Michael often told a joke about the superior mental abilities of an executive, "If you put two numbers on a piece of paper, he can immediately tell which one is bigger." To Grant, this showed disrespect for the people who ran the company, so he never told that joke.

The Dolphin was the Star machine, supposedly. Grant became more and more nervous about it. If this machine had to ship in 18 months or so, it ought to be working pretty darn well by now. It was not. The initial machines were unreliable, they ran very hot, and they were looking expensive to manufacture.

In late April 1978, Grant called Paul, the head of Star software in El Segundo. He knew Paul from chatting with him at SDD staff meetings and considered him a typical Xerox executive. He was affable, businesslike, and devoid of any emotion. Grant felt comfortable with him.

Betty Franco answered his phone, "Paul Juranick's office, may I help you?"

"Hi, Betty. This is Grant Avery. How are you?"

Betty made it her business to remember everyone, "Hi, Grant. Doing great. How about you?"

"Just fine. Is Paul in now?"

"He's in a meeting. Can I have him call you back?"

Fifteen minutes later, Paul called back, "Hi Grant, Betty said you called. How are things up there?"

"Doing great, thanks. Say, I know you're busy, so I won't waste your time. How are the D0 machines working out for you guys?"

Paul remembered hearing some complaints about them at his last staff meeting. He'd overheard an engineer call it the Dog-Zero. But an executive was supposed to know the corporate way to handle this. That's what Xerox paid him for. "I've heard a few concerns. Not sure what to make of them yet. What's the view where you are?"

"Kinda the same. It's giving me a bit of a queasy feeling."

Paul looked for the managerial solution, always. "Are we having a formal acceptance test of the hardware?"

Grant had come to the right place. "Good question. Let me follow up on that."

"One more thing before you go," Paul said, although Grant didn't remember saying he was going. "Are we looking at Large Scale Integration at all? My contacts in the Electronics Division were asking about that the other day."

"LSI. That's another thing I hear rumblings about. I'll follow up on that and get back to you."

"Very good, Grant. I gotta run, but thanks for calling."[1]

Grant made a couple of notes for his next lunch with Michael, which was today. He met him in the PARC cafeteria at their usual table. Richard, whom Grant had been running into a lot lately, was sitting with Michael. He finished whatever he was saying as Grant approached and said, "Hi, Grant." and left.

Grant sat down, and they chatted about the weather and its impact on Grant's weekend bicycling, and then Michael said, "How goes the planning?"

Grant realized he was now "the guy who does the Planning," but he thought, "*Okay, that is my job.*"

"Well, I'm getting a little worried about the Dolphin."

"Oh? What do you mean?"

"Well, the reliability, for one. I'm not hearing great things."

Michael always had everything under control, "Well, we're having an acceptance test pretty soon. I'm hoping that gives us the official word. What else?"

Grant replied, "The cost?"

"Yeah, good point. There's an effort with the Electronics Division to look into an LSI design. What else?"

"*Whatever I think we need to do, someone's already doing it, and Michael knows all about it. And always, I'm the last to know. Well, I might as well gather some information while I have him.*" Grant was silent for a while, "So, this LSI effort… what's the story on that?"

Michael told him what he had been talking to Richard about when he arrived. The hardware designers had been looking into various designs that used Large Scale Integration instead of the Medium Scale Integration that the Dolphin used and what each design did to the Unit Manufacturing Cost. They didn't have an answer yet.

Grant knew it was counterproductive to complain that he was always left out. He just asked some questions about who was doing what for his planning.

"*This is getting old. I have to escape this place,*" Grant said to himself after lunch. "*I need to talk to those printer people in El Segundo.*"

Grant closed his office door to think. He checked his calendar for any upcoming trips to El Segundo. Maybe he could just drop by and visit people without arousing suspicion. He was pleased to see an SDD staff meeting there next week.

Then, he realized that that would normally just be a day trip, with everyone leaving El Segundo together afterward. He really needed to spend the night if he wanted to visit the printer groups.

"But wait! What if I can meet with them officially? No need to even lie about it." Now, he was cooking. The intelligent printer folks wanted to use Mesa and Pilot anyway. It could be a regular meeting, the day after the SDD staff meeting. Grant opened his office door again—this might work. He set up the meetings and booked a hotel room. Michael was thrilled to have somebody doing outreach to other parts of Xerox like this.

Now that he had the beginnings of a plan, he felt better. He went for a stroll around the building to see who was around. In Martin's office, he saw two of his bicycling friends, Chuck and Patrick, standing around, and it appeared to be a social visit. He dropped in and joined them. After 10 minutes or so, Chuck and Patrick left, and Grant asked Martin about the upcoming trip to El Segundo. It turned out that he was also spending the night and staying at Mark's house. They were going to a Go-Kart track that evening with a bunch of the other El Segundo folks, and Grant could join them. My God, he was on a roll. Driving was something he might actually beat everybody at! Somehow, at Xerox Palo Alto, there was always someone better than you at everything, whether it was poker, cooking, biking, chess, or tennis. They were the most amazing group of people he'd ever met.

Martin asked, "Have you ever done go-karting before? I haven't."

Grant laughed, "I haven't raced anything that small."

"That *small?* But you've raced real cars?"

Grant had been a car enthusiast for most of his life. Right

now, he was just driving a crappy Ford Maverick, but he had gone to Germany in the late 60s to buy a BMW from the factory, driven it around Europe, and then had it shipped over. He did all his own work on it, including balancing the four independent carburetors during a tuneup, which was quite an art. He finally sold it when it started breaking down on the road more and more.

A prime attraction of the Bay Area for Grant, aside from the job, was the famous Bob Bondurant Driving School, which was now at Sears Point raceway near Sonoma, north of San Francisco. He'd taken three weekend courses already, and he felt he was almost a decent driver.

"I've had a few lessons. And, I used to auto-cross."

"Wow! I don't even know what auto-crossing *is*."

Grant explained it to him, and Martin was suitably impressed. "It seems like every other person here has some world-class talent you'd never suspect. Did you know Richard was a national champion in sailing?"

Grant did not know that, but somehow, he wasn't surprised. It was something an East Coast guy with a name like Richard Boddington *would* be good at.

At home that night, Grant looked in the Yellow Pages for a Go-Kart track nearby so that he could practice. He found a Malibu Grand Prix in Redwood City. He didn't know if the track in LA was another one of that chain, but he drove up 101 and drove 5 or 6 laps, figuring out the fastest line for each curve. He was ready.

In El Segundo the next week, Mark ran into Janet in the hall and stopped her, "Janet, do you want to go go-karting with us tomorrow night? Martin and Grant from Palo Alto are going to be here."

Janet was pleased to be invited to join Mark's group. It wasn't an exclusive group, but these invitations didn't come often. "Go-karting! Sounds like fun. Can I ask my husband?"

"Sure. Bring him along, too," Mark said as he left.

That night at home, Janet mentioned it to Ken. It wasn't typical that she made the social plans for them. Ken knew their regular group of friends the best since most of them worked at Hughes. They usually asked him first, and then he told her. She was tired of that.

He seemed unenthusiastic, "Go-karting? I don't know... we've never done that, have we?"

"First time for everything, right?"

"Where is it?"

"Malibu Grand Prix, in Sherman Oaks."

Ken made a face. Driving to the Valley at rush hour sucked. "So, who are these people? Your regular coworkers?"

"Some of them. Some are people from the Palo Alto office."

"*Oh, great. A bunch of Bay Area snobs to lecture us about water wasting.*" But he realized that she really wanted to do this, and saying no would probably lead to a fight, so he agreed. "Okay, why don't we meet here and drive over together at about 6:00 pm? We can grab a bite first."

The next day, Grant stopped by her office on his way to the staff meeting, "Hey, I heard you're joining us tonight for go-karting. Outstanding."

"Yeah, should be fun. My husband, Ken, is coming, too."

"Looking forward to meeting him. I'll talk to you later." Grant walked down to Paul's office for the meeting. Mark walked past him going in the same direction and gave a thumbs-up sign without stopping.

Janet and Ken arrived at Malibu Grand Prix at about 6:50 pm. Everyone else was already there. They had a round of introductions, listened to the safety briefing, picked out helmets, saw the course's record time posted on the wall of 47 seconds, and bought their tickets.

Mark went first, and the group stood at the fence to watch. He edged up to the Start line. The green light flashed, and he floored it. The first two left turns were pretty easy, and he managed to straighten them out without hitting his brakes, and then, they lost sight of him. His time was 53.3. He climbed out of his cart and slapped hands with the crew.

"So, how was it?" Martin asked.

"Fun! Want to go next?" replied Mark. He usually didn't say much.

Martin said, "I do!" and got into the next cart. He drove a little more cautiously and came in at 56.1.

Now, it was Grant's turn. He said nothing as he climbed into the cart, put his hands at 9 and 3 o'clock on the steering wheel, and edged up to the Start line. The light flashed green, and he was off. As far as they could see, he was driving the same as Mark and Martin, and then, they couldn't see him very well. He didn't seem to ever exert himself, just zipped around smoothly. Janet noticed that a few of the staff walked over to the track to watch, though, so he must have been doing something right. His time was 49.7.

Everyone applauded as Grant took off his helmet and walked back to the group. "Woo-hoo!" yelled Steve. Grant allowed himself a slight smile, "I think I could do a little better on a couple of those turns."

Janet looked at Ken and said, "Go, Ken! There's your time to beat." Ken had never done this before, but he thought, "*It's just driving, right? You go as fast as you can. Don't brake and turn at the same time, or you'll spin out.*" Once he rode a motorcycle and made that mistake, and he still had a scar on his knee to remind him. He climbed in and eased up to the Start line.

The first few turns were pretty gentle, and Ken's plan was "straighten out the road" because he'd read that somewhere. He kept it floored. A little later, he came to a tighter left turn with the curbs painted with red and white stripes. He took that as a warning and braked early, then turned. Damn, he was going slow now. He floored it again. A bunch more easy turns, then a long, long right, then an easy left, and another right with the red-and-white striped curbs. Damn it, again. He ran up on the left curb and almost lost it. He spun the wheel right, and then, *oh shit!*, a hairpin left, about 180 degrees. He was nearly standing still, it seemed.

His lap time was 59.5. As he walked back to the group, Mark said, "I think we have a winner!"

Ken's face was red, but he managed to say, "You mean for the worst?" Janet took his hand.

They weren't the only people at the track, so now, they had to wait a while. Dan found Grant leaning on the fence watching the other racers, "Grant, I haven't spoken to you in a while. What have you been doing?"

Grant shook hands with Dan, "Oh, the usual. Bicycling on the weekends. How about you?"

"The same, actually. We just did a bike ride with some folks from the Tor project. Do you know about that?"

Grant couldn't believe his luck. Maybe Tor was another name for the printer project he was checking out tomorrow. "Tor… that's some kind of intelligent copier, or printer, or something?"

"Yeah, something like that. We didn't get much into it. I think they're actually using Mesa."

"Cool. What kind of bike do you have?"

They talked bicycling equipment for a bit and were deep into it when Dan's turn came.

He drove and then Steve. While Steve was driving, Janet asked Grant, "Hey, can you show me how you did it?" Grant walked over to a patch of dirt and knelt down. Janet knelt next to him. Using his finger, he drew a diagram of the first turn and drew two lines through it, the amateur and the profes- sional lines. He explained trail braking and how you want to ease off on the brake gradually as you turn the wheel and when you re-applied the throttle. He went over weight transfer between the wheels of the kart and how you applied it to use all the tire adhesion that was available to you. Janet was fasci- nated. This seemed like really simple physics. If you held the wheel with your hands at 9 and 3 o'clock like Grant told her, you felt the road better with more sense of what the kart was doing. She was dying to try it.

Janet drove last. She tried to apply what Grant had told her, but thinking it and doing it were two different things. It reminded her of when she'd played golf with her dad when she was in high school. On most shots, you sucked, but over 18 holes, you might hit *one* good shot that made it all seem worthwhile. On this run, she had one turn where she felt she did it right. Her lap time was 52.8.

They all walked back into the main building. Mark said, "Anyone want to go again?" They all looked at each other. Ken was about to call it a night, but Janet was too excited now. "Me! I want to try it again." Ken flashed her a dirty look, but she didn't notice. She ran back out to the track and ran another lap. 51.6.

Janet walked back, beaming. Grant gave her a high-five. "Wow, this was fun! Thanks for inviting us, Mark."

Ken said, "Right. Nice meeting you all," and he and Janet left.

On the 405 back to Culver City, they were silent. Finally as they came over the top of the hill, Janet said, "Did you have a good time? I'm guessing the answer is no."

Ken said, without a smile, "Yeah, it was great!"

She thought that you didn't need to be married to him to figure *that* out. It was kinda obvious.

After a while, he said, "So, what does this Grant guy do?"

"Oh, he's a planning manager up in Palo Alto. He used to be in charge of Pilot."

"Used to? What happened?"

"I don't know. I guess they needed him more in Planning." They didn't speak the rest of the ride home.

21

DAN MAKES HIS MOVE

I n El Segundo, Brian, David, Todd, Dan, Janet, and a few others were busy writing Mesa code. Finally, it was for real!

They wrote code on Altos because the Dog-Zero machines, as the Dolphin machines were unflatteringly called, were scarce. They were also noisy and not very reliable, so you still needed an Alto.

Dan wanted to specialize in something. He wanted to be the world's leading expert in it, whatever *it* was. When Star came out, big corporations would demand consulting services and add-on software. He envisioned starting a company to provide those services, making a ton of money, and then retiring from computing. He didn't start college wanting to be a computer programmer—that was his third major, after eight weeks in Electrical Engineering and a year in Psychology.

He didn't hate computers, though. He thought of programming as just *one* of the areas he could have gone into, a reasonably interesting one, and definitely well-paid. Debugging was his favorite activity. He still remembered the moment during his first programming course at the University of Illinois, where he'd inserted Print statements to figure out what his program was doing, and went over the output back in his dorm room. This stuff that the computer did incomprehensibly quickly was now captured on paper so that you could follow along. He was hooked.

At Burroughs, he had a second-level boss, Alan, who never got to write code anymore but missed it. Once, an entire group of the programmers was puzzling over a bug that none of them could figure out after days of trying. Alan joined them and said enthusiastically, "Okay, give me a hard bug." No one had a clue what the problem was, and it wasn't even reproducible, but Alan figured it out. That was the level Dan aspired to.

He was thrown into the data management group at Burroughs, and he liked databases well enough. He went to some database conferences, where relational databases were purely a research area. IBM's big money came from a hierarchical database called IMS, and his own database at Burroughs was called a network database, where the user set up links and indexes for common operations. The idea that you could query on *anything*, as the relational model insisted, seemed insane to him. Some of these queries they wrote about would take *days* to run. But all the academic activity was now on relational databases.

Dan decided to use his Burroughs experience on Star. He had worked on a database, designed and implemented a major enhancement that provided record-level locks, visited a major customer, taught classes, and shipped several releases. On the other hand, he had no experience with publishing, or user interfaces, or object-oriented programming, or any of the Xerox Star innovations, but at least he'd done databases. That counted for something. He reminded his boss of that at every opportunity. His motto was, "If you don't toot your own horn, no one else will do it for you."

It was baseball season again, and the Mets were in town on June 14 and 15, 1978[1].The Mets were terrible, as usual, but that meant it wouldn't be a sellout. Mark and his wife Jacki, Randy, Steve, Brian, and Dan all went to Dodger Stadium the first night. Around 5:30, Jacki came over to Xerox, and they all met in the parking lot.

Randy looked around theatrically, "Let's see... who has a car big enough for all of us?" Everyone knew that meant Brian and his Chevy Nova, even though it was old and junky. They set off down El Segundo Boulevard to get on the Harbor Freeway.

Brian asked, "How are the Dodgers doing this year? I haven't even been following."

Dan replied, "Dodgers are only in third place." "Who's in first place?" asked Jacki.

"The Giants. Then the Reds." Dan read the standings every morning and watched the Sports segment of the TV news every night.

"The Giants," snorted Mark. "That won't last."

Dan agreed, but added, "But the Cubs! They're in first in the National League East."

No one wanted to be cruel and say, "For how long?" so they remained silent.

Steve changed the subject, "What I want to know is, how far away is IMO?" Several of them chastised him for talking about work.

Randy snuck in, "It's Juranick's Constant. IMO is two years away. Anyway, let's not talk about anything as recondite as the schedule."

He pronounced it re-CON-dite. Mark pointed out that it was REC-on-dite.

Jacki had brought a copy of the *LA Times* Sports section, mostly to steer the conversation away from work if necessary. She opened it now and read from a story about Ray Kroc, founder of McDonald's and owner of the San Diego Padres.

"His name was Ray Kroc and he owns the Padres. He said his players lacked guts and pride. He said they were responding like juveniles. Excepting Ozzie Smith, Derrel Thomas, Randy Jones and Gaylord Perry, he said they were playing like high school kids."

Steve quipped, "My high school team had five pitchers better than Randy Jones."

Brian laughed, "Wow, you guys had a good team."

Jacki read on,

"Offend the players!" he said, disbelievingly. "Let them be offended! They offend the fans. People voted for Proposition 13 because they were disgusted. I'm disgusted."

Randy shouted, "That's exactly why I voted for Prop 13."

"Because you don't like the San Diego Padres?" asked Jacki.

"No, because I don't like McDonald's."

"Me, neither," laughed Jacki. "Anyhow, he can't top the rant of 1974."

Brian asked, "What rant?"

"He got on the PA system during a game and said, 'This is the most stupid baseball playing I've ever seen.'"

Steve defended him, "Well, it *was*."

Randy replied, "But you don't say that as the owner, though. You just cut their salaries."

Dan was sad, "Supposedly, he wanted to buy the Cubs, but Wrigley wouldn't sell. I wish somebody would buy them."

Mark had the last word as always, "He was probably afraid Kroc would rename it Big Mac Field."

They always exited the freeway at Academy Road since it had less traffic than Stadium Way. They bought $2 tickets for the top deck above home plate, which they called the Nosebleed Seats, and dinner was usually Dodger Dogs and beer.

The Dodgers won behind Tommy John's pitching, with knuckleballer Charlie Hough getting the save. The first baseman, Steve Garvey, whom absolutely no one liked, hit two homers. They honored their tradition of calling out Deuces Wild—whenever the count was 2 outs, 2 balls, and 2 strikes. Bill Russell, the shortstop, made an error, which led Steve to yell, "Randy Carter could have caught that!" Steve peered down at the Dodgers dugout. "I think they're all saying, 'We ought to sign that Randy Carter guy, whoever he is.'"

The game had everything they enjoyed, except for, maybe, a pinch-hitting appearance by Manny Mota. The organist played "On a Wonderful Day Like Today" after the game, as he did every time the Dodgers won.

On the way back, Jacki asked, "How did the Red Sox do tonight? Did anyone check the out-of-town scoreboard?" She had grown up on the East Coast and had a sentimental attachment to the Sox.

Dan answered, "They beat Oakland."

"Aren't they in first place?"

Mark interjected, "That won't last, either."

Steve enjoyed making fun of Dan for being a Cubs fan, "The Red Sox and the Cubs. Two teams with a curse."

Dan was rueful, "It takes intestinal fortitude to be a Cubs fan."

Jacki replied, "Or a Red Sox fan!"

Randy had a smart remark, as he usually did, "You can see a doctor about that."

They listened to the post-game show on the radio the rest of the way home.

The next day, Dan visited Tom's office and told him about last night's game. After Tom's usual sad-but-hopeful comments about the Angels, Tom asked, "Have you given any more thought to the area you want to work in?"

Dan always seized an opportunity if it came along. "Yeah, I'm kinda interested in data management. You know I did that at Burroughs, right?"

"Yep, I remember that. There is some interesting research going on in Palo Alto." It seemed to Dan that no matter what you thought of, someone in Palo Alto was already working on it.

"Yeah, I was reading some docs Ron Warrick wrote. What's the relationship of that to what we're doing?" What Dan was really wondering was, "*Is that anything official or just some wild ravings?*" but Tom would frown on that. Ron had indeed written some think pieces, which is what he meant by wild ravings, but they had a new manager, Frank Lett. To Dan, this meant they were serious now.

"Well… I'm not sure. The new manager, Frank, would be a good person to talk to."

"Yeah, that's what I was thinking. Should I go up and talk to him?" That was what Tom always wanted to hear, corporate bridge-building.

"If you want. It'd be good to find out his thoughts."[2]

They talked some more about what Star might actually do in data management. It was obvious that it was never going to be a big mainframe with tons of corporate data on it. Maybe personal data management? What was that?

Forms and form letters were a good start. Dan had some ideas about this, and Tom and he talked about them. They both felt that a fully relational system for a little computer was a bit much to aim at, but at the same time, limitations were not a popular topic at Xerox. Limitless possibilities was the mood. At the beginning of an ambitious project, a smart manager went with the flow but later, at the right moment, would say, "Okay, we'll do all that, but in Release 2." Dan and Tom both knew the game. Right now, you weren't allowed to say, "No," so they had to play along.

Dan raised a new topic, which Tom surely had something to say about, namely, the schedule. "Do we have a schedule for the Star software?"

Tom did indeed have an opinion, "Ah yes, the schedule. I'm meeting with the other managers this afternoon about that. What are your thoughts?"

"Well, it's hard to tell without knowing what we're building."

Tom was not offended by this and even had a slight smile, "Oh, you mean the FunSpec? That's coming."

"Don't we usually do that *first*, then the Design Spec, and then implementation? I mean… that's the way I was taught. Maybe Xerox does it differently."

Tom replied, "That's what I keep asking, but we seem to be doing them all at once here."

Dan clapped his hands, "Okay, then. All at once, here we go! Two years… that's what I say."

With a barely perceptible smile, Tom made a note on a yellow pad, "Two years. That's what I thought, too."

Dan stood up, "I'll make out a schedule for my part right now."

Tom laughed, "If you can get it to me by 2:00, I can fold it into the master schedule."

Dan sat down at his desk and made a list of all the tasks he could think of for Star data management. He figured on a simple file with an index on some set of keys—for example, a list of customers sorted on last name followed by first name. A Star user might use this to send out form letters to all their customers or maybe to just a subset of them. He didn't even think about a database with lots of related files—he only designed for one file.

This seemed absurdly simplistic to Ron and Frank. They didn't come to Xerox to design a direct-mail system. For them, a fully relational database with atomic transactions was the absolute minimum to aim for. Ron's documents were taking all that as a given and going well beyond.

Dan's database system at his previous job had transactions, which meant that if you started a set of changes to the files and one change failed, then the system had to unwind what you'd already done. That's where the word atomic came from. It either all happened, or none of it did.

Even worse, the database had to save all the changes to a separate file, often a tape, so that if a disaster happened, you could restore the data from backups. Dan had spent countless days writing code for this feature and arguing about all the various cases. He had a healthy respect for how complicated it was. He refused to pretend it was simple. His "basic" system left out transactions.

"Let's see how Tom reacts to some realism." He wrote down a number for the weeks of programming effort each task needed, assuming this sort of simple design. For areas that were completely unknown right now, such as the user interface, he wrote a large number with a question mark. The user interface would be the really innovative thing about Star's database, not the database itself. Right now, nobody had the slightest idea what the user interface was.

He took the sheet of paper with the schedule to Tom's office and showed it to him. "This is just a seat-of-the-pants estimate for a basic, one-file database, sort of an indexsequential." Tom was familiar with index-sequential, a basic sorted file that had been around since the 1950s. "We can plan on more when we have a better sense of what we need to do."

Tom read the schedule over, "This is excellent. Thanks, I'll incorporate this. Why don't we talk about this some more later?"

Dan went back to his office, "*Well, that was easy.*" He reread the file system documentation for Pilot to see what the operating system gave him and drew some diagrams of a record.

22

GOALS

The next morning, Dan and Tom were chatting, and Tom pulled out the schedule Dan gave him and laid it on his desk. "I've been reading this over. This is really great. It's the first actual task breakdown I've seen."

"Well, thanks," Dan said modestly.

"I just have a few questions." Dan slid his chair over to look on with Tom. "Is there some task that we can farm out?"

This was going as well as Dan could possibly expect, "Yeah, I think the logical expression part could be done by someone else. Who'd you have in mind?" Logical expressions are the way a user extracts just a part of the file, such as the customers who live in Arizona or the employees who are managers. Every database has to have them.

"What do you think of having Janet work with you, just for this part?"

"Oh, that'd be great!"

Tom was always very careful to set expectations correctly. He didn't want Dan to think he was now a manager, and Janet reported to him. "This won't be a permanent thing. It'll just be a way to give you some help getting this thing off the ground."

"Sounds great. I like Janet."

Tom folded his hands, "Good, I'll talk to her."

Dan went running that day at around noon. He didn't run every day, but today, the weather was pleasant. The M1 building had a little room with lockers and a shower, which had been built originally for factory workers who got dirty on the job, not for bicyclists and runners, but it still functioned. He put on his running clothes, stuffed his badge in his back pocket, left the building, and turned right, headed west on Alaska, crossed the railroad tracks, and ran through the old industrial neighborhoods. After he finished, showered, and dressed, he went to the cafeteria. It was after 1:00 pm, so the crowds had thinned.

He saw Todd eating alone, so he walked over, "Join you?"

Todd was happy to have company, "Sure, have a seat! Just finishing some lukewarm tasteless garbage."

"Yeah, that's what I come here for, too! How's it going?"

They chatted about Mesa and the coding conventions, but Dan was less interested in talking about work than in Todd's jazz playing.

"So, you're a jazz guitarist, huh?"

"Trying to be. Do you play?"

"Well, not really. I have a Gibson ES-175, but I can't really play much."

Todd was excited, "That's an awesome guitar! Isn't that what Joe Pass plays?"

Dan was thrilled to meet someone who actually knew who Joe Pass was. He considered him the greatest guitarist in the world, and the fact that nobody had even heard of him made it even better, kind of a secret society. Within the jazz world, he was a major figure and had played with some of the biggest names in jazz, but outside of that world, he was a nobody.

"Yeah, it's the guitar on the cover of his *Virtuoso* album."

"That's a great, great album."

"Have you ever seen him live?" Dan asked.

"No, damn it! Have you?"

Dan told him how he'd seen Pass at The Lighthouse in Hermosa Beach, sitting only a few feet from him and how he'd called out "How High the Moon," and Pass immediately played the living hell out of it. Then he said to the audience, modestly, "Someone called for this, so I thought I'd try it."

Todd listened raptly. "That's how these really great players are. They don't *tell* you how great they are... they show you."

When they'd finished eating, they took their trays to the conveyor belt. On the way out, Todd asked Dan, "What are you working on?"

"Oh, I'm starting in on records processing."

"What's that... sorta a database?"

"Sort of. The data management group in Palo Alto has a new manager, so I'm going up next week to talk to him."

"Palo Alto. I want to transfer up there, but I don't know if they'll let me."

"Oh, yeah? Did you ask?"

"I talk to Tom all the time, but he's kinda wishy-washy."

Dan laughed, "That's Tom, all right. Why do you want to move?"

"I grew up in the Bay Area. Also, my wife and I divorced, so I have no reason to be down here anymore."

Dan seized the opportunity to change the subject, "Are you playing in a group now?"

Todd didn't seem to mind at all, "No, but I sit in at this jazz club up in Baldwin Hills. They just call me Whitey. Like 'Hey, Whitey, do you know A Foggy Day in Londontown?'" Baldwin Hills was an affluent black neighborhood in Los Angeles. Dan laughed, "And do you?"

"It starts with Eb, and then the lead sheet says C13b9, but I just play some kind of altered seventh chord. Then Fm7, Bb7, and so on. You've probably got this memorized."

Dan didn't have *any* standards memorized. He wasn't even

sure how you altered a seventh chord. So instead, "That was Gershwin, right?"

Todd had to consider that, "I think that's right."

They were approaching their offices, "Good talking to you. Catch you later."

Dan read his email. After a while, Janet knocked and came in, "So, I guess we're working together now, huh?"

"Yeah, should be fun. I've just barely started on the design for this."

"What should I do now right now?"

Dan thought for a while. He walked to the whiteboard and started drawing boxes. "This is what I was thinking, just for starters. Nothing fancy." He always liked to use concrete examples, so he made it a personnel file, the standard example that programmers had used since time immemorial.

After 15 minutes or so of discussion, Janet said, "This isn't too complicated. Do you have a Defs file for the data dictionary so that I can get started?"

"I'll do that first."

"Great. Thanks, Dan."

She went back to her office and dialed Grant's number, "Hi, it's Janet. How's it going?"

"Hi, Janet. Going pretty good. You sure showed them at the track!"

She smiled ruefully. Ken had been making her pay for beating him, being cold and distant. "Hey... you're the guy with the best time! Did you meet with the printer people when you were here?"

"Yeah, I did. It sounds pretty interesting, but they don't have an opening right now. We'll keep in touch."

"I have a new assignment. I'm working with Dan Markunas temporarily."

"Oh, yeah, I talked to him at the track. Nice guy. What are you going to be doing?"

"Helping out on the records processing system. Doesn't sound too complicated."

"Good, good. Are you coming up here anytime soon?"

Janet needed his help strategizing her career, and a meeting in person seemed the best. "I don't know... maybe I can come up with some excuse."

Grant put on his managerial hat, "We always encourage more ties between North and South."

This conversation was turning stuffy. "Good to hear. Well, I'll let you go now. Thanks!"

Janet thought about their conversation. She wanted to talk to *someone*. In the past, she and Ken had always talked immediately when something interesting happened, but now, that was awkward. Maybe Gwen was around. She walked up to her office on the second floor, "Knock, knock."

Gwen glanced up, "Janet, come in. How goes it?"

Janet sat down in Gwen's guest chair, "Great! I have a new assignment."

Gwen turned her chair toward Janet, still holding the document she was reading, "Oh? Doing what?"

"Helping another guy, Dan Markunas, with the records processing feature."

"Are you happy about that?"

Janet considered her answer, "It... I don't know... it just seems like Tom doesn't know what to do with me, so I'm filling the gaps."

Gwen put the document on her desk. This might be a longer conversation. "Tom and I go *way* back. Have you discussed this with him?"

Janet realized this was what she came up here for, "Well, sort of. I mean... we talk about various opportunities on Star, if that's what you mean."

"That's just Tom's way of sounding you out. Did you tell him what *you* want? And what is that, by the way? You can close the door, maybe." Janet closed the door.

"I guess I didn't. You're right."

Gwen had had this conversation with other young women and some men, too. No one seemed to know how to talk to their bosses about stuff like this. She could help this girl, she thought. Maybe a story would help.

"Let me tell you about when I first started at SDS, before it became XDS. I was fresh out of college, so even less experienced than you."

Janet was half-tempted to think, "*Oh God, not another meaningful lesson from an old guy.*" But she realized this was not an old guy, it was a woman in computers, and those were scarce. And, she'd asked for this by coming up here. "Wow. What were you doing?"

"They had me helping out on the FORTRAN compiler, in charge of the error messages."

"How was that?"

Gwen smirked, "What do you think? It was pretty boring."

Janet was interested now, "How long did that last?"

"Over a year. Going on two."

Janet was shocked, "Oh, my God. But you got out of that somehow?"

"I sat down with my boss' boss since my boss at the time was a total dork. I told him I wanted some managerial responsibility, or I was going to leave."

"That wasn't Tom, was it?" Janet giggled.

"No, someone else. Anyhow, it worked, and they made me the project lead for a new piece of the operating system."

This all seemed too simplistic to Janet, not to mention scary. "*What if you ask, and they say no? Then where are you?*"

Gwen knew what Janet was thinking. Everyone was afraid of asking. "I know Tom pretty well. What do you think would happen if you told him what you told me?"

Janet pondered, "I don't know. Would he be receptive to making me a manager? I mean… we have lots of talented people. Why me?"

"Don't underrate yourself, Janet. You're a smart person. Tom needs to get the most out of his people because that's what he's judged on. And why *not* you?"

Gwen gave her lots more encouragement. Janet resisted, but Gwen patiently kept at it, and finally, Janet agreed that yes, she'd talk to Tom.

23

AT THE GOOSE

G rant was pleased that Janet called him, but he didn't think he'd really helped her out. She probably wanted to talk about her new assignment and what she should do next, but that would be a longer conversation on her next visit.

Ken surely must hate him after he'd turned in the worst lap time at the Malibu Grand Prix. And with Grant's help, his wife had smoked him with a *way* better time. Good! What a dork he was. What was she doing married to him anyway?

The printer guys he visited down in El Segundo were his kind of people. They were Xerox, through and through, and they were building a chunk of hardware that Xerox actually knew how to sell, unlike the Star that nobody had a clue about. If they made him a job offer, he'd move down in a second. But what could he do right now, though? Just keep in touch with them, he guessed. He sent them a thank-you email and then resumed his work.

The Dolphin program was falling apart. The replacement design hadn't taken shape yet, so what was he supposed to do with the schedule? He booked another wearying round of meetings with the people who'd still meet with him. The planners seemed to only meet with each other and never talked to anyone who actually knew what was happening.

But then Grant had an inspiration. Both SDD and PARC people often met after work at the Dutch Goose in Menlo Park. He'd never gone to those things, but hell, why not crash it? What were they going to do, throw him out? Porter Berwick, who ran the Tools group, hung out at the Goose a lot from what Grant heard. Porter reminded Grant of Jerry Garcia, although he wasn't musical. He had a full, bushy beard, often wore a kilt, and seemed to have been everywhere, knew everyone, and had done everything. Porter was always friendly, and Grant had been planning to talk to him some-time anyway, so now was a good excuse. They were meeting at the Goose tomorrow around 5:00.

He drove up to Menlo Park on Junipero Serra Boulevard, which was along the west side of the Stanford campus, and both sides of the road featured trees or bare hills. He'd ridden his bike along here many times since so many Western Wheelers rides started this way, but it made him wistful about moving away. *"Damn, it sure is beautiful here, and LA is so ugly. That part will suck."*

When he visited El Segundo, ugly was his overwhelming impression. Smell Segundo or El Smogundo were the competing nicknames. He remembered the laugh line in the TV show *Sanford and Son* where Fred joked about a religious painting with Moses parting an El Segundo oil spill. Anyhow, he might as well enjoy his stay here while he could.

The Goose had the bar and a large counter on the right, where you ordered food and drinks, and on the left a bunch of trestle tables with benches and the pool table, of course. Peanut shells were all over the floor. Further back were stairs down to the patio, which had more large wooden tables. He found the group seated at one, with a pitcher of beer on the table. He said hello and went back up to order food. Pool players were gathered around the table, and over the bar was a beautiful beveled glass piece with Dutch Goose in large letters, and Anchor Steam below it. While he was admiring it, a pool spectator told him that Porter had done it.[1]

"Oh, you know Porter?"

"Everybody knows Porter!" was the bemused answer. He ordered some food and returned to the table.

Besides Porter, he saw Jim in his signature black jeans and denim jacket; Patrick, the Pilot guy; Lawrence, the head of the Pilot project and Grant's replacement; and Ray Holmberg, whom Grant knew only by name. Grant and Lawrence couldn't stand each other, normally, but as far as Grant had observed, no one liked Lawrence, so he didn't feel too bad about that.

Porter greeted him, "Grant, how goes the Planning?"

"Oh, you know. Same shit, different day." Grant thought, *"That was the right approach for this group."* Generic jokes, nothing too specific. A big bowl of unsalted peanuts was holding them over until the food came. "What's with the bland peanuts? I thought salted-in-the-shell was the big thing here."

Lawrence replied, "Those are the Peanuts of Death. Salt and blood pressure, you know." Grant nodded, "Oh, right."

They were silent for a while. Finally, Porter looked at Grant again, "Grant, we never hear much about the Star software effort down South. How's that going?"

"Okay, I'm in the spotlight, have to expect that. I'm the new guy here," thought Grant. "Well, they seem to be off and running, last I checked. Paul gives me regular updates."

Lawrence spoke up, "They keep hassling me to give them a dummy version of Pilot to test with. I'm not going to. We'll never finish the real thing if we have to keep supporting some dummy shit."

They nodded approvingly. Jim added, "Our last meeting on Mesa planning was nothing but me shooting down their brain-dead ideas."

Grant replied, "But they all say such nice things about you!" General laughter.

Porter laughed, "You're just such a diplomat, Jim."

Grant didn't much want to listen to Palo Alto folks complain about El Segundo—he wanted to hear what they were doing. He figured they'd be more diplomatic about that topic since word might get back to someone they made fun of. Better to just wait and see if they brought it up themselves.

Their names were called for the food, and they went to pick it up. The conversation stopped for a few minutes. Finally, Porter decided he'd picked on Grant enough, so he turned to Ray. "So I hear you've converted to a fulltime Dolphin." Ray had his mouth full, so he just gave a thumbs-up.

Jim Travis said, "Living the all-Mesa lifestyle. Don't think we're not grateful!"

Ray swallowed and answered, "SuchADeal, pre-prototype number 3. It seems to be working. So far."[2]

Patrick smirked, "So far! Did you check the time on it before coming here? I noticed you did get here on time. *Almost*."

Ray played along, "Hey... I've hardly had any trouble with SuchADeal. Someone has to be brave here and use these machines."

Porter played moderator, "Pretty soon, we'll have the Wildflower. Or something. What's the latest name for it?"

Lawrence spoke up, "I was in a meeting with Butler about something else, and he was doodling hardware diagrams."

Porter exclaimed, "That's gotta be it, then. Did anyone get a look at the diagrams? We need to know what we're doing."

This was the information Grant came for. The Dolphin was dead, and Butler was designing something else. Whatever that turned out to be, that was the future of Star. And until Butler was done, nobody would really know anything. He decided to stay silent, just in case anyone said anything more, but no one did. So, Grant brought up one more thing before they left the topic of work. "What do you guys think about artificial intelligence? Is that ever going to go anywhere?"

Porter chuckled, "There's a paper from a few years back called 'Artificial Intelligence Meets Natural Stupidity.' You might want to read that." The other guys laughed.

Patrick announced, "I'll never forget his opening line, 'As a field, artificial intelligence has always been on the border of respectability, and therefore on the border of crackpottery.'"

Porter sat back with a wide grin, "I think they crossed that border several years ago. That's why they can't get any more funding."

Ray said, "Hey, the big breakthrough is only 10 years away. And always will be!"

Grant had the strong impression from their approving looks that they weren't impressed with AI. He wasn't ready to give up quite yet, "Didn't they do some cool stuff, like Blocks World? I loved how you could say 'pick up a big red block,' and it did it."

Ray interrupted, "Winograd's around all the time. You could talk to him."

Grant ignored him and continued, "And the expert programs? And the natural language programs?"

Porter's look changed to professorial, "You can talk to Martin Kay over at PARC if you want the current state of natural language processing. My view is that they're falling down the rathole on that stuff."

Patrick added, "I gave up reading AI papers years ago. As for the expert systems, they might have some promise. Oil field analysis, medical diagnosis, configuring DEC computer systems… that sort of thing might work out."

No one seemed to want to discuss it further, and Grant realized AI wasn't a fruitful topic for this group.[3]

Patrick had been silent for a while, so he decided to bring up the old reliable topic… Porter's cars. "Porter, how's that Dino running? I don't think I saw it in the parking lot."

This was too much for Grant, car enthusiast that he was. "A Dino? You have a Dino? Which model?"

Porter was always more than willing to tell you about his cars, "A 246 GT. I rebuilt the engine myself."

Grant's jaw dropped, "My God. How long did it take?"

"About a year. But that was just working weekends."

Lawrence was not a car guy, "What's a Dino?"

Patrick answered, "It's a car made by Ferrari, but it doesn't have 12 cylinders, so Enzo wouldn't call it a Ferrari." Porter chuckled.

Grant knew all about Dinos, and he was impressed. "Have you driven it on a track?"

"Once, I got it up to 160, but then I got scared. Let me tell you... when you want to stop that thing, it *stops!*" They laughed. "People always talk about how fast it goes, which it does. But man, there are two sides to that."

He was rolling now, "I had this little Italian guy in the passenger seat, and he was wearing these adorable driving shoes. I think he turned 20 shades of white, but he never said a word."

Then he turned to Grant, "You know a lot about cars, I guess?"

"One of my hobbies. I've been to the driving school at Sears Point myself."

"I've been meaning to do that with this thing someday," he replied. "The thing is, if you own a fast car, you sorta have to drive *that car*. You can't leave it at home and drive one of theirs."

Then Lawrence illustrated why nobody liked him, "So... yours won't make it up to Sonoma?"

Porter clearly didn't care to answer that, and Grant saw a chance to ingratiate himself, so he jumped in. "I'm sure it will, but then he'd have to re-tune the Weber carburetors when he arrives." Porter looked grateful.

With that, the conversation moved on to restaurants, how

Hsi Nan was going downhill, and what Szechuan chef was upand-coming now. At the end, they followed Porter's rule for paying the bill at a restaurant, which was that everyone throws a $20 on the bill until it's covered. No analysis of how much you owed was permitted.

Grant thought this trip to the Goose was worthwhile, and he'd have to do it again. If you only learned things through official channels, you were always way behind.

In the parking lot, Porter and Grant talked for at least 15 minutes about what Grant had learned in driving school. Porter told him all about the challenges he'd faced in rebuilding the Dino's engine. Grant was now one of Porter's many, many friends.

24

DECISION POINT

D an and Janet were making great progress in their coding task. Tom had made certain they both understood that this arrangement was temporary. That was one of those managerial things Tom excelled at. If he gave you a task, he was committed to it, and you knew what he wanted.

They spent a lot of time talking about databases and then agreed on a schedule. Even if nobody else in SDD tried to stick to a schedule, which was how it seemed sometimes, they were going to. Tom loved that.

In early July 1978, they met to plan what they were doing. Dan had been talking to some of the Palo Alto engineers about how to lay records out on disk, and he really liked their ideas. He drew some rectangles on the whiteboard to show them to Janet.

The basic idea was that you had a disk block, say 2K or 4K bytes, and within that block, you put as many records as would fit, leaving some space for growth. When you wanted to read in any record, you read in its entire block. He drew a block with several records in it. At the beginning of the block were some "slots" that had arrows going to the records.

Janet asked, "So, what's a record pointer? A block number plus an offset?"

"No, that's the cool part. It's a block number plus a *slot* number. The slot contains the offset."

She took the marker from him, erased, and redrew the records. "So, the records can move around, and the record pointer doesn't change."

"Exactly!" Dan agreed. "If a record gets bigger, or smaller, or you add a new one, you can move all the other ones around."

"Cool… but what if one of them grows too big to fit in the block?"

This was Dan's chance to deploy a word he'd picked up from his Palo Alto colleagues—a tombstone. A tombstone was a slot that said, "The record is not here anymore. It's over there instead." He took the marker back and drew a slot that had become a tombstone. Janet sat back down.

She immediately saw through that scheme, "And then… what happens if it moves again? Do you have a tombstone pointing to another tombstone, and so on?"

Dan had worried about that but didn't have a great answer. "No, at some point, you fix up the pointers and delete the tombstones, I guess."[1]

She looked quizzical, "We'll have to work on that one."

He laughed, "Yeah, let me ponder that. Bit of an issue there… you're right."

Janet laughed, "Anyway. What happens if a record is bigger than an entire block?"

He had a better answer for that one. "We also have the concept of a big block. Let's say the block size is 4K, and you have a record that wants to be 5K. In that case, you allocate two contiguous blocks for it."

She considered that, "So, you're wasting 3K for that one record?"

"That should be rare, though. The block size should be large enough that we almost never have to do that."

She wondered about block sizes and record sizes, but she figured she'd do some calculations on her own. They moved on to the logical expression part that she was supposed to implement. "Is this supposed to be just a logical expression, with ANDs, ORs, NOTs, and all that?"

"Pretty much. What are your ideas?" He was relieved that she didn't have grandiose dreams about it. Maybe, they could actually agree, and then do this thing.

Janet did not, in fact, have a huge ego invested in this project. It seemed to both of them that a lot of folks in SDD were trying to build the world's greatest something, whatever it was, mainly to publish papers about it. She and Dan were proud to be what Michael called "good solid Midwesterners," doing what the job required and nothing more.

"I think we can always make it fancier later if we need to.

Right now, we should do something basic and call it Phase One." Dan had a broad smile, "Great minds think alike!"

Janet liked that. She realized that she and Dan had the same attitude toward this project, even though they hadn't discussed it before. *"Let's just get something done."*

They talked more about records, B-trees, and what Defs files he had to produce and give her. Then as she was about to leave, he asked, "By the way, what did you work on at TRW?"

She sat back down, "Oh, I did this communications stuff with satellites. Most of it was classified, though."

He smiled, "So we both have networking experience, but nothing relevant to now."

"Why, what did you do?"

"My last year at Burroughs, I was in datacomm support. It was all about terminals and slow lines, nothing like Ethernet."

"Support? Did you like that?"

He grimaced, "No, I hated it!"

She was sympathetic, "I don't think I'd like it, either. What were you doing, answering the phone?"

"A little of that. Teaching classes, too, which also sucked."

Janet figured as long as they were done talking work, she could ask him a few things. "So, Dan, do you have brothers and sisters?"

"I have two older brothers. How about you?"

"No, I'm an only child. Where do your brothers live? In Chicago?"

"One does, in the suburbs. The other just moved to Phoenix from LA a few months ago."

"Phoenix! I hear it's hot there."

"Yeah, 110 last week. But at least the housing's cheap." Dan's brother had also been scared off by the LA housing market.

Janet laughed, "Housing is really insane here. You're renting right now, aren't you?"

"Yeah. Are you and Ken in the market?"

Janet had considered looking at real estate with Ken. Deciding on a house together was not an appealing prospect. He'd probably want to buy a house in the Valley, or Gardena, or some other yucky place.

"Well, we talk about it sometimes, but then... I don't know. It's just such a commitment."

"Yeah, me too. And somehow, LA just doesn't seem like home to me. I always figured I'd move somewhere, someday."

"Oh yeah? Where? Do you want to move up to the Bay Area?"

Dan expected that question, "I don't know. It's too similar to here. Just as expensive."

"It's nicer, though."

Returning to his Alto, "Yeah, I'll give you that." With that, Janet went back to her office. She worked mostly on her own over the next six weeks or so, occasionally coordinating with Dan, and finished the Logical Expressions module in approximately the time she'd estimated. Since Dan was able to do the same with his modules, Tom was ecstatically happy. Finally, some code was being finished.

Early in September, on a Friday, she had her regular meeting with Tom. She'd promised herself she would bring up career goals, no matter how much she hated those conversations. She *especially* hated telling her husband about them afterward because he was always nagging her to be more aggressive.

Tom folded his hands, "Well, how goes the records processing project?"

"It's been going great! Dan's really easy to work with."

"Excellent, excellent! I'm so happy when I see things being done instead of just talked about."

She cleared her throat and launched into it, "So... I have something I want to discuss with you."

"Okay."

"It's about my long-term goals."

Tom looked encouraging, "Please."

Now, she was really committed. She'd rehearsed this line in her mind over and over, "I'd like to be a manager eventually. I think I have good people skills and organizational skills. In the time I've been here, I've built solid relationships with both engineers and managers, and I'm ready to take the next step."

Tom seemed positive but noncommittal, "Yes, you definitely have. I've been very pleased with your progress so far."

"Thanks," she said gratefully.

He continued, "I mean... besides finding the wrench and saving the Ethernet." She laughed.

"You've done a great job coming up to speed on Mesa and object-oriented programming, and now Dan and you have been coming along nicely on records processing. And... I'm very pleased with how well you've integrated into the group."

She nodded but thought, *"Now comes the 'but.'"*

Tom put his hands on the arms of the chair, "When we promote someone to manage some area, it's usually when they're already the technical leader of that area."

"Okay." She was searching for a response to that, but he continued.

"Now... I think you've done a great job here. I'd like to work with you on finding an area where you *can* become the leader. When you finish this task with Dan, I want to meet with you again, and we'll see what the next move is. How does that sound?"

Janet tried to look pleased rather than disappointed, "That sounds good."

Tom relaxed a little. The hard part was over. "I want to promote you because we need engineers who can manage, and I have a strong feeling that you'll be very good at it."

She smiled, "Thanks."

"Thank you for coming to me. I always encourage people to be ambitious."

The meeting was over, and Janet felt oddly pleased, even though Tom hadn't given her what she wanted. He said nice things about her, after all, especially that he thought she could do the job. At the moment, she had a real programming task that she *knew* she could do, so she resolved to concentrate on that.

That evening, she was sitting on the couch reading the *Times* when Ken came home. "Well? How'd it go?" She put the paper down, "What... the promotion talk?"

"Yeah, weren't you going to tell Tom today you wanted to be a manager?"

"Oh, yeah. He said not yet. I need to be the technical leader of something first."

Ken looked annoyed, "What? You've been at Xerox *how* long?"

"A little over a year and a half now, Ken."

As usual, he missed the signal that she used his name. He

walked to the bedroom to change clothes, looking determined to say what was on his mind. This was his opening. Back in the living room, he said, "Are we going to Great American tonight?"

"Yeah, just give me a second, and then we can go."

In the car on the way to Santa Monica, Ken said, "I heard today that Hughes is interviewing for a new software lead on the Pioneer Venus mission."

He hadn't brought up leaving Xerox for a couple of months now. Janet had hoped she'd heard the last of it, but apparently not. She didn't want to fight before the evening even started, so she asked some questions about the job without throwing cold water on the idea.

The Great American had a long line outside, as usual. It was pandemonium inside, with people shouting and groups of singing waiters at tables performing songs. They threaded their way through the crowds and found the group at their table in the rear.

"Ken! Janet!" called out Steve. Everyone raised their glasses as they sat down.

"What's new at Xerox, Janet?" Steve asked. "Are you guys shipping anything yet?"

Janet parried, "Not yet. Are you guys relieved that Melvin Dummar isn't your boss?" Ken slapped hands with her as they all laughed. At a trial in Nevada, Dummar had claimed that Howard Hughes' will had left the LDS Church one-sixteenth of his estate, about $156 million, and another sixteenth to him. That will was ruled a fake.

Jim, Steve's sidekick, said, "Actually, it probably would have still been the Medical Institute, not Dummar."

Janet took a beer glass from the waiter and filled it from the pitcher, "Anyhow, how's everyone doing?"

Steve took over again, "Great, as usual. Your hubby is moving up in the world."

"And we're *so* proud of him! And you, too!" Janet said as

she took Ken's arm. He had recently been promoted to technical lead in his systems programming group after Steve was made Section Leader.

"Are you going to interview for that job in the Venus mission?"

Janet saw the plot now, "Ken was just telling me about it on the drive here. I'm definitely going to think about it."

The waiters arrived with the Plank Feast and broke into "Happy Anniversary" to the tune of *The William Tell Overture.* Nobody seemed to care that *every* Friday was Ken and Janet's anniversary.

Jim said, "Anyhow, we'd love to have you back in aerospace. You'd be great in that job." Everyone agreed and raised their glasses.

Steve continued for Jim, "I was the one who spotted that job. I said 'Hey, Janet should be great at that.'"

Janet tried to radiate insincerity, "You take such good care of me, Steve."

Apparently, Steve caught the signal since he dropped the subject, and the conversation turned to the real estate market. Everyone who already had a house recounted how much its value had gone up since they bought it. Nobody mentioned her interview the rest of the night, and Ken didn't bring it up again either.

The following Tuesday, Janet called in sick and drove to Hughes for her interview in her best power suit. She rationalized the interview as "just staying in practice" since it had been almost two years since her last job interview. The job would be monitoring telemetry from the Pioneer Venus Multiprobe, which was launching later in the year.[2]

Janet asked why they were only now hiring a senior software engineer because the project had been in development for years. It turned out that using a general-purpose computer for this sort of critical data-handling, rather than specialized hardware, was still intensely controversial within Hughes. A previous senior engineer had lost the argument and left the company, and they'd concluded they needed someone less wedded to old ideas.

They showed her the PDP-11 that was dedicated to the task. Someone had calculated that the machine instructions on that unit were plenty fast enough to handle the data coming in, so they didn't have to build hardware. It was still being hotly debated whether to use a higher-level language, probably FORTRAN, or if assembler language was required, and this was one of the issues they were expecting her to handle. An ADM-3A terminal would be all hers! They considered that a major selling point of the job.

It sounded fascinating, although she knew that the reality of that job was years—or months, in this case—of crushing boredom, followed by a few days of insanity when the probe reached Venus.

The people seemed exceptionally nice, although they didn't ask much about what she was doing at Xerox. "*Maybe they assume it's all a big company secret.*" Actually, she would have been happy to talk about it, but she figured, correctly, that they didn't know what to ask. On the whole, they treated her job experience as if she just took a vacation after TRW or left to have a child. Her last interview of the day was with the big VP, as usual a middle-aged man who clearly had the final approval. His questions were all softballs. He asked her what she was earning at Xerox, which she interpreted as "an offer will be forthcoming."

When Janet walked into the apartment, Ken was sitting on the couch. He was dying to hear about the interview. "Well… how was it?"

She set her purse on the counter and went straight to the bedroom. "Let me change out of this, and then I'll tell you." A few minutes later, she returned and grabbed a Coke out of the fridge.

"It was fine, and they were nice. I'd forgotten what the rest of the world is like."

"Do you think they'll make you an offer?"

"I don't know. Hard to say," she picked up the Living section of the *Times*. They didn't talk about it anymore that night.

Ken resolved to ask around the next day and see what they'd thought of Janet. At his desk, the phone's message light was blinking. Now that Steve had been kicked upstairs, computer emergencies constantly fell on Ken. He spent the rest of the morning finding out what went wrong with the system, explaining to his team what to do about it, and generally putting out the fire. It made him feel he was a success at his job, but then he thought, "*It would be so great if Janet were here, too, doing more or less the same thing.*"

Ken didn't want to be the nervous husband asking people to hire his wife. That would definitely be inappropriate. But it was fine if Steve did it.

Before lunch, the department held a little celebration in the break room for Steve and his wife, Shelley. They'd married about a year ago, confirming widespread suspicions about their relationship, and now, they already had their first baby, a little boy named Scott. Shelley brought in the baby, and everyone marveled at him. Nobody asked Ken when he and Janet were going to have kids, but he could tell they were thinking it.

At lunch with Steve, Ken asked him, "How did it go with Janet? Do you know?"

Steve was a very busy man as a second-level manager. He had an admin, who was technically supposed to help the entire group, but she thought of Steve as her primary responsibility. She read his mail, answered his phone, and kept his schedule continuously full of meetings, and he hadn't had a moment to himself all day yet. So, he didn't know how the interview went. He agreed to find out, though. "Just between us... it's a done deal. She's a woman engineer, she has a degree from MIT, and she has aerospace experience. What's not to like?"

Ken was ecstatic the rest of the day, imagining Janet at Hughes. They'd commute to work together, maybe. She'd make a lot more money, as he was, and they could finally buy a house. Perhaps they'd even start a family. This was what they'd dreamed of when they were at MIT. This Xerox Star, or whatever they were calling it this week, would be nothing but a bad memory.

25

AND WHAT IF YOU DO HAVE SMART PEOPLE?

A few days later, Tom called Janet into his office. After some pleasantries, he came to the point. "Well, it's been a few days, but I haven't forgotten what we talked about before," he began.

"Me, neither," she replied nervously. She now had a job offer from Hughes, for a 20% increase in salary, but she wasn't sure yet when or if she'd spring it on him. If he stonewalled her, she might have to say, "Okay, I have a better offer, and I'm leaving," but she didn't want it to come to that. Xerox was too fun. Star might never come out, or it might come out and then flop, but she was positive it was the future. She *had* to stay on that train, even if it took longer to arrive at wherever it was headed.

Tom asked, "How do you think our build procedures and release management are going?"

She was surprised at that but figured he asked for a reason. "It's kinda haphazard, I think. The way we're rotating the buildmaster duties won't scale." Tom didn't react, so she continued. "We've been taking turns building, but that's becoming more and more work every month. Everyone does it a little differently. They take longer to learn the job, and they make mistakes. I think we need a full-time Integration Service."[1]

This was what Tom wanted to hear, "I agree. How would you feel about running that service?"

She pictured telling Ken that she wasn't going to Hughes, *"How disappointed he'll be. That won't be a fun conversation."*

She didn't want to say yes too soon, "What does that entail?"

"Glad you asked. It's a promotion and salary boost, first of all." She beamed. Asking how much of a boost was a teensy bit premature, so she restrained herself. Tom continued, "Initially, you'll be on your own, but we're going to open up a req for a person to work under you in the next quarter."

"So, I'll be a manager?"

He permitted himself a small smile, "Without any direct reports, but only for a while. You'll also go to the wonderful Xerox Management Training course next month."

She laughed, "Oh, is that what they call Charm School?"

Tom replied, "That's one term for it." He handed her a folded slip of paper. She opened it to see two numbers, her current salary and the new one, with a (15%) written after it. Her eyes opened wide, but maybe not as wide as he'd been hoping.

"Wow! Thank you."

"No need to thank me. You've earned it. And, I'm certain you'll do a great job in this. Assuming you take it, that is," as he leaned forward expectantly.

This was her moment, "My husband set up an interview for me at Hughes Aircraft, where he works, so I figured I might as well talk to them. They gave me an offer, which kinda surprised me since I haven't done that kind of work."

Tom read this immediately as salary negotiation, so he didn't bother asking what she'd be doing at Hughes. "How much of a raise are they offering?"

"20%"

He whistled, "Let me see what we can do. I don't know if we can match that, though." Janet had nothing more to say.

Tom added, "When do you have to tell them?"

"By the end of tomorrow."

"Let me talk to Paul, and I will let you know. Thanks, Janet."

"Thank you!"

That night, Ken met her at the door of their apartment. He'd heard through Steve at work that they'd extended an offer. "Hey, they made you an offer. Congratulations!"

"Thanks, and it's a 20% raise." She knew this meant she'd be earning a little more than him since she'd received a raise to go to Xerox, too.

"Holy cow! We're rich! Think of the house we can buy now." He hugged her and lifted her off her feet.

"Hang on, cowboy," unwrapping herself from his arms. "I haven't accepted it yet."

Ken was appalled, "But you will, right? I wouldn't try to bargain with them. That's a fantastic offer."

"Let's sit down." They sat on the couch. Ken was exasperated but managed to restrain himself.

"Tom is also offering me a promotion. I'll be able to hire someone to work under me. It's a 15% raise, but I told him about the Hughes offer."

This was too much for Ken, and he stood up and walked in a tight circle. He raised his fists and lowered them again, facing her. "So, what? Hughes was just a negotiating ploy? Wish you'd told me that," he was shouting now.

"Ken, calm down. It's just business," she said as she walked to the bedroom to change clothes.

He followed her, "*Business?*" he yelled. "That's what you call it when you deceive friends of mine?"

"Who's deceiving anyone?" she asked in a calm voice. "People interview every day."

Ken was silent for a while. He left the room in a rush, then stormed in again, "So tell me, what is so *fucking* great about Xerox? Huh? That's what I've never been able to understand." He was still shouting.

She walked back to the couch, "Ken, please lower your voice. And don't swear like that."

A few minutes of silence followed. Ken forced himself to calm down, "I'm sorry I yelled at you." She just nodded. "I just wanted us to work together again, even if it's not directly. We miss you."

"I know, Ken. I'm sorry. I just really like it at Xerox."

"But what is it that you like about it so much?"

Janet wasn't sure what to say. She walked over to the kitchen counter and collected her thoughts. "It's like when I started at Cranbrook or MIT. These are just smarter folks than I was used to."

He looked dubious, but she continued, "And… this technology is so revolutionary. It just *has* to go somewhere, someday."

"Really? Why? From what you showed me… it's just some fancy interfaces. We could add that to the software we already have whenever it's ready." He didn't add, "*Which it's not, yet*," but she knew he meant that.

Janet sat down and picked up the newspaper, but she only pretended to read it. She had a nightmare vision of the future, where her old bald TRW manager instructs her to xerox-ify their ancient software, with no clue what that meant, and pictured Ken turning into that guy.

Ken realized she didn't care for his dismissal of her work as "just some fancy interfaces." He tried a different tack. "Let's say this stuff really does take off and the entire world changes. What's to stop you from jumping on it *then*? In the meantime, you've had fun exploring Venus."

She was dismissive, "I hear it's hot there. Do you want to go to Tito's?"

"Sounds great. Let's go."

They didn't talk about her job offers anymore that night, except Ken asked if she thought Xerox was going to sweeten their offer. She did.

When they were home again and getting ready for bed, Janet went into the bathroom and closed the door. Ken, in his underwear, went to the door.

"Hey, hon'? Are you putting your thing in?"

"You mean the diaphragm? Yes, why?"

"Oh, I don't know. I thought, maybe…"

"Ken, I don't want to get pregnant now."

He slipped under the covers, and Janet joined him in a few minutes, and they entwined. He whispered, "Why *don't* we make a baby?"

"You really want to be a dad, don't you?" she whispered.

"Don't you want to be a mom?"

"Not right now."

They separated, and he said, "But when? We're not getting any younger."

Janet was annoyed. Why was he bringing this up again? "Ken, We're not even 30 yet. My career is just getting going." Now, Ken was annoyed. Her stupid job at Xerox again. He already lost that argument, so he wouldn't bring *that* up again.

"So, what? When *will* we be ready?"

She didn't even want to think about having a baby and taking time off from work. Her own mother never had another child after her. Janet always suspected her mom was depressed for a long time after she was born. No one talked about that then, though. You were just expected to be joyous about doing your duty. When her mom asked about grand-kids, Janet always wondered, "*If it's so great, why didn't you have more kids?*"

"I don't know, Ken. All I know is, I'm not ready *yet*."

Ken stewed. He wanted to roll over and go to sleep. But he was too horny now.

26

BUILD COP

J anet and Ken knew they hadn't really settled anything, except that Janet was probably going to take the Xerox offer. The next morning at Hughes, Steve asked Ken impatiently if she was going to take the offer. Ken played dumb. The manager whom Janet would report to also called Ken. He told him the Venus team was excited to have her and looking forward to resolving the battles about hardware and languages.

As soon as Janet arrived at her office, Tom stopped by and asked if she had a minute. She followed him to his office. He shut the door, sat down, and handed her another slip of paper. She opened it to see the new salary with an (18%) after it. She looked pleased. Tom said, "I spoke to Paul last night, and this is the best we can do, *for now.* But I can promise more will be coming. Lots more."

Janet grinned, "I accept!"

Tom smiled broadly, "Excellent. I know you'll do a great job in Integration."

"Thank you. I hope so."

"I'll let you tell people before I announce this. Then once

you've thought about what you want to do in this job, let's meet again." He held out his hand, "Congratulations."

She shook it, "Thanks, Tom."

She ran up the stairs to Gwen's office and stood in the doorway, "Knock, knock. Guess who's the new manager of Integrations?"

Gwen hugged her, "Congratulations, Janet! Sit down and tell me all about it."

Janet told her the whole story of her Hughes interview, salary negotiations with Tom, and the Integrations job. Gwen said, "I'm so proud of you. You stood up for yourself."

Janet was radiant, "Thanks, it was hard."

Gwen opened the bottom drawer of her desk and pulled out a bottle of Chivas Regal and a couple of glasses. "Just a taste, since it's before noon?" They each downed a *very* small drink.

"How does your husband feel about all this?"

Janet made a face, "Umm... he's not too happy. He wanted me to take the job at Hughes."

Gwen remembered how Janet had gingerly asked her about divorce. She decided not to raise the topic now, though. Janet could bring it up if she wanted. "But he's resigned to it, I guess?"

"Well, he doesn't have a choice, does he? I'm the one doing it."

"Yep."

Janet said after a long pause, "Well, I'd better let you get back to work. Thanks for the advice, Gwen."

"My pleasure, Janet. Good luck in the new job."

Almost everyone congratulated Janet after Tom announced it. She spent the rest of the day questioning the programmers who'd done the rotating build-master assignment since she hadn't had her turn yet. The first person she talked to was Dan. He glanced up as she stood in his doorway.

"Hey, congratulations! I hear we're going to have some reliable builds for a change."

"Thanks, gonna try. Can you walk me through what you did as Build Master?"

"Sure, let's go over to the build machine. It has the giant disk, which we need for this."

They sat down at the Alto with the 300MB Trident disk. El Segundo only had one of these right now, and you had to build on it since the source code wouldn't fit it on the regular 2MB disk packs everyone used.

"The first thing you do is set up your directory structure, the sources here, configuration files here, output files here, tools here," pointing to the folders that were already there from the previous build. "You delete all the files first so that you're starting clean. We won't do that now since we're not actually doing a build."

"Right," confirmed Janet.

"Then, you copy all the current source files from Iris into the source directory." Iris was the file server.

"Won't that make the files look new even if they haven't changed?"

Dan replied, "Well, that'll be up to you. I'd rebuild everything, myself. I'd rather err on the side of caution."

"Hmm. Yeah, that's what I think, too. But eventually, we'll have too much code to always recompile everything, right?"

Dan said, "Which brings up a good question. How long will it take to discover that somebody's change broke the build? Do you have to rebuild everything?"

"You mean someone changes some Defs file, and it makes something else not compile?"

That gave Dan the opening he was looking for, "I guess you know about the Include Checker? A guy in Palo Alto just did this."

"Yep. It looks at the dependencies and figures out what affects what, right?"

"Right. If someone checks in a Defs file, you really need to find out if it broke something right away instead of waiting for the weekly Integration. So… this thing analyzes what needs to be recompiled and outputs a command file to do it."

Janet had been thinking about this. The Star team suffered through screwups where someone broke someone else's code and didn't find out until days later. It was ugly.

"Yeah, I'd like to do partial integrations all the time, if I can."

Dan enthused, "That'd be so great. Do you know how the Pilot and Mesa people do it?"

She'd been thinking about that, too. "No, I'm going up there next week. Porter Berwick is showing me some of the tools they've been developing. And, I'm meeting with the Mesa and Pilot folks, too."

"Excellent." He turned back to the Alto. "We'll skip over what you do when something *doesn't* compile. That'll be the fun part of your job."

She gulped, "I go kill someone, right?"

Dan laughed, "That's for the second time they do it. The first time, you just bash them with the Mesa manual." She pretended to make a note.

"Unless it's me, of course!"

She said, "Right. For you, it's the third time."

He went on, "After it's all successfully compiled, then you run the Binder. We've been doing this with our own code, so you're familiar with that." She nodded. "Then, you *may* run the Packager."

"What does that do?"

"That can rearrange the code for better swapping performance. We haven't really done anything with that yet."

"Okay."

"Then finally, MakeBoot creates a boot file with Pilot.

You'll have to get the latest Pilot release whenever it changes."

"But the boot file is for the D0, right?" He nodded. "Where do we create the version of Star that runs on the Alto?"

"I think you can just let the programmers figure out which libraries they need for that. It isn't really your job."

Janet looked at some of the files and then thanked Dan. She noticed that each of the other people she talked to that day used subtly different methods to build, which was part of the problem Tom wanted her to solve. Star needed a single, reliable process everyone could depend on. It was a management job as much as a technical one.

Grant called later in the day. He'd seen the announcement of her new job. "Hey, congratulations, Buildmeister!"

"Thanks, Grant. How are you?"

"Doing great. I might have some news myself soon."

"Oh? On what, moving down here?"

"Yep. I talked to the managers on the Tor project, and they might have an opening soon."

"Well, great. We can be neighbors."

She meant neighbors at work since Tor was on the second floor and Star on the first, but Grant thought she was talking about neighborhoods in LA.

"I don't know… I was looking at some houses last time I was down there. I was thinking about Manhattan Beach, near Aviation Boulevard. That's not very close to you, is it?"

"No, we live in an apartment in Culver City."

"Are you guys thinking of buying?"

"Ken is always nagging about that. I don't know. I think the prices are insane."

"That they are. But they're not coming down."

Janet was thinking that really, she didn't want to buy a house *with Ken*, but she didn't want to say that to Grant. She changed the topic, "When do you think you might be moving down here?"

"I have another interview next week, and then we'll see."

"Well, good luck. Stop by when you're down here." Grant said he would.

27

FUNDAMENTALLY

Aaron Bickel joined the El Segundo team as one of its first Ph.D.s in late 1978. He came highly recommended by Henry, one of the Functional Spec designers in Palo Alto, since they shared dissertation advisers. Mark and Tom hoped Aaron could provide some intellectual firepower for El Segundo. Prior to his joining, they had almost all practical-minded engineers rather than theoreticians.

Aaron was about 6' tall, slim, and balding on top. He was soft-spoken and polite, but firm and inflexible on technical questions he considered important. If you challenged him on anything, his answer usually began, "Fundamentally,..." and would sound as if he were defending his dissertation. Other engineers in El Segundo might *try* to talk like that since that was the kind of academic environment it was, but Aaron had the authority and professorial heft to pull it off.

Aaron jumped right into the Star effort, taking on the hardest part, the editor and its revolutionary functionality, often called WYSIWYG. No one had ever done this, at least on the scale of Star. Bravo, the text editor, and some of the early PARC prototypes did it in limited domains, but Star was supposed to have documents with embedded graphics frames, tables, equations, and other stuff, all together. If you stretched the graphics frame, the text had to move with it. If *part* of your window became visible because another window or property sheet moved or went away, you had to redraw *just that part.* No one had ever implemented anything like that.

It got even worse. If your code implemented some kind of widget on the screen, it might be forced to do something because of what some *other* widget did. The solution that came naturally to programmers—erase the screen and redraw everything—was definitely not okay. You couldn't have the entire screen flashing and redrawing just because the user typed a character somewhere. It would look ugly, for one thing, and for another, it would be intolerably slow.

Aaron joined Star with a mission to solve this problem. He was busy setting up his Alto when Dan and Brian stopped by to introduce themselves. Brian extended his hand with a grin, "Good afternoon, Dr. Bickell. On behalf of Mr. Markunas and myself, we'd like to welcome you to Xerox."

Aaron played along with the formality and stood up, "I'm very pleased to make you gentlemen's acquaintance."

Dan inquired, "So, have you found the fly-swatting game yet?" Aaron hadn't seen that Alto program, which was where you'd try to swat a fly, and it would evade you unless you were *very* quick. Dan brought it up for him, and Aaron tried clicking on a fly, but it evaded him. He learned to be faster, and pretty soon the dead flies were piled up at the bottom of the screen.[1]

Aaron exited the game and turned serious, asking about their work. Brian talked about the text editing code he was working on, and Dan spoke about records processing. Aaron asked, "What's the overall software architecture of Star? Either of you."

Brian and Dan both looked embarrassed. Dan spoke, "It's sort of object-oriented, I guess, but Mesa doesn't really give us a lot of help." Brian agreed.

"How do we do it now?" Brian went to the whiteboard

and drew some examples of the coding conventions that Gary had laid out months ago.

"And, how is that working out so far?" Aaron asked.

Brian felt even more embarrassed. "Well, it's coming along," and he laughed nervously.

Dan smirked, "It's *improving*. Getting better every day," and they both laughed.

Aaron smiled thinly but didn't laugh, "Can you draw the object hierarchy?"

Brian drew the class hierarchy from memory and tried to describe what each class did. Aaron asked a lot of questions.

Dan was curious, "Aaron, from what you've seen, do you think the final product will be something anyone wants to buy?"

Aaron replied, "I don't think we can really know that. Our job is just to build the thing." Brian nodded. He continued, "Well, I think I have enough to think about for now. I'm sure we'll be talking again soon." Dan and Brian left.

Aaron was reading the Star Functional Spec when Mark came by. He was in his shorts and a Hawaiian shirt, as usual.

"Aaron, welcome."

"Thanks," he said, holding up the spec he was reading., "Just reading the FunSpec, as you advised. Interesting reading."

Mark looked at the chapter Aaron was reading, "Ah yes, I remember that chapter. When you get a chance, come by and let me know what you think." Aaron said he would.

After an hour or so of reading, Aaron walked down to Mark's office. Mark looked up, "Well, do you have it all figured out yet?"

"Piece of cake!" he said. "Is now a good time?" Mark motioned for him to sit down. "First question, who am I reporting to here? Is it you?"

"I guess that would be me until I hear differently."

"Good! Next question, who, if anyone, reports to me?"

"Ah," said Mark. "We haven't formalized anything yet, but I think you already met Brian Lerner, right?" Aaron said he had. "You can let me know what you think after you meet them all, but I was thinking of having him and two other guys, David Bowman and Raymond Wu, work with you."

Three people under him. Well, Aaron didn't know if they'd actually be under him in the org chart sense, but he didn't care right now. They were people who'd *listen* to him, at least.

"Great. I don't know those other two yet. What are they like?"

"Well…" he said, standing up, "No time like the present." He walked down the hall with Aaron following. David was typing furiously in the first office they stopped at. Mark knocked on his door.

After introductions, Aaron said, "What are you working on?"

David cheerfully rattled off four or five things he was doing. He was looking at the Mesa 4.0 opcodes and seeing what had changed from the previous release; checking where the Star code should use the new LONG POINTER feature in Mesa; playing with the debugger and writing up a list of tips and gotchas for everyone; and reading the source code for the Include Checker. The last was a request from the guy in Palo Alto who'd written it. Seemingly all these activities were going on in different windows on his screen, and Aaron had the strong feeling there were others, too.

Mark was used to David's frenetic activity, but Aaron was amazed, "*My God, are they all like this?*" he asked himself.

Mark said, "Well, we'll leave you to it," and they left.

The next stop was Raymond's office. He was staring at his screen but not typing, and before he closed the window, Aaron noticed it had an email from the science fiction mailing list. Raymond had a blissful look and squinty eyes, as though he were stoned. His answers to Aaron's questions were vaguely understated, as if he knew much more than he cared to say right now.

They walked back to Mark's office and sat down again. Mark asked, "Will those do?"

Aaron answered, "Very impressive. What do you want me to do first?"

"Why don't you go through the entire Functional Spec and see if it's all consistent. Then, you can start designing this sucker."

Aaron knew he was dismissed.

28

GRANT LEARNS THE GOSPEL

I t was nearing the end of 1978, and Grant couldn't stand it anymore. His transfer to El Segundo was dragging on and on. The Tor people liked him, they wanted to hire him, but somehow, something was always in the way. First, they had a requisition for his job, then somehow they didn't, then they were getting a new req and some VP had to sign off, but he had to leave on a trip, and his secretary forgot to have him sign it… argh!

In the meantime, he kept going to endless planning meetings. The demise of the D0 had led to a search for a hardware design that SDD could be sure of. Another failure would be fatal, and they knew it. Wildflower, a paper design by Butler Lampson and Roy Levin, was considered a viable contender, and it was hugely influential. Grant's contacts in Rochester and Stamford, clueless as usual, were asking him, with increasing impatience, what the holdup was. To them, hardware was just a chapter in a product plan. You had your cost issues, manufacturability, safety, reliability, and so on, and it was pretty well-understood.

He was about to explain it yet again to a big mucky-muck —he'd hated that term before coming to Palo Alto, but he'd slowly warmed up to it—and he wanted to be sure of the story. Tony kindly offered to help him.

"Hi, Tony. Thanks for offering. Is now a good time?"

"Sure, have a seat. You were at the last planning meeting, so stop me if I'm repeating what you already know."

"I don't know much, so go ahead."

Tony drew five widely spaced lines on the whiteboard.

1. Cost-reduced Alto
2. Fix the Dolphin
3. Custom LSI
4. Vendor-supplied microprocessor, native machine language
5. Vendor-supplied microprocessor, Mesa bytecodes

"These are the five alternatives considered."[1]

Grant copied them into his notebook and put his fist to his chin, "I remember those. The cost-reduced Alto is the one my contacts always ask about. That and the custom Large Scale Integration, which to them sounds like science fiction. "

"Yeah, I enjoy that part, too. First, let's talk about the Alto."

"Please… I'd love to put that to bed."

Tony drew three lines on the right emanating from the word Alto, describing the drawbacks of the Alto.

1. Display size

"The Alto is a 606 x 808 screen. Star is supposed to be big enough for two full-sized documents side by side." Grant wrote that down and nodded.

2. No virtual memory

Grant grasped this, "That takes some explaining for these executives. The fact that IBM now has virtual memory helps. At least, they know it's a real thing. With virtual memory, your program can reference a memory address even if it's not in core. If it's on disk, the operating system brings it in."

"Right. Memory is expensive, but software grows incessantly and arrogantly without bound." Grant laughed at the adverbs.

3. Mesa ops: 200K ips

"The current Alto runs at about 200,000 Mesa instructions per second with the display on. We need more." Grant just nodded. "There are more, but these will be enough for your audience, I'm guessing."

"More than enough. Onward."

"Dolphin is a non-starter and just unreliable. It's too big, too hot, and too unstable. We learned from it, but we have to move on."

"They might ask about it, but I can just refer them to you for details. Onward."

"Custom LSI *seems* attractive."

Grant smiled at this, "I've been doing my research, and LSI seems amazing. Thank God the execs haven't read about it in *Business Week* yet, or they'd be all over us." Tony laughed out loud. Grant continued, "Who's doing these LSI chips? Just Intel?"

"A few other companies, but it's pretty cutting-edge stuff. Xerox just doesn't have the ability to do that."

"Right again. We can't build moon rockets, either. Onward."

Tony looked more serious, like the next item was harder to dismiss.

"Alright, vendor-supplied microprocessor includes a lot of choices. We *are* picking one of those." Grant sat up straight. "A traditional hardware bus allows lots of different peripherals to be attached. Almost all general-purpose computers have one."

"Yeah, that's what I remember."

"The peripherals need some logic to use the bus. What happens when they want to send data, but the bus is busy?"

Grant thought a second, "They need buffering space?"

"Right, and maybe a *lot* of it, depending. The processing gets expensive. Star is not a general-purpose computer,

though. We know what peripherals it needs."

"So that saves money... how?"

He drew a big circle on the whiteboard. "We can think of Star as going through a round-robin every few microseconds. First, it checks if the hard disk needs attention." He drew a line at around 3 o'clock.

"Then, the display." A line at 6 o'clock.

"Then, the Xerox Wire." A line at 9 o'clock.

"Then, the low-speed peripherals, such as the keyboard, mouse, and so forth." Another line at 10 o'clock.

"Then, we let the Mesa interpreter run."

Grant laughed, "So *finally*, we do some actual work."

"In the worst case, if a high-speed device doesn't need its slot, Mesa gets that time, too."

Grant studied the picture, "So... the hard disk always knows it'll be serviced in time, and the display, and so forth?" Tony agreed. "But this depends on having no *other* high-speed devices?"

This made Tony slightly uncomfortable. He knew that engineers habitually tried to one-up each other with a more general design, but on the other hand, he had a task to accomplish. "Right, but Star isn't a general-purpose computer... it just has to handle our office-automation needs."

Grant pondered that, and then he had an inspiration, "Could we call it an appliance?"[2]

Tony didn't care for that word, "It sounds like we're designing a washing machine or something."

Grant couldn't resist, "Or maybe a toaster." Tony was tempted to ask how many bread slots he should plan for but instead said, "Well, let's not call it that. But anyway, we don't have to handle some new high-speed peripheral that comes along next year."

Grant almost wanted to challenge that, but he suspected

Tony was right. Maybe you achieved some cost-savings by settling on a given set of peripherals.

"So, this makes the peripherals cheaper, and thus the entire system?"

"Exactly."

"Okay, but before we make the final choice, this option includes some complete processors on chips, doesn't it?"

Tony looked even more uncomfortable, "Right... there's the Intel 8086, the Motorola 68000, and the Zilog Z8000. The 68K and the 8000 aren't shipping yet, but we have some specs."

"I see that you wrote native machine language. Isn't that obvious? What does that mean?"

Tony suspected this guy was paying attention because he was getting right to the heart of the matter. "You've heard of Mesa bytecodes and PrincOps, right?" Grant nodded. "The idea is that we have a Mesa virtual machine, and it has machine instructions, as it were, which are what Mesa needs. Of course, they're implemented in microcode, not in hardware."

"Yep."

"Periodically, the Mesa group looks at the code the users are writing and tunes the instructions to make the most common ones the shortest, and so forth."

"I've heard that. It makes the compiled code smaller and faster, and life is good."

Tony wondered if he detected some sarcasm, *"Are executives ever sarcastic?"* He went on anyway. "Exactly! It's supposed to mean the hardware is perfect for Mesa."

"You're not convinced, though?"

Tony answered quickly, "It does produce very compact code, no question about that."

"Well, regardless. What does that mean for the Star hardware?"

"It means that our options are very limited. We have to

use hardware that's fast enough, and those commercial chips I mentioned are not."

Grant thought for a long time. Something was wrong, but he couldn't quite put his finger on it. "I'll take your word on that. I have to think they'll get faster over time, though, right?"

Tony felt cornered. This guy was closing in on what Tony really thought, but he wouldn't make any friends in SDD by saying it. "Well, maybe. Anyhow, the compiler's not going to start emitting 8086 or 68000 code or whatever. We could emulate the Mesa instruction set on those processors, but that would be too slow. Maybe 25K to 100K instructions per second."

Grant glanced at his watch. Tony had been extremely generous with his time, but he didn't want to take up his entire day. "So, the final choice is… I've heard the term bit-sliced a lot."

"Right. We use AMD's 2901 processor, which is 4-bits wide and designed to be strung together this way."

"And the performance? In Mesa instructions per second?"

"That depends on the proportion of transfer instructions, such as go-to, because those are slow. But we think it's comparable to the Dolphin, at 400K to 500K instructions per second."

Grant made notes on his pad, "Oh, and it has virtual memory, of course?"

"Of course! Do you need the numbers on VM size and real memory size?"

"Maybe at some point, but these are high-level executives, remember," Grant smirked. "I've taken up more than enough of your time, for now. Thank you very much, Tony."

"My pleasure." Then Tony remembered one more thing,

"Wait, don't you want to hear the name?"

Grant turned around, "Oh, right. What is the name?"

"Since Butler's design was the Wildflower, and we need a

name beginning with D, I'm thinking Dandelion." Grant made a note and thanked him again.

As Grant walked back to his office, he mused about how Xerox reached this design. They started with Mesa, the language, and the Office Information Systems (OIS) architecture long before hiring a lot of people. Then, they worked forward from that. Mesa had its virtual machine, meaning you needed microcode to implement it. In theory, that led to hardware perfectly tailored to Mesa.

In the bad old days, the hardware designers came up with a machine they thought was good, and then, the compiler writers translated a higher-level language to that machine. Nowadays, it seemed like the software folks had taken over, and the hardware folks were trying to be like them. He thought maybe Tony wasn't totally happy with all this, but the last thing he wanted to do was to refight old battles and bruise a lot of egos. He was getting out of all this and transferring to a project to build a plain old boring printer.[3]

29

ANIMAL HOUSE

D an had grown a beard on vacation. He'd never had one in his life and never even thought he could grow one, but now he had one. It was pretty decent, in his opinion. It made him look older, which was a good thing, but his mother was horrified.

Brian made fun of it, "Dan, are you *trying* to grow a beard?"

He had a variety of answers to that, none very satisfactory. Sometimes he'd say, "Trying! How'm I doin'?" imitating New York Mayor Ed Koch. Eventually, the ridicule died down since beards were pretty common at Xerox.

On Friday, January 12, 1979, Dan and Janet were waiting by the printer for Betty to bring more toner. Dan asked, "Did you ever read *Lord of the Rings*?"

"No, but it's on my list to read at some point. Why?"

"Oh, there's a movie adaptation of it out now. I went to see it last night."

"How was it?"

"Well… okay, I guess. It was animated and only covers the first book and half of the second. I think they could have done it better."[1]

"I don't think I can talk Ken into seeing that! He's pushing to see *Animal House* this weekend."

"Hard to beat John Belushi, I guess."

"Yeah. He wants to see *Every Which Way But Loose*, too."

"Too bad… so many great movies are coming out now. Have you heard of *Days of Heaven*?" She shook her head. "And *Invasion of the Body Snatchers*? You might be able to convince Ken to see that. And of course, *The Buddy Holly Story*."

Janet laughed at *Invasion of the Body Snatchers*. Ken liked horror films, and it was one of the few genres they agreed on. She remarked, "It sounds like you go to a lot of movies."

Dan agreed, "Yeah, since I moved to Hermosa Beach, I can walk down to the Surf Theater. They show those old classics everyone sees in college. Except me. Somehow, I never did."

"Like what?"

"*Harold and Maude*. *King of Hearts*. Those kinds of flicks."

"Well, if it makes you feel any better, I haven't seen those either." Dan didn't have an answer for that.

"Is living at the beach all it's cracked up to be? You have movies, at least."

"Yeah. But if I buy a house, it won't be at the beach. Too expensive."

Janet looked interested but frustrated, "I know. Ken wants to buy, but I'd just *hate* living in some crappy neighborhood. Are you looking?"

"Well, more just thinking about it so far. I go to an open house once in a while. You don't have any commitment that way."

"Oh yeah? Which cities?"

Dan looked embarrassed since he'd only been to houses that were *way* out of his reach. "A couple in Torrance. A couple in Redondo."

"And?"

"Well… they're a *bit* out of my price range. But you guys have two incomes, and I only have one."

Janet thought of how Ken kept agitating about real estate. Their marriage was looking more and more doomed, and a house would just make divorce messier. And kids. What a nightmare that would be.

But she and Dan weren't close enough to talk about that, so she just smiled. After Betty arrived with the new toner, they finished their print jobs and left.

On Saturday night, Janet and Ken went to see *Animal House*. Ken had lived in a fraternity at MIT, not because he was the frat-boy type but because it was a good housing deal. He laughed uproariously, and Janet liked it almost as much. "Did we surrender when the Germans bombed Pearl Harbor?" was a joke Ken would probably make for a long, long time. The frat in that movie had special meaning for him.

Ken must have been reading her mind about real estate because after their weekly Sunday volleyball game with the gang, he asked, "So, how'd you like to go to some open houses today?"

She had the feeling that this time the argument would be special, and her intuition was right.

She declined, and Ken said, "Can we talk about something?"

"Sure," she replied, sitting down.

"Do you want to be married anymore?"

"I don't know, Ken. What brought this on?"

"I'm just not so sure anymore. It seems like we want different things."

"What do you mean?"

"Well, houses, obviously, for one."

Janet didn't want to give in too quickly because she wanted divorce to be his idea. "We've talked and talked about this."

"But somehow, we end up doing nothing. If we keep waiting while prices go up, we'll be living in Compton."

Janet laughed, "You mean *you* will. I'm not living in Compton!" She didn't expect this to defuse the situation, and it didn't. He smiled but just briefly.

"Okay, Tarzana then. I think we have to buy something *now*."

"Is this what you wanted to talk about? Or… is there something else?"

"Kids. You don't seem to want them."

"I don't want them right now. Maybe someday, just not now."

Ken was exasperated, "We're not getting any younger, Janet!"

She needed a second to consider her answer, so she got a glass of water, "We're not even 30, Ken." She sat back down.

"So, what are you saying? Do you want a divorce?" Ken was unwilling to just say that he wanted a divorce. It was a mean thing to say. He still loved her and absolutely *hated* seeing her cry. He hesitated, and she jumped in.

"One thing I *have* to know, Ken. Is there someone else?"

Ken ran through the list of women he knew at Hughes, but there weren't many. It was a man's world. Maybe if he were single, he'd meet a woman who actually wanted to buy a house in LA and have kids, and he wouldn't end up as one of those sad old divorced 40-year-olds hanging out by the apartment complex's pool.

"No! Definitely not!"

She knew him well enough to know he meant, "*Not yet, there isn't!*"

"Is there someone else for you?"

She laughed, "God, no!"

Ken felt relieved somehow. "*Could this be an agreeable split? Maybe.*"

"Why don't we sleep on this and talk about it some more

tomorrow? It's too important to rush into." She agreed. Somehow, they'd decided on a divorce without a big ugly scene. He
asked with an imploring smile, "I always hear about wives
throwing their husbands out of the house. You're not throwing
me out, are you?"

She hugged him, "That's for people who hate each other!
I don't hate you. Do you hate me?"

He hugged her back harder, "Not at all, not at all."

30

BEACHY

Janet went straight to Gwen's office on Monday morning, without calling first.

"Ken and I had The Conversation yesterday!" drawing out the words *the* and *conversation*.

Gwen was still drinking her tea and waking up, "The conversation? What conversation?"

Then she realized what Janet was talking about, but she figured saying the word divorce was like asking someone if she was pregnant when she wasn't. Janet could say it.

"We talked about getting a divorce, and I think it's going to happen."

Gwen put her hand on Janet's arm, "I hope it wasn't too awful."

"Amazingly enough, no. We're still sleeping in the same bed."

"My God, that *is* an amicable divorce. Congratulations, tell me all about it."

Janet recounted the conversation, with Gwen interrupting from time to time. "Well, you remember what I said about being young and not having kids yet?"

"I sure do. Thanks for all the help, Gwen."

Gwen hugged her, "I'm sure you're going to end up on your feet, Janet."

Janet walked downstairs to her office. Who could she tell in SDD? No one. She would definitely call her dad but not while he was at work—that would throw him into a panic.

She sat at her desk and thought. Now that she'd told someone, it seemed more real. She started thinking about life as an unmarried woman. Ken refused to go see the movie with that name, which she now found ironic.

Where would she live? Definitely not in the Marina. Ken would move there for sure. Maybe once he found a girlfriend, the two of them could hang out with Steve and Shelley. He could be a swinging single, and they'd go out on Steve's boat and sip Chardonnay. Yuck!

Dan lived near the beach, but he wasn't the type to sit around and drink wine. Maybe she could get some background from him, so she stopped by his office and knocked on the open door.

"Hey, we saw *Animal House* this weekend. It was so funny. Have you seen it yet?"

Dan looked up and laughed, "No, but I can't wait to see it!" Then, he picked up the front page of the *LA Times* that he'd brought in with him.

"Did you read about the horrendous blizzard in the Midwest? Twenty-nine inches of snow and a wind chill of minus 50!"

Janet shivered, "God, I don't miss that."

"This is getting to be my favorite part of every winter… hearing about the horrible weather back East and thinking I used to live in that shit."

She remembered Detroit winters, which weren't quite as bad as Chicago's but pretty close. "So, you live in Hermosa Beach, right?" He nodded. "Do you like it?"

"I do. It's a problem when guests come since there's no parking. But it's great being able to walk down to the beach.

Sometimes on Sundays, I'll just take the radio down there and listen to Vin Scully announcing the Dodgers game."

"What about the traffic, drunken parties, and all that?"

"Well, I'm on Monterey, which is the third street up from the beach. The partiers are mostly right *on* the beach."

"Cool. What's the difference between Hermosa and Manhattan?"

This was a hot button with Dan, "Manhattan's more glitzy. Everything costs more… the bars, restaurants, apartments, everything. All the fancy singles bars are in Manhattan Beach."

"Interesting. It's a little bit closer to work, I guess."

"Hermosa's more of a funky beach town. But hey, this new place just opened, The Comedy and Magic Club, and I can almost roll out of bed and be there."

"I think Ken wanted to go to that. Is that worthwhile?"

"Oh yeah. They have these comedians who aren't quite well known yet, but they're really good. I recently saw this guy David Letterman a few weeks ago, and he was hilarious."[1]

"Okay, I guess I should get back to work. Just curious."

After she left, Dan wondered why she was asking about places to live. Were she and Ken looking to buy a house near the beach? *"Well, two good incomes. They can do that."*

That evening, she called both her parents and told them about the divorce. Her mom tried to be sympathetic, but she and Janet had never been very close anyway. Janet suspected that her mom felt she'd failed in *her* marriage, and now, Janet had failed, too. But she'd never say that. The conversation was over in a few minutes. Her mom asked if she needed anything, and she said no.

Then, she called her dad, Len. "Hi, Dad. Are you sitting down?"

"Uh-oh. I am now. What is it?"

"Ken and I are getting a divorce."

"Oh, sweetie… I'm so sorry."

"Thanks, Dad. I think it's for the best. He just wants the house and kids and I… "

Len interrupted, "And, you want to make something of yourself. Am I right?"

He always had that older generation's way of putting it. She wouldn't have said it that way, necessarily, but he did understand her in a way her mom never did.

"Yeah, something like that. My career is really taking off, and I just want to see how far I can go."

"Sure you do," he said. "And just between you and me, I don't think he appreciates what he has in you. Oh, excuse me, what he *had*."[2]

Janet said to herself, "*I needed that!*"

"He's a good guy. He's never been mean to me, and I wish him all the best."

Len was relieved to hear that. The thought of Janet being with someone who abused her would have been more than he could bear.

They talked about her immediate plans, and he offered to take some time off and fly out to LA to help out, but she politely declined.

31

MOVING OUT, MOVING UP

I t was winter 1979, and Dan and Janet had both become
managers recently—Dan of the Records Processing
group and Janet of the Integrations group. Janet was
actively recruiting for a para-programmer to help her, while
Dan had acquired two junior programmers. Dan went to
Charm School, as they called the two-day Basic Management
course that Xerox gave new managers. They taught him that
managing was not the same as engineering. Even more
shocking to a young engineer, he learned that not everyone
wants to be managed the same way he liked to be managed.

The class was one of the few occasions when he met
people from other parts of Xerox. He went to lunch afterward
with a woman from the class, who told him all about how the
Rosicrucians ran everything in the world and had for
centuries. Shakespeare was a Rosicrucian, and Jamestown, the
English settlement in Virginia, was also a Rosicrucian outpost
where some important relics had been buried 10 feet down
and later discovered. Dan didn't contact her again.

Grant's transfer to the Tor project in El Segundo finally
came through, and he very quickly bought a house in

Manhattan Beach. He'd been scouting the area on his trips down South, and he figured out that he could live a long way from the beach and still have a respectable zip code, without the ridiculous price.

His house was near Marine Avenue, not far from Aviation, and much cheaper than the property west of the Pacific Coast Highway. It was also only a half-hour's walk from work and much less on a bike. He thought it sucked that you paid so much more and received so much less in California. But if he stayed a few years and then moved anywhere else, he'd have a palace on two acres.

The first time he rode his bike to work, he almost screamed at the security guards. They wouldn't let his bike into the building. In Palo Alto, everyone parked their bikes in their offices or the hallway. The first time he rode to work, he didn't have a lock with him and had to ride back home and return in the car.

When he finally got back to work, he bored all his coworkers by recounting the story in excruciating detail. They were all accustomed to the paramilitary Security Department, so no one really wanted to listen. He wrote emails and visited the head of Security in person and, of course, got nowhere. "Fire hazard, plus dripping grease and oil" was their official reason why it was prohibited. Some bike racks sat outside the back door of the building near the loading docks, and there was a guard somewhere nearby, so they claimed your bike would be plenty safe. Grant bought a cheaper bike for commuting.[1]

Grant called Janet on his first day in El Segundo. He'd told her before that he was transferring, so it wasn't a surprise. She used the opportunity to tell him that she and Ken were divorcing. *"Finally! What took so long?"* His first week was completely full with meetings, so he didn't have time to visit the first floor and say hello in person.

Janet moved out while the divorce was pending. She rented a place in Manhattan Beach but much closer to the ocean than Grant. It felt weird living alone after she'd lived for four years with Ken and with roommates in college before that. All her friends were really his friends, so she didn't hang out with them much. Still, she went to the Sunday volleyball games, which was a bit awkward with Ken there as well, but she thought, "*Well ... they'll just have to deal with it.*" Ken seemed to be flirting with this new girl, Heather, but Janet didn't much care. Maybe *she'd* give him some babies.

She went for long runs down the Strand, sometimes all the way to the end at Redondo. The singles bars were too much of a meat market for her, and after one or two visits, she never went again. She was lonely, but work was great, and Gwen had warned her not to rush into a new relationship right away.

Her apartment had fleas from the previous owner's cat, and she was afraid to get her own cat because the fleas would migrate to it. Several times, she'd shut all the windows, set off flea bombs, and left for a few hours while the fumes did their job. Somehow or other, a few fleas always survived, and a month later, she'd walk across the carpet in her bare feet and find fleas on her legs. The landlord finally agreed to call an exterminator after she'd complained multiple times. He warned her that an outdoor cat would just bring in the fleas again. "*Oh, great. So, I have to keep it inside? They hate that.*"[2]

Gwen told her the local Sierra Club had a 21-35 Singles subgroup, and she went on a few of their group hikes and really liked them. There was one moonlight hike at night to a peak with a view of both the Valley and the city. The hikes lasted for hours, so you had the chance to talk to people at leisure. The men usually outnumbered the women, but she made friends with some of the women she met.

She thought it was the perfect alternative to the LA singles culture. The only time she'd ever heard of the Sierra Club before was when they were suing to block a pipeline or something, but they didn't seem to push any politics on these hikes. And, they were free. She was surprised that she'd never heard of it after living in LA for three years, but the LA Chapter had 20,000 members, so it wasn't exactly a secret.

Usually, the hike met at some public spot, like the VA parking lot on Wilshire, where they split up into carpools and rode to the trailhead. There was plenty of time to meet people. When you waited around, were in the car, while you were hiking, and when the group came to a rest or lunch stop were perfect times to talk to someone else. Often, they all went out to a restaurant after the hike.

Frequently when people were saying goodbye, the guys asked for her phone number, but they weren't the hyperaggressive types. Most of the hikers were not in computers, which she found refreshing. If she told them what she did at work, they didn't have the slightest idea what she was talking about.

One morning about two months after she moved out, Dan came in to ask her about the latest Star integration. He noticed her lack of a wedding ring and pulled on his left ring finger with a quizzical look. "Yes, Ken and I are splitting up. I'm living in Manhattan Beach now."

He sympathized, "I'm sorry to hear that, Janet."

She didn't want to talk about the divorce, and she guessed he didn't, either. "Anyhow, now we're neighbors, almost."

Dan asked where she was living and how she liked it so far. She told him about her apartment and the fleas, and he sympathized. He told her his apartment had hardwood floors, and now he understood why.

"Hey, have you ever gone on a Sierra Club hike?"

"No, never even heard of it. I just think of the Sierra Club as a political group. Why?"

"I've been going to some of their hikes. They're not political at all. They're just hikes."

"Really? Where do they go?"

"I've only done a couple of hikes. Last time was out near Malibu, but they go all over. The San Gabriel Mountains, the Santa Monicas, sometimes to the beach."

"Interesting. Do you have to join up or make a reservation or something?"

"No, you just show up." Dan asked how to get the schedule because this sounded interesting.

"Anyhow, what I came here to ask was if you'd heard of Aaron's plans for traits? It sounds pretty scary."

"Yeah, Mark told me I should talk to Aaron, and he sounded pretty serious. Do you know what it is?"

Dan drew a diagram on the whiteboard. "He said every object might be a subclass of *multiple* classes, not just a single parent like now. For example," and he drew a stack of boxes labeled A, B, and C, each with arrows pointing to a fourth box. He pointed at it. "This object has data for classes A, B, and C. So, it has the methods for each class."

Janet stared at it, "Okay, but where is this stuff defined?"

"I think that's where you come in. There has to be some common procedure that analyzes all the class relationships. I should probably let Aaron explain it."

Janet looked concerned, "Oh, boy. I can't wait to hear about this." Dan left.

As if on cue, Mark and Aaron walked in. Mark asked, "Got a minute?" She nodded, and Aaron started drawing on the whiteboard after he erased what Dan had drawn.

```
IS-FORWARD-LINKED-LIST-ELEMENT
IS-TREE-ELEMENT
IS-NAMED
IS-PRINTABLE
```

"These are *simple traits*. So, for example, `IS-TREE-ELEMENT` has the obvious operations `GetParent`, `GetNext-Sibling`, and so on. I won't name them all."

Janet said, "Okay," knowing there was more coming.

"We can also have *compound traits*," and wrote:

```
IS-IN-NAME-HIERARCHY =
IS-TREE-ELEMENT  U  IS-NAMED
```

"In other words, `IS-IN-NAME-HIERARCHY` is specified by the union of the operations specified for `IS-TREE-ELEMENT` and `IS-NAMED`. We can define a directed acyclic graph under the carries relation where an object of the type `IS-IN-NAME-HIERARCHY` *carries* both the `IS-TREE-ELEMENT` trait and the `IS-NAMED` trait."

Janet shifted in her chair, "So, where is all this going? You want to introduce traits into the Star software, I guess?"

Mark piped up, "Bingo!"

Aaron resumed, "The current code is becoming unmaintainable. We find ourselves writing the same code over and over again, and eventually, we're going to hit the wall."

"We're almost at 75,000 lines of code, and sometimes, I think we're there already."

Mark jumped in again, "We haven't even started on graphics yet. Or equations. You get the picture."

"Do each of these traits have data?"

"Fundamentally, yes, they usually do."

"And if an object has multiple traits, how do you lay out the data?"

Mark answered for Aaron, "Raymond and Brian have been working on that, haven't they, Aaron?"

Aaron looked embarrassed, "There are some proposals, but we haven't worked out all the details yet."

Janet realized she didn't have the option to say no, although she wanted to. Mark had Aaron and his entire group working on it. They wanted her to be a team player, not to argue. It was already decided. "Alright, what do you want to do with this?"

It was decided that they would form a working group, with Aaron in charge, and Janet's team would eventually implement a Star-wide trait-analysis program that would be part of her regular Integration duties. "Excellent. Thanks, Janet."

Dan poked his head in after Mark and Aaron had left with a smirk, "So? Have you been baptized yet?" She gave him the finger.[3]

32

TRAITS

T he meeting Janet dreaded was upon her—the traits meeting with Aaron and his group. All she knew was that it was some kind of grand scheme that made *her* group the bottleneck for everything. Now, she'd find out what he had in mind. David, Raymond, Brian, and Mark were there as well. Janet had a new assistant, Angela, who was not a full-time engineer although she could program. Angela also attended the meeting.

Aaron spoke first, "The reason we're here is that fundamentally, the Star software is becoming too complex to manage. We're finding that we're writing the same code over and over again, and we can't keep track of the relationships anymore."

No one spoke, so he continued, "Up to now, we've had a system of subclassing where each class is a subclass of, at most, one parent class, so the system forms a tree." He drew a tree on the board, a data structure that every computer science student learned in school. It had a circle on the top with A in the middle, and below that, two circles B and C, each with a line to A. B had circles D and E below it as children. C had children F and G.

Mark interrupted, "Aaron, we don't need to show the entire Star class tree. Why don't you skip right to your design?"

"Thanks, Mark. What we want to introduce is a class *graph*, rather than a tree where a given node on the tree can have more than one parent."

He drew a line from C to D so that D now had a line from B and C. It wasn't a tree anymore. "So, class D now inherits from both B and C. We say that D carries the *traits* B and C."

Raymond exclaimed, "This is the cool part… it's now a graph."

"A directed acyclic graph, actually," Brian explained triumphantly.

Aaron said, "You win the prize, Brian."

Janet spoke, "Okay. A few questions?" Aaron held out his hand, palm up.

"Actually, a lot of them. Let's start with… how are these relationships defined?"

Raymond was eager, but Aaron answered, "There's a trait manager and a language where you declare the relationships. Raymond's working on that."

"So, that has to run before anything else?" Aaron nodded. "And what does that do?" Aaron looked at Raymond for the answer.

Raymond took the marker from Aaron and drew tiny boxes next to each circle. "Each trait has its own data. That's these little boxes. When a class carries a trait, it has its own copy of that trait's data."

He drew a stack of two boxes next to D, one labeled B and the other C. "Each D object has both B *and* C data."

Aaron interrupted, "Don't you want to show the language where the relationships are defined?"

Raymond looked impatient but drew some syntax on the board where the trait relationships were defined. "We have some obvious language where you define what trait goes with what. Do I need to go into that?"

He clearly wanted to skip that, and Janet confirmed, "Not right now, but obviously, we need to see it at some point."

Raymond was eager to continue, but Aaron took back the marker, "Excuse me, Raymond, but there's something important here."

He pointed to the stack of boxes next to D and the single box next to E.

"So, the thing we've been struggling with, and we might need your help with, is the trait data for C is at an offset of zero for E, but something non-zero for D because B data comes first. In other words, it's not at the same offset in every class."

Janet stared at that for a few seconds. She said, skeptically, "In other words, an object doesn't know at compile time where all its data is."

Aaron replied, "That's what we're trying to avoid because an execution-time lookup would be slow."

Brian interjected, "Actually, the *trait* is what needs to know its data."

"Right. An object is made up of traits."

Janet was absorbing all this, "You want to precompute all the offsets somehow? Is that what you're thinking?"

Raymond stood up, dying to expound on all the ideas he'd been working on. Aaron had heard them all and was anxious not to scare Janet with them. He motioned to Raymond to sit back down.

"That's what we're thinking... a Trait Analysis step before the main compilation step is one way. Or, we could ask the compiler people to help out, somehow. What do you think?"

Angela had been silent the entire time, but now, she spoke up, "What would this Trait Analysis thing do, in terms of files? What would I do?"

Janet agreed, "Good question! Aaron?"

Aaron turned to Brian, "Brian's been thinking about that."

Brian took the marker and drew a flowchart. The words Trait Analysis were in a box with an arrow pointing to another box labeled `TrtDefs.mesa`.

"Basically, Trait Analysis would analyze all the individual trait defs files and spit out a file `TrtDefs.mesa` that contains the compile-time constants. Then, all the Pack files reference `TrtDefs`. The first line of each function is a call to `MyData` to get a pointer to their trait data. `MyData` references `TrtDefs` to compute the pointer."

Janet looked dismayed, "That's what I was afraid of. So, we have this global file that everyone depends on, and it's generated?"

Angela added, "And, Janet and I have to generate it."

Mark said, "Unless you all can come up with something better. Sorry, but I have to run to another meeting."

Brian continued, "It's a little more complicated. I'm working on a scheme where *some* of the traits are always at a fixed offset, while others have to move around. We can have an inline procedure that tells you which is which, so we don't need execution-time lookup."

Aaron didn't want to deep-end into that, "Thanks, Brian. We can write that up when we have all the details worked out."

Janet realized that traits were a done deal. Mark had made that clear. Still, she had to take charge of it somehow—at the very least, don't piss off Mark. That would be career death. Maybe she could even turn this into a plus for her.

Finally, she spoke. "Clearly, we have some details to work out." Aaron agreed. "How about conversion? How do we convert all the code we already have? Like Records Processing.

This would invalidate everything, wouldn't it?"

Aaron said, "Yeah, good point. We touched on that briefly yesterday, but nothing definite yet."

"First, let's work out the details of Trait Analysis and put it in a technical doc for everyone to see. Who's going to do that?"

Aaron looked at Raymond and Brian, "Can you two work on that? Janet, do you want to be in on it as well?"

"Yes, and Angela. *And*, we have to bring in the users of it. Dan for one. Next, we have to plan the transition so that we don't break everything until the conversion is done."

Angela asked, "So, we have to have two sets of Defs files?"

Janet looked at Aaron, who nodded. "For a while. I don't see a way around that. Do you guys?" looking at Raymond and Brian, who also signaled assent. "But let's get the design details hammered out. When can we have that design document?"

They agreed on dates and assigned people tasks. Janet felt she was getting the hang of this management stuff. Instead of complaining about the situation, she was making the best of it and focusing on the tasks. Mark would be pleased. Tom would be, too.[1]

33

BIG-TIME PROFESSIONAL MANAGEMENT

D an's group, which consisted of two people besides himself, was spending virtually all its time on the visible part of Records Processing (RP), not the actual database. The code that actually stored the data, called RpNucleus, was long finished, and no one wanted to touch it, except Dan. He wrote most of it so that was fine. He'd written B-tree code to maintain the sort order, and Janet's logical expression code allowed queries.

In the data processing world outside Xerox, a records file would have been called an ISAM file, which stood for indexed-sequential access method. IBM had created that for mainframes, ages and ages ago, and commercial databases had moved well beyond it. But the hard part was getting the data onto the screen and editing it. That was almost an afterthought in the rest of the data processing world. Programmers there just designed a bunch of terminal screens and called them the user interface.

Star's database, or records file, was a personal database. This was brand new. In the rest of the world, if you needed computing help, you went to the company IT department to get a new file or request a report. Maybe if you were lucky, they already had a program for you. Star users had to do it for themselves without learning some new command language.

RP's interface had to be the same as Star's, meaning users needed to rely on the MOVE, COPY, DELETE, and PROPS keys, for instance. This forced much soul-searching in Dan's group about what those functions should mean in every context. There might be rich text with fonts, subscript and superscript, and all that. The text might even be in Japanese. A Star document could have a table in it, and the operations on tables had to work the same way whether there was a records file behind it or not.

Janet thought this was interesting, in principle. A lot of things in Star were, but she didn't have time to learn about all of them. The engineers depended on her to do the builds regularly, and she had to keep Angela busy.

Janet and Angela discovered that the Build Cop's lot is not a happy one. Almost every day, someone checked in code that made someone else's code not compile anymore, and one of them had to tell the offender. Often, that person was not happy to hear it and blamed someone else for not changing their own code in time. They would tell Janet or Angela to go bug them.

After a couple of times trying to be nice, they reverted to saying, "No, *you* tell them, and in the meantime, we're pulling this change." Instead of the "good cop, bad cop" routine on TV police dramas, Angela and Janet played "bad cop, *really* bad cop." No one liked to see them knocking on the door.

Peter Eisen, a young UCLA graduate, worked in Dan's group on tables. It was slow going since the user interface objects he had to use were continually being redesigned. Peter was frustrated a lot, with the endless bickering over the proper way to do object-oriented programming in Mesa. Dan regularly had to tell Peter about some new rule in the coding conventions, and Peter inevitably made a face. After a while, he usually stopped complaining and just did it. Dan was afraid that someday, Peter would become frustrated enough to leave.

Dan was not looking forward to convincing Peter to convert to the new traits stuff Aaron was foisting on everyone. Besides the tables code being sort of embryonic, to put it charitably, Peter now had to revise everything he'd already done. He'd complain extra about this one.

RP also had a forms interface. A document might have fields in it, and the fields had names. A field with the name Name was filled in with a given record's Name field, and if the text had to break across a line or wrap around a graphics frame, that had to be handled. You could take a personal letter —Dear <Name>. You've won a <Prize>!—and use it to output a direct-mail campaign or do something less commercial. Since RP depended on documents and documents were the very heart of Star, Dan couldn't possibly just ignore them and do his own thing. This was an integrated system, and RP was part of it.

Dan had Cyril Costos, an XDS veteran, working on the document fields code. This part was also very slow going, but Cyril kept his head down and didn't complain. Somehow, he had survived the layoffs after Xerox went out of the computer business, and now, he was a solid nine-to-fiver who just did his work. Cyril didn't hang out with the UCLA Mafia or any other social group in SDD. He had his own friends from the XDS days and went to lunch with them or ate at his desk.

Aaron's group finished their traits design document and were now ready to explain it to the rest of the engineers. The meeting was billed as a design review, but everyone understood that no wasn't in the cards. Rather, the goal was to flesh out the details and find issues that Aaron hadn't thought of. Everyone filed into the large conference room.

Aaron stood at the front with the overhead projector and a small stack of transparencies alongside it. He put up the title slide that said, "Traits: multiple inheritance subclassing," followed by the names of his people.

"Thanks for coming. I'll assume you all read the document. What questions do you have? Does anyone need to hear the rationale for traits?"

Janet raised her hand, "Angela and I definitely need to be able to explain it to other people." Peter nodded in agreement.

Aaron's face reminded Dan of a math professor who reluctantly agrees to explain what proof-by-induction is, even though he feels everyone should already know that.

"Fundamentally, traits provide sharing." He continued into an overview of object orientation, how Star heretofore used single inheritance subclassing, and traits simply extended that to allow an object to combine several component abstractions. He talked about types and the operations defined by a type and how all that applied to Star objects. This was old hat to most of the engineers, but Angela hadn't heard it before. Finally, Janet intervened and offered to host a smaller session for her and others who needed to hear the basics. Aaron thanked her.

Dan put up his hand, "Can you start with an overview of the process? From defining the traits graph to the final integration."

Aaron smiled broadly, "As a matter of fact, that's the next slide," switching to a transparency with a flow chart. Everyone stared at it and waited for Aaron to say more. "You define the traits and the classes that include them here on the left, and then that file goes through Trait Analysis."

David spoke up, "So, that's a single point of failure for the entire system?" This was a rude question but a fair one. Everyone else in Aaron's group looked embarrassed.

"Yeah, that bothers us, too. Raymond's working on some solutions for that. We don't have anything that we're ready to talk about, though." Raymond looked eager to hold forth but held back after looking at Aaron, who continued.

"Trait Analysis uses the Mesa compiler to process the Defs, so we know how much data to reserve for each trait in each object."

Peter raised his hand, "Is the offset to a given trait's data the same in every class?"

He already knew the answer to this, and Aaron knew he knew. "No, Peter. It can be different. That's what Brian's been working on. Brian, do you want to explain?"

Brian dutifully stood up and wrote `MyData()` on the board. "The `MyData` proc is an `INLINE` that every trait calls on entry."

Brian went on to explain that, for some traits, the offset was the same in every object and thus a compile-time constant, but for others, it needed a runtime lookup. This resulted in a lengthy discussion involving almost everyone in the room. Dan could tell that this was something Aaron's group had argued long and hard about, as they deferred to each other often. Raymond was clearly fascinated by the computer science-y aspects of it. Brian took a broader view but respected Aaron's learning too much to openly contradict him, and David was always the systems guy who did what Michael called pick-and-shovel engineering. It was clear that traits was not what David would have designed.

David asked, "What's the runtime cost of all this?" "Right. As opposed to what we have now," added Peter.

Aaron countered, "In what sense?"

Peter waited for David to expound. "Does it *actually* save object code size? Have we done any measurements?" Dan looked pleased that the right question was being asked. Wasn't this how real engineering was supposed to be done, by measuring things?

Aaron started, "Intuitively, it has to because…"

Raymond interrupted, "You can prove it by counting lines of code. Instead of repeating the same code over and over in every class. Now, we just have it once."

David was always polite, "That's an *intuitive* argument, as Aaron said. What about hard numbers?"

Aaron stepped in, "Once we convert everybody, we'll be able to get those numbers."

Dan refrained from saying, "*By then, it'll be too late.*" Mark would not be pleased by open warfare breaking out in the Star team, and Dan and David both had to keep working with these people. Instead, Dan asked, "Have we talked to the Mesa compiler people about any of this?"

This was Aaron's department, "I *have* had discussions with them. They're fully committed for the next year, at least, but they've promised to address it after that."

The meeting continued with Janet explaining how she and Angela would run Trait Analysis and maintain two sets of Defs files during the conversion. The group talked about INLINE procedures and how much time they really saved and the impact on the working set of Star, meaning how much of the code had to actually be in real memory.

After the meeting ended, Peter and Cyril followed Dan back to his office. Peter closed the door and started ranting, "Why are we doing this? I think it's stupid!"

Dan was coming to hate this part of managing. Peter was only eight years younger than he was, but sometimes, it felt like an entire generation. Dan was supposed to be the grownup who kept his people motivated and productive, and supposedly, Charm School taught you that. But nothing prepared you for the reality of an unhappy employee.

Peter was right in many ways about traits. Furthermore, the Star project was not going his way, and he was pissed about it. He might quit, and while that might not be a *complete* disaster, it would be inconvenient. How long would it take Dan to hire a replacement, assuming he was even allowed to? Besides, Peter was productive and a lot of fun most of the time. They'd had a lot of spirited discussions on New Wave music, which Dan was strongly tempted to condemn entirely, but Peter defended it. Once, Peter persuaded him to see the Mystic Knights of the Oingo Boingo with Danny Elfman at a club in West LA. Dan thought they were a little over the top.[1]

Dan knew that having Peter talk to Mark wouldn't win him any points with Mark. Dan was supposed to manage this kind of thing, not just hand it off to higher management. "Well, it's a done deal. What can we do about it now?"

Cyril had been silent up to now, "Probably nothing. We should just figure out how to work with it."

Peter persisted, looking even more annoyed, "Can we talk to Mark?"

Dan felt anxious because he didn't want to take every little issue to Mark. But maybe for this one, it couldn't be avoided. Maybe Peter needed to hear it from the voice of authority, which Mark unquestionably was. No one ever won an argument with Mark, on any topic.

"Sure, go ahead. I've already talked to him about it." Peter left.

Cyril got right down to business, "So, what do you want me to do?"

Dan and Cyril talked about the next steps in the conversion to traits. Cyril explained the internal interfaces he was using now and asked how those were changing. Dan didn't know, so he said he'd set up another meeting with Aaron to iron it all out.

34

HOUSES

One morning in May 1979, Dan and Janet were going over a problem with the latest build when Grant knocked, "Hi, I can come back later if you're busy with something."

Dan looked at Janet to see if he should leave. "No, come in. Dan was just being a jerk as usual." Dan tried to look hurt.

Grant said, "I'm all settled in now. You should come up."

Dan looked confused, "Wait... I thought you lived up North."

"No, I transferred down here to the Tor project."

"Wow, I thought people only moved from South to North."

"I'm starting a new trend."

"Are you up on the second floor now?"

"Yep. Come up and visit sometime."

"What a thought. Is it like here?" Dan had never been on the second floor or anywhere else in the building.

Grant went to the door and made a show of looking in both directions, "Looks very similar. Anyhow, what are you doing for no-driving day tomorrow?" He looked at Janet, who had a quizzical expression.

"The company just said we're not supposed to drive alone tomorrow because of the gas rationing. They're going to station guards at the parking lots to check."

Dan already knew about this, but Janet didn't. "Don't know. Maybe Dan can come by and pick me up. Then, we'd be a carpool."

Grant flashed a look of displeasure for an instant but quickly erased it. He was hoping Janet would come to his house, and they could walk to work. "Do you live near Janet?"

"Hermosa. Janet's right on the way."

Grant recovered, "I *was* going to suggest we meet at my house and walk to work. It's only about a half-hour walk."

Dan asked, "Where do you live? Hawthorne?"

Grant looked vaguely insulted at the suggestion that he might live in Hawthorne, "Manhattan Beach, near Marine and Aviation."

"We could pick you up, too! You're right on the way."

Grant wasn't expecting this resolution, but there it was. He wrote his address on the whiteboard, which Dan copied down into his notebook. They agreed on a time tomorrow, and Dan and Grant both left.

The next day, Dan picked up Janet and then drove to Grant's house. It was a nice but modest tract house, like most of the homes in that part of Manhattan Beach. Dan honked the horn, and Grant came out and sat in the back seat. "Morning. How's everyone today?"

Dan answered. "Great! I saw a house this weekend that I'm making an offer on."

Janet slapped him on the shoulder, "Woohoo! Congratulations. Where is it?"

"Hawthorne. Or actually, the unincorporated part of Hawthorne. A little over a mile from work."

Grant said, "Can we go see it?"

"What, you mean now?"

Janet exclaimed, "Why not? It's close by, right?"

"Well, we can't go in. People are still living in it."

"But we can at least drive by," countered Grant.

Dan continued up Aviation and turned right on 135th. Neither Grant nor Janet had ever been over here, even though it was only a short walk from Xerox. It was the village of Hawthorne, famous, if at all, for the Beach Boys, who all grew up there, and the Mattel Toy Company on Rosecrans. Now, it was a solidly working-class suburb, with narrow streets and small houses that were fairly close together. Dan continued under the 405 freeway for a couple of blocks and turned on Shoup Avenue. He came to a corner, pointed out the window, and said, "There it is."

"Ooh, it's pretty!" exclaimed Janet. Grant agreed. Dan's new house, if he bought it, was a relatively large one-story home, which had obviously been built as a small two-bedroom in the 1950s and added onto at the back twice. It had a detached garage and a cinder block wall on the property line.

"How many bathrooms?" asked Grant.

"One and a half. The extra one was added on." "And they had permits for the additions?" Dan winced, "Who knows?" He drove on.

"Well, congratulations. What's the asking price, if you don't mind the question?"

Dan didn't. "$89,000. I'll probably offer 85."

Grant did some mental arithmetic, "So, you have to put $17,000 down unless you get a second mortgage." Janet interrupted, "I don't have that kind of money!"

Dan answered, "Me neither, and lenders frown on seconds. I'm going to borrow some money from my dad and brother, and they have to sign a statement that the money is a gift, not a loan, and that it doesn't have to be paid back," he laughed.

"But everyone knows it *does*."

Dan put his fingers to his lips, "Shhh!" They all laughed.

Grant asked, "What kind of interest rate are they quoting nowadays?"

"10.5%, hopefully."

Janet had never dealt with numbers this big. She was horrified to think of being chained to a mortgage for 30 years, but still, she figured she'd do it eventually, so she might as well find out. She asked, "So, what will the monthly payment be?"

Dan grimaced, "About $650, plus the payments to my dad and brother, *plus* property tax, *plus* insurance."

"Ouch," she said.

"Todd and Don are going to say they're rooming with me and paying me rent, too."

"And are they?" asked Grant.

"As a matter of fact, they are."

At Xerox, the guard at the parking lot entrance checked the number of people in the car and waved them through.

"Thanks for driving, Dan. And congratulations on the house." Janet agreed.

"Janet, when are *you* buying a house?"

Janet was embarrassed, "I guess I should before it's too late."

"Well, that's what everyone thinks. 'No one ever lost money on California real estate' is what the realtors all tell you."[1]

"With my luck, I'd be the first."

35

GAMES

I t was a Saturday in July when Dan moved into his house in Hawthorne. He'd bought the house for $85,500 after he'd offered 85K, and the seller had countered 86K. He had an epic scene in the real estate office, where he learned a life lesson—what your real estate agent *really* cares about, and it isn't you. He sat in her office, and she relayed the 86K counteroffer to him, "Offer them $85,500." The agent was distraught, "Oh, Dan! You don't want to lose the house for $500."

"Make the offer." She did, and it was accepted. At 3%, which was her half of the commission, Dan's counter-counteroffer had cost her $15. If the sale had fallen through, she'd have lost the entire commission—hence her anxiety.

He moved in with Todd and Don. Originally, it had two bedrooms that took up the entire width of the house, but one of the owners had added on two additional rooms, each the whole width. They didn't bother putting in a hallway to the additions, so you had to walk through one of the bedrooms. It was a one-of-a-kind floor plan.

Don took the bedroom that you had to walk through, and Todd took the second addition at the very back, which was more of a walled-in patio than a regular room. You could tell it was a patio at one time because a sliding glass door led to it, and you stepped down to ground level when you entered. It had two doors and so many windows that you couldn't possibly make it dark, but Todd didn't mind.

The first addition was set up to be their music studio. Todd and Don played jazz together a lot and had even put together a band with Don as the leader. They had a drummer and bassist but no horns. They named the house Shoup Street Studios, and Dan had matchbooks made up with that title. They practiced while Dan was in the front of the house, and since there were two walls between them and him, it wasn't too loud.

At work, a new multiplayer game, MazeWar, appeared that took advantage of the network and the fact that everyone had their own Alto. Your screen showed a big maze, and you were a rat in it, or actually a giant eyeball. You had a global view of the entire maze, but it only showed your rat, and below that view, you had a rat's-eye view down the corridors where you saw the other rats. When you saw one, you fired. If you hit them, they were randomly relocated, and you earned a point. If they saw you first, you were the one who was killed and relocated. Then, someone else would see you first and kill you again.

The controller was the keyset, which all Altos had, but almost no programs used. Most users just stored theirs out of sight somewhere until MazeWar came along, and they dusted them off. Often, they didn't work well anymore, and the Support group was flooded with repair requests.

The keyset was about six inches by six inches, with five keys, each slightly larger than a stick of gum. You moved forward or backward, turned, peeked around corners, or fired. It was insanely fast, and it was almost certain that some player was much quicker than you, and you got killed over and over. Dan played it for a while, but it was just too twitchy for him. A lot of programmers were hooked, though. You'd walk down the halls and hear people yelling as they killed someone or got killed.[1]

Dan preferred the Trek game, which was also networked and multiplayer, because it was more cerebral. Your ship fired phasers or photon torpedoes or put up its shields to defend against other players' weapons. The shields used your energy, so you couldn't just fly around with shields up all the time. It had 10 or so star systems, named after the brightest stars like Arcturus, Vega, and Sirius, and you jumped between them by hitting warp speed. You could lay down bases, which let you recharge, but other players could see and destroy them. Once you had bases in every star system, you won the game. That was the goal Dan worked for. He didn't engage in combat unless he had to.

Dan figured out that he could lay bases way out in the far reaches of the star systems where other players wouldn't see them and stealthily put one in each star system, without anyone catching on. It was a little like shooting the moon in Hearts, except that in Hearts the others figure out you're doing it and warn each other. In Trek, sometimes no one knew you were close to winning, until that magic moment when they were told they'd lost. If someone saw you, though, you'd have to fight them and maybe lose everything you'd built. It appealed to Dan more than MazeWar.

Several times, Dan stayed late playing Trek after everyone had gone home, which meant 7 or 7:30 at the very latest. He was too hungry to stay much longer, and there was no food available except vending machines, and no restaurants were nearby. After a couple of weeks of this, he tired of it and never played Trek or MazeWar again.

He'd arrive home and find Todd and Don already there. The two of them never seemed to cook. Dan was used to buying food at the supermarket and making dinner for himself, but their attempt to share cooking duties and make dinner for each other didn't last much more than a week. Dan was never really sure what they ate or when. They definitely were not into cooking. Sitting down together to eat was not something they ever did.

Todd was a Christian, although he didn't seem to go to church often or even talk about it much. He didn't swear, but he didn't have any problem with anyone else doing it. He also didn't engage in premarital sex, although Dan didn't want to ask about it.

Don was the more driven of the two, musically. He wrote songs and hectored Todd to practice sight-reading more. He'd had a lot of piano training when he was younger and had played in bands full-time. He always warmed up with "Joy Spring," which turned Dan on to Clifford Brown, the great trumpeter.

Their drummer, Mark, was from a wealthy family and lived up in Palos Verdes. He also wrote music. One of Mark's songs changed time signatures in almost every bar, and it was naturally called, "Can You Find the Time?" It was insanely difficult to play, so it required endless practicing. Dan couldn't stand it.

Dan had always been a musician wannabe. If he'd only practiced the guitar more as a teenager, he thought, he would have been in rock bands, played in front of thousands of fans, all those fantasies every guy had. Later in college, he'd started taking jazz records out of the library and going to see the acts who came to campus—Herbie Hancock, Chick Corea, and lots of less-famous names. Now, he was living with *actual* musicians and having other ones come to his house. He was thrilled.

One Saturday afternoon a few weeks after they moved in, Todd and Don held their first full rehearsal in the studio. They now had a bass player, Ted, who played a bass that was guitar-style but fretless. Dan hung out while they set up. He already knew that music rehearsals are not performances, but even so, he was quickly bored. Don had sheet music for some of his original songs, and he distributed it to them all, along with Mark's original songs, "Can You Find the Time?" and "You Know What I Mean, You Know?" They worked through the songs, rarely playing one all the way through.

Todd had seen Don's songs before, but he hadn't learned them thoroughly enough for Don's exacting ear. The other guys, of course, didn't know them at all and had to sight-read. Mark's songs were so difficult to play that Dan eventually decided he'd rather undergo a root canal without anesthetic than listen to that. He went back to the front of the house. Fortunately, jazz bands aren't usually as loud as rock bands. They didn't play any songs he recognized.

After a couple of hours, they took a break, and Dan met the bassist and drummer. After some preliminaries, Dan was curious about what they hoped to do. "So, do you guys have a name?"

Don answered for them, "No, we haven't even talked about it."

Ted and Mark threw out some wild ideas, but they were all too obscene to actually use.

"So you're doing all original music? I didn't hear any standards."

They looked at each other, and Mark said, "We already know how to play the standards. You can't get ahead unless you play your own music." Everyone nodded.

Dan wanted to say, *"But your original songs aren't any good,"* but he realized that would not be well-received.

Don added, "If you go see any of the jazz guys who are happening now, they *might* play a few standards, but they emphasize the original stuff."

Mark agreed, "Also, to put out an album, you need your own stuff. If you do other people's songs, you have to pay royalties."

Dan was getting schooled in the realities of the music business. He found it disillusioning. The more they talked, the more he realized that they didn't listen to jazz for its own sake, either—it was market research. They'd passed the passive-listening phase a long time ago. He mentioned that he'd seen Art Blakey at The Lighthouse, and they were respectful of that, but Blakey was too old for them.

That night, everyone but Dan headed up to The Baked Potato in Studio City to see Lee Ritenour or Larry Carlton or someone trendy, he forgot who. Dan wasn't much interested in finding out who was making it commercially. He thought that most of those guys were technically really skilled and could sight-read a chart and play it perfectly in one take, but they still had no soul.

He went to bed early because he was going on a Sierra Club hike the next morning. He packed a lunch and drove up to the VA building parking lot on Wilshire, where the group met at 8:30 to form carpools. Today, they were hiking in the West Valley and were going to walk through the set for *M*A*S*H*. [2]

A collection of cars in the middle of the vast empty parking lot signaled the Sierra Club group. He parked and joined one of the little groups clustered around a leader with a clipboard. In one of the groups, he saw Janet in a circle of mostly guys and waved to her. He figured they'd talk later on the hike. She had told him that he would have time to talk to almost everyone on these hikes.

Dan did a quick check of how many women there were—less than half, but still quite a few. He found these hikes a surprisingly good place to meet women. In fact, for a while, he was leaving with someone's phone number on about half the hikes he went on. This one looked promising, too.

After 10 minutes or so, the leader asked for everyone's attention and delivered his standard lecture about where they were going, how long the hike was, when they'd stop for lunch, and when they'd get back, and asked them to form carpools to drive to the trailhead. Dan hated driving a full car, so he usually tried to get in someone else's carpool. "Anyone who's willing to drive, raise your hands. Everyone else, line up behind them." The Sierra Club had a standard per-mile fee that each rider paid the driver for gas, actually a pretty generous amount, so you made a few dollars by driving.

Dan stood behind a burly guy in a T-shirt that said, "Rule 1: Don't sweat the small stuff. Rule 2: It's all small stuff." He was driving a 1974 Chevy Monte Carlo, which was a gigantic boat of a car and not very Sierra Clubby. *"This guy didn't make much money from the gas allowance."* The back seat had lots of room, though, and three others rode in the car.

Bill got on the 405 at Wilshire and headed over the hill. The five all introduced themselves. Bill was a clerk at an auto parts store, and the other person in front, Will, was a math teacher at a private high school. In the back, besides Dan, were Cathy and Jacki. Cathy was a lawyer with the EPA, and Jacki was a nursing supervisor at a major aerospace company. Dan occasionally met another computer programmer on these hikes, but they seemed to have normal jobs. Oddly enough, considering what the rest of the country thought about Southern California, there was never anyone from the film, TV, or music industries. Dan didn't know what those people did on weekends, but they sure didn't go on Sierra Club hikes.

Going on one of these hikes was a complete break from high tech, and Dan loved that. He didn't worry about confidentiality. If he told someone *exactly* what he was working on at Xerox, they'd say, "Xerox? Do they make computers?" He could tell them anything, including the truth, and they wouldn't remember any of it.

They talked about other Sierra Club events they'd gone on. Will was very proud of having done the 10-week Basic Mountaineering Training Class (BMTC) that the chapter held every winter. He held forth about BMTC for most of the drive —how you learned to use an ice axe to arrest your fall down an icy slope, orienteer with a map and compass, and rock-climb at Joshua Tree out in the desert. The climax of the class was a snow-camping expedition in the Sierras. Jacki and Cathy asked him a lot of questions about the class. Dan thought that camping in the snow didn't actually sound fun, but he made a mental note to sign up for the class next winter. If this was a rite of passage for Sierra Clubbers, he figured he should go through it.[3]

They exited the 101 at Las Virgenes in Calabasas and drove to Malibu Creek State Park, where most of the carpools had already arrived. Everyone gathered in the parking lot, and whoever had to use the bathroom headed off. The leader waited for everyone to return, and they set off.

On the trail, the group naturally broke into little clusters of two to four, small enough that everyone could hear each other. They walked through the *M*A*S*H* set, which was deserted except for security guards. They saw where the opening scene with the helicopter was shot, supposedly in Korea. The trail went right past the mess tent, the OR, and all the buildings you saw on TV. "Only in LA!" Dan said to the guy he was walking with. "Everything is a movie set."

He figured Will *must* know all about the movie sets you could visit on a Sierra Club hike, and he was not disappointed. Will went on for at least 20 minutes about Vasquez Rocks, in the desert near Palmdale, which had appeared in the *Star Trek* movies, *Blazing Saddles*, *Gunsmoke*, *Maverick*, and tons of other Westerns. Will told Dan that he really needed to check the schedule for a hike up there. He said he would.

He talked to several women on the hike, but he really didn't connect with anyone. Still, it was nice to have a relaxed conversation without having to shout over a crowd. No one had the slightest knowledge about what Xerox was doing in computers and weren't much interested, either. It was wonderful. Someone from the Palo Alto office once told him that if you went to a party in Silicon Valley, they might ask you at the door, "Hardware or software?" and then direct you to the appropriate group. LA was not that way at all.

The group went to dinner afterward. As they separated, Dan saw several guys ask Janet for her phone number, which she appeared to give them. He got back home around 7:30. Don and Todd were out. He read the Sunday *LA Times*, which he hadn't had time for in the morning, watched the news, and went to bed.

The next morning, Todd rushed into the kitchen, toasted a slice of bread, spread peanut butter on it, and ran out holding it. He and Don roller-skated to work sometimes since it was only about a mile, and today was one of those days. Dan was in his office when Todd appeared, out of breath and holding his roller skates.

"You won't believe what just happened to me!"

"You roller-skated to work, I guess?"

"Yeah, but after I got to Xerox!"

It didn't look like he'd skated through the halls, so Dan had no clue.

"A Security guard chased me through the parking lot!"

Dan laughed out loud, "I guess they're not used to roller skaters."

"He was shouting, 'Sir, this is private property!'"

"You're lucky he didn't fire his gun. Did you flash your badge?"

"No, I just yelled back, 'I sure hope so!'"

Making fun of the Security guards—the week was off to a good start already.

Janet appeared and caught the tail end of Todd's tale. She asked Dan if he'd enjoyed the hike. He didn't want to ask about the guys she'd met, but he told her about the Basic Mountaineering Training Course. She was interested, and they both thought they'd sign up for it this coming winter.

36

THE BIKE TRIP

Todd returned from his 1979 Christmas vacation engaged to a woman he'd just met. Don and Dan were shocked, but not that shocked. It was the sort of thing Todd would do.

He'd gone to Seattle to see his family at Christmas, as usual, and somehow he met Marge, who was a Christian just like he was. One thing led to another, and now, they were getting married. Todd was going to move out of the house, as soon as his transfer to Xerox Palo Alto could be worked out. For some reason, Marge was willing to move to the Bay Area but not to Los Angeles. Transfers from South to North were generally discouraged, on the theory that *everyone* would move if they could, and Xerox didn't want that. In any case, it was allowed for family reasons.

Todd went to work as a Mesa tester, which might have been a demotion in most engineering groups, but Jim, the manager of Mesa, didn't see it that way. The testers had to write programs and understand Mesa as well as any of the developers. If the system was buggy, it failed.

Before that, however, Todd and Don's jazz group had a gig. Mark's parents, who were wealthy and prominent in Los

Angeles society, were hosting a fundraiser for Governor Jerry Brown's Presidential campaign. It was at their Palos Verdes house, and the group was invited to play. Don and Todd's jazz group would not play their original songs. Their orders were to play quietly with nothing too loud or obtrusive.

Dan invited himself along, and he was so excited. Maybe the Governor would bring Linda Ronstadt to the event. They had been dating, although he wasn't sure if that was still going on. Dan's friends from college used to joke about a single Governor's Ultimate Pickup Line, and the winner was, "Hey, how'd you like to be First Lady for the night?"

The night of the fundraiser came, and Dan drove up to PV with Don and Todd. Security guards checked the guests for weapons, and Dan helped the group set up their instruments. This gave him a chance to use a line he'd always wanted to speak, "I'm with the band!"

Waitresses circulated with glasses of champagne and trays of hors d'oeuvres, and elegantly dressed women and besuited men hobnobbed and acted important. Dan was disappointed to find out that the Governor himself was not attending, let alone Linda Ronstadt, but he sent his father, Pat Brown, a former Governor, in his place.

Dan was standing at the food table when the former Governor walked in, surrounded by his aides and hangers-on. Dan shook hands with Governor Pat, who was about to start a conversation with him when an aide leaned over and whispered in his ear, and they walked on. Dan figured the message must have been, "Don't bother with that guy... he's nobody." He was amused and not at all offended since, in a fundraising sense, he *was* nobody. The Governor had important donors to court.

Before the wedding, Marge came down to visit, and Dan met her. Marge and Todd slept in separate rooms since they weren't married yet. She was an accountant, quite conservative, and apparently more religious than Todd was. When she recounted how they became engaged, she said, "God told me to follow this man!"

Todd moved out, and now it was just Don and Dan. Don was somewhat depressive. He did not have the infectious good humor that Todd had, and Dan realized that the two of them had little to talk about. They didn't fight about anything, but Don was now more of a lodger than a roommate. Raymond from work had come to the house occasionally before, but now, he seemed to hang out almost every day. Dan realized that when you have a roommate, you also get all their friends.

Don and Raymond hung out almost every night, smoking pot and playing chess. He came to realize that if Raymond always looked stoned, it was because he really was. Dan couldn't stand him. He was an acolyte in Aaron's traits team and really believed that Aaron's multiple inheritance system was almost divinely inspired. Whenever Dan or any of his group had some practical question about Aaron's code, which was often, they all avoided Raymond if anyone else was available.

Dan began to hate the sight of Raymond's car parked in front of the house when he came home at night. He'd come in the front door and find the two of them playing chess at the dining room table, with the smell of pot heavy in the air. It only took a month or so of this before he had a talk with Don and asked him to move out. Don was not at all offended, and they continued to be friends. Finally, Dan had his house to himself. His salary had continued to rise, and he didn't need the money from roommates anymore.

At work in early 1980, SDD was now under a Dallas organization, the Office Products Division, with a new manager, Harold Esposito. Dan didn't experience any change in his day-to-day work, and management reassured everyone that nothing would. "OPD is fully committed to the Star program going forward blah blah blah," was what they all heard.

"Maybe we'll get a new T-shirt out of it."

The Star effort was growing rapidly. The product code was well past 75,000 lines, with over 25 programmers, including a group working on JStar, the Japanese Star. They had regular meetings everyone had to attend, thankfully not every day. Dan often went home around 6, ate dinner, and then came back to work. Usually, a few other programmers who'd never left were still working. It was beginning to resemble all large software development projects.

On a Wednesday in June, Dan was talking to Brian, who mentioned that he'd bought an Apple II personal computer.

Dan was incredulous.

"You spent $3,000 for a computer? What the fuck for?"

Brian was not defensive, "I just thought it'd be fun."

"And is it?"

"Well... it has some good games on it," Brian laughed.

Dan didn't see any reason to make fun of Brian, but he was not especially curious about it. He used a computer all day long, and the last thing he'd ever want to do was go home and do it some more. He mentioned Brian's expensive little toy to Grant when he ran into him in the cafeteria, and Grant told him about how Apple had visited PARC in 1979. Dan was only mildly interested. He knew that PARC was always giving demos. Researchers flowed back and forth between PARC and Stanford, as well as other universities. The Alto had been around since 1973, so it wasn't exactly a secret. He was pretty sure they hadn't shown them Star. That was the real secret Xerox was working on, but it was barely functional.

"Really? What did they see?"

"I think they just saw an Alto with Smalltalk. Not sure."

"Did we tell them about Star?"

"I doubt it."

Grant was leading a bike ride the coming Saturday, June 7, which Dan and Janet were both planning to go on, so they talked about that for a while. Dan asked Grant how he was getting along in LA and how it compared to the Bay Area, but

Grant didn't say very much. He asked him about the Tor project but didn't find out much about that, either. "*Typical Grant. Won't tell you what he's thinking, ever.*"[1]

On Saturday, Dan and Janet met at Grant's house since his car had a bike rack on the roof big enough for all three bikes. They hoisted the bikes up and tied them down, Janet hopped in the front seat and Dan in the back, and Grant drove over the hill to Westlake Village in the Valley.

Grant broke the silence, "How are things in SDD-land? Star moving along?" He didn't want to say anything sarcastic yet.

Janet answered for the two of them, "Steaming ahead. Do you miss it?"

Grant chuckled, "Oh, every day. It's so *boring* working on something Xerox can sell."

Dan jumped in, "Wait… I didn't know they built copiers up on the second floor. I thought those were all in Rochester."

"A little-known fact, Dan… the laser printer is actually a worthwhile product."

Janet said, "Now, we feel better. But no more work talk. It's a Saturday."

"Just one more thing, though. I told Dan about the Apple visit to PARC last year. Did you hear about it?"

Janet hadn't, and she'd barely heard of Apple. Dan explained that it wasn't the Star that they saw, just the Alto and Smalltalk. She didn't show much interest.

Grant was dying to hear about Janet's personal life post-divorce, but with Dan in the car, he couldn't risk any personal talk. "Janet, what do you do when you're not at work?"

She knew what he was looking for, but she played dumb. "Oh, work keeps me pretty busy these days. Sometimes, I go on hikes with the Sierra Club. Dan does those, too."

"Yep. Janet introduced me to that!"

Grant pretended interest, "Hiking, huh? Sounds like fun. Where do they go?"

Dan and Janet told him about some of the hikes they'd gone on. Dan almost said that he saw Janet give her phone number to a guy at the Malibu Creek Park hike, but he thought better of it. Instead, he asked Grant, "Are you doing much bike riding down here?"

Grant told them about the Los Angeles Wheelmen, a cycling club he'd joined. They hadn't heard his stories about trying to be a serious bike racer when he was younger. Neither of them knew anything about racing, so that topic occupied them most of the way up to the 101 in the Valley.

As they were heading west on the 101, Dan decided to risk a little political talk. Neither Janet nor Grant seemed very passionate about it—at least, he'd never heard Janet say anything political.

"Janet, did I tell you I shook hands with *former* Governor Brown?"

Grant exclaimed, "Wow. And to think we actually know you." They all laughed.

"It was at a fundraiser for Jerry Brown's Presidential campaign. Todd and Don's jazz band played at it."

Janet was confused, "Wait. Brown's not running for President, is he?"

"Not anymore, he's not."

"And he didn't even come to his own fundraiser?"

"Governor Moonbeam... he'll never live that down."

Dan mentioned that it was the columnist Mike Royko from Chicago, his hometown, who gave him that nickname, and it stuck.

Grant asked, "Can I do a *little* bit of work talk? You guys know we put Altos in Congress and the White House?"

Dan said, "Yeah, I heard about that. How's that working out?"

"Alright, I guess. The reason I mention it is that the program is being run by ASD, Jerry Elkind's group, and they were the ones who told me about the Apple visit."

"Interesting. Why did *they* hear, and we didn't?"

"They talk to different people, I guess. It's not like it was a big secret."

Janet interrupted, "Seriously, that's enough work talk!

Grant, where do we get off the freeway?"

"Lindero Canyon Road. Quite a ways to go yet."

"Does anyone have any vacations planned?"

Grant had a bicycling trip in the south of France planned for July, and they talked about that and other trips Janet and Dan were taking, which weren't nearly as exotic as Grant's. They exited the freeway and parked near an elementary school, where a few of the others were already setting up their bikes. When all the riders arrived, Grant told them about the rides they could take, and let them choose. One group chose a route that went up Mulholland Drive to Malibu Lake and set off, with Grant in the lead. Grant didn't have route sheets printed up, so they just had to follow him and stay together. Grant planned to wait at intersections for the group to reform. He was the strongest rider by far, so he stayed in front, leading the way.

Dan rode with a couple of engineers, Steve and Sandy, who he knew only slightly. The rest of them were in small clusters behind him. Janet rode with Peter Eisen and another guy Dan didn't know, and behind them were three men and a woman from the LA Wheelmen, the bike group Grant belonged to. They looked like they were conserving their energy for a big competitive sprint up the hill.

When Dan joined Steve and Sandy, they seemed to be in the getting-acquainted phase. Steve was in his late 20s, around 6' or so, although it was hard to be sure since he was on a bike. He was neither skinny nor fat nor muscular—he was average in every way. He'd gone to a Big Ten school, too, so straight down the middle again. He recounted how someone questioned his eating pizza for dinner when he'd just had it for lunch, and he quipped, "Help me out here... I don't see the problem."

Sandy was a Japanese-American woman, fairly short, who'd gone to MIT. Both of them had been at Xerox for a couple of years, starting right out of school. Steve and Sandy asked him a lot of questions about the Star project. "How are you guys still on Star? We hear all these stories."

Dan smirked, "What have you heard? No one tells me anything!"

Sandy laughed, "Oh, just that the hardware is a failure. And, it moves further out instead of closer."

Steve said, "Yeah, like that."

"Oh, that? Old news." Dan chuckled. "We killed you in softball, though." The Star softball team had, in fact, beaten the Tor team last week, after a mighty home run in the last inning by a guy in Operations, someone Dan didn't even know before the team was formed. Dan had noticed the Palo Alto people were always surprised to hear they played softball down in El Segundo, too. *"Maybe they thought they invented softball."*

Steve realized the topic of Star was going nowhere, and they moved on to softball, biking, and other neutral subjects. Dan didn't deal with printers, so he couldn't ask them much about what they were doing. He already knew it was some kind of lower-cost laser printer that used Mesa, and a lot of people were working on it, but he didn't find out much more than that. He wasn't too interested in printers, which he felt guilty about since that was Xerox's business. On the other hand, most of the folks he worked with on Star felt the same way. They were not old Xerox hands like Grant—they were here for the Office Information Systems projects.

The ride was around 25 miles, with about 1,800 feet of climbing. It was quite a workout, or at least it was for everyone except Grant, but nobody complained because it was what they came for. The people from Grant's bike club suddenly came alive when they reached the hill, and the three of them plus Grant awed everyone else with their hard pedaling. They had a very late lunch in Westlake and then headed home.

Dan took the back seat again. He figured Grant wanted to talk to Janet more than to him. They were much less talkative than on the ride up since everyone was tired.

Janet wanted to know how Grant was coping with his move down South, "How's the house working out?"

"Oh, it's fine. Smaller than the house I had in Dallas, but that's California for you."

Grant asked Dan about his house, while Janet waffled, as usual, about whether and when she'd take the plunge into real estate. Grant wondered if maybe she was expecting to remarry and that was part of her indecision. He pictured her moving in with him, and he was glad he bought a larger house than he needed.

They arrived at Grant's place, and Dan took his bike down off the roof, thanked Grant, and left. Janet lingered behind.

37

EVEN DADS HAVE HEARD OF PCS

J anet drove down Marine Avenue toward home. "*What just happened?*"

Grant had invited her in, and not wanting to be rude to a guy who'd just asked her on an outing and driven her to it, she agreed. Grant's house was immaculate. It looked as though nobody lived in it, and his taste in furnishings was impeccable. Everything was smart and modern, but nothing too outlandish. She couldn't imagine him ever having a dog or cat. It would be way too messy.

He'd opened a couple of beers for them, and they sat out on his patio. She decided to keep things professional and stick to safe topics since they'd never seen each other outside of work, and maybe, he wasn't even interested. Or perhaps she wasn't. She asked him about his experiences buying his house, and they talked about Manhattan Beach traffic and the gas lines. He kept trying to be her mentor, though. He asked about her management training classes and the people from the rest of the company who attended and told her about his contacts in Rochester and Stamford and what the corporate politics were around printers. It was interesting, but she heard enough business during the week. Some people never know when to turn it off.

When Grant talked about his move to the Tor project and how smart it was, it reminded her of when Ken pushed her to go to Hughes. But at least he picked up on her lack of interest much faster than Ken had. Jeez, *that* guy just never quit! But Grant backed off—she had to give him that.

She didn't want to stay a long time, so after about a half-hour, she pleaded the need to go home, leaving the impression that she had a date that night, although she didn't. At the door, she went to hug him, and he kissed her on the lips. It was quick, but she kept replaying that moment. *"Was he trying for more?"* Did she want more? *"Not now, for sure."*

At home, she checked her telephone answerer. This thing was so cool and was one of her first purchases after the divorce. It cost a couple of hundred dollars, but it was so worth it. No more sitting at home in case someone called, and she didn't have to talk to people if she didn't feel like it.

At first, the people who called were freaked out that they were talking to a machine and not a human, but they got used to it. Except for her mother, who would probably never leave a message longer than, "This is Mom!"

She had a message from her dad, Len, *"Hi, sweetie! I just had some questions for you since you're the computer whiz. Give me a call."*

Len was a financial analyst for Chrysler. Her parents were divorced, and she'd grown up with her mother. But her dad had always encouraged her in her technical pursuits, attended her graduation, and boasted to his friends about his computer genius daughter. She called him right away.

"Hi, Dad! I got your message."

"So, these telephone thingies really work! How's the weather out there?"

"Oh, it's perfect, as always. How about there?"

"Not too bad, considering. How's your health?"

"It's fine. I was out bicycling when you called."

"I'll get right to the point... one of my colleagues at the office brought in his personal computer. Aren't you working on something like that?"

"Well, ours isn't out yet. What kind is it?"

"It's an Apple II."

"I haven't seen those. How is it?"

"It's cute. Like a little TV set on top of a box. Is that what you're building?"

"Well, I think ours is a little bigger. Is he using it for work, somehow?"

"That's the interesting thing. It has this program where you put in all your numbers, and when you change one, the others all change automatically. The kind of stuff I spend hours doing, and this thing does it in a flash!"

Janet knew the numbers-crunchers at Xerox and TRW had programs like that on their terminals, but she had never used them. Computers were really good at doing arithmetic. This was why big companies bought them in the 1950s and 60s. But her dad was excited enough to call her, so maybe she was missing something. "Can't you get your computer department to program that for you?"

"Yeah, but they say they have a six-month backlog for new applications. And then, you have to sit through meeting after meeting justifying it. Who has time for that?"

"Okay, but then how do you load the data *into* the Apple?"

"Well, you key it in manually, I guess. That's the only bad part I can see."

"Yeah. Are you going to buy one?"

"I don't know. I'm intrigued, but it's a lot of money, and Chrysler won't pay for it. You can't get me a discount, huh?"

She laughed. "'Fraid not, Dad! Different company."

"Just thought I'd ask."

"Maybe when the Xerox one comes out, I'll see what I can do!"

They talked about the family back in Detroit and her life since the divorce. He asked if she was seeing anyone, and she said she wasn't. Len liked Ken well enough, but he'd never really thought of him as a son, so he didn't much regret losing him. Janet said she'd see Len and the entire family at Thanksgiving, as always.

After the call, Janet thought. Two mentions of Apple in a single day just *had* to be a sign. But nobody at Xerox had mentioned it. She decided to ask around on Monday.

Back at his house, Grant mulled over Janet's visit. He had a master plan to entice her to leave Star but for some job not working with him so that Xerox corporate policy wouldn't prohibit their relationship. He could be her mentor as she rose up the corporate ranks. With two big Xerox salaries, they'd be filthy rich and could buy a house anywhere.

But did she really think of him *that* way? It was hard to tell. She didn't pull away when he kissed her goodbye, but she didn't exactly respond, either. Was this going to be, "I just want to be friends with you," yet again? He hadn't actually asked her out on a regular date, however. That would be the real test.

His move to LA had worked out. He had a great job managing people again and was working on a product with a real business plan, and moreover, it was one that Xerox's 4,000 salesmen knew how to sell. He lived only a couple of miles from the beach, so the smog was almost non-existent, and in LA, he didn't find this suffocating sense that you *had* to be liberal, wine-drinking, and snobbish. In LA, everyone took you as whatever you said you were.

He'd discovered that, whereas people in the Bay Area hated LA folks and felt immensely superior, the feeling was not reciprocated. "*They hate us? Why? We don't hate them,*" was what most Angelenos would have said. He washed his car and watered his lawn and didn't feel the slightest shame about it. He read the *LA Times* and thought every day about how much better it was than the *Chronicle* or *The Mercury News* up in the Bay Area. LA had better museums and just as many great restaurants, although they were spread out more. The downtown wasn't much, admittedly, but then, nobody went downtown.[1]

38

A MANAGER'S LIFE IS NOT AN EASY ONE EITHER

Dan was checking his mail at 9:00 am Monday when Janet knocked. "Hey, great ride Saturday!" He agreed. "So, you'll never guess what my Dad called about on Saturday."

Dan pretended to think, then said, "Umm... nope. I don't think the coffee's kicked in yet. Tell me."

"He said some guy in his office is using his personal Apple computer at work, and it runs some kind of financial program."

Dan laughed, "I bet their MIS department is thrilled! Did he say what the program is called?"

"I think to him... it's just *the computer.*"

"You know, Brian bought an Apple. Maybe he can give us a demo."

"I'll ask him. I wonder why Apple wanted an Alto demo at PARC?"

"Maybe they can finish Star before we can. Speaking of which, what time will the integration be ready?"

They talked about the build schedule and the other changes that were going in, and Janet went back to her office. Just then, Peter walked in, and Dan braced himself for more

Peter unhappiness.

Aaron's traits system had become the default system. Multiple inheritance subclassing was the law of the land. Dan's Records Processing system had two views onto a records file—the table view and the form view. The form view was more for direct mail. Everyone thought it'd be pretty cool if the form letters you received in the mail didn't look so stupid.

Dear Mr. SMITH , You and the SMITH family at 123 Main St.

Anytown, Ohio

Have won a valuable prize blah blah blah!

The table view was a set of rows and columns, and since tables were something that existed in documents, too, RP was completely dependent on the tables code. The table view was being done by the number one favorite person in the world for both Dan and Peter, Raymond.

Peter sat down, "How was your weekend?"

Dan told him about the bike ride and asked him about his weekend. Peter had gone to two concerts by groups Dan had never heard of. Dan figured he must have a reason for being here. "So, what's happening?"

"The tables code doesn't work," Peter said with an expressionless face.

"What specifically doesn't work?" suspecting this was going to be a painful conversation.

Peter confirmed his suspicions, "Everything."

Dan just made the "come here" gesture with his right hand, asking for more information.

Peter walked around the room, "Raymond said his new tables code wouldn't affect RP, but now, I can't even open the table. I'm so sick of this shit!"

"Did you tell him about this?"

"Not yet. I thought you'd want to know."

"So right now, RP won't work at all in this integration?"

"Nope!"

Dan yearned for a person who'd solve problems on his own instead of bringing them to him, but that wasn't who he had. He could tell Peter on his performance review that he expected him to do that, but that was months away. Somehow, Mark never seemed to have this problem. If you complained about somebody to him, he'd just tell you to bring it up with them, and off you'd go.

He'd noticed that Peter would sometimes do that, too, but only after he'd vented. Dan tried that now, "Alright, I'll get Janet to hold up the integration. Can you try talking to Raymond?"

"Alright," Peter got up and left. *"Success!"* Maybe with any luck, the two of them could thrash it out, and he wouldn't have to go to Raymond, let alone Raymond's boss, Aaron.

Dan walked down to Janet's office. She wasn't in, but Angela was next door, and he told her about the RP problem. While they were chatting, David came in with a question of his own. Dan walked back to his office with him. He was one of the quickest and smartest programmers Dan had ever met, and he almost always learned something from him. "What's new with you?" Dan asked.

"Oh, I'm writing the specs for a new Mesa instruction, TextBlt." David pronounced it text-blit, and every engineer knew that blt stood for block transfer.

"TextBlt! I like it, BitBlt, but for text."

"Right. You know how BitBlt lets us move massive amounts of bits from one place to another, and we couldn't possibly do a bitmapped screen without it?" Dan nodded. "Well, taking a bunch of text characters, fetching their font representations, and applying their looks, like bold and italic, uses an ungodly number of cycles."

Dan winced. The slowness of the Star software was depressing for everyone. "That's for sure. TextBlt sounds a lot more complicated, though. You do a font lookup, you might have to transform the character if it's a superscript, or whatever… "

David cringed, "Well, yeah. I'm having a hard time bounding this thing. You don't want to hear all the details."

"Bounding the time it takes? I guess not. Anyhow, if it's a Mesa instruction, then it's done in microcode, right?"

"Right. I'm reading up on the microcode language right now."

"Have you shown this to the Mesa group yet? They're always making snide remarks about Star slowth. Maybe that'll shut them up."

"Next week, I'm on the calendar for their regular meeting."

Dan was impressed. Maybe Star *would* be fast enough someday. He knew that David always had a bunch of projects underway, though. "What else are you doing?"

David loved to talk about whatever he was doing, "I just got more memory, maybe enough for my Star machine, finally."

Dan winced again, "Yeah, you kinda need that to even run Star."

"Maxed that machine out. This is *way* more than we're planning on shipping."

"Way more."

"What does all this do to the unit manufacturing cost?"

"No clue."

"And now I'm wondering… what's the working set of the document editor?"

"You mean how much code has to be in memory all at once?" Dan knew perfectly well what working set meant, but he was stalling.

David finished his question, "So that it's not spending all its time swapping in code from disk? Yeah, that's a working set alright."

I don't think anyone's measured that," Dan answered.

"It'd probably be easy to get the size of the code brought in when you type a character."

"Is someone doing that?"

Dan realized he was now a representative of management in David's eyes. He could have told him they had a plan to do memory analysis soon when the software was stable, but he didn't see any reason to BS him. And, David wouldn't fall for it anyway.

"Not that I know. Maybe you should."

David laughed, "In my copious spare time?"

Dan replied with a smile, "Well, back to it!'

On his way back to his office to check his to-do list for the week, Dan had one of those regular reminders that constant interruptions were the price of being a manager. His boss stopped him in the hall.

"Marksy! Got a minute?" He had nicknames for everyone, usually a riff on their last name. Dan followed him back to his office, and he closed the door. Since he remained standing, Dan did as well. "Paul is super pissed about the general state of the development effort, especially the schedule. So... since

I'm taking it in the shorts, *you* are taking it in the shorts, too."

Dan just said, "Okay."

He continued, "We're having a managers' meeting at 1. I'll see you there."

Dan made it back to his office without someone stopping him, and he shut his door. He looked at the last schedule he'd set. Sure enough, they'd missed it, or at least, one could argue that they'd missed it. Some of the milestones were dependent on the tables code, and Peter had spent most of the last month struggling with that. Should he tell Peter that he, too, was taking it in the shorts? He debated with himself. Everyone had to be aware of the schedule and report when they couldn't make it.

On the other hand, what would Peter say? "*I told you the*

tables code didn't work." In fact, he had told Dan that to the point of nagging. No point in yelling about it now.

Managing sucked. *"Why did he want to do this again?"* The key must be in having a really thick skin like his boss did. Dan didn't have that. Or maybe, you needed to believe in your own rightness so completely that *nothing* was ever your fault, like Aaron. Dan didn't have that, either. Fuck it. He decided to go outside for a run and headed over to the locker room.

After his run, he ate at the cafeteria. It was still early, not even noon yet, so it was pretty empty. He saw Brian. "Mmmm! Lukewarm tasteless garbage," he said as he sat down.

"That was the daily special, but I just got the burger. Did you just come back from a run?"

"Yep. What's new with you?"

"Oh, just slogging, as usual. I went to see *The Empire Strikes Back* over the weekend."

"Oh, yeah? How'd you like it?" Dan and Brian had gone to the original *Star Wars* together over three years ago. With all the excitement back then, they'd waited in line for two hours. This movie had been out for a few weeks now, so it was a little saner.

"I really liked it. Especially the AT Walkers."

Dan laughed, "And finally, we have a black person in space."

"Yeah, what was his name again?"

"Lando Calrissian. Changing topics... how's your Apple computer working out?"

"Oh, it's still fun. I don't have that much time to play around with it nowadays, though."

"A lot of personal computers these days." Dan came to the point, "Anyhow ... did you hear Xerox gave the Apple guys a demo?"

Brian stared at him, "A demo of what? Why?"

"I heard it was just Smalltalk on an Alto. As for *why*, I have no idea."

Brian still looked incredulous, "Who gave it? The Smalltalk group? When?"

"It was at PARC, but I don't know who exactly. It was the end of last year."

Brian shook his head, "What's Apple going to do with it? Their own Star? Don't we own the patents?"

"You can't patent software."

"You can't?"

"Nope. You can't patent a mathematical formula, either. Or any law of nature."

"So, we don't have any protection at all?" Dan shook his head.

Brian leaned back and smirked, "Well, I'm sure there's a *very* good reason for all this. I'm just going to go work on documents now." He picked up his tray, and Dan followed him.

39

BUT THE SOFTWARE IS ALWAYS LATE

J anet arrived at the 1:00 pm managers' meeting with a feeling of dread. She was pretty sure Mark was unhappy, and since the latest integration was late, maybe the crowd would gang up on her. But she didn't think he'd stand for it. It was pretty hard to fool him.

Dan and Aaron came in looking expressionless. Ralf Richter, a recent addition to the group and the head of Graphics, had his typical Prussian stern expression. Howard, who was always pleasant and somehow never offended anyone, sat down with a smile and greeted everyone. Mark entered last and spoke first, "This last integration was kinda shitty. What went wrong? Anyone?"

No one spoke for a few seconds, then Aaron answered, "We've had a lot of trouble ironing out the kinks in the traits system, but the guys are working as hard as they can to overcome it. I think we're making pretty good progress, all things considered."

Dan somehow always had to be the naysayer, "The code doesn't work, though, except on Raymond's machine."

Ralf was a friend of Aaron's from graduate school and

nearly always defended him. He did so now, "My group has all the Graphics traits defined, and we're coding as we speak."

Mark was unimpressed with the happy talk, "That might be, but the schedule called for this to be done May 23."

Aaron had a sheepish look, "Oops."

Dan had the urge to do Steve Martin, "*Well, excuuuuuuuuu-uuuuuse me!*" but he stifled it. "*Neither the time nor the place.*"

Mark said, "This isn't a research project anymore. We have outside executives tracking our progress, and they notice when we miss a deadline."

Howard, always helpful, offered, "The range of uncertainty for something like this is pretty high. I wonder if we're setting unrealistic deadlines?" Aaron and Ralf nodded.

Mark was impatient, "But you signed up for them."

Everyone but Mark had the same thought, "*This really is a research project. No one knows how the fuck long it's going to take.*" But they knew that was not the answer Mark wanted to hear.

Janet felt relief that no one was pointing fingers at her. Mark was taking command as always, "Alright, here's what we're going to do."

Everyone sat up. "Janet, I want you to run unit tests before you accept a submission."

Janet made a note in her notebook and said, "We don't have a whole lot of unit tests right now, except for a few from Dan's and Howard's groups."

Aaron and Ralf knew the spotlight was on them. In the academic world where they'd both come from, testing was an afterthought, if it was done at all. The grad students just got their code working well enough for the professor to satisfy the funding agency, and then, the semester was over, and they left. Dan, Howard, and Janet had all come to Xerox from the industry, so they were more accustomed to unit tests.

Aaron tried to be helpful, "That's going to slow us down, but I can have David look into it." Ralf agreed.

Mark wasn't falling for it, "I'm afraid I need more than

that, Aaron. Janet, can you coordinate our testing strategy for us?"

Janet made another note, "What about the Star testing group? Can we ask them to help?"

Dan smirked, but everyone else remained expressionless. Mark eventually said, "They're focused on testing the finished product. Writing Mesa code is not their charter."

Dan knew, dimly, that he shouldn't be negative about other people in meetings like this. He just couldn't help himself now, though, "So what *are* they doing since we don't have a finished product yet?"

Mark looked ready to reply, and with exaggerated patience, but Howard spoke first, "I've seen their test plans."

Mark ignored Howard. "They're doing whatever they're doing. It's not *our* job."

Since Janet had the action item, she spoke, "I have some ideas on what a unit test should do. Should I put those in an email when the meeting is over?"

Mark looked appreciative, "Please."

Ralf objected, "Are we going to spend as much time on unit tests as we do writing code?"

Dan realized again how much he hated Ralf. Whereas Aaron was sort of passive-aggressive, Ralf left out the passive part. This time, for once, Dan resolved to let someone else carry the load.

Mark took it up, "Ralf, your code has to *work*. You aren't saving us any time if you check it in faster, but it's still flaky."

Ralf stiffened, and Aaron stepped up for him, "We can also end up writing test code that just becomes obsolete. When the code is fluid like it is now, what's the point of test code that just gets thrown away?"

Dan couldn't hold back any longer, "If you're not sure about the code, why are you checking it in?"

Aaron was about to respond, but Mark interrupted the

brewing fight, "Okay, okay. I think we have our direction. Is there anything else?"

Silence. Everyone just wanted to leave. Mark continued, "Remember, on July 28, we have an all-SDD meeting with Harold Esposito."

Ralf looked quizzical at that name, so Mark added, "The head of the Office Products Division. The boss of all of us."

Janet felt relieved. They hadn't tried to blame everything on her, and she was now in charge of fixing things, or at least *some* of them. She followed Mark back to his office. He sat down and invited her to sit as well.

"So, Janet. Are you up for riding herd on this crew?"

"Riding herd? I thought it was just coordinating unit tests."

"Depends on how you look at it, I guess."

Janet decided to just stick to the task. "How much testing do you want people to do? Basic sanity-checking, all-out coverage of every line of code, or something in between?"

She knew Mark had definite ideas, but he could be kind of Delphic sometimes. You had to draw him out. "I think we all want to avoid the sort of disaster this last integration was."

She laughed, "For sure!"

"People are just throwing code over the wall and saying, 'here, try this.'" She nodded. "So, do Ralf and Aaron have any test programs at all?" Janet shook her head. "And Dan and Howard have some, at least?"

"They have some. Not enough, but at least it's a start." Mark was silent. Janet offered, "How about if we start by saying every major component has to have some kind of test program? We can leave the level of detail open for now so that they can start small and build on it."

"Sounds like a plan. Let it go forth."

Janet was about to stand up, but then she sat back down, "Can I bring up something else?" "Of course."

"Performance. This thing is *awfully* slow."

Mark didn't want to talk about that, "We don't have our real hardware, the Dandelion, yet. You know what they say about premature optimization, right?" Janet didn't. "Something about it being the root of all evil."

She looked unconvinced, so he continued, "Contrary to what I said in the meeting, this really *is* a research project. We're doing something nobody's ever done."

Janet nodded, "It sure seems that way."

"Look, we have documents with embedded graphics frames, fonts, tables, the whole nine yards. Who else has ever done that?"

"Nobody I know of."

"When we have the software working on the real hardware, then we'll have to do some serious optimizing."[1]

Janet was unconvinced, but she didn't expect to make any more progress. She stood up, "Anyhow, thanks. I'll put

together a document about the testing."

"Yeah, let me know if you need me to do anything."

"Oh, boy. Am I being set up to take the blame?"

40

A FINE DAY OUT

Janet had four messages on her telephone answerer when she arrived home on Monday. The first was from Grant, the next from Ron, a guy she met on yesterday's Sierra Singles hike, one from Janie, a woman friend she'd met recently, and the last from Shelley from the former Hughes gang.

She called Shelley first. Ever since the divorce, Shelley kept her up to date on all the gossip in the old group. One of Shelley's hot items was that Ken was now seeing a woman who'd been on the UCLA tennis team, and it looked semi-serious. Ken self-consciously bragged about how she would let him win a point once in a while when they played tennis. She had an MBA from USC, worked in finance, and was probably making a bunch of money, maybe as much as Ken.

Janet thought she knew why Shelley always told her this stuff—she was married now and had one kid already and another on the way. Apparently, she couldn't fathom why anyone didn't want that. One of these days, Janet had to tell Shelley to knock it off, and that she didn't care what Ken did. Still, it was interesting. She was annoyed with herself for being interested, though. "*What a liberated man he is. Hope they're very happy together*," she muttered under her breath.

Grant had been asking her out for weeks now, plus there was the kiss, and it was getting awkward to keep putting him off. He did have some interesting date ideas, she'd give him that. He'd asked her to see Todd Rundgren at the Greek Theater back in May, but she'd pleaded other plans that time. One of these times, she'd probably go out with him, just for fun.

Ron, the guy she met on the hike, was an outdoorsy guy who worked for LA County in a job that didn't sound like it was well-paid. At first, she found the hikes refreshing because she met ordinary people who didn't work in aerospace or computers. But she discovered that normal people didn't earn much money, either—at least the ones who went on those hikes. Going out with a guy who's been brought up to pay for everything was weird when he knows you make more than he does. Maybe she'd return Ron's call tomorrow and go out with him once or twice.

She called Janie right after Shelley. Janie was a masseuse who lived in West LA, and she'd been active in Sierra Club for much longer than Janet. She'd taken the Basic Mountaineering Training Course last winter and had lots of tales of ice ax practice up in the San Gabriel Mountains and snow camp in the Sierras. Janie was a serious runner, and a couple of weeks ago, the two of them had run from Manhattan Beach to Venice and back. That was the farthest Janet had ever run.

Janie had gone on a weekend backpacking trip with another group in the Sierra Club, so they talked about that for a while. They made plans to meet up at the Singles hike on Saturday. But in the meantime, her cat Rocky was climbing on her shoulders, where he liked to rest. She'd been planning to go back to work after dinner, but she could feel her resolve melting as Rocky relaxed. "*Maybe tomorrow night.*"

The next day, she and Grant both flew up to Palo Alto and ran into each other in the departure lounge. Neither had known the other's plans. Grant wondered why she hadn't called him back, but he didn't want to ask.

Grant's job became more stressful when the 5700 copier/printer was announced. It used Mesa and an early release of Pilot, and since everyone knew he'd actually been in charge of Pilot, he was the go-to guy for all software issues. Now that the PARC technology was passing into the real world, the messy realities all fell on him.

Janet was sitting and talking with someone Grant recognized but had never met. He sat down next to Janet after introducing himself to the other person. Her name was Angela, Janet's assistant. "Janet, happy Tuesday. What are you doing up there today?"

"This is Angela's first trip up. We have a bunch of Star developers in Palo Alto now, so we're just paying a visit. How about you?"

Grant made the wiping my brow gesture, "Oh, man. You know we announced the 5700, right?"

"Vaguely."

Angela said, "Is that the new laser printer that uses Mesa?"

"Well, we're using the same technology Star's using... Ethernet, the Dolphin processor, the Mesa language, the Pilot operating system, the whole nine yards." "Oh, boy," Janet muttered.

"I guess that was sympathy?"

"Don't think we're not grateful to you for testing it for us!"

Grant laughed, "So now, we're the pioneers with arrows in our backs."

"And how's it working out?"

"It's, uh... challenging. That's why I'm going up there... to see if we can get some better hardware and a few other things."

"Well, Angela and I are visiting because we have new responsibilities."

"Oh, did they put you in charge of everything?"

"Almost. We have to coordinate unit testing now."

"Who was doing it before?"

Janet looked sheepish, "Well, it was kinda haphazard."

"Let me guess. *No one* was doing it?"

Janet pretended to be offended, "Well, not *no one!*" Grant laughed.

Angela had been smiling at the banter, but now she spoke up, "It varies by group. We're trying to bring everyone up to a minimum level so that we can run sanity checks when we do an integration."

"Makes sense. So Angela, what were you doing before this job?"

"Well, I have a degree in biology, but I wasn't finding a lot of good jobs in bio, so I took night classes at El Camino College, and then, I was a tech at The Aerospace Corp for a couple of years."

"And now, here you are."

Angela agreed, "Here I am."

"And, we're so lucky to have her," said Janet, putting her hand on Angela's shoulder.

Just then, they started boarding the plane. Janet and Angela sat together, and Grant was farther back, almost in the smoking section but not quite. He hated how his clothes reeked of smoke, merely from being in the airport, and then if he had to sit near the smokers on the plane, it was even worse. He made a note to himself to get to the gate earlier next time to get a better seat.[2]

At SDD, Grant's first meeting was with the Pilot group. Besides Lawrence, who had taken over after Grant left, there was Patrick and Phillip, whom Grant remembered, and a couple of new people.

After everyone sat down and exchanged pleasantries,

Lawrence opened the meeting, "As you probably know, Xerox announced a copier/printer built on Mesa and Pilot. Woohoo!" Everyone applauded.

"Grant is here to give us a progress report on the 5700. Hopefully, it's all good news?"

Grant smiled broadly, "Indeed. It's great to see our stuff actually being used. I use the word *our* loosely here since I haven't been part of Pilot for quite a while now."

Patrick said, "Wait! I thought I saw a module with your name on it."

They all laughed. "Someone forged my name!"

"But I suppose there are one or two *tiny*, insignificant little problems you came to talk about?"

Grant stood up and pretended to leave, "No, we're done here. That was it!" More laughter.

He sat down again, "Well, as you know, the memory situation is the big one. It's pretty slow."

Lawrence tried to remain expressionless, "Ah yes, the memory chips." Patrick and Phillip looked uncomfortable.

Grant continued, "And without a keyboard or console, it's difficult starting up the thing at times. Remember, this is a standalone device in our users' minds, not a computer."

Patrick replied, "Yeah, we're sorry about that, but I think we have a solution for you."

Grant looked pleased, "Excellent. Before I forget, one long-term thing, which I'm sure we're not going to resolve here, but I want to put it on the table." They stared expectantly, so he continued, "Mesa hardware. We'd like to drive the unit manufacturing cost down. I think a Mesa chip is something we ought to be talking about."

Lawrence said, "A Mesa chip. We were just talking to Michael about that yesterday. I can fill you in on the thinking."

They talked for a half-hour about Grant's issues. It turned out that someone in Procurement had gotten a great deal on memory chips and bought a gigantic quantity but, unfortunately, not the latest and greatest or the biggest. So, the Tor printer had to make do with the smaller ones, which limited it to 128KB when they'd been planning for 192KB. This had some unfortunate effects on their performance, and since pages per minute was what customers cared about, losing some of that was a big deal.

The biggest issue was the hardest to resolve, and that was the Dolphin processor. Star was not planning to use it and was beginning to test the real machine, the Dandelion. But Grant was stuck with the rejected old machine. It didn't really work reliably, and no one seemed to know how to fix it or make it cheaper, either.

"This is why I get the big bucks. The impossible takes a little longer."

The Pilot team consisted of software guys who didn't design hardware. They could sympathize with him, but their main focus was Star, not the 5700.

At about the half-hour mark, Lawrence spoke up, "We need to halt this because we have other issues to cover. You're welcome to hang around if you want, Grant."

Grant said he might leave, but he'd stay for now, and he'd try not to ask questions.

"Where are we on the Mokelumne release?"

He turned to Grant, "Actually Grant, this concerns you. Mokelumne is our next major release, scheduled to enter system testing on August 4. It's based on Mesa 6.0, and it supports the 10Mbps Ethernet."

Grant wrote the dates down in his notebook. He asked how Mokelumne was spelled. Phillip was about to quip, *"With one N,"* but Lawrence spelled it for him, explaining that the releases were named after California rivers.

A major piece of pride for SDD was that the Ethernet had been endorsed by Digital Equipment Corporation and Intel, so it was on its way to being a standard. This would make installing it a much easier decision for companies. Grant asked, "Is this the standard Ethernet we're pushing with DEC and Intel?"

"Good question. We do have a draft of the public spec, but we may or may not get DEC's and Intel's agreement by then." Grant made a note. Lawrence continued, "This release *will* be supported on the Dandelion, the hardware the Star will use. We're seeing really good reliability on that, which is excellent."

Grant thanked them and wandered out. He had some free time before his next meetings and wondered if Tony was around. Tony had given him a fantastic summary of the Star hardware situation, and he thought surely he would know what was happening on the Mesa chip or if such a thing was even planned. As luck had it, Tony was in. After some pleasantries, Grant brought up the issue.

"We just met with Michael yesterday about that. Lawrence was there, as you probably heard, and Ray."

Grant nodded, "I don't know Ray, but go ahead."

"Ray Holmberg. Anyway, various ideas were kicked around. Everyone knows that a VLSI version of Mesa is the way to go. The question is… who wants to do it? And especially, who's *able* to do it?"

"It's a big investment, I guess."

"Exactly. We meet with Intel all the time, and they obviously have the factories. So that's one possibility, but getting them interested is the hard part."

"A little Xerox money might help."

Tony answered, "Perhaps more than a little, but I doubt that Star's production volumes are big enough. But the most promising alternative is Fuji Xerox."

Grant sat up, "Japanese money. I like it already. So, do they want to do it?"

"Well, they love forward-looking projects like this. We just have to convince them that this is the right one."

Grant made a note. Tony identified the people at Fuji to talk to, and they discussed the fabrication facilities Fuji already had and were building, the lead times for a processor chip, the quantities needed to make it interesting for Intel and other U.S. manufacturers, and other issues. Grant thought this was a promising lead, although it would take a very long time to come to fruition. It was a huge commitment, and the Japanese took forever to decide anything. But he absolutely loved Tokyo. He'd even dabbled with learning a little Japanese before his last trip, and he'd learned business-card etiquette— always hold it with both hands and treat the card with utmost respect.

He spent the rest of the day meeting with the Mesa group about the plans for the next release, the hardware people about the processor his printer was using, and generally making people aware of the 5700. All in all, Grant thought it was a pretty good day. He passed Janet and Angela in the hall a few times but didn't do any more than wave.

Janet and Angela spent their day meeting with their new charges in Palo Alto. Two years ago, all product development for Star was in El Segundo, but by mid-1980, Star had become a vacuum cleaner for talent. They didn't have enough engineers down South to do it all, so several Palo Alto people were now contributing as well. Martin, who'd led the Functional Spec effort that defined the user interface, was currently leading the graphics effort, while Brooks owned Customer Programming (CUSP), a sort of macro language. Star had nearly 40 software engineers in all and about 125,000 lines of Mesa code.

Janet explained how she and Angela combined everyone's code and built it, with only a 56KB leased line linking North and South. However, within each location, they had the much faster Ethernet, so it was manageable most of the time. They didn't get enough credit for keeping the whole thing going, she felt, and it was a struggle to keep smiling sometimes. She was losing that struggle more and more lately, as people grated on each other.

The Star programmers in Palo Alto, however, were mostly new to Xerox. Having come straight from college, most had never worked on a large project or used any sort of source control system, so all this was a revelation. Angela walked them through the basics of synchronizing with a snapshot, checking your code in, and what the Integration team did with your code after you checked it in. She skipped lightly over the part where she or Janet told you when you'd broken the build, but the message was clear that you don't want to be the one who holds up the show. It was an exhausting day.

Janet, Angela, and Grant met and sat together at the San Jose airport. They all looked much less chipper than they had in the morning. Grant spoke first, "How was your day?"

Janet answered for the two of them, "Busy. How about you?"

"Same. I can't say it was a huge success, but we're making progress."

41

MEET HAROLD

T he SDD-wide meeting was happening this afternoon on video. It was July 28, 1980, and Harold Esposito and Michael Adams were hosting. Harold was based in Dallas and was the head of the Office Products Division (OPD), where Star now lived. This was one of those major executive reorgs that Dan and most of his colleagues had learned to ignore. "Same monkeys, different trees," was the common sentiment. Still, most of SDD was full of hope that a reasonable plan to make and sell the Star now existed. The promise of the technology, which was once the motivation for everyone, was now in the "show me the proof" stage.

Frank from Palo Alto was down in El Segundo that day to meet with Dan, among others. He was a scholarly, serious, balding man who'd published several papers on operating systems before coming to Xerox. Frank ran the Data Management group, which had six people, way more than Dan had. They were defining a database system that went well beyond anything in Star 1.0. It was a relational system, with transactions and all the modern bells and whistles.

Having a competing group was normal for Dan, and this

being his second job, he was familiar with such politics. He had long since stopped thinking of implementing Frank's group's ideas, and even they would sometimes admit that their work was a prototype for some future version of Star. It was tricky for him, though, since the natural question in SDD politics was, "Shouldn't Records Processing be up in Palo Alto?" After all, they had the people with doctorates, which was important at Xerox.

On the other hand, RP had to be tightly integrated with the rest of Star's user interface, and all of that was being implemented in El Segundo. That was the winning move in the political game—integration. Dan's group was building Star, after all, and Frank's group didn't have anyone who wrote Star code. That was a pretty big hurdle to jump, as it turned out.

But Dan couldn't *completely* ignore Frank's group since they were responsible for the way a user interacted with RP. So, he had regular chats with them about user interface questions. He and Frank met in the morning, and they went over all the projects Frank's group was pursuing, and Dan recapped his. At one point, Frank commented, "I think we might want to move you up to Palo Alto at some point."

Dan had thought about that over the years. He knew the Bay Area was just as expensive as LA, and he always thought he might move to some cheaper state someday. "I just bought a house last year, though."

Frank was ready for that, "Well, of course, Xerox pays for your relocation expenses." Dan was silent, so Frank continued, "An Eichler in Palo Alto costs about $140,000." [1] Dan didn't know what an Eichler was. They moved on to other topics, and in the afternoon, they went to the cafeteria. It was the only room large enough for all of SDD South, which was over a hundred people now, and it had a movie screen set up for the video. Harold and Michael were in Palo Alto, and the camera showed their cafeteria, with all the SDD North staff.

Harold was the type of executive who business journalists called brash. He opened the meeting with a short movie of him driving his Mercedes to work, playing a motivational tape. The voice enthused, "You're a terrific person! Everything about you is terrific! And you're going to have a terrific day!"

He arrived at work, and his secretary greeted him, "Good morning, Harold! How are you today?"

"Terrific!"

Harold put up a chart of the new OPD and explained how it had its own dedicated sales force, its own manufacturing, and conformed to Xerox's rigorous financial rules. The part about the sales force was intended to allay the fear in SDD that Xerox salesmen could only sell copiers. Many Xerox copiers had a meter for the number of copies made, and each month the meter would be read and a bill sent. It was the same as the gas company reading your meter. The checks just rolled in, making for a cushy life, but could salesmen accustomed to that life sell a complicated computer system with a network? But no worries, OPD would have its own salespeople now.

OPD sold the 860 word processor, and it also had a new electronic typewriter to challenge the crushing dominance of the IBM Selectric. The 860 would soon have an Ethernet card so that it could talk to the file servers. The word processor and the typewriter would bring in revenue right away, while the Office of the Future products were maturing. It seemed like a good business strategy—use the current products as cash cows to pay for the future.

Harold also addressed the growing concern about personal computers, especially now that office workers were starting to bring them to work to run VisiCalc. He even mentioned the shocking rumors that IBM was going to make a PC.

As Harold explained it, the world was starting to adopt Xerox's vision that office workers needed computers. This was validation that Xerox had the right idea almost 10 years ago. But the office desktop was *our market*, and Xerox had to protect it.

To prevent competitors from hijacking the revolution, Xerox would now sell the 820, its very own personal computer. The design of the 820 was largely outsourced to other companies. It would be based on the Zilog Z80 processor and run CP/M, the most popular PC operating system. The program was being run out of Dallas, and most of SDD had not been asked to support it in any way. It seemed rather hasty to Dan. Harold declared that the 820 was designed to "hold our place on the desktop" until Star was ready to assume it.

Then, he and Michael opened the floor for questions. The obvious ones came up concerning the other parts of OPD, the demand for the 860 word processor, why Xerox could sell a typewriter and make money from it, and so on.

Tim, the man who'd figured out how lightning brought down the Ethernet, asked, "Does the 820 have an Ethernet connection?"

Harold looked at Michael, who answered, "Hi, Tim. We'll be talking to you about that."

Dan whispered to Frank, "So, it's not a network citizen. Too bad."

Ron, the Palo Alto guy whose office Janet had had to extricate herself from once, spoke, "I heard that PARC gave a demo of our technology to Apple. Why did we do that?"

Harold and Michael exchanged glances again, and then Harold answered, "Yeah, this was organized by Xerox's venture capital arm. We've invested in a lot of small companies, Apple among them."[2]

Frank and Dan looked at each other. They both thought that Harold's answer left an awful lot of questions. But they knew only fools would argue with senior executives in a big meeting. The Palo Alto camera focused on Ron again, and he looked like he wanted to argue anyway, but even he knew enough to stifle it.

The questions went on for another 15 minutes, and then the meeting ended. As they walked back to the A&E Building, Dan asked Frank, "Did you know about the Apple visit?" He hadn't heard of it. Two of the people walking in front of them turned around. They didn't know about it, either.

Dan went to Tom's office. Tom asked, "What did you think of the meeting?"

"I don't know. It's great we'll have our own sales force now."

Tom was doing his management thing and asking all the questions, so Dan waited for the next one. "And Harold Esposito? What did you think of him?"

"Oh, he's... what's the word I'm looking for?" "Brash?" They both laughed.

"Maybe brash is what we need. What about this new 820 machine? Are we supposed to be supporting that now?"

"I haven't heard anything about that. Until I do, we just stick to the path we're on."

"Okay," Dan had assumed as much.

"Did you and Frank have a good meeting?" Tom always knew exactly who was meeting with whom.

"Oh, yeah. They're doing a bunch of stuff for Star 2.0 or 3.0 or something. But we're still cooperating on the user interface."

"Excellent. Well, keep me posted."

As Dan was leaving, Tom called out, "Dodgers beat the Cubs yesterday. That must be a tough one for you!"

Dan turned back, "Yeah, I guess I'm for the Dodgers unless they're playing the Cubs. That way, I win either way." Tom smiled and turned back to his Alto.

Janet dropped by Dan's office. She knew he was into the

blues, so she had some exciting news, "Hey, Grant and I saw the Blues Brothers this weekend."

"Oh, yeah? How were they?" Dan immediately picked up on the Grant angle, but he had no idea what he could tactfully say about that, so he just let it go.

"They were great! It was kinda like seeing them on *Saturday Night Live*, though."

"That's one hell of a band they have with them. I'll say that."

"They were really good. I think I'll see the movie now."

Dan had already seen it and thought it was a little over the top, with the gigantic car crashes. "What'd you think of the meeting?" They'd both heard about the Apple visit, so they didn't waste time on that.

"Oh, it was interesting. I wonder if we'll have to fly to Dallas now."

"Please, no," cried Dan. "That's a much longer flight than Palo Alto."

Janet smirked, "Oh, *excuse* me. I think they're delivering my 820," and left.

Dan chuckled and called after her, "Hey, I want to book some time on that thing!"

Of course, no 820 was in her office or anyone else's in El Segundo. [3]Angela was waiting for her, though. The two of them spent the rest of the day untangling the latest build failure and chasing down the guilty parties. It was only Monday, and it was starting already. For the past two months, that was all they'd been doing.

When Janet arrived home, she had yet another message from Grant on her telephone answerer. She'd finally gone out with him, but only because the Blues Brothers concert sounded fun, which it was. Gwen at work had warned her not to do it, and Gwen was right once again. Gwen had given her an old copy of *Pride And Prejudice* with the first line highlighted in yellow:

"It is a truth universally acknowledged, that a single man in posses-sion of a good fortune, must be in want of a wife."

"That's okay," she said to herself, *"I'm not marrying anyone again for a long, long time."* She didn't call him back that night.

42

SATURDAYS AT XEROX

It was Saturday morning, January 10, 1981. In the A&E Building, every Star developer was at work because they had to be. Saturdays were mandatory, starting this month.

The Friday before the holidays, Paul had held one of his rare all-hands meetings to announce this. The large conference room could hold everybody only if extra chairs were dragged in, and still, the latecomers had to stand against the walls.

Paul began as he always did, in his low-key, semi-apologetic way, "Well, it's been a while since we've all gotten together." Dan and Brian glanced at each other and suppressed a smirk. "Thank you all for being here. I wanted to update you all on the Star program." No one spoke. "We are announcing Star in April, and demoing it in New York, and then again at the National Computer Conference in May in Chicago. After almost five years, we're at the finish line! I really want to thank all of you for your incredible hard work." Applause. "That was the good news," he said with a grin.

"And what's the *bad* news, Paul?" asked Mark, trying to sound like Ed McMahon with Johnny Carson.

"We're going to start working on Saturdays after New Year," he said while pretending to duck. Nobody made a sour face since that might be a career-limiting move. "We will have lunch brought in. I know this is a sacrifice for you, and we wouldn't be doing it if this wasn't *very* important. We have competitors who agree with our vision, and they're bringing out their own computers. But this is *our* vision, and we have to get out there with it. Mark, do you want to say anything?"

Even though he was not at the top of the org chart, Mark was the driving force in Star engineering. Dan often felt Mark was going to will it into existence. For the last six months at least, he was the one who answered all the naysayers. Xerox had an active email culture, and anyone could express an opinion about anything, even if it wasn't in their job description. Some people in Palo Alto, especially, were growing nervous that The Office of the Future didn't live up to their dreams.

"*It's not going to be ready!*"

"It will be," he answered.

"*It's too slow!*"

"It'll get faster as hardware improves," he countered.

"*It's missing at least five key features!*"

"We'll add those in Release 2," he promised.

Mark was terse, as always. "Okay, gang, we're in the final push. We need you to fix whatever keeps us from shipping Star. Anything else can wait. Are there any questions?"

Raymond raised his hand, "We have a lot of cleanup in the traits mechanisms to do. I think it's going to cause a lot of new bugs if we don't do it now."

Mark showed no annoyance, but he didn't look sympathetic either, "Aaron needs you to talk over anything risky before you do it." Aaron nodded in agreement.

"Anything else?"

Janet figured she could ask the question about performance that was on everyone's mind since she built the product after all. Without more memory than Star was supposed to have, it was just abysmally slow, and every developer had extra memory on their personal machines. David Bowman, probably the best programmer in El Segundo, had quit after he realized that.

"What about memory? We can't even run the product in 192K, and yet, that's the official configuration."[1]

Paul and Mark glanced at each other. Finally, Paul answered, "I've been bringing that up with Michael every week. Believe me... we're not ignoring it. I may have some good news in a few weeks."

Mark added, "In the meantime, pray for 64K chips."

Paul spoke again, "Thanks, Mark. For the newer people, we expected that the industry would be delivering 64K memory chips in quantity and at the right price by now. Unfortunately, it's not happening quite as fast as we predicted. So, that leaves us with some difficult choices. But please, don't worry *too* much. We're on it!"

Peter raised his hand, "Are we sure it's just a memory problem?" looking at Aaron, who ignored him.

Mark said, "We also have a Performance Working Group, which I'm a part of. We're doing some interesting stuff, and if you have spare time on your hands, we'd love to put you to work."

The meeting dispersed. Dan happened to be walking with Gary, whom he hadn't talked with in a long time. "Gary, what do you think?"

"Oh, the Saturdays? About par for the course."

"For Xerox, you mean?"

Gary stopped and lit his pipe, "In the job I had before XDS whenever we had a big release, everyone had to work Saturdays, and you had to bring your *own* lunch. If you went out, you only had 45 minutes."

Dan laughed, "I guess we're spoiled."

"You don't know how good you have it."

"No, I do, I do. When we had the big snowstorm in Chicago and the buses weren't running, my dad walked two miles to the train station. Then when he got to work, no one was there, and he turned around and came home."

"Now that's dedication. Where did he work?"

"At Swift, in the stockyards."

"Swift... I think we have Swift's Premium bacon at home." Dan nodded approval.

On the Saturday after the first full week in January, the policy went into effect. As Janet was headed out the door that morning, her phone rang. It was her dad, Len.

"Hi, Dad, I can't talk very long. I have to go to work."

"Work? On a Saturday? Do you get overtime for that?"

Janet chuckled. Her dad worked for Chrysler. Office people didn't work on weekends, and if the factory workers had to, they got time and a half. The union was always pushing for double-time when a new contract was negotiated. "No, Dad. I wish!"

"I know you're in a hurry, so I'll get right to the point. I'm going to buy one of those Apple computers."

"Really? Wow! How come?" Janet guessed it must be for that spreadsheet program he mentioned before, which she'd found out was called VisiCalc. She was right.

"Well, this analyst keeps showing me the financial model he runs on his, and I gotta say... it's pretty impressive. Stuff that used to take me all day, and he does it like *that*!" snapping his fingers.

"Great! You'll have to tell me how it works out."

"Okay, you have to go. Is Xerox's computer going to have a program like that?"

Janet was embarrassed. Spreadsheets seemed to be a hit with some part of the office market, but she wasn't even sure the Star was going to have one. She made a mental note to ask about that.

An all-hands meeting for Star developers was held at 10

am to make sure everyone was focused. Dan and Brian arrived early, and while they were waiting for the others, Dan thought Brian looked especially tired and haggard. For some reason, maybe the accumulated fatigue they all felt, Dan was in a teasing mood, "I was just reading about this new psychological test they have."

"Oh, what's that?" asked Brian.

"It's called the Maslach Burnout Inventory. It's a test that measures how burned out you are."

Brian looked alarmed. Dan noticed his obvious distress but continued anyway, "The concept of burnout started with medical and clinical workers, but now, they're seeing it in workers in other industries as well."

Brian got up and left the room. The other people started filtering in, and eventually, Brian came back and sat as far away from Dan as he could.

Tom took the floor, "Thank you all for being here. I know it's a Saturday, and we wouldn't do this if it wasn't important. Mark wants to say a few words."

"Yes. Lunch at 12:30."

At 12:30 in response to a lunch-is-here email, Dan went back to the conference room, which was already half full of people. Besides the usual soft drinks, they had brought in beer, which made Dan think they really were serious. At Xerox, it was supposedly a firing offense to have alcohol in the building. This was generally ignored in Palo Alto but adhered to in El Segundo.

Long ago, Gary had told him that this policy was a legacy of Xerox Data Systems history. Xerox was ostentatiously liberal and pro-union, so the factory staff was unionized. The union contract specified no alcohol because if the factory workers had to give up their beer, then dammit, the executives were going to give up their martinis, too.

After lunch, Mark had a few words for the troops, "The Pilot guys tell us we'll be getting the release definition of

Rubicon on January 20. If you're up on your Roman history, you know that this is the big river to cross."

Dan remembered again what he'd loved about Xerox from the very beginning—it wasn't just a bunch of engineering nerds. Major software packages weren't named with some contrived acronym the way they were in the rest of the industry. For a while, PARC had a convention that names had to appear in *The Sunset Western Gardening Book* (Laurel, Juniper, Poplar, Cedar), although Laurel was followed by Hardy, and of course, now we had the rivers theme for Pilot releases.

Before everyone left, Mark had one more announcement, "Oh, and for those who haven't heard. Carroll Molnár is leaving us for, get this… Microsoft!"

Aaron said, "What's he going to do, put Bravo on CP/M?" Almost everyone laughed, but there were a few puzzled looks.

Mark said, "CP/M is the leading PC operating system, if you didn't know that. Run by our very own 820."

Raymond asked, "But who's Carroll Molnár, and why should we care?"

Mark replied, "Who knows, maybe you shouldn't. Aaron will tell you all about him. See you all on Monday."

43

THE HIT OF THE SHOW

I t was finally happening. After almost five years of labor by 250-plus people, the Office of the Future was here. Despite the prayers for them, 64K memory chips had not appeared. Michael had gotten corporate approval to increase the manufacturing cost with an extra 64K words of memory. Star now had 256K words, or 512K bytes of main memory. The performance was still poor, but at least it was tolerable now.

Star had been announced and demoed in New York already, and this week was the National Computer Conference in Chicago, starting Monday, May 4, 1981 and lasting until Thursday. Dan had volunteered to man the Xerox booth for all four days. He flew out to Chicago on the Sunday morning before it started, but with the time change, it was past dinner when he finally arrived at McCormick Place.

He checked into the hotel, ate dinner, walked over to the vast show floor, and after a short search, found the Xerox booth. The machines were already set up, and at the front, both sides had a large TV monitor up on a stand. Two Star machines sat at the back of the booth, and this was where Dan would stand.

Dan chatted with the show manager, Gary, whom he didn't know. Gary had experience running shows like this for Xerox, so he carried a large wad of $100 bills for paying off the union chiefs. Dan had grown up in Chicago, so he wasn't surprised to hear that if you didn't pay the unions to do all the *electrical* work, including carting your machines in, you'd find that none of it worked at showtime. Other Xeroids were shocked to be told, "Don't touch any wiring."

Henry Davis was standing around, and Dan shook hands with him. "Hey, we're finally here, huh?"

Henry smiled broadly, "I have to admit ... there were times I never thought we'd make it. How long are you staying?"

"The entire week!" Dan became pensive, "My God, so many times, I thought we were doomed." Henry agreed. "Like all the times anyone noticed how the software was so *fucking* slow."

Henry laughed, "And still is! I have to be careful what I demo because a lot of it crashes."

"Anyhow, I grew up here, you know."

"That's right... I forgot. Do you still have family here?"

"Just my brother. My parents moved out to LA a few years ago. But I have a lot of college friends here."

"Well, you'll have to show us around. Where exactly did you grow up?"

Dan was used to this question. His old neighborhood had completely changed racial composition, and everyone he knew had moved out. People not from Chicago didn't understand this "white flight" phenomenon, so he'd learned it was best just to leave such things vague. Also, Henry would naturally assume he was going to stay with his brother, Jack, on the weekend, whereas he was staying with his college friend, Tom. He'd visit Jack on Sunday since he and Jack were on good terms but not especially close.

He remembered Jack's attitude when he was in college, "You're smart. You should be a doctor.'

Dan protested, "But I'm not interested in biology and chemistry."

Jack snorted, "Who cares? You'll make a ton of money." Jack didn't go to college, and he now managed a tiny adhesives factory in Skokie.

Dan told Henry, "I grew up on the far South Side. But my brother and all my friends live in the north suburbs, so that's where I'm going after the show."

"Well, good to talk to you. I'll see you tomorrow."

Dan didn't see anyone else he wanted to talk to. He asked Gary if he could help out, but everything was under control. He knew that McCormick Place was well away from downtown and not near anything you'd want to walk to, so he went back to his hotel room. It was almost 9:00 pm.

Dan read the Sunday *Chicago Tribune*. He had fond memories of walking with his dad to Sam's Drug Store at 111th and Emerald on Saturday nights to get the Sunday *Tribune* and walking back with Dad as he read. But now, he just wanted the hometown news. The University of Illinois, his alma mater, had been sanctioned by the Big Ten for athletic eligibility violations. A parade had been held for Polish Constitution Day—Chicago having an enormous population of Poles—and the Solidarity union's struggles featured prominently. There were ads for Marshall Fields, Wieboldt's, Goldblatt's, and Polk Brothers, which were stores he hadn't heard of since leaving Chicago.

In the Sports section, the Cubs won, the Sox lost on Saturday. Today, the Cubs played the Braves at Wrigley, and the Dodgers were in Montreal. Maybe he'd find out who won on the 10 o'clock news. The Sox were leading the American League in team batting—how the hell was *that* happening?—and in the Fishing report, some very large walleyes were being taken in Michigan and Wisconsin lakes. And of course, a dissection of the University of Illinois's misdeeds that won them the sanctions.

In Business, CompuShop was offering an Apple II starter system for $1,595. But then buried deep inside the section, Dan found what he was looking for, a story about the Star. It began:

Xerox terminal has symbols, not codes

Managers and professional workers haven't been the best customers for automated office equipment like computer terminals.

Maybe it's because they are more accustomed to pointing and selecting material rather than typing out explicit commands.

Maybe it's because they can't type.

The article quoted a Xerox marketing executive, who explained that the Star was aimed at "managers or professionals who produce documents, reports, or charts." It explained how the mouse worked. The executive went on to explain that the Star system cost $15,595, but "technological advances will allow price reductions in the future." Star would be demonstrated at the National Computer Conference at McCormick Place this week.

This "typing is for secretaries" thing was a big deal, apparently. Dan never quite understood that since he'd taken a typing class in summer school after his sophomore year in high school. It was just one more hurdle for the Star. Maybe a price tag of $16,000 would make managers realize it wasn't a clerical tool.

Dan skimmed the rest of the paper and learned that Bob Dylan was coming in June. He watched the local news and went to bed. Turns out, the Cubs lost.

Janet came in on a different flight, probably one that let her leave at a civilized hour instead of the crack of dawn like Dan's flight. Unfortunately, that meant she arrived really late, so she didn't have time to go to the show floor. Her phone's message light was blinking when she walked into her room. It was Grant—this was getting annoying. She didn't call him back.

The next morning, Janet saw Dan eating breakfast and joined him. He was dressed in jeans and a T-shirt.

"Morning! All ready for the show?"

"Yup. Just gotta change into my suit."

"What a relief! I was afraid you were going like that."

Dan laughed, "Ever since I dripped maple syrup on my tie at a job interview, I started putting the suit on *after* breakfast."

She was already in her power suit and glanced down to make sure it was still clean. "Smart. Have you been over there yet?"

"Last night. So exciting!" He told her the story of the payoffs to union guys. Since she was from Detroit, also a union town, she wasn't too surprised.

"After all these years. Do you think Star's going to be a big deal?"

"No idea. The *Tribune* had one little story on it, in the back of the Business section."

She showed him today's paper, opened to Xerox's two-page ad for Star. It was the one on the plaque they'd all received. The headline was, "How do you explain something that's never existed before?" and had a caveman showing his friends his new invention… the wheel.

So cool! The financial might of Xerox was finally being brought to bear on all their hard work. Now, they were going to find out what the world thought of it.

"Well, I need to go change. Do you want to wait for me, and we can walk over together?" Dan said, standing up.

"Thanks, but I'm going to go over and check out the booth. I'll see you there." Janet waved and headed for the outside door.

Dan arrived half an hour before the doors opened to the public. Inside the booth, almost everything was ready. The Xeroids were standing around, chatting and reading the official program. Most of the engineers in El Segundo didn't volunteer for this show, which Dan couldn't understand. How could you *not* want to be here? Lots of the Palo Alto people were here, including Martin and Henry. Of course, Michael, the head of it all, was standing by the TV monitors where the demos would be shown. Everyone seemed excited but nervous. The rollout in New York had gone okay, but this was for the general public.[1]

The actor who played Brother Dominic in the 1977 Xerox Super Bowl commercial, where a monk amazes his superior by making hundreds of copies of his manuscript in seconds, was gliding around in his habit, smiling beatifically. By now, he'd become as much a symbol of Xerox as Colonel Sanders was of Kentucky Fried Chicken. The fact that he was actually a Jewish comedian and not a monk or even a Xerox employee made it all the funnier.

A female engineer from Palo Alto approached him, "Can you bless me, Brother Dominic?"

He looked down at her chest, "I see you're already twice blessed!"[2]

A voice came over the intercom, "In five minutes, the doors will be opened." The newspapers were folded up and hidden away behind the desks, along with anything else the Xeroids were carrying. The first attendees trickled in. It was on!

The demos were held every hour on the hour. The first, at the show opening, seemed to pull in passers-by so that almost 50 were watching at the end. A few strays stopped by the desks to ask questions. Dan explained the mouse, the icons on the screen, and most of all, the price. After telling them it was $16,000, he explained that you also needed a file server and a print server, at about the same price. He even had to tell them what a server was.

Dan, Janet, Martin, Henry, and the rest of the Xeroids were continuously busy, explaining the Star to curious attendees. Visitors could try a mouse, and lots of them did—almost no one had ever used a mouse before. A technical staffer had brought a box full of spare mice and swapped in a new one every hour since the accumulated dirt and finger oil from all the guests made the steel balls in the mice sticky.

As each hour approached, people began gathering around the monitors to see the demos. By noon, they were waiting 10 minutes before the hour. Michael stationed himself near the left side monitor, where he kept busy talking to reporters, executives, and random attendees. Michael watched the crowd closely, and he noticed that Steve Jobs, one of the Apple founders, came every hour, surrounded by other guys Michael didn't know. He knew that Jobs had visited PARC the year before last for a demo of the Alto and Smalltalk, but he hadn't seen Star before. He had supposedly asked, "Why isn't Xerox doing anything with this?" Now, he found out they were.[3]

Michael had heard rumors that Apple was working on its own computer with a graphical user interface, but he wasn't sure how serious they were. If Jobs was coming to every demo, he *must* be serious. Michael passed the word to the other Xerox staff that they were to be polite to guests from Apple, or any competitor, but no more than that, and to be on guard against questions that were too probing.

The crowds for the demos started gathering earlier each hour. Eventually, the crowd spilled out of the Xerox booth and into the IBM booth next door, which caused the IBM staff to complain to the conference management. Dan's throat became sore from talking so much. The Xeroids kept stealing glances at each other, as if to say, "Isn't this crazy?"

Finally, the closing announcement came over the loudspeakers, and the crowds cleared out. Dan and the rest of the

Xerox staff were too excited to just have a quiet evening at the hotel, and McCormick Place was pretty far from any decent restaurants. Dan had rented a car and agreed to drive as many as it would hold for some real Chicago food. Janet said she was meeting some friends from school and didn't join them.

They met his college roommate, Tom, at Miller's Pub downtown on Adams, and most of them had ribs, which were excellent. On the way back to McCormick Place, Dan drove on a roundabout route through Lower Wacker Drive. He pointed out Billy Goat Tavern, the inspiration for the *Saturday Night Live* "cheezborger, chips" sketch. [4]He felt it his duty as a Chicago tour guide to explain the curse of the billy goat—how the owner of the tavern had tried to bring his pet goat to Wrigley in 1945, the last time the Cubs were in the World Series. He was refused entry and laid a Curse on the Cubs so that they would never be in another Series. The Curse was holding so far. The Cubs hadn't been in a World Series in Dan's lifetime.

None of the others were baseball fans, so they just listened politely and changed the subject as soon as they could. He was about to tell them how the real Eliot Ness from *The Untouchables* went to his high school but figured, "*Screw it. They're not interested right now.*"

The rest of the show was crazier day by day, as word of the Star spread. Dan was exhausted long before the end. In the infrequent downtimes, he had memorable conversations with Patrick Wolfe, a Pilot engineer. Patrick was familiar with the startup scene in Silicon Valley, which Dan had only heard vague rumors about. Late Wednesday afternoon when the crowds were thinning, Patrick explained to Dan and Janet how it worked.

"Yeah, so, my buddy Dennis is working at a startup ..." he named it, but the names all sounded alike, and Dan immediately forgot it. "And I visited him one evening, and everyone was still there."

"Wow," murmured Dan. At Xerox, most people were gone by 5:30, unless it was *really* close to a deadline.

"They were all hunched over their VAX terminals," he continued.

"That's what you get if you leave Xerox, a terminal to a VAX!"

Patrick agreed, "It's a sweatshop. But the stock… they'll all be millionaires if it goes public."

Janet asked, "Is that really true? Does a regular engineer get that much stock?"

"Dennis told me how to evaluate a stock offer. Let's say they offer you 100,000 shares, and you don't know if that's a lot or a little."

"Sounds like a lot to me!" exclaimed Dan.

"You have to ask … how many shares are there total, and what percentage do *you* have?" They let him continue. "Suppose there are 10 million shares. Then, you have one percent of the company. Now, let's say it goes public, and the market cap is a hundred million. Your one percent is one million." Joy spread from Dan's face to Janet's. "Of course, one percent is a lot. Almost no engineer, except maybe the very first, gets that much."

Dan asked, "So, how much do you get?"

"A tenth of a percent is a pretty typical offer for a grunt-level engineer."

Janet said, "But that's a $100K, assuming a 100-million market cap."

"Right. But a market cap of 100 million is pretty small. Apple's IPO created 300 millionaires, supposedly."

Janet wondered, "*Okay, how do I figure out how much I'd make if I joined Apple now?*" But she couldn't ask that.

"Suppose they offer you those 100,000 shares? Do they just *give* them to you, or do you have to pay for them, or what?"

Patrick answered, "I think they usually have a very low

share price, 10 cents or something. But you do have to buy them."

"For that example, it's still $10,000?"

"Yep. It *is* possible to lose money on your startup and not get rich."

They both laughed. "What determines the market cap?"

Patrick was about to answer, but Dan interjected, "I'll try this one. Suppose they have a $100 million in sales, and their profit margin is 50%."

Patrick laughed, "That's a pretty high margin, but we can go with that for now."

Dan continued, "So that's $50 million a year in profit, or earnings. If the market gives it a price to earnings ratio of 30, its market cap is…"

Janet did the math in her head, "One and a half billion!"

Patrick agreed, "So, a tenth of a percent of *that* is still a fucking lot of money!"

Just then, a pair of show attendees walked up, putting this conversation on hold.

Janet knew her father understood all this financial stuff backward and forward, and she made a mental note to call him this weekend. But since Apple was already public, maybe the easy money had already been made.

Dan had been assuming that consulting for Star customers would be the way to make money or maybe writing custom software for them. That was what you did in the mainframe era. Now, he realized there were other, quicker ways. But how did you get into a startup early enough? Was it just about who you knew? He needed to ask around.

44

NEVER MAKE YOUR MOVE TOO SOON

When Janet heard that Steve Jobs and his Apple cohorts were at the NCC, she decided to be bold. Jobs himself was in the public eye and too risky to talk to, so she followed one of his lieutenants away from the Xerox booth. She gave him her business card, and they shook hands. He asked if he could call her at the hotel. "Looking forward to it!" She left, hoping no one from Xerox saw the encounter.

On Wednesday night after the show, she had a message from him at the hotel asking her to meet for dinner. Finally!

Jobs was not at the dinner. Apparently, he was not directly involved in the development of their new computer, but this Star demo really convinced him on the graphical user interface. Janet felt like they were selling *her* on Apple more than she was selling herself and that she had some kind of halo for being on Star from the beginning. They assumed that she knew everything Xerox was doing. She wished she'd been more active and asked more questions at all the talks about hardware, networking, printing, and everything else. But she found out that whatever she did know, it was more than they did.

But this wasn't her final interview. They mentioned that they would be inviting her to the main Apple campus in Cupertino. She left dinner, practically floating, and called her dad as soon as she could. "Hi, Dad! Guess who I had dinner with?"

"Um… Lee Iacocca? Where are you?"

"No, silly. Some guys from Apple! I'm at a conference in Chicago."

She expected him to comment on how much this call was costing, but he surprised her, "Apple? The computer company?"

"That's the one!"

"So, are they going to make you their CEO?"

"I think they have one of those already. Maybe just an engineer for now."

"Wow! That's my girl! Did they make you an offer?"

"Not yet. I still have to visit their headquarters in Cupertino."

"Cupertino? Where's that?"

"Somewhere in the Bay Area. I'm not sure."

"Hang on, let me get my atlas." He put the phone down. She tried to tell him not to bother and she'd figure it out, but it was too late. A few minutes later, he came back.

"I found it. It's right next to San Jose."

"Thanks, Dad."

"When are you going there?"

"I'm not sure. They're going to call me."

"Well, I'm going to call my broker and buy some of their stock. If you're working there, it's going to go through the roof!"

"Yeah, we didn't talk about stock options for me yet. Hopefully, I'll get some. But remember, I don't have an offer yet."

He ignored the caution, "Stock options? At Chrysler, those are only for the big executives!"

"It's different with these little companies, Dad. Almost everyone gets them. Hey, that reminds me... I have some questions for you."

"Shoot!"

"What determines the price/earnings ratio of a brand-new company like Apple? I know you work with stuff like that."

"Whew, you're asking a tough one," Len dropped the fatherly stuff and adopted his work voice. He explained that, traditionally, companies without a long track record of rising profits and dividends were regarded suspiciously by Wall Street. That's why his group of finance guys at Chrysler was so interested in the Apple IPO. It seemed to break all the rules they'd learned in school.

He mused, "But nowadays, who the hell knows. You have little companies like Apple with *some* profits, but their stock is mostly hope. I know the stock sale was banned in Mass-achusetts because the price was too high."

"Really?" Janet was amazed.

"That IPO was insane. It was supposed to come out at $14, but they had to raise it to $22 because of demand. At the end of the day, it was $29, so their market cap was almost $1.8 billion."

"What was their P/E ratio?"

"Who the hell knows if they even *had* any earnings? It didn't matter."

"What was their... I think this is the right question. What was their gross margin?"

Len snorted, "Gross margin? Who knows that, either? I can tell you it was a lot."

She realized Apple was an outlier. They were already public, unlike all the startup companies springing up in their wake. "Anyway... thanks, Dad! I'll let you know if I get an offer."

"Before you go... why do you want to leave Xerox? It's been a good job, hasn't it?"

Janet asked herself the same question. "Um... I'm not sure I do. I just don't know if Xerox can actually sell this stuff."

"Why do you care? You're in Engineering! You're not paid on commission, right?"

Janet had a vivid image of herself standing in a Chrysler-Plymouth showroom trying to sell cars and laughed out loud, "No, thank God!"

Len chuckled, too. "There you go. Anyway, interviewing with Apple. I can't get over this. Janet, I'm so proud of you."

She never tired of hearing that. Her dad had always encouraged her in her scientific pursuits. Maybe he'd always wanted a son, and she was filling that role, but whatever.

She flew back to LA on Friday morning. With the two hours gained flying east to west, she arrived at work by early afternoon. She spent most of her time telling people about the conference. Aaron's group was pretty much ignoring all the excitement and writing code as if nothing had happened, which she found somewhat depressing. *"What's the matter with you? Your work was the hit of the show!"*

Apple invited her up for interviews on Monday, May 18, after a week of her being nervous about it!

During NCC week, Grant was at work since the Printing Systems Division wasn't part of the show. Grant was annoyed that Janet hadn't returned his calls. She went out with him once, after all, and it seemed like a good date, but she'd shown a pronounced lack of enthusiasm for their relationship ever since. His grand plan of moving to LA and marrying Janet might need to be rethought. *"Let's not be too hasty. Maybe she just needs more time after the divorce."*

Grant was learning he was now both Mr. Mesa Chip and Mr. Fuji Xerox. Whenever anyone in SDD or the Printing

Systems Division (PSD) brought up the subject of "better hard-ware for Mesa" or "Japanese Star," his name invariably came up. He didn't even have anything to do with J-Star. It didn't matter because his name was on at least half the documents. And since he'd been in Tokyo meeting with Fuji Xerox every other month, he'd become a point of contact for half of Japan, or so it seemed.

Early on Thursday morning, May 7, his phone rang. He knew what it was going to be about before they even spoke. "Good morning, this is Grant Avery."

"Hi, Grant, this is Jim Travis from SDD North. I hope you remember me."

Grant was surprised not to hear a Japanese voice. "Hi, Jim, sure I do. How are things in Palo Alto?"

"Oh, about the same. Hey, I'll come right to the point. Fuji Xerox is asking for a liaison in Japan for a short time, and naturally, we thought of you."

"Naturally," he muttered. *"Oh, boy. They played Musical Chairs, and I'm the one left standing."*

"And what would this lucky person do?"

"As near as we can tell, head up the Mesa hardware effort, among other things. I understand you have something to do with that?"

"There it is. Say Mesa chip, and you just said Grant Avery!" Grant continued, "We've been in discussions, yes. I haven't heard that they committed to it yet, though."

Jim persisted, "Well, who knows? Anyhow, do you want to call them?"

Grant knew that he was being tagged as the Mesa Chip Guy, but he could always ask his own management to untag him. He wrote down the contact information and exchanged pleasantries, congratulating him on a successful NCC.

It was the middle of the night in Japan, so he didn't need to call them right now. He sat and thought a little, *"Is this really an offer I can refuse? Maybe they're not asking me, they're telling me?"*[1]

He reviewed how it reached this point. The 5700 printer/copier used the Dolphin processor, which Star had abandoned years ago. He'd *volunteered* to talk to his contacts in SDD Palo Alto about a better solution. SDD used the Dandelion processor for everything, but their printer was only about half as fast as the 5700 needed. He'd thought of persuading Fuji Xerox to solve the problem with all their money. If they announced that, he'd be on the next rung of the Xerox management ladder, probably back in Dallas. He didn't want to stay around for all the messy work of actually making the product. The thing to do was to keep moving. He wasn't sure Janet would even want to move to Dallas, but he could cross that bridge when he came to it, *if* he did.

Now, where was he? The planning meetings with the Japanese were stretching out into infinity, and Janet wasn't returning his calls. On the other hand, he was getting to know all the flight attendants on the Japan Airlines flights to Tokyo. He loved having ultimate authority when anyone here talked about sushi or sake. All he had to do was drop the names of his favorite hole-in-the-wall joints in Tokyo, and that was the end of the argument. His karaoke repertoire was expanding, and he knew that when someone said, *"Hai,"* it didn't mean they agreed with you. He liked this Japan thing a lot.

As he was lost in thought, Steve and Sandy came in. They seemed to arrive together every morning, come to think of it. Were they living together now or something? He wasn't much for the interoffice gossip, so he figured this was something everyone else had known about forever. Instead of just walking by as usual, they knocked on his door and walked in, "Hi Grant, we have some big news!" He looked expectantly.

"We're getting married!"

Grant stood up and shook their hands, "That's fantastic! Congratulations, you two. When's the big day?"

Sandy answered, "We haven't set a date yet, but we hope you'll come to the wedding."

"I'd be honored."

Steve added, "Especially since you were the one who brought us together at that bike ride."

Grant smiled modestly, "Wish I could say I did that deliberately." No one spoke, so he added, "I guess you're living together already?"

They both looked just a teensy bit embarrassed as they nodded. Sandy said, "We'll probably buy a house, but we're not sure where yet."

"I can help with that. I did a hell of a lot of looking before I bought my house."

Steve replied, "Yeah. You live pretty close to here, don't you?"

"Manhattan Beach. Near Aviation and Marine."

Sandy exclaimed, "That must be so great! So, you can walk to work?"

"Technically, yes, although I hardly ever do."

"Well, we have a bunch of people to tell."

"*I'm a yenta! At least, I'm good for something. Where was I... oh, yeah, Japan.*" He made a face, "*And Janet.*" He had a meeting soon, so he gathered up his materials and put her out of his mind for now.

On Monday, May 11, Dan returned to work. "*What do I want to do now?*" he asked himself. "*It feels like everything should be different.*" He spent an inordinate amount of time reading his email.

SDDers were erupting with opinions. Not about what Dan should do, of course, but what Xerox should do. The personal computer revolution was heating up, and rumors flew about both Apple and IBM. Some folks assumed Xerox had thought of personal computers at work, and therefore, the market belonged to them. They especially felt that graphical user interfaces were theirs. Now, the panic was spreading. Other companies were going to steal it all! When people realized that PARC had given a demo to Apple, for God's sake, they felt betrayed.

Microprocessors were becoming pretty powerful, much more so than when Xerox was choosing its hardware. Companies were springing into existence, fueled by venture capital, to take advantage of them. Headhunters were calling up engineers to join them and get rich. That last part didn't seem to apply to Dan, at least not yet. *"Maybe you had to live in Silicon Valley to get those phone calls."*

Everyone seemed to have an opinion on what Xerox should do now. "We should switch to Unix!" was a popular theme. "We should switch to the Motorola 68000 microprocessor!" If you wanted to make yourself unpopular, you could jump on the "We should dump Mesa!" train. Most people had at least some sense of self-preservation and stayed off that last one. A computer science professor on sabbatical presented his work on "Converting C code to Mesa code automatically." It was a very naughty joke that he should have been working on converting Mesa to C.

Xerox top management had no immediate reaction to this torrent of criticism. They were not used to the troops telling them they were doing the wrong thing, and especially, that they had to change *right now*. In the world they'd grown up in, management made the decisions, and then everyone carried them out, over many years.[2]

Dan had his weekly meeting with Tom the next day. He knew Tom too well by now to think he was getting carried away by any of this. Tom opened, "So, you went to NCC. Was it as exciting as we heard?"

"It really was! The crowds were lining up to see the demos 10 minutes before they started."

"That's what I heard. It must have been quite a thrill after all these years of work." Dan agreed. "Sometime, maybe not right now, you and I need to talk about what you want to do next."

Dan stayed seated, "Now is fine. I think I'd like to do

something different. I've been on RP for almost four years now."

Tom was sympathetic, "Has it been that long?" He thought for a second. "Let's see… 1978, 1979, 1980, and here we are. Pretty close to four."

"Anyway, I'm not sure what, exactly, I'd like to do. I had some talks with Martin at the NCC about maybe joining his Advanced Development group."

They agreed that Tom would find another manager for Records Processing, although it might take some time, and he'd appreciate it if Dan continued in that role until then. Dan agreed, of course.

Back on his usual job for now, Dan had time to think. He was disillusioned with Xerox management. Did they really not understand the magnitude of the opportunity they had? Everyone else in Silicon Valley did.

This "join a startup and get rich" thing seemed pretty appealing! But how to do it? The startups were all in the Bay Area. Maybe if he was working for Martin up in Palo Alto, he'd have a good excuse for being up there often, and then, he could interview with them. He still had to figure out how to *find* the startups. They didn't exactly put ads in the *LA Times* or the *San Jose Mercury-News*. It seemed to be all word-of-mouth.

He'd have to work on that problem.

45

INDECISION

On the morning of Thursday, May 14, Dan was reading his email and noticed that everyone seemed to be writing a scholarly paper about Star, Pilot, Mesa, or whatever. Maybe he should write a paper, too. The Star database wasn't too impressive as a database, but this one was intended for normal, non-computer people to design and use. Maybe that was publishable. And, Dan had brought it into being. Of course, Dan wasn't the only designer of the UI, and actually not even the principal designer. That was Joel Byrne up in Palo Alto. Dan decided to call him.

"This is Joel Byrne."

"Hi, Joel, it's Dan Markunas."

"Dan, nice to hear from you. Congrats on the NCC."

"Thanks! Yeah, it was a thrill. Hey, I had an idea."

"I'm all ears."

Dan couldn't resist, "I think you mean 'I'm all a-tingle!' don't you?"

"If you say so, " Joel wasn't much for repartee.

"I'm so glad. Why don't we write a paper about Records Processing?"

"A paper is a great idea. I was just thinking about that myself."

"Great minds think alike. What was your idea for it?"

Joel turned professorial, "We've devoted an incredible amount of effort to formalizing a user model of the data and mapping it to Star documents. So, I think that's the thing we did that's really a contribution to the science."

They talked about the paper's main points and which conference to present it at. Joel had definite ideas. They agreed that Dan would write a preliminary outline and send it to Joel for comment. Dan proposed adding Peter Eisen to the list of authors since he'd been intimately involved with RP almost from the beginning. Of course, Xerox had to approve their publishing it, but the company seemed all in favor of getting Star concepts out in public.

Done! This would definitely be a great resume builder, and besides, Dan liked to write.[1] This was a good morning already and now was a great time to go running. He headed out to the car for his gear.

Janet had her Apple interview this coming Monday, and she really wanted to tell someone about it. If she went up to the second floor to see Gwen, she might run into Grant, which would be awkward. But finally, she called her, explained the situation, and proposed meeting for lunch instead.

Janet didn't want to go to the cafeteria since they might run into Grant there also, so they decided to meet in the parking lot and drive to Murray's on Manhattan Beach Boulevard. Over sandwiches, Janet recounted the dinner with the Apple folks.

Gwen asked, "How do you feel about leaving Xerox? And the LA area?"

Janet thought a while, "It makes me sad, kinda. The people are so nice at Xerox. On the other hand, Ken is here." She made a face.

"You don't have to see him all the time, though, the way you would if you had kids."

"No, thank God for that."

"So, why leave Xerox? You've been pretty happy here, haven't you?"

Janet recalled her dad asking the same question, which she'd been mulling over since. "I don't know… I'm just afraid Xerox is going to mess this up. They don't seem to understand what we have here."

Gwen nodded, "No, they never did." She waited for Janet to say more.

"You should have seen the crowds at the show. We did it! After all these years, it's real."

"Yeah, I heard. But you know, they aren't the decision-makers."

Janet felt a little annoyed. Was Gwen too old-fashioned to get Star? Maybe selling a copier meant schmoozing with the department manager, but Star was a computer.

Gwen changed the subject, "How were the Apple people you had dinner with? Did you like them?"

Janet hadn't spent a lot of time on that, "Yeah, I guess so. It's funny… I didn't think about that too much. I just focused on making a good impression."

Gwen pressed on that one, "It's important, though. How would you compare them to Xerox?"

These were tough questions. "I don't know… they seem more aggressive, I guess."

"You find that at smaller companies. A lot of the rules we take for granted at Xerox don't really apply outside."

"Really? Like what?"

"Like basic politeness. Like treating other people with respect. It's a cutthroat world out there. At least, that's the impression I have."

Janet was silent. She found it hard to believe a successful company in the computer industry could be *that* different.

Gwen could see Janet was resisting her warnings, so she continued, "And something we haven't talked about much, namely, how women are treated. We have it pretty good at Xerox. It's easy to take that for granted."

"Yeah, I guess we do. I don't know what Apple is like."

"Were any women at the dinner?"

Janet shook her head. She remembered they all seemed to be guys in their mid-30s, and all dressed more or less the same, with khaki pants and button-down Oxford shirts. "I guess you're kinda negative on this?"

Gwen protested, "No, I wouldn't say that. I'm just giving you some things to think about."

"I really do appreciate it, Gwen."

They talked about Gwen's project for a while, and then, she told Janet she had two pieces of gossip to share. "So, have you heard Grant's considering a temp assignment in Japan? We're not supposed to know about it. But of course, everyone does."

She was shocked, "Japan? Really?"

"Yep. He's been sitting on it for a week now."

"Wow. That sounds great. Doesn't he want to go to Japan?" Janet wondered whether *she* had anything to do with this. Now, she felt guilty for not calling him back.

"Your guess is as good as mine. You haven't talked to him lately?"

She shook her head, "No, I haven't. You said two gossip items. What was the other one?"

Gwen beamed, "Happy news! Steve and Sandy are engaged. You know them, right?"

Janet remembered them from the bike rides, "Oh, yeah, I've met them a couple of times. That's so great!"

"I wish I could say I saw that coming."

They drove back to work, and Gwen said she'd take Janet someplace nicer if she actually quit.

Janet thought about the news about Grant, Steve, and

Sandy, but pretty soon, Angela came in with another integration problem, and they spent the afternoon on that.

Dan finished his run through the industrial neighborhoods near Xerox, took a shower, and went to the cafeteria for lunch. Getting a burger and fries, his default choice, he put them on his tray and looked around and saw Todd eating by himself. Todd had moved North a long time ago, but everyone came down here once in a while, so it wasn't too shocking to see him. He sat down. "What it is, bro?"

Todd looked up, "What it is. What it was."

They said, "What it shall be," in unison and shook hands.

"What brings you down here?"

Todd glanced at his watch, "Teaching a Mesa class this afternoon. I gotta watch the time."

"You get *all* the plum assignments, don't you?"

"Somebody has to do it. As the low man on the totem pole…"

"So, how is it being in Palo Alto?"

"It's different, man. We go roller-skating at lunch. There are trees."

"Yeah, I always like going up North."

"How are things with you? I guess you asked Don to move out."

"Oh yeah, without you, it was just the two of us in the house. We really didn't have a lot to talk about."

"Yeah, I'm not surprised. How's work?"

"Oh, I'm thinking of moving up North and joining a start-up." Todd was the sort of guy you didn't have to beat around the bush with.

"Really? Good for you. I'll probably book outta here eventually, too. Which one?"

"Well, that's the problem. I don't know how you find one of those before they get so big there's no money in it anymore."

Todd didn't see a problem at all, "You just call them up,

man. We are *so* hot right now. Everyone wants to hire a Xerox guy."

This was news to Dan. He'd always thought you had to send a letter and a resume and wait. Or else, you had to know someone. "Really? I haven't noticed that."

"That's 'cause you're down here. You need to be up North!" Todd looked at his watch, "I gotta teach the class. Good to see you, man."

Dan finished lunch. *"Okay, I have to join Martin's group. Then at least, I'll have an excuse to go up North all the time."*

Around the end of the day, Grant sat in his office, lost in thought. Fuji Xerox would be arriving at work right about now. Tomorrow was Saturday over there. He'd been sitting on their offer for a week now.

Janet had still not returned Grant's call from the week before. He was becoming more and more annoyed the more he thought about it. Should he just walk down to the first floor and drop in on her? She'd probably apologize and plead forgetfulness because of all the excitement of the conference. He'd been down that road before with her. She always had some excuse.

His own management was asking, ever more insistently, if he'd made a decision yet on the Tokyo assignment. In his professional life, Grant always cultivated an air of being unflappable, but it required a lot more effort this week. He kept wondering what he'd do with his house while he was gone. Pay someone to house sit for him? Rent it out? If he sold it, then he'd miss out on all the real estate inflation and come home priced out of the market.

He could rent it, but he'd heard horror stories about renters who trash the place and refuse to move out. How the hell can you stand to interview all those smelly people and choose one? And then, what if they call you every time the damn toilet clogs? And if you have to evict them, how can you do that if you're in Japan? Was he going to have to hire a property manager to do all that for him? And how do you pick one of *those*? A gigantic pain in the ass.

He could advertise the house on one of the internal mailing lists, but then everyone would know he was taking the Tokyo assignment, and this was supposed to be a secret. What to do, what to do? He was a *Manager*, goddammit! He was supposed to be able to assess the facts and make a decision. Besides being annoyed with Janet, he was annoyed with himself for being stuck on this conflict.

46

SAYONARA

Finally, Janet and Angela straightened out the latest build problem, and Janet had a moment to think again. She reluctantly decided it was finally time to stop ducking Grant, so she headed up to the second floor.

Grant was still turning over the options in his head when she knocked on his door. "Enter." She did.

"Hey, I'm sorry I haven't called you back. I guess I could plead the excitement of the conference, but there's really no excuse."

"At least I don't have to hear that again." He motioned for her to sit, "It must have been insane the last few weeks. How are you holding up?"

"Oh, lots to talk about. But first, I heard you were considering a temp job in Tokyo."

Grant was shocked momentarily, but then, he realized that nothing was ever a secret for long around here. "Word gets around. Yes, I'm having a hard time making up my mind."

"How come? It sounds fabulous to me!"

"Oh, lots of things, starting with my house. I can't leave it empty. I don't want to sell it, so what the hell do I do?"

Janet considered the heartbreak that someone with an

appreciating asset endures when he has to decide how best to hold on to it. She tried to be sympathetic, "Can't you just rent it out? You could advertise it on email so that you would rent to a Xeroid, at least."

Grant was stuck. He hated the idea of advertising his personal business on email to hundreds of strangers and maybe having them come to his house, even if they *were* Xeroids.

After receiving no response, she continued, "You don't care for that idea, I guess."

"Well… not that much. I'd rather rent it to someone I already know."

"But there's no one?" He shook his head. A long silence, and then she brightened, "Aren't Steve and Sandy getting married?"

"Yeah. So?" he raised his eyebrows.

"Are they going to buy a house now?"

Grant remembered asking them about that, "They're just thinking about it, as far as I know. Why?"

She stood up triumphantly, "So, why don't you rent your house to *them*?"

Grant was taken aback. Sandy *did* say his house was in a great location, after all. But, but, but… "But what if they buy a house and move out? Then, I'm stuck without a tenant again."

She sat back down, "Hmm… I didn't think of that. Why don't you talk to them?"

The sky was clearing. Maybe if they rented with an option to buy… something like that? He thanked Janet profusely and walked over to Steve's office. Steve was surprised to hear Grant's offer, but he seemed excited about it and said he'd talk to Sandy, who was out of the office at the moment. Steve also offered that maybe if they did move out, they would find a new tenant for him.

Grant returned to his office, called his colleagues in Japan, and accepted their offer. They were as ecstatic as the Japanese ever get. After the glow of finally making a decision wore off, he realized that he might still need a property manager, in case Steve and Sandy didn't rent it or if they rented it but later moved out. He got on the internal want ads list and asked if anyone knew a property management company, and three people with first-hand experience answered. He loved it that someone at Xerox always knew whatever you needed to know.

He sent Janet a thank you email for the idea. She wrote back and offered to buy him a drink. They met at the Shellback Tavern near the Manhattan Beach Pier. It was full, which was usual at this hour.

The waiter brought Janet a glass of white wine and Grant a beer. She sipped her wine and put the glass down, "Are you going to Japan now? I'm so jealous!"

Grant smiled broadly, "Yes, I finally made up my mind. And thanks once again."

Janet was modest, "I'm sure you would have figured it out on your own."

"I'm not so sure about that," he demurred.

She cleared her throat, "Anyhow... I think I owe you an explanation for the last couple of months."

He held up his palm as if to say, "No need."

She paused and then said, "You remember I was married right out of college, right?"

"I knew you were married."

She took another sip of wine, "Yeah... with hindsight, it was way too young, but live and learn, right?"

"That's for sure."

"Anyhow, it's over, and I sorta don't want any relationship right now. So if I'm kinda remote, I guess maybe that's why."

Grant groaned inwardly, "*Hey, it's yet another 'I just want to be friends!' speech.*" But he just said, "Yeah, I kinda figured."

"Yeah." Long pause, "But I have something else to tell you, *if* you promise not to repeat it." He raised his fingers in

Scout's honor. "At the NCC, I had dinner with a bunch of Apple people. I'm interviewing up there on Monday."

Grant's jaw dropped, "Apple? Why in God's name would you want to work *there*?"

"Well, they might take this great technology and actually do something with it. I don't think Xerox will."

"Hell, that was clear to me four years ago. Xerox is not a computer company."

"Is that why you transferred to Printing Systems?"

He nodded, "The laser printer is *definitely* a Xerox kinda product. That's the future of this company."

"At least, we agree on something," she laughed.

He put his elbows on the table and leaned forward, "So, is Apple doing some kind of bitmapped computer? With a mouse and everything?"

"I don't know that much about it yet. Also, I can't talk about it. But yeah, it looks that way."

"What will you be doing?"

"I don't know much about that either. I think they're just getting started."

He sat back, "So, you'd move up to the Bay Area?" She nodded. "Wow. Well... good for you! I'm so happy for you."

"Thanks! It's pretty scary."

"I'm sure you'll do great, Janet."

She smiled gratefully, "How about you? How do you feel about living in Japan?"

Grant had a policy of not talking about his feelings, but this might be the last time he ever saw her. "I'm excited! I've visited Tokyo a lot, but living there is a whole different thing."

"Do you know where you're going to live?"

He shook his head, "Fuji has a relocation department, and they have special housing for *gaijin* if it comes to that." She was puzzled by the word *gaijin* for a second but figured it must mean non-Japanese. "Tokyo is very expensive, isn't it?"

"Yeah, Xerox has a cost-of-living adjustment in the salary, but I have no idea if it's enough."

"Well, I'm really happy for you, too! Give me a call when you come back. Of course, I don't know where I'll be living."

They worked out how to reach each other and then hugged and said goodbye. On his way home, Grant wondered why he'd ever thought he needed to be married. His parents bugged him for grandchildren, but he didn't like kids and didn't want any. He kept worrying that he'd never be promoted to a senior management job unless he had the requisite wife and 2.1 kids. At least being single made it easier to take a fun assignment like this. He resolved to travel all over Japan and Korea while he was there. This was going to be a gas!

Back in her apartment, Janet reflected. Grant was a nice guy, for sure. He had a lot of skills that she admired. But being with him would be pretty much the same as being with Ken. Thirty years from now, he'd probably still be at Xerox. Janet took a day of vacation on Monday and flew up to Cupertino. The Apple engineers weren't quite as impressed by her background as the guys at the conference, but it was still a pretty easy day. They seemed to want her to do more or less the same thing she did on Star. But Apple didn't have the massive staff and codebase Xerox had, so she was mainly going to be managing developers at first. She described the system modeling tools she used at Xerox and their build procedures, and they seemed rapt.

She kept wondering when Steve Jobs or Steve Wozniak would walk in, but when she asked, they said Jobs had already interviewed her. Apparently, he was one of the guests she'd talked to while she was on booth duty or maybe he was standing nearby listening, and she didn't even realize it in all the excitement. Anyway, he was still traveling. As for Wozniak, no one knew.

At the end of the day, she was pretty sure she'd get an offer, but they didn't even have a verbal one ready yet. This would really be a different experience than Xerox. That was for sure. They knew they had to ship a product quickly, and it had to work. No excuses accepted.

She wasn't quite sure who was calling the shots, though. They were kinda vague on that. She was worried she'd be stepping into some big-time politics of the sort that Michael handled for them at Xerox. But still, they were a hot company, and it would be great for her resume if nothing else.

Dan went up to Palo Alto on Tuesday to talk about his transfer to Martin's group, Advanced Development. He decided to try flying into SFO instead of San Jose airport, just for yucks, and he took 92 over to 280. Driving down 280, he looked over at the Crystal Springs Reservoir and all the open space around it, and he marveled, "My God, it's so beautiful here. LA is so *fucking* ugly." He'd always been a little ambivalent about moving to the Bay Area, but this was potent.

Joining Martin's group did not require any hard selling. They all knew him and really needed someone in El Segundo, especially someone who knew the Star code and could make a demo with the actual product. Martin mentioned some research prototyping that he might do, maybe voice annotation of documents. It sounded fun.

He didn't have an agenda of meetings, so he was free to wander around and talk to his friends. He always made a point of chatting with Rosalind whenever he was here, so he dropped in on her and gave her the news, "Hey, I'm joining Martin's group!"

"Wow, that's fantastic! He needs more people who know Star."

Dan liked to hear that. All those years of slogging through Trait Analysis were finally paying off. "Yeah... you don't work in that group right now, do you?"

Rosalind always had to remind herself that people outside Palo Alto thought org charts meant something. Up there, you might be *borrowed* to work on some other manager's project, and no one was too upset about their perquisites being violated. "Well, we're kinda loose about org charts here. Right now, I'm not working with him, but I could be in the future. So, we might be working together at some point." Dan smiled at that prospect, so she continued, "Do you know what you're going to work on?"

"Oh, he mentioned a few possibilities. Voice annotation of documents was one."

Rosalind beamed, "I think I wrote a paper about that. Let me see if I can find it for you," She turned and thumbed through a stack of paper on her desk. While she was doing that, he got up and closed the office door.

She didn't find it, and when she turned back, the door was closed, "Uh-oh. What's up?"

"I'm starting to think about life outside of Xerox. I know… hard to fathom."

Rosalind smiled ruefully, "You and everyone else."

"Really?"

"People are starting to figure out that Xerox is going to blow this opportunity."

"Yeah. Plus, we can get rich!"

She laughed, "And there's that."

Dan was relieved that this was not a forbidden topic, "So, how do you find these hot startups? Do you have to know someone?"

Rosalind replied, "Maybe you just need to know *one* person, such as the headhunter they all use."

"*Now, we're getting somewhere!*" Dan thought. "And his or her name is…?"

"Kim Burdette, I think it is. Wait, let me check." Rosalind looked in her card file, "Yeah, that's it. Do you want the number?" He nodded, and she read it off.

This was too easy. Maybe being a smart Silicon Valley guy wasn't that difficult after all. Dan put the piece of paper in his pocket, "Thanks! What are you planning to do? Stay here?"

Rosalind looked unperturbed, "Oh, I don't know. For now. I'm still doing good work and enjoying the people I work with, so as long as that continues... I'm not super-motivated by money."

He didn't think that was intended as criticism, but Dan was so sensitive he took it that way. "Yeah... this is still a pretty amazing place, isn't it?"

She smiled, "It's grad school, but with better food."

Dan spent the day talking to the people he'd be working with in his new job. A couple of people mentioned Tony Webb as someone who knew a lot of startups, so he dropped in on him. He didn't know Tony that well, so he left the door open and just kept his voice down.

Tony mentioned Sun Microsystems as one startup that was a real sweatshop but seemed to have good prospects. They were adapting Unix to a windowed environment with a mouse, which had to strike some of the old Bell Labs people as newfangled nonsense. Dan had never used Unix, so he wasn't sure about that one, but it wouldn't hurt to check it out.[1]

He also mentioned a company whose name he forgot that was building a really portable computer, not a luggable one— one you could conceivably put on your lap. They were using some weird language called FORTH to save on memory space. Tony and Dan both figured that *someday* a laptop might be practical, but right now, they'd have to find some special- ized market niche that required the portability. But that was the good thing about a small company—you didn't have to conquer the entire world like Xerox was trying to do with Star.

Tony mentioned yet another startup that was commercial- izing Ada, this new language that the Department of Defense was standardizing on. They both had their doubts that Ada would take over the entire world just because the DoD was adopting it, but who the hell knew? One more company to call.

Of course, a zillion little imitators were trying to make personal computers. Dan had seen a bunch of them at NCC, and he figured that it was the first *and* last trade show for most of them, so he didn't bother getting their names from Tony.

Dan and Joel went over the organization of the paper they were writing. One major conference had a deadline for papers coming up, so they had to hurry and write the thing. Dan congratulated himself on recruiting Joel. He had a Ph.D. and could give it academic respectability.

Dan reviewed all these moves, and it sounded good from the outside. He was writing an academic paper, working with new technology, plus now he had some contacts in the startup world. But he lived in LA and owned a house. The housing market was shit right now, with interest rates through the roof, so how long would it take him to sell the place? Startups always had to move fast, so they wouldn't want to wait two months for him to move.

He also didn't really *have* a specialty to sell, like networking or graphical user interfaces or Unix kernel. A lot of engineers seemed happy to be compiler guys, kernel guys, or user interface guys their whole lives, but Dan had no interest in doing one thing forever. He thought of himself as a Renaissance Man. The thing he loved about Xerox was that it had a lot of people like that, and he didn't have to apologize for it.

In most engineer's minds, he was the database guy, but the Star database was, let's face it, just a single file. And the dirty little secret was that he didn't even like databases. It was an area that they'd handed him at Burroughs, and he'd stuck with it long enough to carve out a niche on Star. But now, he wished he could get into networking, somehow or other.

Maybe the ideal would be to find a startup that did something with networking but be hired for something else and then move over. But he realized, sadly, that you don't always find exactly what you want.

47

THIS IS THE END, BEAUTIFUL FRIEND

J anet was on pins and needles all the rest of that week. Would Apple make her an offer or not? They didn't give any hints when she left on Monday, and she didn't want to appear insecure by calling. So, she just had to wait—Tuesday, Wednesday, Thursday, still no word.

Finally, on Thursday night, she arrived home and found an envelope from Apple propped up against her door. They must have had it delivered by courier or something. It had to be an offer! It was.

Janet called her dad and told him. Len was ecstatic. She couldn't really ask him whether the offer was fair since to him, *any* stock options were more than he'd ever received. He just repeated that this was a fantastic opportunity, and he was very, very proud of her.

She tried to think of *anyone* she could ask about the offer, but everyone she knew was only familiar with jobs down in LA with giant companies. No one knew about little up-and-coming companies like this. Of course, she knew Xerox people in the Bay Area, but she wasn't close enough to any of them to ask this. The advice she received at the NCC was all about offers from pre-IPO startups, but Apple was already public.

Lying in bed Thursday night, she realized that she wanted to take it, and they probably weren't willing to bargain in any case, so she'd call in the morning and accept. Then, she went to sleep. The very first thing she did at work on Friday was to go to Tom and tell him. He seemed a little surprised, but not much.

"Tom, I've just gotten a job offer from another company, and I'm going to take it." She was about to add the obligatory words about how much she'd enjoyed working here, but this was an opportunity too good to pass up, but Tom interrupted.

"An offer? Good for you? Who's the lucky company?"

"It's Apple." She was half-expecting him to call Security and have her escorted out of the building, but he didn't. Sometimes companies did that if you were going to a competitor.

"Apple? Wow. I've heard they're building something like Star. When did this happen?"

She didn't want to say that she'd approached them at the NCC, but at the same time, Xerox would be concerned if Apple was actively poaching. So she left it vague, "A couple of weeks ago. My dad was telling me how his employees were bringing in their personal Apple computers to use VisiCalc, so I looked into it and called a friend there."

Tom sat back, "Well, I'm really sorry to see you leave. But I know this is probably a good opportunity for you. When's your last day?"

"How about two weeks from today?"

"That'll be great. Have you told anyone else yet?"

"No, not even Apple!"

"Okay, then can you hold back, and let me announce it myself?"

How could she say no to that? "Sure." She figured if he held back from announcing it for too long, she'd just tell a few people and ask them to keep it quiet. What could he do? Fire her?[1]

An hour later, Tom sent out a department-wide message:

Janet Saunders has announced that she'll be leaving us. Please join me in thanking her for her great work on Star and wishing her all the best in her future endeavors. Janet's last day will be June 5.

Within a minute, people were lining up at Janet's door to ask about her plans. Dan was first, and then Angela and Brian joined him shortly.

"So… where are you going?" Dan asked.

"I'm going to work for Apple," hoping no one would throw things at her. Dan looked disapproving but didn't say anything.

"On their Lisa project?" asked Brian. She nodded. "Wow! Is Lisa like Star, but better?" She laughed, "I can't say."

Dan asked, jokingly, "How many buttons on the mouse?" She held up one finger. The rumor that Apple was using a one-button mouse had already spread around the Star team, so this was confirmation.

"Who's going to organize the goodbye lunch?" Brian asked.

Angela raised her hand, "I'll do it!" Dan and Brian left, while Angela stayed.

Janet smiled at her, "I'm sorry I couldn't tell you about this, Angela."

"Oh, I understand. Who's taking over *this* group?"

Janet wished she could just designate Angela, but she knew that wasn't how it worked. "Tom and I didn't talk about that. I don't know what he wants to do." She was emphasizing that it wasn't up to her.

They talked more about the Star project and where it was going. Janet asked her what she wanted to do, and Angela said she didn't have any ideas right now and needed some time to figure that out.

After Angela left, Janet shut her door, called Apple, and accepted the offer. They expected her to give two weeks' notice, and she asked if she could take an extra week to get settled up in the Bay Area, which was fine with them. They included relocation expenses in the offer, which were pretty minimal for her since she didn't own a house. She was so glad she'd held off on the real estate thing when everyone else was plunging in. Otherwise, this would be much messier.

The rest of the day seemed to be just Janet telling everyone about it. Most people were congratulatory, but not everybody. She'd worried ever since she met the Apple guys at the convention that Xerox people would consider her a traitor. After all, Xerox had invented the graphical user interface, and here these nobodies were coming in and stealing it.[2]

The next week was pretty boring. Whenever she walked past a group talking about future plans for Star, they suddenly went silent. It reminded her of the time at TRW when a Russian guest had been escorted through her area, and everyone was instructed to hide all their classified materials. A few people became noticeably cool. Whenever she passed Dan in the hall, he would nod and keep walking. Did *he* think she was being disloyal? She wondered how she could clear this up or if she even could. He'd been a good friend for all these years.

Mark didn't seem at all judgmental about it. She was walking past his office a few days after the announcement, and he called out, "So, Apple, huh?" She stopped and went in.

"Yeah, 'fraid so."

"What are you doing there?"

"More or less what I'm doing here, except also managing some developers. Maybe."

"Excellent! Did they give you a good offer?"

"I think so. It's hard to tell."

"Well... I expect they'll have a lot more Xerox people before this is over."

She was surprised, "Really? I was worried people thought I was joining the enemy."

He laughed, "Well if Xerox isn't going to use this technology, they can't really complain if someone else wants to."

Janet thought about that, "That's kinda the way I see it. I think a few folks here don't."

"Really? Who?"

"Well, Dan, for one. He's been standoffish."

Mark snorted. "Marksy? He's probably just pissed it's not him."

She laughed for a second, "I don't know what's up with him."

"Well, I wouldn't worry about it. Anyhow, have fun at Apple."

She thanked him and left. Janet thought Gwen deserved to hear it in person, so she paid her a visit. As she approached her door, Gwen called out, "Here comes the traitor!" Janet hesitated for a second, worrying Gwen was serious, but the smile gave it away. She sat down in the guest chair.

"I guess you heard already, huh?"

Gwen smiled broadly, "Cyril told me. Well, congratulations! Are you excited?"

"Nervous really."

"Well, I'm sure you'll do great. But I'll be sorry to see you go."

Janet said, "Gwen, you've been such a help all these years, with my divorce and everything else. I sincerely want to thank you."

Gwen smiled modestly, "It was nothing. I enjoyed hearing what it's like for women just coming up. You have a lot of advantages I didn't have."

They talked some more about Janet's plans. Gwen didn't want to raise concerns about Apple at this point, and she'd already done that the last time they met anyway. Gwen followed through on her promise to take Janet to a nice restaurant for a goodbye lunch.

Her last week made her sure that she'd made the right choice. The developers were treating Star 2.0 as just another software release—what Star 1.0 *should* have been. Of course, Tom, Aaron, and Mark would admit that "performance is a problem," but they were dealing with it. They saw no reason to panic about Apple or anyone else, Janet thought, "*No, you do need to panic!*" but she refrained from telling them that. Rumors that IBM was making their own personal computer were rife, and all the jokes about how it would be like teaching an elephant to tap dance were fading as it became clear that they were serious about it.

Friday, June 5, her last day, finally came. Angela had everyone sign a great big card for her, and she had lunch delivered to the large conference room. At the end, they had a presentation of gag gifts, which seemed to be part of the tradition at all companies, as far as anyone could tell. Many people were unable to resist the "apple" pun, so there were a lot of apples, real and plastic. Tom presented her with a giant copy of the Star announcement, which had been signed by everyone. Tradition also called for the guest of honor to give a speech, and Janet did. As far as she could remember afterward, it was just, "Thank you. It's been great working with you all. Please look me up when you come up to the Bay Area."

She was actually free to go after she visited HR and turned in her badge, but she wanted to see if maybe, just maybe, she could leave on even slightly better terms with Dan.

Down the hall, Dan was talking to Peter and Brian about Apple and the PC revolution.

Brian said, "Well, I think it's just fine. Xerox doesn't own anything."

Dan was annoyed, "Except the graphical user interface, the mouse, the Ethernet, the laser printer…"

Peter, always eager to correct anything even slightly inaccurate, pointed out, "Not the mouse! That was Doug Engelbart."

Brian continued, "Anyhow, Xerox doesn't have patents on any of that."

Dan had to admit that they didn't own the graphical user interface. But it still bothered him, "Look, they got a visit to PARC and saw everything, and now, they're doing a knockoff."

Peter retorted, "Whose fault was that? Nobody made us show it to them."

No one had an answer for that. Brian said, "Anyway, it's probably *not* a knock-off. They have the advantage of starting fresh."

Just then, Janet walked in. Peter looked at her, "Isn't that right, Janet?" They all laughed.

"It's not a knock-off. I'll tell you that much," she laughed. Dan said, "Except intellectually."

"Maybe so," she agreed.

Dan turned to Peter, "I'll come and talk to you in a second. I have some notes from Joel I want to go over." Peter took this as the signal to leave, and Brian followed him. Only Janet was left.

After a long silence, she spoke, "Hey! I just wanted to say goodbye in person."

"Yeah, thanks. Good luck!" He thought maybe she wanted something more than good luck, but that was for her to initiate.

After a long pause, she said, "You've been kinda distant since I announced I was leaving. Is it the Apple thing?"

"By *the Apple thing*, you mean jumping to someone who's ripping us off?"

She didn't want to get nasty, "I guess you *could* look at it that way." He was still silent. "Or, you could look at it as they're great ideas, and Xerox doesn't know how to exploit them."

This was too much for Dan, "I thought that was what we spent the last five years doing."

She saw an opening to change the subject, "And, they've been great years, haven't they? The bike rides, the night at Malibu Grand Prix…"

Dan couldn't help smiling, but only for a second or two, "Still going on, though."

Janet felt maybe she'd turned the corner, "I know, and that's what I hate about leaving. This is really the best bunch of people I've ever been a part of."

This time Dan thought a while, "So, I bet these Apple weenies are going to parade around and act like they invented it all."

"Probably," she admitted. "I can try and remind them where it came from, though."

"Yeah, good luck with that!" No one wants to tell people what they don't want to hear, and he didn't think she would, either.

"Thanks. Anyhow, it's been great working with you, Dan, and I hope we can stay in touch."

Dan got up, and they hugged, "All the best, Janet!"

After she was gone, Dan walked over to Peter's office to talk about their paper on RP. Back in his office, he called Kim Burdette, the headhunter whom all the startups were working with. She'd been expecting his call.

EPILOGUE

I'd like to pay tribute to all the Xerox folks who are no longer with us.

SDD
>   Bob Ayers
>   Linda Bergsteinsson
>   Don Charnley
>   Larry Clark
>   Ron Crane
>   Jim Cucinitti
>   Bill English
>   Jerry Farrell
>   Steve Glassman
>   Forrest Howard
>   Pitts Jarvis
>   Phil Karlton
>   Robert Kierr
>   Charlie Levy
>   Ted Linden
>   Bev Manes

Ev Neely

Patrick Olmstead

Steve Purcell

Smokey Wallace

John Wick (yes, he had that name before the movies)

PARC

Jim Horning

John Ellenby

Giuliana Lavendel

Greg Nelson

Ken Pier

Frank Squires

Gary Starkweather

Howard Sturgis

Bert Sutherland

Bob Taylor

Warren Teitelman

Larry Tesler

Chuck Thacker

AFTERWORD

The cover image has a story of its own. Dave Smith told you, in the Foreword, that the person "playing" MazeWar is his son, Jeffrey, and that he was, in a sense, born because of MazeWar. (Well, he would have been born eventually, but the giant eyeball hastened it!) On the next page is the raw photo that Jonathan Sainsbury worked from. I had previously met with Scott McKellen, a professional photographer, at the home of a computer historian, Josh Dersch. Josh had many vintage computers (I counted three VAXs), including two working Xerox Altos. Jeffrey was "playing" the same MazeWar game we played in 1979.

NOTES

1. The First Day

1. "Ham and limas" is the one special dish I can remember. I asked everyone, and no one remembers any others.

2. The Alto

1. Getting a ticket for parking "backward" actually happened to me, although not on my first day.

4. The Power Couple

1. LA was an aerospace town back then. It seemed like everyone with a high-tech job worked for Hughes, or TRW, or Rockwell, or one of the giants. Not me, though.

6. The Trip to Palo Alto

1. It was true—bean bag chairs were terrible for meetings.

7. Back in Reality

1. The Great American Food & Beverage Company isn't around anymore, but they did have singing waiters and the "plank feast."

8. Dan Moves to the Beach

1. The Lighthouse is featured in the movie *La La Land*.

11. Ethernet and Smalltalk

1. The original speed goal for the Xerox Wire was 20 megabits/sec. The first controller, for the Dolphin, had independent send and receive buffers, but could only be made to fit on the board using 10-Mbps CRC chips from

Fairchild. Furthermore, in the lab, Tony found that 20-Mbps signaling caused spurious collision detects on the cable due to transceiver tap reflections.

12. Let's Get This Show on the Road

1. The "I've never seen a man type that fast" story really happened.

13. Breaking Up Is Easy to Do

1. I did have that experience with Dave Liddle, which blew me away. I'd been there only four months and never met him, but he casually said, "Hi, Bob!" as we passed in the hallway.

14. Corporate Politics, Hot and Sour Soup, and Softball

1. There was indeed supposed to be a "competitive evaluation" of word processors, although the actual event proved to be a bit of a dud.
2. I did eat at Hsi-Nan. As I recall, it was excellent.
3. I played softball as a guest, twice. I don't remember when or anything else about it, but I'm pretty sure it was at Stanford. Willie McCovey did come to a softball opening day, although I wasn't there.

15. Palo Alto Explains It All For You

1. The Ethernet had no security, and the HR department had their own for confidential matters.

16. Lightning Strikes!

1. All this is the way it happened, except of course, I inserted Grant and Janet into the story, without letting that alter any of the basic facts. It was a hardware tech who discovered the wrench. I don't know which Xerox executives were flying out for a demo, but it was probably not Peter McCulough.

17. Back to Normal

1. "Tape-O" actually was an idea that we had. Ironic that now it's called a "loop" and is totally normal.
2. I did actually use a baseball card to get past the video camera once.
3. All the Arcy Eyes stuff is true. I thought of including actual sheet music for *The Suzanne March*, but you know, typography, copyright...

18. A Celebrity In Our Midst

1. Sadly, I never met Judy Resnik, RIP.

19. We Have Liftoff

1. "How many buttons should the mouse have?" was a burning issue for a long, long time, and everyone had a strongly held opinion.
2. "How to do object-oriented programming in Mesa?" was just as contentious an issue, and it continued for far longer. I don't recall if there was one big meeting like this where the coding conventions were discussed; it was probably many, many meetings and email exchanges instead.
3. The Notification Queue was the first coding I did for Star.

20. Meanwhile, Back in Palo Alto

1. The Dolphin, or "D0," was a failure. It was a classic example of Second System Syndrome, a well-known phenomenon you can look up on Wikipedia.

21. Dan Makes His Move

1. We did go to lots of Dodgers games, but I don't remember if we went to that one.
2. This "cooperation" with the Palo Alto data management group did go on, right up to the release of Star and after. Jerry Farrell, RIP, was a co-author of my Records Processing paper.

23. At the Goose

1. The Dutch Goose is still there, and I went there for lunch as research. I had to check, though, on how it was Back In The Day. There are no peanut shells on the floor anymore. The patio has a roof over it now, but it didn't back then.

2. SuchADeal was a real D0, and it was eventually bludgeoned to death with sledgehammers in the parking lot since people were so sick of it.
3. The late 70s were the first AI Winter. Everyone had given up on AI ever achieving anything.

24. Decision Point

1. This is how Records Processing evolved. I received good ideas from the Palo Alto folks and incorporated them.
2. As best I can determine, the Venus mission was being planned at Hughes right about then but hadn't launched yet. I consulted the Hughes employee list on Facebook, and they conceded there might have been a data collection team in place, but I don't know any more than that. The speed of FORTRAN and whether Assembler was required to process all the data fast enough was indeed a big issue, *in general*.

25. And What if You DO Have Smart People?

1. The job of Build Manager was done by LeRoy Nelson assisted by Vanessa Otto. Janet and her assistant are not modeled on them in any way; rather, I stole their biographies in order to place her somewhere in Star.

27. Fundamentally

1. The fly-swatting game was real, and the Support group classed it as "mouse practice."

28. Grant Learns the Gospel

1. This list of the five alternatives for hardware is real and exists on Bitsavers. Special thanks to Robert Garner and Bob Belleville for checking over this chapter.
2. The word "appliance" was indeed floated as a term for what we were building, but not everyone was comfortable with it.
3. I had assumed that no one ever transferred from North to South, but Dave Liddle reminded me that Ron Rider did to build laser printers, just as Grant does.

29. Animal House

1. There *was* an adaptation of Lord of the Rings before Peter Jackson's. It wasn't a big success.

30. Beachy

1. I did see David Letterman at The Comedy and Magic Club. I don't remember if I saw Jay Leno or not. Leno still performs there sometimes.
2. Len is my favorite character in this book, if it's not obvious.

31. Moving Out, Moving Up

1. The part about Security not allowing bicycles in the building is true. They put in a bike rack near the loading docks, which was (supposedly) under the watchful eyes of the guards.
2. Fleas were a horrendous problem back then. Vets didn't offer the medications you give your pets now, except for flea powder, which was horrible. You'd close all the windows, flea-bomb your apartment, and leave for a few hours, after which it would smell bad, and the fleas would return in a few days.
3. The part about multiple-inheritance subclassing and Trait Analysis is all true.

32. Traits

1. Meetings like this happened, but this particular one is a composite.

33. Big-Time Professional Management

1. I did see Danny Elfman at a club, before he got into scoring movies. He was manic, that's what I remember.

34. Houses

1. 'No one ever lost money on California real estate' was what the realtors always told you. Now they have.

35. Games

1. For whatever reason, I'm not really a Gamer. But I did try these games and was (briefly) hooked on Trek. Many other Xeroids played MazeWar all the time.
2. I did go on Sierra Club hikes through the sets for M*A*S*H and Vasquez Rocks, but I don't remember when.
3. I did eventually take the BMTC course. It's no longer offered because ice axe practice, years later, led to a serious accident and a lawsuit, and the

Sierra Club's insurance went through the roof.

36. The Bike Trip

1. At the time, I knew many, many people who worked on Tor, and I tried as hard as I could to find someone now who could tell me more about it. I failed.

37. Even Dads Have Heard of PCs

1. It would have been a surprise to Bay Area folks that Angelenos didn't return their hatred, for the most part. We thought, "Yeah, it's great up there, but it's great here, too. What's the big deal?"

39. But the Software Is Always Late

1. The software *was* appallingly slow. It's part of the purpose of this book to give some insight into how something like this happens.

40. A Fine Day Out

1. The machines *were* called "telephone answerers" at first, and not "answering machines." That didn't last long.
2. It's hard to imagine now, but at the time, the back part of the plane was for smokers. And yes, the smoke did travel up to the "no smoking" rows.

41. Meet Harold

1. The part about Eichlers costing $140,000 is real. That was a lot of money then.
2. There was a meeting like this, but I don't know if it was on July 28, 1980. Someone did ask about the Apple visit to PARC, and the answer was accurate, that the Xerox venture capital arm had pushed for it, and Xerox had invested in Apple.
3. We did ignore the 820, and in fact, I don't think I ever saw one.

42. Saturdays at Xerox

1. For the longest time, management insisted Star would run in 192K of memory, while almost no one really believed it. Finally, they relented, and we had 256K, which raised the Unit Manufacturing Cost considerably.

43. The Hit of the Show

1. The National Computer Conference in May 1981 was the highlight of my professional career. I hope this chapter conveys the excitement. People lining up 10 minutes before the demos and spilling over into the IBM booth—it just doesn't get any better than that.
2. The Brother Dominic incident really happened.
3. It was Dave Liddle who told me that Steve Jobs came to our demos. At the time, I'm not sure I even knew what he looked like, so it's possible I saw him. I don't remember.
4. The Billy Goat Tavern now has a branch at O'Hare Airport. The "cheezborger, chips" routine was huge for them.

44. Never Make Your Move Too Soon

1. I don't actually know if an American went over to Fuji Xerox to be a liaison person, let alone to work on a Mesa chip. This part is possible but fictional.
2. There was indeed an avalanche of emails about what Xerox should do next. The NCC was the beginning of a multi-year mass exodus from Xerox.

45. Indecision

1. My paper was called, *The Design of Star's Records Processing: Data Processing for the Non-Computer Professional.* It's possible to find it for free on the Internet Archives.

46. Sayonara

1. I visited Sun in 1982 and met Bill Joy, not really an interview. It did seem like a sweatshop at the time. What can I say? I was ignorant.

47. This Is the End, Beautiful Friend

1. I double-checked with a former Star manager, and you were not escorted out of the building immediately if you said you were quitting for Apple. Xerox was pretty civilized that way.
2. What I tried to indicate here is, a few Xeroids did in fact have hard feelings and took it as disloyalty to leave for Apple, but most did not.

ACKNOWLEDGMENTS

The people who worked at Xerox back in the day continue to be a community. Prior to the pandemic, there was a reunion of sorts at least every year, where many of us kept in touch, and of course, there's a Facebook group and a mailing list. I made lifelong friends there. In writing this, I found that for almost every chapter, there was someone I needed to check some facts with. More to the point, reliving Xerox 40 years later was almost as much fun as being there the first time. As you'll see below, I talked with almost everyone who's still around, and that was one of the best things. Nearly everyone was delighted to talk about it, although I have to say, memories do fade after all these years.

The website "bitsavers" is a treasure trove of contemporaneous documents about SDD, and I can't express enough gratitude to whoever put them all there.

First of all, Dave Liddle, our leader in SDD, without whom Star would never, never have made it through the treacherous reefs of Xerox politics. In phone calls and emails, he helped me set the stage for how Xerox decided to do Star in the first place, and in so many other ways.

Robert Garner, of the Computer History Museum and

designer of the Ethernet NICs (Network Interface Cards) for the Dandelion (10-mbps) and Dolphin workstations (3- and 10-mbps), and Dandelion CPU card, kindly reviewed two of the chapters and helped me make sense of the hardware issues, for which otherwise I'd have been hopeless.

Dave Redell, Paul McJones, Jerry Morrison, and Brian Lewis were extremely helpful in writing about the early days of Star, the history of Pilot (the operating system), and Mesa (the programming language).

Charles Simonyi, the inventor of Bravo, kindly allowed me to use him under a pseudonym. I only worked with Charles for a few months and enjoyed it immensely (but if only I'd gone to Microsoft with him)!

Other thanks go to (and I apologize profusely if I left someone out), alphabetically:

Pete Alfvin

Mary Artibee

Bob Ayers

Larry Baer

Marney Beard

John Beeley

Bob Belleville

Bill Bewley

Heidi Buelow

Fred Bulah

Karla Collett-Robson

Dave Curbow

Gael Curry

Yogen Dalal

Daniel Davies

Dan DeSantis

Steve Finkel

Bill Fisher

Jim Frandeen

Alan Freier

Randy Gobbel
Jim Guyton
Bruce Hamilton
Chris Harslem
Eric Harslem
Steve Hayes
Bill Hostrup
Rich Johnsson
Derry Kabcenell
Barbara Koalkin
Hugh Lauer
Robert Levine
Alan Luniewski
Bill Lynch
Milt Mallory
Shannon McElyea
Bob Metcalfe
Hal Murray
LeRoy Nelson
Ron Newman
Roy Ogus
Vanessa Otto
Victor Schwartz
Dave Smith
Dick Sonderegger
Dan Swinehart
Ed Taft
Peggy Buell Thomas
Geoff Thompson
Tim Townsend
Don Woodward

ABOUT THE AUTHOR

Albert Cory is the pen name for Bob Purvy, a retired software engineer who worked on the Xerox Star. In his career, he also worked at Burroughs, 3Com, Oracle, Packeteer, and Google. Bob lives in San Jose with his dog Ernie, who was named after Ernie Banks, the greatest Cub who ever lived.

ALSO BY ALBERT CORY

Constructing the Future, working title for Book II, set in the 1980s.